TRIBRID N
THE ORACLE OF AEON DRA SAGA
BOOK 3

Tribrid Nexus

The Oracle of Aeon Dra Saga, Volume 3

Bria Lexor

Published by Bria Lexor, 2024.

This is a work of fiction. Similarities to real people, places, or events are entirely coincidental.

TRIBRID NEXUS

First edition. November 6, 2024.

Copyright © 2024 Bria Lexor.

ISBN: 979-8227161574

Written by Bria Lexor.

The Flames Omen

The Oracle of Aeon Dra Saga
Rebels Flame
Flight Games
Tribrid Nexus

The Vampire Society Saga
Hunter of Destiny
Kiss of Flames
Sentient of Twilight
Red System Rises
Innocent Hunter
Eternal War

Watch for more at https://brialexor.wixsite.com/brialexor.

Onizuca Series
Return To Outer Earth

Origins of Onizuca
Fall of the Skraxiz Empire

Shaman Academy Saga
Year One

Shamanic Princess: Ruler of Darkness: Origins of Darkness
Ruler of Darkness

The Enchanted Saga
Twisted Fate

The Gargoyle Redemption Trilogy
Gargoyle Redemption

The Lightworker's Saga
Elysium

The Lyric Lockheart Story

Also by Bria Lexor

Card Masters Saga
Invited by the Elements
Tournament of Wars
Champion of Power

Heir of the Octopus Saga
Hero of the Fallen Empire

Hell's Guardian Chronicles
Crimson Savior
The Force of Vengeance
The Final Glory
Vampire Candidate
Rise of the Cruxim
Reluctant Secrets

Holiday Academy Saga
New Year's Blood

Table of Contents

BRIA LEXOR 1
DISCLAIMER: | Readers should be aware that this book includes explicit depictions of violence, strong language, the deaths of minors, adult-oriented content, and sexual scenes. Proceed with caution as you read 2
LANGUAGE: | The Lost Language of the Celestials. 3
ONE | -SIXUS- 4
-MELFINA- 5
TWO 14
THREE 24
FOUR 33
FIVE 44
SIX 53
SEVEN 62
EIGHT 71
NINE 80
TEN 93
ELEVEN 105
TWELVE 119
THIRTEEN 131
FOURTEEN 141
FIFTEEN 151
SIXTEEN 161
SEVENTEEN 169
EIGHTEEN 178
NINETEEN 187
TWENTY 196
TWENTY-ONE 206
TWENTY-TWO | -SIXUS- 218
-MELFINA- 221
TWENTY-THREE 229
-SIXUS- 235
-MELFINA- 237

TWENTY-FOUR	240
TWENTY-FIVE	249
TWENTY-SIX | -SIXUS-	259
-MELFINA-	264
TWENTY-SEVEN	270
TWENTY-EIGHT | -TIMBRAX-	281
-SIXUS-	284
-MELFINA-	287
TWENTY-NINE	294
THIRTY	305
THIRTY-ONE	315
-SIXUS-	322
TO BE CONTINUED	324
COMING SOON! | THE ORACLE OF AEON DRA SAGA | BOOK 4	325
TRIBRID NEXUS PLAYLIST:	326

Dragons burn the fire and shed light upon the world. You are the dragons. Keep shining your flames.

In memory of Auntie B. Thank you for being a light in my life. Love and miss you Brandi.

BRIA LEXOR

DISCLAIMER:

Readers should be aware that this book includes explicit depictions of violence, strong language, the deaths of minors, adult-oriented content, and sexual scenes. Proceed with caution as you read.

LANGUAGE:
The Lost Language of the Celestials.

ONE
-SIXUS-

Melfina lay unconscious in the dorm room. I couldn't hide my secrets from her forever. Timbrax cleared his throat, drawing me out of my thoughts. I looked at him.

"We had a deal, Sixus," Timbrax spoke as he removed his scarlet trench coat and matching gloves before handing them to me. "Our little alliance was temporary and... now I'm leaving." He turned and walked out of the open French doors and stood on the balcony.

"I'll see you out on the battlefield," I said as he climbed up on the marble ledge and stood still before opening the astral thread with his right palm. "Victim Commander."

I watched as Timbrax flipped backwards and entered the thread before it closed behind him.

A moment later, a bright green light flashed inside the room, and the shaman returned. They stood before me and kneeled before standing.

"We're ready for your orders, Solas," Varric nodded curtly at me as he glanced at Nyxie, who had been knocked out after Orion electrocuted her with a lightning bolt. "You can't keep erasing her mind."

"I'm telling her the truth about us later, Varric," I sighed as I gazed at her. "I'm reawakening her shamanic powers."

I just hope she won't be too pissed at me for protecting her.

-MELFINA-

My eyes shot open, and I tasted electricity. I slowly sat up and found Sixus standing near the entrance of the open French doors, gazing out into the night sky. I climbed to my feet when he turned and rushed to my side as I fell, after losing my balance.

"You need to rest, Mel," Sixus whispered down to me as he gently led me back to the bed and sat me down on the edge. He kneeled down before me. "Orion struck you with his lightning bolt before re destroying the Xeonada Empire."

"What?" I asked, stunned.

The doors slid open, and three shamans entered my dorm room and walked up to Sixus as though they knew him personally.

"Did you tell her yet, Solas?" the guy demanded.

"She *just* woke up," Sixus hissed through his teeth. I felt his annoyance through his end of the bond. "Varric, I can't just unload everything on her like this."

"What's going on Sixus?" I demanded. "And don't you dare lie to me."

"I've been wiping your memory for years," he admitted. "I gave you a new identity to protect you."

"Protect me from what?" I asked.

"From Claus," he sighed. "He's a Spellbinder like his sister Phyre was before you killed her."

"Nyxie killed her," I said. He gave me a look. "Didn't she?"

"You and Nyxie are the *same* person, Mel," Sixus said. "Just like Solas and *I* are the same person."

"No," I gave him a confused look. "How can you possibly be some other guy?"

By snapping his fingers, Sixus changed his appearance. He looked like the other guy who was with the shaman earlier tonight. He snapped his fingers and was back to himself.

My eyes widened in surprise. Sixus was, in fact, Solas.

The alarms sounded around the institute, and I stood and walked out of the French doors and stood on the balcony. I saw Orion, Largo Croix, Tasia, Timbrax and a legion of Victim standing outside of the gates.

"Why the hell is Timbrax back with Orion?" I asked Sixus.

"Our alliance was short-lived," Sixus said as he walked out, standing beside me. "He's returned as the Victim Commander Mel."

Timbrax and the others leaped over the wall, and I climbed up onto the marble ledge of the railing. I leaped down, rolling and standing. Sixus and the shaman leaped down, rolling and standing as a unit.

"I guess I didn't strike you hard enough, Melfi." Orion stated. "I intended to kill you with my lightning,"

"You struck my kingdom again," I spat. "Why can't you leave us alone?"

"My life's mission is to kill you, dearest sister," Orion replied bluntly. "I see you have aligned yourself with the shamans."

Orion altered his appearance like Sixus had, and he, too, looked different.

In my mind, I saw a vision.

Claus and Phyre standing beside each other back on Erda facing off against Solas, me and the entire battalion of shaman came to me.

It dispersed rapidly.

I felt Timbrax unbind himself from me and Sixus. I turned my attention towards him as he stared a hole into my soul.

"You gonna stare?" I spat as my rage boiled to the surface. "Or are you gonna fight me Victim Commander?"

"Victim," Timbrax spoke as he pulled his sword out from behind his back and held it out in front of him in a defensive stance. "Bring the oracle to me alive," he paused. "And kill everyone else!"

"Firelash Power!" I shouted as I transformed into the superheroine vampire Hell's Guardian. Draped in a pale blue and white corset dress, I adorned myself with long, pale blue boots that ascended to my knees, white gloves that extended to my elbows, and a dragon mask that enveloped my eyes and nose. I pulled out the Valistik sword and slashed at a Victim as he rushed at me with his fingers crooked. "Gotha bitch!"

Instead of turning into a dark pile of ash at my feet, the Victim fell transforming into a demon. He slowly rose, and I slashed it again. Blood seeped out of the wound, but he sneered at me.

"The fuck?"

I thought.

"Do you like the upgrade I made to Victim?" Orion asked. "Makes it harder for you to kill them now, doesn't it, Melfi?"

Then I remembered the dagger Nyxie had given me earlier that night. Or I had given myself, I guess? This shit was confusing the fuck outta me. I grabbed it and put the Valistik sword away. The dagger transformed into a sword.

"Whoa."

Sixus said in my mind.

I slashed a demon, and his head rolled to the right. It fell, turning into a dark pile of ash, as did the body.

"Holy shit!" Sixus said as he and Timbrax exchanged glances with each other briefly in shock.

"Looks like I found your kryptonite," I smirked at Orion. He gazed at me and became pissed. "Kill the demons with the shaman's daggers!"

The vampire hunters stood behind us. The assassins, dragon knights, and mecha pilots all flanked behind them. Sixus snapped his fingers and daggers appeared in everyone's hands who wasn't a hunter.

I rushed towards Timbrax, and our swords clanked as we were an equal match. We snarled at each other before we backed up a step to regain our composure.

"So," I said panting. "Did you just use me to get what you wanted or what?"

"Something like that," he smirked. "I hadn't anticipated falling in love with you, Melfina."

"Fuck you dude!" I spat. "You only love my power!"

Timbrax was about to reply when Orion snapped his fingers and Zyra appeared in a dark cage. She looked around in confusion and terror. She was a human and didn't know about our world after I revived her and wiped her memories and her vampire abilities.

"What is this, Orion?" Timbrax snarled as he shifted his gaze towards my brother.

"Prove your loyalty to me, Victim Commander," Orion replied as he released Zyra. She screamed as she fell. Timbrax caught her by the throat, and she kicked at him to let her go. "Kill your ex-wife."

"What?" Timbrax's surprise was evident as he stared at him in disbelief at what he was asking him to do.

"Let me go," Zyra begged with tears in her eyes as she gazed down at Timbrax. "Please?"

"I'm sorry Z," Timbrax whispered as he regained his composure. He brought the blade forward, thrusting it deep into Zyra's abdomen. Her eyes widened in surprise as he stabbed her. "Please forgive me, gorgeous."

He yanked the blade out and tossed her body, making it land before the feet of the stunned vampire hunters.

"MOM!" Zara screamed as she rushed over to her mother's side. Chaos also ran over to comfort his daughter before she died. Tears streamed down her cheeks as she looked at her father. "You're a monster, dad!"

"Welcome back, Victim Commander," Orion nodded curtly at him as he licked Zyra's blood off the blade. He kept his eyes fixed on me. "I was worried you had forgotten your mission there for a moment after the Flight Games fell apart on us."

"You sick fuck!" I snarled at Timbrax.

"You're just as demented as the rest of us, Melfina," Timbrax smirked at me. "I find that darkness within you to be sexy as fuck."

"Hunters!" Tork spat. "Attack!" The vampires started shooting their acid bullets towards Victim. Once they transformed, Sixus stepped forward.

"Assassins, dragon knights, mecha pilots, shaman!" Sixus shouted. "Attack!"

The purple magic seal exploded from my body as I slashed at the demons. I turned my attention back towards Timbrax. He stood there waiting for me to attack him. He slammed his sword against mine and my power shot him backwards. His back slammed into the wall behind him, cracking it.

"We did what we came to do," Orion shot to Timbrax. "Fall back!" They turned and leaped over the wall.

"I'll be back," Timbrax spat. "Melfina is your reigning queen of the Dark Region!" he shouted to the vampire hunters. "I look forward to you coming after me!" He opened the astral thread leaping backwards into it. It closed behind him.

After my rage dissipated, the sword transformed back into a dagger. I placed it in the sheath and took in the carnage as the outfit disappeared as well. Bodies of slain assassins, dragon knights, mecha pilots, and vampire hunters littered the lawn of the Abraxis Institute of Union grounds.

"You sold me out to save yourself, Brax."

I thought.

"I did."

Timbrax replied in my mind.

I walked over to a slain female dragon knight and kneeled before her. I recognized her immediately. She was one of the blonde twins who had spoken to me on my second day here. Blood splattered her face; she had a gaping hole in her chest.

"CLAIRE!" a female voice shouted as I turned and saw her twin sink to her knees. She pulled her twin into her lap. "I should've stayed with you!"

"I'm so sorry for your loss," I whispered to her. "Claire's death won't be in vain."

"Thank you, my queen," she whispered. "I will avenge my sister's death!" When I hugged her tightly, she began crying even harder. I released her as I quickly climbed to my feet.

I walked over to Zyra's body, and I gently picked her up. Across the courtyard, I turned and carefully placed her body on a long black table that the hunters had prepared for the blood-draining process. I crossed her arms over her chest before I gently placed my hand across her face, closing her lifeless eyes.

I gazed up at Sixus, and he nodded. He approached and lifted the lifeless body of a male mecha pilot. Moving towards me, he placed the body on the table next to me and replicated the same steps that I had just carried out.

The others saw us and silently followed our lead. We were their royals. We had to show strength in dire times such as this.

As the final bodies were laid out on the tables, the sun began to rise. Sixus had sent everyone to their beds and had canceled classes for the entire week, giving us the opportunity to perform the ceremonies in honor of the deceased before their bodies were sent off to be buried by their families.

Sixus walked up to me and wrapped his arms around me before kissing me on the forehead. "How are you holding up Mel?" he asked quietly.

"I'm constantly on the move," I sighed quietly. "If I don't stop and think about it, then it can't affect me, you know?"

"Timbrax-"

"I'm killing that dead son of a bitch!" I spat. "He killed Zyra… he swore he loved her!"

"You should help the hunters drain the bodies," Sixus whispered in my ear. "You transformed into Hell's Guardian and need to feed."

"I can't," I shook my head. "Those are *our* people laying there, Sixus."

"I know," he agreed sadly. "Mel, I won't compel you to go against your humanity in any way."

I was still a half-Draconian. My conches didn't allow me to feed on our people. Or anybody I didn't want to feed on.

Right before we were about to enter the institute, I felt a sharp sting from a needle in my neck. It alerted me to someone injecting a cold liquid into my vein.

After tripping on the lawn, I lost consciousness.

***

Upon awakening, I found myself on the familiar black couch. Gradually, I sat up and got to my feet. I had on a short black dress with matching heels. Sixus groaned as he woke up and climbed to his feet. The doors slid open, and we walked towards them. We stepped out into the hallway and our shoes clicked on the black marble floor. We stopped in front of a door, and they slid open. Upon entering, we walked past the table filled with the other royals representing their kingdoms. We took our seats at the end of the table and the doors slid closed and the lights dimmed. The meeting was underway.

"Our deepest sympathies go out to you Sixus and Melfina." Prince Feran Rakia of the Pheacisea Dynasty said to us. He was in his early twenties, just like me and Sixus, full of youth and energy. His short, blonde hair framed his striking blue eyes and complemented his light skin complexion. With a chiseled and defined jawline, he possessed a remarkable handsomeness. Dressed in a black tuxedo, he exuded an air of elegance and sophistication with his slim physique. The news of the tragic loss reached their ears, and it included the heartbreaking story of an innocent mundane from Erda.

"Thank you," Sixus nodded curtly. "The vampire King Timbrax DeRaps has returned as the Victim Commander to aid Orion."

"War is upon us," Feran spoke for the other royals. "We must prepare the dragon knights, assassins, and the mecha pilots to protect Tellus at once."

"What about the Tribrid?" another king asked. "We must protect and keep the oracle out of harm's way to ensure that Orion and Victim do not take control of Tellus." another king stated.

"Did you not watch the Flight Games?" Feran scoffed. "She will lead the war if you don't recall us making that decision recently."

"Orion," I spoke, making them turn their attention towards me. "Has altered the DNA of Victim, causing them to turn into demons."

"How are you supposed to kill them now?" Feran asked.

"We have received aid from the shamans from Erda," Sixus spoke up before I could say anything. "They have sent their best fighters, and that is how we could dominate the demons and kill them."

"Perfect." Feran clapped his hands together as he placed them on the table. "We must meet with their king at once."

"My father," Sixus spoke, choosing his words carefully. "Was the former Shaman King before his untimely death... I took his place both on Erda and here." The room fell eerily silent, and I glanced at Sixus out of the corner of my eye. "Melfina and I will lead the charge in the war against Orion, Timbrax and Victim," Sixus spoke. "And we will win."

My intuition kicked in, alerting me that danger was near. I leaped to my feet and stepped away from my seat just as glass tubes shot up from the floor as soon as the alarms sounded around the building. They protected each royal in them. The doors slid open and Orion, Tasia, Largo Croix, Timbrax entered the room flanked by twenty Victim.

"You seem to have forgotten our invitations," Orion spoke to the royals as he gazed around the room. "Bring the Tribrid to me Victim Commander."

My purple shamanic seal shot out of my body and protected me from them. Victim hissed as they stepped into the left corner of the room.

"I'll get her myself," Orion spat as he walked towards me. He reached his hand through my seal and gripped me by the throat. "Too easy Melfi."

"Let her go!" Sixus snarled, as he formed thick icicles in his closed fists. He slammed them against the glass, they shattered on impact. "Mel!"

A pale blue flame shot out of my body and merged with the purple magic seal, causing it to transform into a blue-violet color. Orion released me and stumbled backwards in surprise.

I felt my powers increase as my three forms balanced each other out. With the Valistik sword in hand, I made my way to Sixus tube. I placed my hand on the glass, shattering it without even trying. He shielded his face with his arms. He lowered them and stepped out of what remained of the tube.

I pulled the Venin dagger out and tossed it to Sixus. He caught it and pulled out his shaman dagger.

Victim rushed at us, and we slashed them. A moment later, they transformed into demons. With a swift motion, I extracted my dagger, causing both mine and Sixus' to transmute into swords.

We slashed demon's limbs clean off their bodies. They soon turned to dark piles of ash on the ground. All twenty Victim were dead in seconds.

I locked eyes with Timbrax, before I felt him reform the bond between us, Timbrax gazed at me and tied our souls together once more.

Sixus snarled. His soul was bound to Timbrax's again as well.

"We're tied to fate, Melfina."

Timbrax thought.

He smirked as he opened the astral thread. I watched as Orion and the others ran through it. Timbrax walked slowly through it, never taking his eyes off of me as it closed behind him.

I sighed in relief as the glass tubes dropped back through the floor, releasing the royals from their safety boxes.

"This location has been compromised," Feran shouted over the alarm. "We will find a new secure location!"

Our swords transformed back into daggers as we put them away. Sixus handed me back the Venin dagger, and I put it and the Valistik sword back into their sheaths.

The royals all shoved each other out of the room as they raced for the door. They slid open, and the mess was left for Sixus and me. We headed for the door, and they slid open. Someone guided us towards the elevators as we stepped out into the hallway.

"I'm going to bed when we get back to the institute." I stifled a yawn. "Killing vampires and demons all night and most of the day is bullshit."

Sixus agreed as we stepped inside of the elevator. The doors slid closed, and I saw my reflection in the silver panels. I looked like Nyxie, and Sixus looked like Solas. We just had slight alterations to what we looked like on Tellus. I looked at Sixus and found him gazing at me.

"We got our shaman abilities from our parents, Mel."

Sixus said in my mind.

"Imagine a thick brick wall and you'll be able to block Timbrax from feeling your emotions and reading your thoughts."

He added.

I closed my eyes and imagined a thick black wall and I couldn't feel Timbrax's end of the bond. I opened my eyes and Sixus smirked at me.

The bell dinged, and the doors slid slowly open. We exited the elevator and walked through the lobby for the last time. The lobby was completely deserted. The doors slid open, and we walked outside. Sixus white limousine was waiting for us. We walked up to it and climbed into the backseat. The driver closed the door and got in the driver's seat. A moment later, the vehicle moved and pulled away from the curb.

After we were a suitable distance away, a loud explosion rocked the limo.

I lay my head down on Sixus' lap and closed my eyes.

I drifted off into endless nightmares.

TWO

I awoke to total darkness. By motion, the light turned on as I sat up. As I got to my feet, I realized the dorm room was entirely vacant. With the velocity of a vampire, I snatched a fresh double-sided uniform and accompanying undergarments. After entering the bathroom, I took a quick shower. I put on my clothes and pinned my hair in place. Once I put my boots on and zipped them up, I strapped my weapons onto my body. I put my jackets on just as the doors slid open.

Cy walked up to me and gave me a hug. I returned her hug before she removed herself. She looked sad.

"What's wrong?" I asked.

"The vampires returned to Erda," she whispered. "They are burring Zyra's body in the Dark Region."

"Will they be coming back to aid us in the war against Orion and Victim and Timbrax?" I asked.

"I don't know," she shrugged. "Dad doesn't want you to overdo it, mom."

"I can't make any promises." I forced a smile. "Let's go-"

My intuition kicked in and I covered Cy with my jacket before a loud explosion erupted behind me from the balcony, sending us both flying to the floor. Instant pain shot up through my right side. Alarms sounded, and the doors slid open.

"Cy!" Sixus shouted as he rushed over to her after entering my dorm room. I moved, and he pulled her up. "Help me put out the fire!"

Both of them flicked their wrists and a thick layer of ice sprayed out over my head. They put the fire out in no time. They flicked their wrists, and the ice vanished.

"Mel!" Sixus rushed over and pulled me up. "Are you hurt?"

"No," I shook my head. "I was worried about protecting Cy more than myself."

"Let's get out of here." Sixus grabbed us both by the arms and headed for the door. They slid open, and we rushed out into the hallway. The three shamans met us, and they flanked us. "Did anyone see who tried blowing up my daughter and my wife?"

"A dragon was seen leaving the perimeter after the explosion," Varric said as we walked into the lobby. After pushing open the heavy door, he rushed us down the steps and directed us towards the oracle dormitory. His stature was impressive - tall, slim, and with a noticeable muscular build. The light danced in his captivating brown eyes, highlighting the sharp angles of his oval face, particularly his chiseled chin and prominent cheekbones. Although he was attractive, his no-nonsense attitude left a bad impression on me. "The guardian's primary duty was to protect the queen and the princess, ensuring their safety at all costs."

"Obviously Varric," the beautiful girl with long dark hair rolled her eyes at him. With her slender frame, her muscles were visibly toned and defined. The harmonious balance of her face is evident in its oval shape, petite nose. As you look into her hazel eyes, you can feel their piercing intensity. "We've only been doing our job for the past four years, you know?"

"Angelina," Varric spat. "Our worlds are merging!"

"I know," she replied nonchalantly. "And it's Melfina's job to fix it before we're all dead."

"Excuse me?" I asked as I stopped outside of the door. I stared at her, clearly not liking her attitude towards me.

"If she hadn't blown up earth." Angelina rolled her eyes at me. "Nyxie and Solas would have never merged into *their* bodies in the first place!"

"I gave the order A.J.," Sixus spat. "Blame me not Mel."

"You are taking the blame for her pulling the trigger is, sad Solas," A.J. scoffed. "She needs to own her mistakes like an *actual* ruler would do." She walked up to me and shoved me hard in the chest, sending me flying backwards. I caught my balance and snarled at her.

"You wanna go, bitch?" I asked. "I'll beat your fucking ass!"

"Don't," Varric shot A.J. a warning look. "She's the fucking queen!"

"Like I give a shit who the fuck she is!" A.J. spat. "I'll kick her ass and make her-"

With the velocity of a vampire, I snatched her by the throat. I held her up and tossed her over my head. I turned, and she landed in a crouching position before standing. As she charged towards me, I effortlessly somersaulted over her, delivering a powerful kick to the back of her head.

A.J. fell, catching herself. She scrambled to her feet and tapped into her shamanic powers. Her pink magic seal shot out and so did my blue-violet magic seal. I brought the human part of me to the front so I wouldn't break her arm or any other limb she may need to kill demons with.

I grabbed her arm and twisted it behind her back easily. She screamed in pain as I popped her shoulder out of socket. I released her and she stumbled into Varric, caught her quickly. He grabbed her arm and popped the bone back into place. Our magic seals vanished, and I stood there gazing at her to see if she wanted more.

She didn't.

"You got lucky," Sixus said, looking at A.J. "You pissed off the dragon or the vampire in her and she didn't kill you."

"Show your queen some fucking respect," Varric snarled in her ear. "I don't like this situation any more than you, but they are our rulers now, Angelina."

"We have ceremonies to get to," Sixus spoke in a scary, calm voice. "I expect to see you all there to honor our fallen allies." He nudged his head towards me and Cy. We walked over to him and walked up the lawn back towards the institute.

A quick glance was cast towards the remains of the balcony. The balcony caught my eye as it was both burned and covered in ice, while debris of cement lay in ruins below. I had to temper my rage before I really killed that bitch. Prior to anything else, I had to make it through the ceremonies.

***

Sixus did the assassins' ceremony first. I couldn't attend the ceremony because I wasn't part of the Order of the Assassins.

I stood in the front of the room in the Order of the Dragon Knights with the other instructors and Cy beside me. Sixus entered the room dressed in his dress uniform of jade green slacks and jacket and took his place beside me. I wore a gem green jacket and skirt. I wore my red mecha pilot boots.

"Tonight, we honor our fallen dragon knights," Sixus spoke, making his powerful voice boom off the silent walls. "We will defeat Orion, Timbrax, Victim and all the enemies who align with them as they have initiated this war upon Tellus, Erda, and Outer Earth!"

"Hail King Sixus!" the crowd shouted. "Hail Queen Melfina!"

"Dragon Knights!" Sixus shouted. "The dragons shall rise and defeat our enemies," he paused. "Either fly or face demise in the skies!"

"Dragon Knights never die!" The crowd shouted in unison.

"Dragon Knights," Sixus shouted. "Dismissed!"

We walked out and rushed to my dorm room. The circular doors slid open, and we entered. They closed behind us as Sixus slammed his fist against the button on the wall. The room rotated counter counterclockwise, adding to the surreal atmosphere as we ascended to Intelligence Order Annihilation. (Or commonly referred to as I.O.A.)

We used our vampire speed and changed out of our uniforms and put them in the laundry basket before changing into our mecha pilot dress uniforms. Sixus and my uniforms comprising a long white long-sleeved jacket with crimson red markings on the edge, black pants, long white boots, long sleeve shirt with a collar. Despite not attending the institute for another five years, Cy wore the same uniform as us.

When we made our way to the door, they slid open. We walked out and headed up the hallway, and then we entered the room where the entire mecha pilots and repairers were lined up in formation. We took our places. I stood with the other six deity pilots and Cy stood beside her father on the right.

"Tonight, we honor our fallen mecha pilots and repairers!" Sixus spoke, making his voice boom in the silent room. Sixus' voice boomed in the silent room as he declared, "We will not forget their lives as we head into this war against Orion and Victim!"

"Yes, King Sixus!" They spoke in unison.

"Company!" Sixus shouted. "Salute!"

All cadets placed their closed fists up against their hearts with their arms extended sideways in unison with us.

"Commence Cor Hyme!" Sixus shouted.

The band played the song of the Kingdom of Eozadion to send off the fallen pilots and repairers to be buried by their families. After the final casket passed, it was time to get out of here.

"Company!" Sixus shouted. "Dismissed!"

The room cleared out, leaving us behind. The memories of doing this exact ceremony for Cora only days ago came flooding back. My best friend was gone. She wouldn't get to graduate or be my repairer after we left the institute the following year.

I quickly regained my composure as I followed Sixus and Cy out of the room. We walked up the hallway and stood in front of the dorm room. The doors slid open, and we entered. Cy walked into the bathroom and closed the door behind her so she could change out of the uniform.

Sixus walked over to the button on the wall and pressed it. The floor descended slowly clockwise as it returned to the dormitory of the dragon knights.

We changed in silence as we got dressed in our double-sided uniforms. The floor shook as it snapped into place. I turned and witnessed the steam and smoke leaving behind only an enormous hole where the balcony once stood. The floor showed signs of singeing from the French doors.

Cy emerged from the bathroom, and all of us tossed our uniforms into the laundry basket.

"SIXUS WESTIN!" A pissed off female voice shouted from outside. Judging by the annoyance coming from his end of the bond, he knew the woman.

"What is she doing here, dad?" Cy spat. "I don't wanna see her!"

"I'll deal with her," Sixus sighed as he walked towards the opening. "Be right back." He leaped down, and I heard them arguing within a matter of seconds.

Cy and I ran leaping down onto the grass. We rolled and stood in unison and walked over to Sixus' side.

"My brother is dead because you are an incompetent king!" she spat.

"Go home, Exrah!" Sixus growled. "I have a war to prepare my people for!"

"I want my daughter!" Exrah added. "Tandenth!" she called, looking towards the doors, waiting for the little girl to emerge. "Mommy is here to bring you home, darling!"

"That's not her name," I whispered. "She hates it."

"Excuse me?" Exrah scoffed, turning her attention towards me for the first time. She gave me the once over with her eyes and dismissed me quickly. She was beautiful, her heart-shaped face and her long dark hair complemented her beautiful green eyes. "Who the hell are you?"

"Queen Melfina Aeon Dra-Westin," I replied, extending my hand out to her to shake. "It's a pleasure to meet you… lady."

"You married *her*?" Exrah scoffed, laughing lightly as she rolled her eyes at me. "Such a downgrade from *me*, Sixus."

Trying to control my anger, I lowered my hand and clenched it into a fist. I held my arm to my side.

"I'm going inside, dad," Cy sighed in annoyance. "Night."

"Can you send my Tande out please?" Exrah replied.

"No," Cy shook her head. "She hates you."

"Who is this juvenile delinquent?" Exrah scoffed. "Such a rude young lady."

"I hate the name Tandenth." Cy narrowed her eyes at her mother. "I changed it to Cymmuphoa."

"Tande?" Exrah gasped, taking her daughter in wide eyed. "You grew so fast?"

"That's what happens when you feed me," Cy shook her head. "I'm outta here."

"What did you do to my *daughter* Sixus?" Exrah became enraged. "She's supposed to be a six-year-old *child*!" She huffed. "Not some mouthy teenager!"

"She's sixteen now," Sixus shrugged. "Half-Draconian children grow up faster than the average human does."

"You will *never* be her mother," Exrah shot daggers my way. "She will never love you; you bitch!" Before I could say a word, Exrah pulled her hand back, bringing it forward. She slapped me as hard as she could in the face. She pulled her hand back to her side and gave me a satisfied look.

"Get the hell off my property!" Sixus snarled. "And I have full custody of Cy since you gave her up after you gave birth to her six years ago!"

"I'll be back!" Exrah spat as she turned and walked furiously back towards her waiting limo. She climbed inside and looked at us. "You'll regret this Sixus!"

"Who the fuck is she?" I asked, glancing at Sixus, who looked annoyed.

"That was Exrah Minetta," Sixus sighed heavily. "Cy's bitch of a birth mother who left her with me so she could focus on her repairer career."

A vision started to take shape.

The driver slammed the door and rushed to the driver's side, where he left the door open. Settling down, he closed it behind him. He left the engine running and quickly pulled out of the driveway. He exited through the gates when the limousine exploded.

The image faded away, leaving me with only a moment to act.

Without hesitating, I shot my hand out as the limo neared the gates. The astral thread appeared, and I leaped through it. I sat beside Exrah in the backseat.

"How the hell did you get in here?" she demanded. "Get out!"

Without speaking a word, I grabbed her by the hair and tossed her through the astral thread behind me. She screamed in fear as she flew through it. I grabbed the driver and tossed him through it as well. It closed, and the car exploded with me sitting in the back seat.

I heard someone smash the glass and pull me out as I was losing consciousness. The flames weren't burning them. Weird. I was waiting for Sixus to spray his ice. But it never came.

"Who the fuck is this?"

I thought.

"I got you," a familiar male voice said as the astral thread opened and he leaped inside. "Melfina, they left you for dead."

The sound of the astral thread opening as he stepped out carrying me in his arms. He walked into a room with a bright light. He walked over and placed me down on a metal cot. I stared into his white eyes with red rings around the edges.

"I can't believe she fell right into your trap, Victim Commander," Orion spoke from the door. "Impressive work in distracting Sixus while you managed to get her out unnoticed."

I slowly sat up, and Timbrax placed the silver handcuffs around my wrists, snapping them into place. The stinging and burning hit me instantly. I was a prisoner on a Victim ship. I was in space. Outside, the pitch-black small window was adorned with thousands of tiny stars in every direction.

"MEL!"

Sixus screamed in my mind.

"Where are you?"

I didn't wanna reply to Sixus with them still in the room. So, I didn't.

"You may be my wife," Timbrax said, drawing me from my thoughts as I looked at him. "Melfina, I consider you to be my foe, and I will treat you accordingly."

"Fuck you!" As I leaped to my feet, I spat and found myself standing mere inches away from him. "Just kill me like you did, Zyra."

"Where's the fun in that?" Timbrax scoffed. "Orion needs you to locate something important, so we need you alive."

I repositioned myself, sitting back down and bringing my knees up while embracing them.

"She will not give up her powers so easily, will she Victim Commander?" Orion sighed Bordley. "I'll get the toucher chamber prepared for you at once." He turned and exited the room, leaving me alone with Timbrax. I felt Timbrax unbind himself from me and I felt Sixus panic on the other end of his bond.

"Don't you dare break Mel."

Sixus snarled in my mind.

"I'm coming to get you!"

He added.

"Sixus! I'm on a Victim ship!"

I screamed in my mind.

The link fell silent as I kept my gaze fixed on Timbrax. He crouched down before me as he placed an icy hand on my cheek. The heat within his body only came out when he used his Pyro Lancer powers.

"You're aware of my love for you, right?" Timbrax gently asked.

I did not give a response.

With a pocketknife in hand, he forcefully separated my cheeks. I put my tongue out and prepared myself for the ensuing pain.

Out of nowhere, Magnetic started playing at full blast in the room. Possibly to mask the screams that were about to erupt from me.

Overwhelmed by the sensation of burning hellfire, he pressed the silver blade further. He severed my tongue within a matter of seconds.

I remained calm without uttering a scream. I stayed in one place without moving. Nevertheless, the animosity evident in my eyes revealed my true sentiments towards him.

After licking my blood off both sides of the blade, Timbrax pocketed the knife. With a forward lean, he initiated a tender kiss on me. I could still detect the metallic taste of my blood. He pulled away; his mouth covered in my blood. He stood and removed the handcuffs from around my wrists. There were signs of swelling and red rings around my wrists.

I felt my wounds heal instantly after Sixus had used the Holistic sword on himself. Our souls were still bound to each other. If I died so, did he.

Timbrax turned to face me. He pulled his sword out from behind his back and thrust it through my stomach. Dark blood seeped out of my wound, staining my uniform.

"I trained you to be a lethal weapon, Melfina," he whispered in my ear as he yanked the sword out of my body. "Don't disappoint me."

He pushed open the door and stepped out. I followed him silently up the long hallway. My mecha pilot boots echoed off the silent walls. They stuck to the metal floor with each step I took. I gingerly held my wound, trying to stem the flow of blood, as I left a crimson trail behind me.

"This is gonna be a long fucking night."
I thought.

He entered a familiar room. I followed him inside and found Largo Croix licking his lips as I passed him. Orion stood with Tasia beside him. Once they smelled my blood, the Victim scattered around the room grew excited.

I saw the familiar chair and sat down as Orion strapped my wrists and my ankles and my throat down.

"Tell me what I want to know," Orion spoke as he stood before me. "Or I will electrocute the shit out of you, Melfi."

I smiled at him. I flipped him off with both hands before he stuck me with his first lightning bolt!

The electricity caused my body to shake uncontrollably before I blacked out into total darkness.

I had to stay alive, feeling every second ticking by, until Sixus came.

Or we were both dead.

THREE

I had lost all sense of time. They regularly beat me, either during the day or at night, using various forms of torture. I was lying on the metal cot in my not so cozy cell, doing my best to recover from another beating.

"Why isn't it working, Orion?" Largo demanded. "You should've been able to extract her flame easily, like your father did before he died!"

"Her life has been altered since then," Orion reminded him. "She's died twice and had been reviewed both times."

"I say," Largo laughed maniacally. "We kill the Tribrid bitch before she kills us!"

"I need her alive," Orion replied. "As does the Victim Commander."

"I'm surprised," Tasia whispered. "That he hasn't fucked her in his room yet."

The door was unlocked and Timbrax entered the room, followed by Orion. I slowly sat up as they stood before me.

"I require information from you, Melfi," Orion replied. "Or you will continue to be tortured."

Timbrax opened the astral thread and walked through it. He left it open. When he returned, my eyes widened in surprise as I saw him holding the black and blue dragon egg in his hands. The astral thread closed.

"Kill it," Orion ordered. "It's an abomination."

"No," I said as I stood. My wrists were cuffed, and the thick metal chains rattled. "Timbrax... don't do this."

He met my gaze. He raised his hands high above his head and with a mighty force brought his hands down. The egg smashed onto the metal floor. The sound of the shell cracking echoed off the silent walls. White goop slimed out into a puddle as the cracked eggshell oozed around it.

"NO!" I screamed as I sank to my knees and tried to put the shell back together. "You killed my baby!"

"I shall see you out in the hallway Victim Commander," Orion replied as he walked towards the door. "Now we are down to one Tribrid." He exited the room, leaving me alone with Timbrax.

I started sobbing uncontrollably. Timbrax killed our unborn child!

"I killed the other twin first," Timbrax replied coldly. "I'm not fucking around here, Melfina!"

"Get the fuck out of my cell!" I screamed. I pulled his wedding ring off my finger and tossed it at him. He caught it and pocketed it. "I am going to kill you myself on the battlefield Victim Commander!"

"I expect nothing less from you," he replied. "Now get your ass to bed and forget about these dead dragon babies!" He turned and walked out of the door and closed it behind him. He locked it and I heard two sets of footsteps walking away.

Tears filled my eyes as I settled on the cold, hard floor, cradling the shells in my hands until I eventually cried myself to sleep.

***

I awoke laying on the metal cot. I found myself hidden beneath a bloodstained blanket, a stark contrast to its original white hue. Now, the object appeared to be a dull, brownish shade, and as I reclined on the pillow, I could feel the stickiness of dried blood. The smell, a mix of iron and decay, was a grim reminder of the dried blood. My own.

The door to my cell opened, and Tasia entered and walked over to me. I slowly sat up and tossed the filthy blanket off of me. I turned and allowed my feet to dangle off the edge of the cot in case she wanted to sit down. Not like we were best friends or anything. We were far from it.

"Sign this Melfina," Tasia handed me a clipboard with a piece of paper on it. I picked up the pen and signed my name before handing it back to her. "You forgot to add you other surname."

I rolled my eyes but added DeRaps after Aeon Dra-Westin.

"Now we both filled out our divorce papers from our shitty husbands," she sighed. "They both murdered our babies, and they don't deserve us!" I averted my gaze and stayed silent. "You stink," she made a face. "Victim Commander!"

Moments later, Timbrax entered the cell and stared intently at us.

"Take her to get a shower," Tasia ordered. It is your responsibility to take care of her. With a swift movement, she directed herself towards the door. "In case you weren't aware, she's ending your marriage and seeking a divorce."

Tasia exited the room, and he walked silently towards me. He unlocked the shackles, and they dropped onto the bed. I slowly climbed to my feet, and he gently picked me up and carried me out of the room. He walked up the hallway and entered the bathroom. He set me on my feet and closed the door.

I took off my boots, undressed myself, and simply dropped my clothes onto the floor. Stepping inside, I closed the glass door behind me. The water started running on its own and regulated itself to the temperature of my body. I cleansed both my hair and body before shaving. Upon opening the door, the water ceased running with no intervention. Stepping outside, Timbrax gave me a clean, black towel.

After I had finished drying myself, I observed that he had brought clothes from Erda. Before I styled my hair by brushing and pinning it up, I changed into my outfit. I equipped myself with my mecha pilot boots and bundled up in my two jackets. I walked past him and pushed open the door, stepping out into the hallway. He joined me and I waited for him to lead me back to my cell.

"As of this moment," Timbrax spoke calmly as he placed a hand on my back and gently steered me in the opposite direction of my cell, saying, "We do not consider you a threat to anyone on this ship, so feel free to walk around."

I gave him a look, not believing him, and he rolled his eyes at me as we entered the kitchen area. Thankfully, it was empty. I walked to an empty table and sat down. Timbrax walked over and set down a glass of soda and a box of pizza from Erda. He opened it and placed a slice of peperoni pizza on a plate, and I gingerly picked it up and took a nibble. The flavors instantly popped in my mouth. I was starving, and he knew it.

"I'm sorry for my actions that resulted in the death of the twins," Timbrax said, but I didn't acknowledge him. "Nevertheless, it is crucial that I remind you of the initial motivations behind your father and brother's selection of me as the Victim Commander, Melfina."

"I never forgot."

I thought.

"Are you aware of the Nexus, Melfina?" Timbrax asked. As I shook my head, I quickly glanced up at him. "It is imperative that you acquire the location from the shamans and inform Orion about it."

I fixed my eyes on him in complete silence.

"Could you take on the role of a double agent for me once more?" He asked. "You are still my wife, so I won't sign those divorce papers."

I indicated my disagreement by shaking my head. I couldn't allow him to hurt me again. He took me by the hand and helped me to my feet. He rebound his soul to mine, and I instantly felt his pain and turmoil for killing the twins. I instantly placed the block up, and he was stunned by my new trick. I moved past him and exited the room. He followed close behind, curious as to what I was doing.

I walked up the metal steps and sat down at the top of them. Timbrax walked over and sat down beside me. I kept my gaze fixed out of the window, seeing endless space and many stars.

He pulled out his cell, and Masterpiece started playing. I wasn't falling for his shit. He stood and took me by the hand and led me down the stairs. We walked up the long hallway and I noticed nobody was around. I stopped in front of my cell, and he released my hand. I stepped into the room, and he walked past me and picked up the bloody pillow and blanket. He exited the room and returned with clean bedding. I watched as he fixed the bed for me and fluffed the pillow.

I sat on the bed and waited for him to chain my wrists. He shook his head, and I just sat there in silence.

He fled the room, prompted by the sound of alarms, taking care to close and secure the door. Prior to the angry voices, I could hear multiple sets of footsteps racing around in the hallway.

"Who the fuck are you?" Timbrax spat. "How did you get in here?"

The sound of fighting reached my ears moments before the door crashed into the wall. Timbrax was unconscious, and as the door fell, it bent inward with him trapped inside. I was taken aback and filled with hope as I prayed Sixus had finally managed to find me.

With his skin glowing in a vibrant shade of blue, a male stepped into the room. He was clad in a black ensemble, complete with boots and long gloves in the same shade. His ears extended in a way that reminded one of an elf or fae, pointing outwards. When he shifted his gaze, his eyes, which resembled the eyes of a cat, appeared to be massive. They had a blue hue.

He walked towards me and then carried me in his arms. With a single toss, he hoisted me onto his left shoulder and swiftly fled from the cell. Excruciating pain instantly spread throughout my body, causing me to wince. I breathed in the smell of him. His fragrance was that of a potent, earthy man from Erda. With significant force, my purple magic seal shot out of me and struck Victim, propelling them into the walls and leaving them unconscious.

"Holy shit! Did I do that?"

I thought.

Walking up the stairs, he entered the hangar. As he raced through the door made of vibrant green gel, the heavy black cords whipped around my body, released by his actions. With the flick of a switch, the lights illuminated, and a smooth, feminine, computerized voice filled the air.

"Welcome Pilot Melfina. Prepare to launch in 5... 4... 3... 2... 1... GO!"

The Aeon Dra deity burst out of the hangar at an astonishing speed, rivaling the force of gravity. I redirected my gaze to the man who was being forcefully pushed out of the door. Without any sort of face covering, he was freely floating in the vastness of space! As he turned, a word instantly formed in my mind.

"ALIEN!"

With his finger in the shape of a gun, he shot a blue beam. After a brief moment, the ship designated as the victim exploded. I was forcefully propelled forward due to the shockwave. He flew back towards Erda before he vanished, and I was able to witness it.

"Mom!" From the intercom, Cy's voice rang out loudly. "I'm programming the coordinates to bring you back to I.O.A."

In a surprising turn of events, the Aeon Dra deity shifted directions and started heading towards Tellus. I lost consciousness.

***

The sudden stop of the mecha's movement jolted me awake moments before the cords set me free. My body was instantly flooded with intense pain as I dropped to the floor. Using my strength, I pushed myself upwards and successfully made my way out through the door, which was composed of a thick green gel. With a sudden loss of balance, I came crashing down hard onto the unyielding metal grate.

"Who the fuck gave the order for the Aeon Dra to depart?" In a voice full of annoyance, Sixus shouted from the ground as he rapidly ascended the metal steps and stormed up the metal grate, his boots pounding forcefully with each step.

"You did, sir," a timid female voice replied. "A Westin gave the order, sir."

"I was in the middle of an important royal meeting," Sixus spat. "My arrival here followed the information I received about the Aeon Dra leaving Tellus." Sixus exclaimed.

"I did, dad," Cy's quiet voice said from behind him. "Mom needed help."

"You don't have the certification to be a repairer." Sixus calmed himself down. "Someone could have been harmed due to your actions."

"I brought mom back," she said. "She's right there."

Sixus glanced in my direction, and then hastily made his way towards me. In a gentle motion, he picked me up and swiftly moved past everyone. "Let's go, Cy!" Down the metallic staircase he went, and as he did, the doors gracefully opened. As he strolled along the corridor, I suddenly lost consciousness.

***

Startled, I opened my eyes and realized that I was back in my bed in my dorm room at the institute. I found Sixus sitting in a chair, gazing back at me. Cy stood beside him.

"I hid Frudi and Xeyva, thinking I was protecting them from Orion," Sixus whispered. "Only for Timbrax to kill them both."

"Timbrax murdered Xeyva right before my eyes, Sixus." Choking on my tears, I managed to utter. "I tried to mend the broken pieces of her egg, but my attempts were in vain."

"I understand." As his eyes filled with tears, he gave me a smile tinged with sadness, much like Cy, and spoke, "Mel, we will find retribution for our beloved children."

"What happened to Exrah?" Sitting up and discarding the hot comforter, I changed the subject. I rose to my feet, secured my mecha pilot boots by zipping them up, and then stood upright. Getting up, he motioned for Cy to put the chair back behind the desk and handed me my weapons. I took them and carefully placed them on my body. My jackets were thrown by her, and I proceeded to wear both of them.

"She was adamant about not leaving here." Sixus displayed a disapproving look. "Mel, she provided assistance in finding you and ensuring your safe return home."

"Oh," I replied. "Got it."

"Varric and the shamans fixed the balcony," Cy perked up, pointing her index finger towards the French doors. "It looks amazing!"

"It's beautiful," I gave her a sad smile. "Playing on it would have been something your sisters would have loved." Emotion overwhelmed me, and tears flowed freely from my eyes. I was pulled into a tight hug by Sixus, and then Cy came running over to join in, hugging the three of us together. We cried in such an intense and emotional manner that we reached a point of exhaustion from crying.

Cy and Sixus separated themselves from me, and we all used tissues that suddenly materialized to wipe our faces. Utilizing my supernatural speed, I effortlessly transformed my attire into a clean, reversible uniform. Once this was accomplished, I equipped my weapons and re-donned the two jackets. Once more, I brushed my hair and applied a fresh coat of makeup. I was the fucking queen. I couldn't look like shit in front of my people.

With purpose, we proceeded towards the exit and discarded our tissues in the trashcan. We stepped out into the hallway after the doors smoothly slid open. As we made our way up the hallway, I felt the scrutiny of every person as I purposefully passed by them. Sixus and I held hands, our fingers entwined together.

Casting a quick glance in his direction, I noticed his determined gaze fixed upon me. As we made our way into the main area, he used a strong shove to open one of the weighty metal doors. Stepping outside, we proceeded down the cement staircase. The three shamans met us at the bottom.

"Welcome back, your highness," Varric and the women greeted me with a bow before meeting my gaze. "It's a relief to see that you're not dead."

"They need me alive," I replied. "And thank you for the warm welcome."

The astral thread opened behind the shaman, and they turned, getting in defensive stances as we awaited whoever was coming out. Zara and the vampire hunters returned. I breathed a sigh of relief, and the shaman relaxed. Sorta.

"You came back," I said. "Is everything okay?"

"We did," Zara agreed. "Sixus told us my father killed my twin sisters." She shook her head in disgust. "He has turned into a despicable man."

"Yes," I agreed. "Will you be joining us in the war against him, Orion and Victim, then?"

"Absolutely," Zara agreed. "All our homes are on the line."

Setha walked up to me and placed a hand on my shoulder. I felt her absorbing my darkness until it became balanced once more. She removed her hand, and I nodded a curt thank you.

"While I have everyone here," I said as everyone turned their attention towards me. "Orion is after the Nexus."

"Fuck. Me!"

Sixus thought.

"What is it?" I asked. "They beat my ass for days because I don't know what the hell it is."

"My father," Sixus chose his words wisely. "In an attempt to keep it away from Claus and Phyre, the Nexus was hidden in the vastness of space."

"The hidden whereabouts of the Nexus remain a mystery to all shamans." Varric replied. "That's the explanation behind his belief that he could enlist your assistance in finding it."

The astral thread opened up, revealing the emergence of Timbrax. Employing his supernatural speed as a vampire, he swiftly snatched me by the throat. My body was forcefully pulled backwards by him, and I could feel the stinging touch of his knife against my throat.

"Do you know the whereabouts of the Shaman King?" Timbrax snarled.

"He's busy," Sixus snarled as he formed icicles in his closed fists. "You killed my child, you bastard!"

"I killed mine too," he scoffed. "She was an abomination and needed to die!"

"What the fuck do you want?" Sixus snarled as he took a step towards us.

"I owe that fucking shaman king a damn receipt!" Timbrax spat. "Tell him to bring his ass out here now!"

The hunters all raised their weapons towards Timbrax's head.

"Don't shoot!" Velzy spat. "We might miss and hit the queen!"

The shamanic seal appeared on his right forearm, glowing a bright red color.

"Ah!" Timbrax snarled as he released me. I ran and Sixus shoved me protectively behind him. "What the fuck is this?"

"How was he able to acquire a shamanic magic seal?" Varric inquired of Sixus.

"His soul is now connected to both Melfina and me," Sixus snarled angrily. "Our fate is linked to his, so if he dies, so will we."

"So," A.J. asked. "Let me get this straight. You're saying we *can't* kill him?"

"We can't proceed unless he frees his soul from ours." Shaking his head, Sixus indicated his disapproval. "Ironic," he said mockingly. "A person who is no longer alive, yet still experiences fear towards death!"

"I'm not afraid of a damn thing!" Timbrax snarled. "Remove this shit!"

"Once you detach your soul from ours, it will vanish," Sixus said with a smirk. "Just do it!"

Unbinding his soul from ours, Timbrax let out a fierce snarl. His forearm was instantly void of the seal. Before executing a backflip into the astral thread, he emitted a hissing sound towards me. Once he went inside, it simply vanished.

As the alarms blared, Tork nonchalantly shrugged, capturing the attention of everyone around. "I'll make arrangements to have it fixed." Her reaction was to roll her eyes at us. "The former queen was hastily buried in an emergency situation."

I was in need of a good laugh. Due to my anticipation of the following sequence.

A violent massacre awaited us.

FOUR

I underwent rigorous training with both Sixus and the shamans. The presence of Sinergy within me allowed Nyxie's memories to come forward, enhancing my ability to connect with her and quickly develop mastery over my newfound powers. We didn't have time to fuck around.

My rock music was blaring, and it took the other shaman some time to drown it out. I relied on that approach for my training and combat. They had no choice but to deal with it, damn it.

Outcome was currently playing.

"Take all four of us on at once, Mel," Solas said. "Or Nyx... whoever you are right now."

They closed in on me and launched an attack. I managed to block all of their attacks by raising my sword. By administering a strong kick to his stomach, I sent Varric flying through the air and across the room. I propelled myself into the air, executing spins and twists, ultimately delivering a strong kick to A.J.'s back. I caused her to soar and collide with Nell. They both traveled to Varric by air.

Solas and I revolved around each other, maintaining a constant distance. I caught a smirk directed towards me from him. The intensity of that smile was so overwhelming, it felt like it could be the end of me. As I bent backwards, he came running towards me, swinging his weapon through the air. The blade of the sword swiped across the place where I was previously positioned. My foot got grazed by him, causing me to lose my balance and fall. One-handed, he caught me and looked down at me with a triumphant smile.

With a sudden kick to my foot, I swiftly made him fall and land on his back with force. With a sudden leap, I rose from the ground and witnessed my sword changing back into a dagger. I applied pressure to his neck with it.

"Mel, you've won," Solas conceded, reverting to his original form as Sixus. "It's evident that you're training as a dragon knight is yielding results, isn't it?"

Varric's exclamation of "Holy shit" was followed by them leaping up and rushing over to us. I rose to my feet as Sixus did the same. Transforming into a dagger, he safely stowed away his sword. I carefully stored my dagger back in its sheath as well. "It was beyond Nyxie's understanding to perform that task."

"Melfina is highly skilled in multiple areas," Sixus replied. "The instructors who have trained her are among the best I have ever seen."

"I'm glad she's on our side," Nell whispered to Varric. Eleanor Nightingale, a timid shaman, preferred to observe from the shadows. With her tall and slender frame, she appeared to have a lack of muscular definition. Behind her thin, wired glasses, her eyes sparkled with a vivid shade of blue. Her beauty was undeniable, accentuated by the way she wore her long, dark hair down her back. "In terms of raw power, she far exceeds Nyxie."

"Is there a possibility of bringing her and Solas back?" A.J. inquired. "I was told that you possess the power to resurrect individuals."

"Changing the current timeline will inevitably lead to consequences," Varric warned her. "Let this be, and don't bother with it."

With time frozen, the shaman remained immobile. I blocked out my vision and honed in on my thoughts.

"Spirit Guide Naphirie?"

A thought crossed my mind.

"Tell me, oracle, what is your desire to destroy or revive?"

She posed a question.

"In order for the shamans to have authoritative figures to follow, we should bring back Evan Reigns, the Shamanic King of Light, and Nyxie Reigns, the Shamanic Queen of Light, to our present timeline."

A thought crossed my mind.

Silence.

"The task is complete. Is there anything else you wish to destroy or revive oracle?"

She asked.

"No. Thank you Naphirie."

I thought.

"Until our paths cross again, oracle."

Naphirie said.

Time started moving again, and to their surprise, Nyxie and Solas were now standing next to Varric, looking utterly perplexed.

"You've returned!" Nell's voice filled the air as she held Nyx in a tight hug, shouting with excitement.

"Did we go anywhere?" Nyxie posed a question to them.

"No idea," Sixus shrugged. "I am pleased to see the two of you here."

"Thank you," Solas nodded curtly at him. "Elder brother."

"Can you repeat what you just said?" Sixus asked, shooting him a glance.

"The timeline was altered," Solas responded. "This indicates that there were slight modifications made to our current timeline."

Nyxie's purple magic seal and Solas's dark blue seal were expelled from us and reentered their bodies. The lights slowly dimmed, and I felt a weight lift off my shoulders, as I no longer had to carry her powers.

A radiant pale blue magic seal, adorned with a menacing dragon visage, illuminated the space around me. Prior to the lights vanishing, Sixus had a dark blue face featuring a dragon, which then entered our bodies.

Whispering to Solas, Nyxie revealed, "It's them," and he shared the same level of shock as the rest of the group. "They are the Universal Shamanic King and Queen of Light Solas!"

Synergy and Helios departed our bodies and dissolved into thin air. Sixus and I grew exhausted as we made our way to the door.

"Hey!" Solas angrily shouted in our direction. "I'm not done speaking to you, Sixus!"

"We'll talk later!" Sixus shouted as he walked away, "We're going to bed!"

As alarms blared throughout the institute, I couldn't help but hope that it was Tork coming to fix the damn system again. I became aware of an imminent danger through my intuition. In a quick motion, we left the sparing room and proceeded to race up the hallway. Bursting through one of the side doors, he propelled us outside, and we swiftly made our way into the crisp night atmosphere. As we made our way around the building, we were surprised to find Orion, Timbrax, Tasia, Largo Croix, Claus, and Victim waiting for us behind the gates.

A group consisting of shaman, assassins, dragon knights, mecha pilots, and vampire hunters appeared and joined us, standing in the back. Cy advanced and positioned themselves next to me.

"I've been looking for you." Timbrax stared intensely at Solas and spoke. "Shaman King, I haven't forgotten about the receipt I owe you!"

"For what?" Solas asked, giving him a questioning look with his raised eyebrow. "I have never had the pleasure of seeing you until now, Vampire King!"

Leaping over the wall, Timbrax swiftly unfastened his sword from its sheath on his back.

"He's really serious, isn't he?" Solas asked Sixus.

Timbrax wasted no time and tapped into his vampire speed, rushing towards Solas even before Solas could respond. Sixus tightly clenched his fist around a solid icicle and forcefully struck the ground beneath him with it. The dark blue magic seal enveloped him, emitting a blinding light that left us temporarily blinded. When it dispersed, I gazed at him and my jaw dropped a bit. Before my eyes was the blue alien, the one who had saved me from the Victim ship.

Sixus caught Timbrax's gaze, prompting him to snarl.

"Surprise, bitch!" With a smirk on his face, Sixus quickly shifted to a more serious demeanor. "I'm the one who knocked your ass out on the ship after you killed my baby!"

"Victim!" Timbrax emitted a menacing snarl. "Eliminate every single one of them!" He turned his attention towards me. "Aside from my wife!"

"Hunters!" Chaos snarled. "Initiate an attack!"

"Assassins, dragon knights, mecha pilots!" Sixus shouted. "Attack!"

"Shamans!" With a glance at his team, Solas said. "Attack!"

In a swift motion, Timbrax moved towards Sixus, initiating a battle where their swords clashed.

Victim were turned into a demon when the vampire hunters shot them with acid bullets. They were mercilessly stabbed by everyone else with their daggers, resulting in their transformation into dark ash piles.

I grasped the hilt of the Valistik sword and the dagger, swiftly removing them from their sheaths. A sword replaced the dagger through a transformation.

Right as I was preparing to make a move, Timbrax unsheathed a knife and threw it, propelling it towards my midsection. By crossing my two swords, I successfully blocked it. Despite that, he flung a throwing star at me, which ended up stabbing the left side of my neck.

"Ah!" I lowered myself onto one knee. With a firm grip, I held both swords in one hand and forcefully extracted the metal from my neck. With a swift motion, I flung it to the ground, and I could feel the heat of my wound as sticky blood began to seep out. "You son of a bitch!"

"I caused her to bleed!" Timbrax's shout echoed towards Claus. "It's your chance!"

I glanced over at Claus, who was completely engrossed in Nyxie. He was in this place! Using his abilities as a dark shaman, he crafted a gigantic bird cage to trap her within. Catching both her and the other shaman off guard, he lifted her up. Metal spikes grew and became prominent inside the cage. Her body was forcefully struck by them, resulting in a combination of pain and shock that made her scream. She found herself on the black floor as the cage fell away. Without warning, the victim sprung to their feet and began biting her.

"Nyxie!" As he fought off demons with his sword, Solas shouted and made his way towards her. "I'm on my way!"

The sound of her screams ceased when Victim leaped down. Falling towards the lawn, Solas swiftly caught her body as he leaped up. He touched down beside me, cradling her lifeless form in his embrace. Her body was marked with bites, and her garments were ripped and ruined. Her wounds were bleeding. She was nearing death. It came to my attention that her heartbeat was gradually getting slower.

She softly spoke the words, "Evan, I love you," as her hand quivered and made contact with his cheek. "I am giving Sinergy and my abilities to Melfina as my final gesture." Her hand dropped and came to rest on my leg. As her life slipped away, I observed a purple magic seal emerging from her body and entering mine, only to vanish shortly after.

"Nyx?" Evan delicately moved her body with a shake. There was no movement from her. "NO!" he shouted. A slender string of red color shot out from his body and flew into mine before disappearing. I was able to sense the pain he was experiencing. His gaze lingered on me, a mix of uncertainty and puzzlement evident in his eyes as he questioned the inexplicable connection that tied us together.

I struggled to get up from the grass, wiping away the tears from my eyes. It didn't concern me that I was experiencing severe bleeding. With a scream, I began slashing anything that moved that wasn't an ally. I ensured the demons were eradicated by continuously eliminating Victim.

The sword underwent a transformation, reverting back into a dagger, which I promptly returned along with the Valistik sword to their sheaths. With labored breathing, I dropped onto the grass. My consciousness was slipping away.

"Mel!" In his human form, Sixus promptly rushed to be by my side. After stowing his dagger, he gently placed his hand on my neck. In order to stop the bleeding, he used a thick layer of ice to seal my wound. "I got you."

Handing Nyxie's body to Varric, Solas walked over to me and stood beside me. Timbrax took his time to approach us, making sure his weapon was constantly pointed at me.

"It has begun!" Claus couldn't contain his maniacal laughter. "The Tribrid will find the Nexus for us and destroy three planets!"

"What the fuck is he going on about?" Snarling, Timbrax glared at Sixus and Solas. A faint glow of dark blue light emanated from Sixus' body and seamlessly transferred into Solas' body. From Solas, a brilliant dark blue light appeared and then shifted into Timbrax. A red light, originating from Timbrax, entered Sixus' body. "What is this shit?"

In a mesmerizing spectacle, my body soared upward and levitated as the three lights positioned themselves in the shape of a triangle. As a searing pain enveloped me, a luminous purple magical seal erupted from within, eliciting a cry of anguish. Alongside it, a pale blue seal featuring the menacing countenance of a snarling dragon materialized. Sixus had a dragon companion that perfectly matched his attire, both in color and style.

The purple one that Solas had was just like Nyxie's. Timbrax's was red, and it had vampire teeth in the center. Prior to separating into two distinct colors, my two hues combined to form a stunning blue-violet tone. One flying towards Erda. Before it disappeared, the other one was going towards Outer Earth. I dropped onto the lawn, desperately trying to catch my breath.

"To unlock the stages of the Nexus," Claus said calmly, "The Tribrid is required." There was a temporary pause in his actions. "In order to bring about the downfall of everyone, I needed a Tribrid who could only be defeated by a royal female possessing the unique abilities of a vampire, a shaman, and a Half-Draconian."

As the lights disappeared around the three men, Timbrax quickly flipped back to join Orion and the rest of the group. His connection to me became stronger, resulting in a snarl from Sixus.

"Tonight, our mission is finished," Orion stated calmly. "Move out!" They gracefully bounded over the wall and disappeared into the otherworldly plane. The astral thread closed, leaving us alone.

"Everyone go back to the institute and go to sleep!" A shout escaped Sixus' lips. "Well done tonight!"

"How do you define a successful night?" While Sixus was helping me up, Varric spat. "In the act of safeguarding your queen, our queen lost her life!"

"Return to the academy," Solas spoke in a quiet voice, glaring at A.J. "I'll meet you three there and we can bury Nyx."

"Solas," A.J. began. "I didn't anticipate this happening."

"Once we are back at the academy, I will handle your punishment, Miss. Battle." He stopped momentarily. "Go!"

Without wasting any time, they rushed through the green light before it, and they disappeared from sight.

"I need to see if Melfina still holds the Shamanic Queen of Light's powers in her body," Solas said, looking at Sixus. "For the sake of my mental well-being, big brother."

"Just do what you have to do," Sixus sighed. "Mel, I don't have any intentions of going anywhere."

Stepping closer to me, Solas took the initiative and kissed me. He backed away and simply gazed at me. In addition, Sixus was staring at me.

In a matter of seconds, my skin illuminated in a soft purple hue and then vanished. When I turned my gaze towards Solas, he greeted me with a sorrowful smile.

"You are now the Shamanic Queen of Light, Melfina." Solas whispered. "Fate, chose me as your partner as your Shamanic King of Light."

"Oh," I said, taken aback that I had a third mate. "Is there a method to delegate the power to someone else?"

"The only way for that to happen." In a gesture of negation, Solas shook his head. "Death is the only path."

"Yeah," Sixus said, shaking his head in a disapproving manner. "Sorry, Mel, but that is not a viable choice."

"Looks like I'm stuck with her abilities now." I offered them a smile filled with sadness. "I regret messing with the timeline... I'm truly sorry for the loss you've experienced, Evan."

Solas nodded with a curt gesture, expressing his gratitude. "Your actions were influenced by Angelina, and she will receive severe punishment."

"You can take as much time as you need," Sixus stated. "I will protect Mel from Orion, Timbrax, Claus, and Victim."

"In case you didn't know, all three of us were actually triplets." Solas directed his words to Sixus. "Until you needed me back on Tellus, my dad made some slight modifications and kept me concealed on Earth."

"Our mother was a dragon," Sixus informed him. "You, along with Faron, Cy, and I, can become skilled ice wielders."

"I'm aware," Solas smirked knowingly. In a display of his extraordinary abilities, he fashioned an ice rose seemingly out of nothing and presented it to me. His back muscles flexed as he removed his black T-shirt, revealing his white dragon wings that exploded out. "It was my father who ensured that my mother came to Earth and taught me how to wield my powers, older brother." While a blue light flashed, he pivoted and moved away. After entering, he disappeared, taking it along.

Sixus forcefully removed the Holistic sword, who then stabbed me in the leg. As the wound on my neck healed, a bright blue light flashed and then vanished. Sixus placed it back in the sheath and then bit into the rose. While walking up the steps, he chewed on the ice. As he pulled the heavy metal door open, I entered first, and he quickly followed before it closed behind us. We moved through the main area and then proceeded up the hallway on foot.

"You're not jealous of Evan, are you?" I expressed my disbelief. "He is assuming Feron's position."

"I'm not feeling jealous," Sixus said with a frown, as he took another massive bite of the ice rose and pondered over it. I gave him a disapproving glance, and in response, he rolled his eyes. He was damn well aware that his envy was evident in our bond. "He is more attractive than I am!"

"You're joking, right? He's your identical twin, Sixus," I scoffed. "You dumbass, he's supposed to look just like you!"

When Sixus shot me a look, I immediately became aware of it.

"I say that with love, Sixus."

I expressed my thoughts to him.

We came to a stop right in front of my dorm room in the dormitory. With the doors sliding open, we made our way inside and were greeted by the illuminating light triggered by motion. The moment the doors closed, we wasted no time in shedding our clothing stained with blood and disposing of them in the nearest trashcan. Stepping into the bathroom, Sixus pulled back the shower curtain, and we followed suit, entering the shower area.

With a twist of the knobs, he unleashed a torrent of water that soaked us. We rapidly cleaned ourselves and he promptly turned off the water. After he opened the curtain, we dried off before putting on our clothes. After we left the bathroom, the sight of a teenage girl standing greeted us on the balcony, observing us intently. She had divided her hair into two colors, with one side being purple and the other side being blue. The florescent lighting cast an unnatural glow on her red eyes, making them appear even more striking. Her appearance was stunning.

I confronted her, stating that she was responsible for the balcony fire and had attempted to take my life, to which she responded with a smug expression. "May I ask who you are?"

"I am Vizzeirra- The Kind- Aeon Dra," she responded, mimicking Orion's style. "I happen to be the younger sister of Dynastra."

"She died reviving you," I said. "Did your father send you here to assassinate me?"

Entering the bedroom, Vizzeirra chuckled at my words, clearly amused.

"I am determined to seek vengeance and take the life of Orion for the brutal murder of my sister and cousins," Vizzeirra stated firmly. "I am willing to become your second guardian, Auntie Melfina, and join you in the battle in the sky."

"What makes you reliable and trustworthy?" I asked. "You have already made an attempt on my life, do you remember?"

"If I had any intention of killing you." She remarked with a nonchalant shrug, "I would've done it while you were sleeping."

"If you betray us," Sixus warned in a chilling, resentful tone. "I will freeze your heart, extract it from your body, and bring it to your parents, causing them immense pain."

"It would be beneficial if you had more confidence in me, Uncle Sixus." In a sarcastic tone, Vizzeirra replied, "Dynastra was taking care of me and my baby cousins until we met our unfortunate demise."

I observed the slender red string fly out of her body, and into mine before it disappeared. I was now bound to her ass. The instant the doors slid open; Cy entered with such fury that I could feel it in the air.

"If you make another attempt on my life or my mother's, you'll regret it." Cy's voice filled with anger. "I will personally ensure that you meet your demise, you bitch!"

"Alright," Sixus sighed and massaged his tired eyes with his index finger and thumb. "You and Cy will be sharing a room."

"Father!" As her anger reached its peak, Cy stomped her foot in frustration. "Are you actually serious?"

"The only alternative we have is to choose that, as risking Orion returning to harm her again is not an option, Cy." With a sidelong look, Sixus observed her. "Bed... now!"

Stepping out from the astral thread, Timbrax appeared. Employing his exceptional vampire speed, he swiftly caught hold of Vizzeirra by the throat and cautiously stepped backwards towards the open blue portal.

"Damn it, Brax!" I let out a snarl while making my way towards him. His gaze met mine as he untethered his soul from Sixus, Solas, and me. "Stop killing children!"

"I have only one mission." With a menacing glare, Timbrax spoke in a frigid tone. "My intention is to inflict the maximum amount of pain on you, Melfina."

"Well, I must say congratulations!" I spat. "You have achieved your goal!"

Vizzeirra was flung into Sixus and Cy by Timbrax, causing both of them to be knocked to the ground. I was forcefully pulled along through the astral thread as he tightly grasped onto my arm. It was closed once he was gone.

"MELFINA!"

In my mind, Sixus shouted with intensity.

"Kill me!" I uttered in a bitter tone.

Backed up against the cold blue wall, I felt his snarl intensify as he loomed over me. After licking my neck, he proceeded to sink his fangs into my skin.

A snarl escaped me as his endorphins were activated. After retracting his fangs and tasting my blood, he turned his head to meet my gaze without a hint of hesitation.

"Do you stand with me or with them?" Softly, Timbrax asked his question.

"I will always choose," I managed to say amidst the tears in my eyes. "Sixus!"

"I feel abandoned by you too," Timbrax said, his expression filled with sorrow. "When I'm given the order to kill you," he laughed dryly. "Melfina, you will meet your end at my hands!"

At the exact moment he uttered those words, the astral thread suddenly opened up, compelling me to forcefully push him away and rush out into the secure arms of Sixus, who was patiently waiting for me.

"When I kill her," Timbrax shook his head as rage filled him. "Rest assured, I'll ensure you're there to see Sixus!"

With the closing of the astral thread, an overwhelming pain gripped my heart.

The tension between Timbrax and I was thick, our rivalry fueling a constant state of conflict.

There was no alternative except for me to eliminate the Victim Commander.

My heart will part ways with my love for him, no matter the sacrifices I have to make.

FIVE

Understanding the risk to my life, I took my training to the next level. I had added weights on both my wrists and inside my boots. Three days had elapsed since Orion and the others last targeted the institute. There was still no sign of the shamans coming back from Erda.

As I stood on the flight strip, Vizzeirra loomed behind me in her majestic, two-toned dragon form. With the saddle in place, she was ready to go.

"Mount up!" Sixus' loud shout jolted me out of my reverie. He walked up to me as I was about to leap on Viz's back. "What do you think you're doing, Mel?"

"My responsibilities as a dragon knight." I gave him a glare. "Now back up before Viz stomps on your ass, will ya?"

"It's too dangerous for you to leave the institute unguarded, Mel," Sixus replied. "Stay your ass here!"

"I'm training!" I hissed under my breath, so the other dragon knights didn't hear me. "You can't stop me."

"I'm pulling Mel from her duties today," Sixus said to the other instructors. "Your dismissed Dragon Knight Aeon Dra-Westin." I was about to argue with him when he pulled rank on my ass. "Disobey a direct command from *your* king," Sixus snarled, emphasizing the potential consequences. "You, Dragon Knight Aeon Dra-Westin, will have 26,000 demerits added to your account by *me*!"

Everyone's eyes were fixed on us, and I had to make sure I didn't lose my temper. I wore a forced smile as I hurried past him, my anger palpable as I stormed away from the flight field.

"I didn't dismiss you!"

Sixus snapped in my mind.

"Get your ass back here, Mel!"

He demanded.

I constructed a wall to shield my emotions or thoughts from him. As soon as I threw my hand out, the astral thread materialized. I made a quick leap inside and the door shut immediately.

After a brief moment, the other side of the thread opened, and Timbrax swiftly entered before it closed behind him. I kept my gaze fixed ahead of me. As he walked over to where I was sitting, the odor of death became more prominent, and he sat down beside me.

"I'm just sitting for five minutes," I whispered. "I'll be gone after I calm down."

"He pissed you off," Timbrax sighed as he moved closer towards me. I pretended not to notice. "Vent."

"I'm good," I sighed. "I won't come here anymore."

Timbrax reached out and brought me close, settling me onto his lap. As he held me tightly, I found comfort in resting my heavy head against his chest. Despite everything, he continued to have feelings for me. And I still loved him. There was no need for us to speak. Our understanding of each other reached new heights through our shared experiences of training and battling side by side in the Flight Games.

"You're starving yourself to death," Timbrax said in a quiet voice. "Feed on me before you leave." I shook my head. "That's an order from your Victim Commander!" he said, pulling rank on my ass. These men loved doing that shit to me. "Now Melfina."

I expressed my frustration by rolling my eyes, then lightly licked the side of his neck before finally sinking my sharp fangs into his neck. I quenched my thirst by drinking his blood until I was satisfied. After removing my fangs, he wiped my chin with his thumb to get rid of any remaining blood.

"You're not planning on signing those divorce papers, are you?" I asked him.

"No," he chuckled. "Melfina, I love you."

"I've witnessed the way you treat the people you claim to love." I mocked. "Right before my eyes, you ended both of their lives."

"We can have another baby," he sighed sadly. "Melfina, once you give them what they want, all of this will be finished."

"I have to leave," I exclaimed, quickly getting up from his lap and standing. Taking his time, he got up and peered down at me, then bent down and kissed me with intense desire. As I closed my eyes, I welcomed his kiss and allowed him to hold me tightly. Fuck. He desired my immediate presence. I couldn't allow myself to be under his power. As I pulled away, my breath came out in short pants. "Bye."

The feeling of illness overwhelmed me, and I doubled over, vomiting blood until there was nothing left inside me.

"What the fuck did you do to me, you sick bastard?" I asked as I struggled to catch my breath.

Walking towards me, Timbrax reached out and lifted me up in his arms, his intense gaze focused on me. "Now that you have pledged your allegiance to the shaman king," he frowned in disapproval. "Melfina, my blood is lethal to you."

"So, why did you force me to consume it?" I inquired.

"Cause I'm an asshole," he smirked, his voice dripping with arrogance. Opening the astral thread, he ventured outside. To ward off the dizziness, I closed my eyes while he walked. "There's that jackass dragon now."

"Mel!" With a shout, Sixus quickly came over to us. He guided me attentively, and I sensed the mingling scent of cranberries and snow emanating from him. I felt a sense of security wash over me. "What did you do to her?"

"She drank my blood," he replied, shuddering at the memory. "I think it's poisonous to her at this point."

There was a burning sensation on the inner side of my right wrist. The moment I woke up, a glistening triangle came into view, breaking apart into three distinct pieces. My arm went numb and dangled, finding support on top of Sixus' arm.

"Can you tell me what she has on her wrist?" Timbrax asked. "We obtained it too."

"Mel is the oracle," Sixus spat. "I'm getting her to I.O.A."

"You know I'm not going to harm her, right?" Sixus froze in his tracks upon hearing Timbrax's statement. "Do whatever it takes to keep her protected from Orion and Claus, alright?"

Upon lowering the barrier, Sixus quickly understood and shared my pain. I sensed Timbrax reconnecting his soul with us moments before he vanished.

I fainted and everything around me became completely dark.

***

Upon awakening, I realized that I was still in my bed inside my dorm room. I had Sixus and Solas sitting in chairs right beside me.

"Mel, I specifically chose you to venture into the enemy's territory." Shaking his head, Sixus expressed his disapproval. "I regret not giving you the opportunity to fly."

"No," I shook my head. "If only I had heeded your direct instruction, I wouldn't feel this remorse…"

"Let's move beyond this," Solas interrupted, redirecting our discussion. "Mel, our top concern is to protect the secrecy of the Nexus from the enemy and to ensure your survival."

"Absolutely," I concurred as I flung the toasty comforter aside and they both rose, aiding me in standing upright. "To ensure Timbrax's toxic blood doesn't contaminate me, starving the vampire seems like the only viable option."

"And have you ever succumbed to your vampiric nature, leaving a trail of death and destruction in the institute?" Solas' head shook in denial, his eyes widening with surprise. "Mel, I have a specially crafted mouth guard that provides a fresh and innovative way for you to consume your blood."

I took the gold mouth guard from his outstretched hand, marveling at its luxurious appearance. I picked it up and proceeded to open my mouth. Placing it inside, I eagerly bit down, and the taste exploded in my mouth. My saliva activated the dry goop. It slid easily down my throat. Before opening my mouth and removing it, I made sure to completely drain it. With a flick of my wrist, I tossed it into the trash can, and we stood there, the silence broken only by the sound of our breaths.

"Is there any noticeable difference in how you feel?" Solas asked.

I stood there, waiting for the sickness to overcome me. There was no occurrence or incident.

"No?" I skeptically raised an eyebrow, to which he responded with a smug smile. "I can manage to keep the blood from coming up."

"Great," Solas nodded. "Mel, I'll get the vampire hunters to work on this special blood for you as soon as possible." he promised.

"Thank you, Solas," I gasped, my eyes wide with surprise as I tried to comprehend what had just happened. "Your… kind."

With a wink, he confidently claimed, "I know exactly how to cater to a woman's needs." With a hint of annoyance, Sixus rolled his eyes at his brother's predictable behavior. "Everything I learned goes against what Sixus believes."

"So," I sighed. "Can you share the details of our plan?"

"We prioritize your safety," Sixus replied straightforwardly. "You never stray from us, Mel, under any circumstances."

"Normally," I sighed inwards. "I would say something fucked up, but you're right... again."

"I'm always right," Sixus smirked cockily at me. "You just hate to admit it."

"Where is your kingdom, Melfina?" Solas inquired.

"Over there." I gazed out the open French doors and could see the pile of rubble from miles away. "In a heap of devastation."

"That," Solas searched for the words to say. "Sucks."

"I would rebuild it again," I sighed. "But I don't want Orion to infiltrate and destroy it, you know?"

With a silent nod of his head, Solas expressed his agreement.

"Can I go for a fly if you two accompany me?" I pleaded with my eyes looking at Sixus. "Please?"

"I'm not a fan of the whole flying thing." Solas shook his head. "Fear of heights."

"You twins really have the same fears, don't you?" I smirked at Sixus.

"Hey," Sixus shot me a warning look. "I wasn't expecting that rollercoaster ride from hell during the Flight Games."

"I heard," Solas gazed at him. "You passed out and screamed like a little bitch."

"That shit doesn't leave this room!" Sixus glared at him.

"Well," Solas inquired. "How did she learn how to fly?"

Sixus and I exchanged glances with each other before I spoke.

"By embracing the darkness within me," I said, lowering my head in shame. "I thought I was protecting Sixus, but... I was wrong." Keeping my gaze on Solas, as I observed him. "Now I live with that regret daily and it's why I had to prove myself to everyone in the Flight Games."

"I'm not doing that shit." Solas shook his head. "Going through what you've both did," he sighed. "It strengthened your relationship, trust, and love with each other, didn't it?"

"I'd like to think so," Sixus agreed, looking at me. "Even though that fucking vampire infiltrated her emotions with his manipulations... he loves her, too."

"Timbrax," I frowned as they looked at me. "Refuses to sign the divorce papers," I scoffed. "I didn't hesitate to sign them."

"Timbrax is protecting Melfina from the inside of enemy territory," Solas said to himself. "He is embracing his inner darkness to do it, though."

"Is that why this triangle symbol appeared on all our wrists?" I asked as I flashed my wrist his way.

"You got your first shamanic marking, Mel," Solas nodded. "It appeared on everyone who is bound to you."

The astral thread appeared in the room with Timbrax standing there, shooting daggers towards Solas. "Remove it," Timbrax snarled as he flashed his right wrist towards us. "NOW!"

"I can't," Solas shrugged. "You chose your path, vampire king."

"Unbind your soul from us," I whispered. I felt Timbrax unbind himself, freeing us from his grasp once more. We watched as his marking disappeared from his right wrist. As he walked into it, he paused and faced away from me, his presence casting a shadow on the ground. "Now stay the fuck out of my life!"

I raised my hand and made a fist, closing the astral thread, and it disappeared as I lowered my hand to my side.

"Mel," Sixus rushed to my side and placed his hands on my cheeks, forcing me to look into his eyes. "I will *always* choose you."

Hearing those words always broke me. He knew that. Hearing his voice brought me back to reality.

"Sixus?" I whispered as he gave me a sad smile. I reached up and placed my hands on the back of his neck, pulling him towards me. I crushed my lips hungrily against his. He kissed me fiercely before breaking it. "Thank you."

"I won't let him take you away from me again," he whispered. "Our love will burn them to the ground!"

My gaze shifted towards Solas, who attempted to look unbothered. Seeing his shamanic queen with another man was breaking his heart. The strength of the bond was evident, as I could feel it coursing through his end, a powerful and unbreakable link.

I stepped away from Sixus' side and walked up to Solas. He gazed down at me, not knowing what to say.

"I love you too, my shaman king." Softly murmuring, I extended my hands and delicately placed them behind his neck. I drew his face towards me and closed my eyes as I kissed him. His body tensed up before he relaxed in my arms. He returned my kiss before breaking it. "You will always have me by your side."

Solas pulled me tightly into his arms and buried his face into my shoulder as he sobbed uncontrollably.

Sixus walked over and hugged us both. Solas regained his composure, and we released him.

"Thank you," he whispered. "I promise I will love and protect you with my life, Mel."

"I know you will, Solas," I gave him a small smile. "Welcome home."

"Time to get your ass a guardian, little bro," Sixus slapped him on the back. "If you don't die falling off dragon mountain."

"What?" Solas' eyes widened in surprise.

"Have fun becoming a dragon knight!" I called as Sixus grabbed Solas by the arm and ran out of the open French doors and stood on the balcony. He leaped down with a screaming Solas behind him.

The astral thread opened, and Timbrax stood there staring at me.

"I decline your offer Victim Commander," I said, standing my ground. "I look forward to killing you on the battlefield."

"You're making a mistake," Timbrax snarled. "There will be no more chances for you."

"I know," I replied, not caring as I slowly made my way into the astral thread. He backed up, eyeing me suspiciously. I yanked the Venin dagger out and stabbed him in the left side. He snarled as he gazed up at me. I pulled it out and licked his blood off the blade. The silver burned my tongue as I smirked at him. "My parting gift to you... is my hate for killing my babies!"

"You," Timbrax breathed as blood seeped out of his wound. "Are one demented bitch you know that?"

I laughed as I strolled out of the astral thread, stepping back into the dorm room. "You helped create me."

Timbrax used his vampire speed and stood before me. As he sank his sharp fangs into my neck, I snarled up at him just before his endorphins kicked in. When he yanked them out, I lost my balance and fell forward. He caught me and carried me over to the bed, laying me down.

"You need to stay away from me, Melfina," Timbrax whispered down to me. "My blood is turning the darkness within you even darker than I could've ever imagined."

He ran through the astral thread, and it disappeared.

I closed my eyes and fell into a deep sleep.

***

"Mel!" Sixus voice was filled with panic as he shook me awake. "Why is Timbrax's blood in here?"

Confused, I opened my eyes and sat up with a jolt. I gazed around the room and saw a large pool of blood beside Sixus' feet on the tile floor. The Venin dagger lay beside it.

"I stabbed him, I think?" I shook my head, still in a dazed state. "He bit me, and I stabbed him."

"Other than getting bit," Sixus asked. "Are you hurt?"

"I'm fine," I nodded. "I don't remember him even coming in here to be honest with you."

Sixus froze the blood and placed it in a protective ice box. He lifted it off the floor and tossed it to Solas who caught it.

"I'll get the vampire hunters to analyze it," Solas replied as he headed for the door. "There's gotta be something in his blood to keep Mel from embracing the darkness even further." The doors slid open, and he stepped out. He ran, and the doors closed.

"You knew?" I whispered.

"Of course we did," Sixus nodded. "We had to get you to turn on him and it worked."

"The darkness," I shook my head. "It's trying to take complete control over my body."

"I know," he sighed heavily. "That's why we had to place a massive amount of it into another host."

"Who?" I asked as the doors slid open. Tork and Velzy escorted a familiar female into the room, with her hands handcuffed behind her back. "You?"

I was face to face with Phyre Wix, the Shamanic Princess of Darkness, who stood before me in a haunting, undead state. The smoothness of her flawless, tan skin was the envy of everyone around her. Her hair, long and dark, hung straight as her deep brown eyes held a mysterious, dark hue. With her tall and slender figure, it was evident that she maintained an athletic lifestyle. With her oval face as a frame, her body seemed even more statuesque and striking. The sight of her beauty filled me with a sense of unease and insecurity. It seemed like everyone was effortlessly stunning, which only highlighted my own insecurities about my appearance.

"You look surprised to see me, Universal Shamanic Queen Melfina," Phyre smirked. "I owe my brother some payback."

"How do I know that we can trust you?" I asked as I slowly climbed to my feet.

"You don't," she laughed evilly. "I represent your best opportunity to keep the Nexus away from Claus."

"If you entertain the idea of betraying us, Phyre." I stated in response. "I will end your life."

"This alliance is going to be fun," Phyre smirked. "Let's get started, shall we, Tribrid?"

I didn't trust this bitch at all.

Despite everything, she was our top choice for keeping the Nexus secure and away from Claus's grasp.

I just hoped that I wouldn't look back on this later and wish I had chosen differently.

SIX

I restored the Xeonada Empire and placed a protective cloaking shield over it to keep Orion and Victim and their gang out. Solas had bound Phyre's powers using symbols and bangles to keep her from using them against us. She was our enemy, after all. We were in the air patrolling the skies for any sign of Victim. We found nothing.

"So," Phyre shouted up to me. Viz was carrying a glass tube with her inside of it. It swayed back and forth as she dangled from the thick metal chain in her clawed talon. "Where is the Nexus, Melfina?"

"If I knew," I shouted down to her from the saddle. "I wouldn't tell your bitch ass!"

"No wonder Nyxie chose you to harness her powers," Phyre laughed to herself. "You both had the same personality types!"

I snarled, as I did my best to ignore her ass. It had only been a few days, and she was pissing me off relentlessly. The cold sea air stung my face as I kept the flight goggles over my eyes. I had forgotten what it had felt like to be a normal dragon knight. My life had become chaotic ever since stepping foot in the Abraxis Institute of Union last year!

Sixus and Solas were my wing men. Solas had obtained two guardians and was getting used to his Half-Draconian life that had been denied to him while living as a mundane on Erda.

"Listening to music up here helps!" I shouted to Solas. "Trust me, I know!"

"I'll try that!" Solas shouted over the roar of the wind. "Thanks!"

I sensed danger approaching.

"Watch out!"

Viz screamed in my mind.

A giant mecha flew out of the sea and used a sword slashing open the glass tube. A hand grabbed Phyre as she fell.

With a sudden release, Viz let go of the chain, and the top of the tube descended into the sea with a resounding crash, sending a powerful spray of water shooting upwards.

"It's an ambush!"

Viz shouted in my mind.

Orion appeared before me, using his wings to fly. Viz was surprised when he head-butted her.

Viz roared as she shot up, flapping her wings to stay in place. My magnetic boots prevented me from being moved as I flew backwards. I got bad whiplash, though.

Claus released Phyre from her bangles, and her powers rushed to the surface.

"*Shit!*"

I thought.

"*VIZ GO!*"

I added.

Viz snarled as she shot upwards, and Orion followed us as he flapped his red dragon wings rapidly to catch us.

I unclipped my boots and stood, immediately noticing the weightlessness in my legs. I raced up her body, my heart pounding in my chest, and launched myself into the air from her head. As I flexed my back, a rush of air filled my ears and the sensation of my pale blue dragon wings springing out gave me a sense of exhilaration.

Viz transformed into her human form as the saddle plummeted into the sea below us with a crash. She snarled at Orion as he gazed at her intently.

"I smell Aeon Dra blood flowing through your veins," he said. "What is your name?"

"Vizzeirra- The Kind Aeon Dra," Viz spat. "And I'm killing you, father!"

Viz screamed as she flew at him. He grabbed her by the throat and squeezed the air out of her. She used her sharp nails and tore at the flesh on his wrists. He didn't budge. Instead, he tossed her to the right and a black birdcage formed around her, enclosing her inside of it. She slammed the back of her head against the metal bars and fell to the floor, unconscious.

"Give me back my guardian, Orion!" A snarl escaped my lips.

"I gifted you a guardian," Orion sighed boredly. "I'm taking this one in return as payment, Melfi."

"Viz is bound to me!" I shook my head. "She's *mine*!"

"Not for long," Orion snapped his fingers. "Claus!"

My gaze shifted, and to my disbelief, I watched Claus snatch a shaman dagger before mercilessly thrusting it into Phyre's heart. In her final moments, she chuckled with a wickedness that sent chills down the spines of those around her. As his hand extended, Orion absorbed her body, leaving only a faint trace of blood in its wake. With a swift motion, he turned towards the cage, unleashing a powerful burst of darkness that consumed Viz's body.

"NO!" My screams filled the air as I desperately flew towards the cage. As it vanished, Viz was left suspended in the air, defying gravity. When her eyes finally opened, they revealed an unsettling sight - they were blood red, giving off an eerie glow. As she grinned, her teeth sharp and menacing, I felt her release her bond from me.

"Let's go," Orion said to Claus and Viz. "I am grateful to you, Melfi, for looking after my daughter and keeping her out of harm's way."

As Claus mysteriously disappeared, Orion and Viz took flight towards the north, their wings slicing through the air with a gentle whoosh.

"Mel!" I could hear the sound of Sixus and Solas' voices growing louder as they finally caught up with me. The presence of the mecha made their task even more difficult. They blew it up, causing a deafening explosion that reverberated through the air. "Where's Viz?"

"Orion took her." My vision blurred with unshed tears, and I blinked hard to keep them from falling. "Claus killed Phyre and put her soul into Viz's body before she unbound herself from me."

"We should return to the institute," Sixus whispered softly, guiding me into his embrace. "Mel," he said reassuringly. "Please understand that none of this is your fault."

"It's easy for you to say," I murmured quietly as Ivrem flew towards the institute, with Solas by his side on the back of his guardian. "Your guardian wasn't just lost to the enemy."

"We'll get her back!"

Sixus said in my mind.

I hoped it would be so.

Lost in my thoughts, I was suddenly jolted back to reality as Ivrem smoothly touched down on the flight strip, signaling that we had reached our destination. With a leap, I descended, and a moment later, both Sixus and Solas joined me. Their guardians shot upwards and headed towards the dragon sanctuary.

"No." Sixus placed his hands on my cheeks, and I met his gaze. "Don't you *dare* fall into yourself... this wasn't your fault, Mel."

"I should've traded myself for her freedom," I whispered. "Viz is only a *child*!"

"Once a guardian *willingly* unbinds themselves from their dragon knight," Sixus said. "You can never have them back!"

"What?" I gasped. "That's... not an option for me, Sixus!"

"Your other guardians died, Mel," he whispered. "Viz is your first guardian to survive and has willingly unbound herself from you... her *former* dragon Knight!"

"I shouldn't be a fucking dragon knight then!" I snarled as I pushed my way past him and headed towards the institute.

Cy pushed open the heavy metal door and ran down the steps and into my arms. I hugged her tightly. "I need you, mom," she whispered. "Please stay as my dragon knight?"

"Always," I whispered as the men made their way over to us. I experienced frustration directed towards myself, not any of them. "I'm not going anywhere Cy."

"There's something I wanted to ask you," Cy said, pulling me closer and taking hold of my hand. She yanked me up the steps while the guys hurriedly ascended the staircase. The door swung open under Solas' forceful pull, and without hesitation, Cy grabbed my hand and pulled me inside. They followed us as Cy pulled me towards the mess hall. "Over dinner, of course!" She pulled me into the dark room, and someone flicked the lights on.

"SURPRISE!" the packed room yelled. "HAPPY BIRTHDAY MELFINA!"

Balloons and streamers filled the room, cascading around me as Cy tugged me in. It was a moment of utter disbelief, leaving me completely stunned.

"Say something!"

Cy spoke in my mind.

"Oh, my God!" I exclaimed, my voice filled with shock and disbelief. My words fading into the quietness of the room. "I can't believe I completely forgot about my own birthday!"

Everyone laughed as someone played music. Everyone moved around and danced. Sixus led me to an empty table near the back of the room and sat me down in a chair.

"We had to get your out of here to set up," he gave me a sad smile. "It was supposed to be a joyful surprise for you, Mel."

"It is," I laughed lightly. "Thank you all for this amazing surprise party!"

"You deserve one night," Sixus shouted over the blaring rock music playing around us. "Tonight should be about having fun and not having to kill Victim!"

"Your right," I shouted. "I need a drink!"

Alcohol was being served to me all night, and I was getting fucked up! It was my twenty-first birthday, and the air was filled with excitement and anticipation. Finally, I had come of age on Erda and could now experience the vibrant atmosphere of the bars while enjoying a drink. Indulging in my go-to Erda delicacy, I savored every bite of the mouthwatering pizza. I enjoyed the best chocolate cake. I opened my presents. Feeling the need for some air, I excused myself and went outside. I walked over to a cement bench hidden behind a wall. Leaning against the icy wall, I closed my eyes. Everything was spinning, and I had to sit still, so I didn't spew everywhere. The sensation of the cool air against my sticky, hot skin was incredibly pleasant.

The familiar hum of the astral thread opening made my eyes shoot open. I was no longer sitting on the bench. I was sitting on my bed in the Xeonada Empire!

Timbrax stood before me, and I knew I was fucked!

"I won't hurt you, Melfina," Timbrax spoke as he sat down beside me on the bed. "I need to get that alcohol out of your system."

"No," I said, as I tried shoving him away. "It's my birthday, asshat!"

Timbrax grabbed me and sank his sharp fangs into my neck. I gasped as he drank my blood eagerly. I felt his endorphins kick in. He removed his fangs as he laid me down on the bed. "You're a lightweight," he laughed in amusement. "You should feel better soon."

"What do you want, Brax?" I asked him.

"To keep you safe," he whispered as he rebounded his soul to me. "This is the only way I know how to do that."

"You're my enemy now," I said. "I-"

Timbrax gently kissed me. I closed my eyes and returned his kiss before he broke it.

"That's what makes our forbidden love so-"

A loud explosion was the last thing I heard before the world fell silent.

***

The first thing I experienced upon waking up was a relentless attack, leaving me battered and bruised. A sudden blow to my face came from a boot's heel, leaving me dazed and disoriented.

"Enough!" Timbrax's snarl filled the air as he closed in on me, his powerful hands reaching out and hoisting me up with ease. It hurt to breathe. "She doesn't know shit!"

"We need to ramp up the intensity of our attack on her!" Largo Croix laughed maniacally. "Victim Commander, I insist on doing it myself!"

With a heavy sigh, Timbrax resignedly headed towards the door, his disappointment palpable in the air. "Maybe later," he muttered to himself. "She requires some rest."

My eyes followed him closely as he nonchalantly passed by the cell where I had been imprisoned before. I heard a door open, and he entered the room. With a tender gesture, he led me to a comfortable bed and carefully laid me down; the doors closing softly in the background.

I hacked blood, causing Timbrax to instinctively reach out his arm to assist me.

"I promise my blood isn't toxic," he frowned down at me. "They've been manipulating your visions, Melfina."

Holding onto his arm, I punctured his skin with my fangs. I gulped his blood until I was full. I retracted them and felt my wounds healing.

"You should kill me," I breathed. "Before I kill you!"

"I need you alive," he replied. "As does your brother."

I sat up and climbed to my feet. Timbrax stood, and we walked towards the door. They slid open and Victim stood there hissing at me as I exited the room. Timbrax had bound his soul to me, and they couldn't touch me.

But I could touch them, I stabbed them with the daggers, and they turned into demons, then dark piles of ash.

As I entered the room, I found Orion, Tasia, Claus, Largo, and Vizzeirra gathered there. They all turned and looked at me.

"Looks like the Tribrid slut wants another ass kicking." Largo laughed as he walked up to me. I pointed the dagger's tips towards his neck. All I had to do was stab him.

"Yeah," Timbrax sighed as he stood beside me. He lowered my blades as I put them back in the sheaths. "I wouldn't piss my wife off, Largo."

"How do you get her to listen to you?" Orion asked.

"By drinking my blood," Timbrax chuckled triumphantly. "I've had her under my control since day one." He gave me a smug smirk. "I told her my blood isn't toxic to her, but it is."

"Then make her kill the dragon king," Orion ordered. Claus has larger-scale strategies in mind for her. "I'm tired of his shit!"

I turned and silently exited the room. As I held my palm out, the astral thread opened. I leaped through it and Timbrax joined me as it shut behind him.

Timbrax placed his hands on my cheeks as he gazed down into my eyes. I felt him unbind himself from me once more. I felt sick after drinking his blood.

"You are doing so good, my love," he whispered into my ear. "I will reward you soon." He gently kissed me, and I returned his kiss before he broke it. He held out the astral thread, and I stepped back. I turned and walked out, and it closed behind me. I stood in my dorm room.

The doors slid open, and Solas and Sixus entered the room.

"You look like shit, Mel," Sixus whispered as I walked up to him. "Did you do it?"

"The shit I do for you," I smiled wearily. As per Sixus' mission, I journeyed to the Victim ship, where I meticulously collected their blood on my blades, an essential step in the quest to discover a cure for the vampires. I would often receive his orders in my dream state, a strange and unsettling experience. Originating from Tellus, their blood was infused with the transformative properties of Timbrax, which resulted in them becoming Victims rather than Varacolaci. Living on Erda for two years gifted me with the blood of Varacolaci and Stregoni Benefici, a fact that defined my heritage. "Yeah, I stabbed some Victim and demons leaving their ashes behind on the ship."

"Good," Sixus replied bluntly. "Now get that shit pumped out of your system so the shaman can detoxify it and put it back in your body."

"On it." I stepped away from him and the doors slid open. I exited the room and stood in the hallway. "The Victim Commander fucked around with the wrong Tribrid."

***

My eyes shot open, and I found myself laying in my bed in my dorm room. I sat up and tossed the hot scarlet comforter off my body as I climbed to my feet. I gazed out of the open French doors and saw it was still dark outside. The light turned on and I glanced down at myself. My eyes widened as I took in my new double-sided uniform. Red dragon scales were on the right. While jade dragon scales were on the left. The hood even had them on it. I bent down and saw the new mecha pilot boots had them in red as well. Someone had sewn them into the uniform and boots for me.

Once I slipped my feet into them, I carefully zipped them up in the back. Standing on the balcony, I discovered Sixus and Solas. I heard them whispering. I walked out of the French doors and gazed up at them.

"You look better," Sixus smirked down at me. "You ready to get a new guardian at dragon mountain?"

"Thanks." I gave him a small smile. "Let's do this."

All three of us flexed our backs and our dragon wings exploded out of our trench coats. Just like Sixus and Cy, the vampire hunters had created a jacket for Solas that was a replica in style and design. The dragon's scales glistened with a captivating, iridescent blue hue. We all climbed onto the marble ledge and kicked off. Our wings caught the air, and we flapped higher and higher in the sky as we headed for dragon mountain.

I inhaled the fresh air deeply and smiled at Sixus, who smirked at me.

It was time for a new guardian.
And this time. They would survive.

SEVEN

I stood on dragon mountain alone. Sixus and Solas waited for me at the bottom. I took a deep breath and ran out of the mouth of the cave. I leaped off the ledge and plummeted downwards. Dragons of all different colors, shapes, and sizes flew around me. I wondered if any of them would even want to bind themselves to me.

A purple dragon with red eyes flew beneath me. I gripped her scales and climbed up her back.

"My name is Xemret- The Scary!"

He spoke in my mind.

"Thank you, Xemret!" I shouted over the roar of the wind.

He tilted to the left, and I flew off, landing on the back of a black dragon.

"My name is Norlos- The Dark!"

She said in my mind.

"Thank you, Norlos!" I shouted as I gripped her scales tightly. Blood seeped out of my palms as she swooped down to the ground. Xemret was waiting for me as I leaped off her back. I was taken aback to see Sixus standing beside a new guardian.

"I needed a new one too," he casually shrugged. "Meet Indantos- The White One."

I nodded a curt hello to him. He was white with piercing blue eyes. I could tell he was an ice wilder right away. His mother looked exactly the same as this new guardian in color.

The three dragons shot upwards and headed towards the dragon sanctuary, leaving us behind.

Sixus, Solas, and I all flexed our back muscles, and our dragon wings exploded out of our backs. We kicked off the ground and our wings flapped, taking us higher and higher into the sky. We headed towards the institute.

"This is great, isn't it?" Sixus shouted to me.

"What are you up to?" I asked, glancing at him out of the corner of my eye as we reached the institute. We descended and landed on the lawn. We each helped one another fold our wings back inside of our jackets.

"You are going back to Erda with Solas," Sixus whispered. "For a few days until this blows over, okay?"

I felt anxious about going with someone I didn't really know. Both men exchanged glances with each other before Sixus continued.

"Cy will go with you," he smiled. "I need to be sure both of my girls are safe and out of reach of Victim's hands, right?"

"Alright," I sighed as I turned to look at Solas. "Let's go."

"We'll be on standby, Solas," Tork said as I turned and saw the vampire hunters standing on the steps. Cy ran down them and stood beside me and her father. "Have fun training with the shaman's dragon royals."

"You're coming with us?" I asked, looking at Sixus.

"Obviously," Sixus smirked cockily. "I need to learn how to control my oracle abilities, just like you and Cy do, don't I?"

A bright blue light flashed, and Solas nudged his head towards it. Upon running through it, he followed us in. The massive, gated building was where we stood outside. Passing easily, the barrier allowed us to proceed after walking through the gate. We followed Solas up the steps as Varric met us and held the door open for us as we passed him and entered the building.

"I would like to welcome you to the Sovereign Academy of Shamans," Solas said. "Your training begins now." Solas moved his hand, and our clothes transformed into Erda's clothing. Jeans, T-shirts and tennis shoes. "Don't need you guys standing out any more than you already do, right?" Solas chuckled in amusement. "Follow me."

We walked towards a door, and he pulled it open. Upon entering the room, darkness was the main feature. A room with water didn't thrill me as a large waterfall sat at the end. With the closing of the door, the room was transformed into a dimly lit space, illuminated only by the pale light of the torches that hung on the walls. My anxiety was rising. This place wasn't to my liking.

"I can't swim," I said, looking at Solas as he, Varric, Nell, and A.J. all stood to the right of us. "During the Flight Games, I had a near-drowning experience with Sixus."

"She ain't lying there," Sixus agreed. "We did nearly drown."

"You don't need to worry," Solas said, looking at me calmly. "Just to clarify, you're not required to enter the water, okay?"

"That's good," I sighed in relief. "Then why the hell are we in here?"

I didn't like the way Solas looked at me, his smirk filled with a mix of amusement and something darker. As I looked around, it became apparent that we were the only ones in this room, creating a sense of solitude. Weren't we?

Then I saw them. The room was full of the dead. Nyxie was amongst them.

"Don't be afraid, Melfina," Nyx said, stepping forward. "We're all here for you."

"Why are you here?" I asked cautiously.

"Do you know why Claus wants to find the Nexus so badly, Mel?" Solas asked me.

"Not a clue." I shook my head. "Why?"

"So, he can rule over the dead army of shamans," Solas sighed heavily, the weight of his duty sinking in. "The Nexus was a secret that we guarded closely, and that meant keeping it hidden from everyone, yourself included."

"That's... not good," I murmured softly, the words lingering in the air. "What do I have to do with them?" I asked, nudging my head towards Nyxie and the dead shaman behind her.

"Your job," Solas replied calmly. "Is to protect all of them by protecting the Nexus with your life."

"Protect the door leading to the army of the dead shamans." I nodded. "Got it."

"She's fucking with us, isn't she?" Varric asked Solas.

"Defiantly," Solas nodded in agreement. "We kept it from her for a reason."

"But wait," I gasped. "There's more, isn't there?"

"The Tribrid," Solas continued. "Is the goddess of the entire universe, Melfina."

"Please tell me," I groaned, knowing I didn't like this. "You have another Tribrid hidden somewhere around here?"

"I wish that was the case," Varric pressed his lips together tightly, making them turn white. "But we only have... *you*."

"It's been a pleasure meeting all of you fine dead people," I forced a smile. "Please excuse me."

I turned and pushed my way through the many deceased shamans standing around the room. Right as I was getting close to the door, Solas halted me. I turned my head and met his gaze as he lightly gripped my left wrist, keeping me pinned to the spot I stood.

"Lead the army of the dead, Melfina," he whispered. "There is no one else who can do it but you."

"Aren't there enough dead leaders amongst them to do it?" I whispered. "I'm already in charge of the living army and protecting three fucking planets from getting annulated from Orion and Victim!"

"All the Tribrid's are dead, Mel," Solas went on. "You're our only hope of defeating Claus."

"Fine," I breathed quietly. "I'll be the goddess leading the army of the living and the dead, okay?"

"Thank you, Mel," Solas gave me a sad smile. "Protecting earth is our top priority."

"Don't I know it?"

I thought to myself.

I glanced around the room and noticed it was empty. Only the living were standing in here. The sound of the waterfall pouring into the pool below reminded me of wanting to get the hell out of this damn room!

"Can we please get out of here now?" I begged. "Water freaks me out."

"Absolutely," Solas nodded as he released me and walked towards the door. He opened it and I rushed out, sighing in relief. A moment later, the others followed, and Varric shut the door behind him. "That was all the business I needed from you, Melfina."

"So?" I asked, giving him a confused look. "We can go back to Tellus now?"

"Sure," he replied. "Or you can spend the rest of the day on earth and be normal for a change."

"Dad," Cy begged him. "Can we go to an amusement park and ride some rides, please?"

"No." Sixus shook his head with wide eyes as he remembered the roller coaster ride from hell during the Flight Games. "Never going to one of those damn places."

"You three can take her," Solas replied. "She'll have a blast."

My intuition kicked in, alerting me that danger was upon us. Alarms sounded around the academy, and shaman ran all around us.

"I can't be here," I shouted to Solas. "Claus found me!"

Solas opened the portal and the blue light appeared, and Sixus grabbed Cy and me by the arm before leaping inside. The next thing I knew, we stood back on the lawn of the institute and the light vanished.

"Something's wrong," I shook my head. "I can't feel Evan's essence anymore!"

The blue light appeared, and the four shamans rushed out. It closed behind them, and they all appeared bloodied and with their clothes torn to shreds. Solas fell forward and blood seeped out of his wound on his lower abdomen.

"EVAN!" Startled, I let out a scream as the vampire hunters dashed out of the institute. "Help him!"

With Chaos taking the lead, they swiftly gathered him in their arms, ensuring the other three were secure as well, and hurriedly made their way back into the institute and up to I.O.A.

Sixus wasted no time in instructing Tork to go to Erda. "Verify the shamans' well-being and swiftly create a safeguarding barrier around the perimeter!"

As Setha opened the astral thread, Tork's reply echoed with deference, "Yes, Sixus." The human hunters ran through, leaving behind a trail of hurried breaths and the scent of adrenaline. "Leave the premises!"

As they moved forward, Setha quietly joined their ranks, blending into the shadows. It closed behind them.

Alarms sounded around the institute and the dragon knights, assassins, and mecha pilots exited with the vampire hunters who remained behind. My intuition kicked in and I looked up to see Orion standing there with Claus, Viz, Largo, Tasia, and Timbrax.

"What were you doing at the shaman academy, Melfi?" Orion asked casually.

"Taking a tour," I spat. "Did you destroy it too, Orion?"

"Not my domain to ruin," Orion calmly responded, stealing a quick glance at Claus. "But he did."

"Did they tell you where the Nexus is located?" Claus asked me.

"No," I shook my head. "We were going to an amusement park until you assholes showed up!"

"She's telling the truth," Timbrax whispered to him. "I sense no deception coming from her."

"I suppose we destroyed the academy prematurely." Claus shrugged. "That place needed an upgrade, anyway."

"You need to feed Melfina," Timbrax said, looking back at me. "I can't have this dragon starving you."

"I'm good," I shouted to him. "Your blood is toxic to me, remember?"

"You'll come back to me," Timbrax smirked. "When the darkness within you needs me."

"The Shaman King of Light is still alive," Claus frowned. "For now, anyway."

The rage fueled within me. My shamanic seal exploded out of my body and the power shot outwards. hitting Claus. He narrowed his eyes at me as his black magic seal pushed back against mine. A loud explosion erupted, leaving a massive hole that was deep in the ground before me as the dust settled.

"How are you learning how to control your powers so quickly?" Claus asked.

Nyxie and Sinergy appeared beside me. I stood my ground, and he grew pissed off at the sight of them. Zyra and Cora also appeared beside me to the left.

Timbrax's eyes widened when he saw Zyra. They vanished, and Timbrax flipped over the wall and disappeared through the astral thread.

"What's wrong?" I asked. "Your Victim Commander can't possibly be afraid of ghosts, can he?"

Orion looked around and didn't realize Timbrax was gone until I said something.

"We'll be back!" he rolled his eyes. "Let's go!" They leaped over the wall and vanished.

My magic seal disappeared, and I exhaled, not realizing I was holding my breath. I looked at the hole and back at Sixus, who just stared at me silently.

"I'm not getting demerits for that giant hole in the ground," I asked, making a face. "Am I?"

"I," Sixus snapped out of the daze he was in. "Didn't even think about it, Mel."

"Me ether," I forced a smile. "I'm gonna patrol the skies-"

A hard kick landed on my back. I flew into the wall with a dominant force, resulting in a crack.

"MEL!" Sixus snarled as I groaned and pushed myself out of the hole I was in. As I turned around, I caught sight of Timbrax standing there, snarling back at me.

"I'm good," I called to him. "I got this Sixus!"

"Why aren't you following my orders, Tribrid?" Timbrax snarled.

"What orders?" I asked as I walked up to him. I kept at least twenty feet between us.

"Don't fuck with me," he scoffed. "You know damn well what I told you to do!"

"Kill Sixus?" I asked him as he looked at me. "Not happening!"

"You disobey a direct order from your Victim Commander?" Timbrax arched an eyebrow my way.

"You aren't my superior," I snarled. "Now fuck off Victim Commander!"

"You need me to discipline you again, don't you?" Timbrax smirked before growing serious.

"Firelash Power!" I shouted as I transformed into Hell's Guardian. With a flex of my back, my dragon wings erupted out of the trench coat. I kicked off the ground and flew over his head. I had to lead him away from the institute.

"Get your ass back here!" Timbrax snarled as he grabbed a flying motorcycle he had hidden on the institute grounds. He started it and flew after me. I opened the astral thread and flew inside it. It shut behind me. I leaped through the wall and landed on Erda.

I emerged back in the Dark Region. This was Timbrax's territory. With the velocity of a vampire, I swiftly made my way into the castle's backyard. I saw the maze made of thick bushes and raced through it. I stopped and hid in a random bush.

"Of all the places you could've gone to Melfina," Timbrax snickered as I heard him walking into the maze. "You came home?"

"This place isn't my home!"

I shouted in my mind.

"Of course it is," Timbrax said as he walked past me as he burned the leaves, causing them to catch fire. He was trying to draw me out of hiding. I wasn't moving. He walked past me and all I heard was the crackling of the surrounding fire. He returned and pulled me up by the throat. I shot daggers down at him, and he smirked at me. "Got you."

He released me, and I landed on my feet. I kept my gaze fixed on his chest. I could feel him burning a hole in my brain. He flicked me in the side of my temple, and I made a face as I gazed up at him.

"I need to discipline your ass," Timbrax whispered down to me. "You know that, right?"

"Drink my blood then," I shrugged. "Sixus hates when you bite me."

"Does he now?" Timbrax smirked down at me as he moved the collar of my jacket back and sunk his sharp fangs into my neck. I grunted as his endorphins kicked in. He drank his fill before he removed his fangs. He licked my blood off his lower lip before he gave me a strange look. "Why does your blood taste... different?"

"I'm a Tribrid remember?" I shrugged as I fixed my jacket. "My blood is constantly in a state of change, I guess?"

"That's probably it," Timbrax agreed. "I feel..."

A moment later, he fell forward and was knocked unconscious. I shoved him off me and he fell to the left, laying on the lawn.

"Sorry Brax," I whispered down to him. "How does it feel to have tainted blood in your body for a change?"

His eyes shot open, and he sat up, kneeling on one knee as he glared up at me. I pulled the Valistik sword out and pointed the blade beneath his chin.

"You aren't under my control anymore?" Timbrax's eyes widened as he realized what was happening. "What's changed between us, Melfina?"

"Oh, you know," I shrugged. "I became a goddess thanks to all of you fucking with my DNA."

"That's," Timbrax was in shock. "Impossible?"

"You never should've listened to my father," I said in an icy voice. "Who's the bitch now Victim Commander?"

"It's not in your nature to kill me," Timbrax spat my blood out onto the lawn beneath our feet. "Unless you're in your dragon or vampire form."

"Your right," I said as I moved the Valistik sword and placed it back in the sheath. "Zyra," I said, looking over his shoulder as she appeared behind him. "He's all yours."

"No," Timbrax scurried to his feet and faced her. "You can't be here!"

As I threw my hand out, the astral thread opened up. I leaped through as it closed behind me. I walked through the other side and stood in my dorm room back on Tellus. It shut behind me.

I picked up my ear pod box and opened it. With the purple ear pods in my ears, I turned on my music. I could hear Timbrax's screams in my mind as Zyra let him have it. I placed the shield up and his screams stopped.

When he returned to Tellus, was he going to be even more pissed and want me dead?

Yes.

Was getting payback worth it?

Also, yes.

And I was looking forward to it.

EIGHT

I was flying on the back of Xemret patrolling the area when he growled. I sensed danger move towards us.

"Vile vampire is approaching!"

Xemret snarled in my mind.

"I know!"

I replied.

The roar of a motorcycle pulling up beside me made me turn my head to the left. I found Timbrax glaring back at me as he kept my speed.

"You did that shit on purpose!" He shouted over the roar of the wind.

"Did what exactly?" I shouted back with a slight smirk on my face.

"I can't deal with the dead!" Timbrax shouted. "They freak me the fuck out!"

"Xemret is gonna bite your ass if you don't get to the fucking point Victim Commander!" I shouted.

A bolt of lightning cracked above my head, and I knew Orion was around. I flipped Timbrax off and he made a hard left to get the hell away from what was about to go down between us siblings. He wasn't really my biological brother. Outside of the castle, my father raised him, away from the grandeur and luxury.

"Those shamans taught you how to use the dead to your disposal, haven't they, Melfi?" Orion sighed as he hovered before us. Xemret stopped but snarled at him. "Is there nothing beyond your control?"

"I'm not interested in whatever you offer, Orion!" I spat.

"How did you break free from the Victim commander's grasp?" Orion demanded.

"He is my enemy," I replied. "Pretty easy to do when he wants you dead."

"He loves you, Melfi," Orion frowned. "I presented you to him, as our father had requested."

Xemret opened his mouth, and a massive purple fireball shot towards Orion. He flew out of the way as Xemret turned and headed back towards the institute.

"Get back here, Melfina!" Timbrax ordered.

They didn't bother chasing after me, as I was really close to the institute. Xemret shot downward and landed on the flight strip. With my boots unhooked, I removed the flight goggles from my head. I tossed them in the satchel and buttoned it. I stood and leaped down. He shot upward and headed back to the dragon sanctuary.

Sixus and Solas were standing there, waiting for me. I walked up to them, and we walked off the strip and headed towards the institute.

"Did you get any additional details on what Claus is up to Mel?" Solas asked.

"No," I shook my head. "They were more interested in how I can harness the dead and how I broke free from Timbrax's mind control."

"You didn't tell them anything?" Sixus asked. "Did you?"

"No," I rolled my eyes. "Timbrax is still pissed off because he drank my poisonous blood and Zyra went after him."

"Serves him right," Solas murmured under his breath. "He shouldn't have killed her."

We walked up the lawn and to my surprise, Exrah was standing there waiting for us. She kept her gaze fixed on Sixus.

"I owe you an analogy." She cleared her throat. "To both of you, actually."

"Thank you." Sixus gave her a confused look, but regained his composure. "Let's move past this Exrah."

"I see why you love her!" she cried as we started moving past her. We stopped dead in our tracks, and I glanced at Sixus out of the corner of my eye. "I'm not able to put others before my own selfish needs!"

"I'm married, Exrah," Sixus spoke as his rage was boiling through his end of the bond. "You left my heart in pieces, and it was Mel who patiently restored it."

"I-"

She started coughing up blood, and we staggered back from her. When she slowly rose back up, she had transformed into a Victim! She hissed at us and pounced on me. A gunshot rang out, and she fell backwards, falling on her back. She slowly sat up, transforming into a demon. Sixus grabbed his dagger and threw it at her neck. She screamed as she turned into a pile of dark ash.

I turned and found Velzy lowering her weapon. Sixus retrieved his dagger, and we all exchanged glances with each other.

"What the fuck was that?" Cy asked nobody in particular as she pushed open the heavy metal door and stared at the pile of ash that used to be her birth mother.

"The Victim Commander," I whispered. "He's infiltrated the institute with Victim blood."

My intuition kicked in as the alarms sounded around the institute.

Timbrax stood outside of the gates with a legion of Victim behind him. "It only takes one," he shouted to me as he raised one finger high in the air. "To infiltrate and infect an entire institute with Victim blood!"

"No," I whispered as the doors opened behind me. I heard many people walk down the cement steps and walk past me. They were dragon knights, assassins, mecha pilots. Timbrax pushed open the metal gates, and they walked past him to join his army.

"Everyone!" Solas shouted as a blue pill fell in everyone's hand. "Eat the antidote quickly!"

Cy, Sixus, Solas, the vampire hunters and everyone who wasn't infected quickly swallowed the pill. I gazed down at the pill in my hand and looked at Timbrax. He stared at me as I opened my mouth and popped it in. I swallowed the enormous gel pill.

"I warned you there would be consequences, Melfina!" Timbrax narrowed his eyes at me. "Now you get the pleasure of killing your own people!"

I screamed in rage as my shamanic magic seal shot out and struck all the Victim turning them into demons, then into dark piles of ash. The rest of them vanished before it could touch them. Timbrax flipped into the astral thread, and it closed, striking only the former humans from the institute.

"Cleanse the water supply," I shouted to Sixus and Cy. "The rest of you check the food supply and the surgical tools in I.O.A.!"

"Yes, my queen!" everyone said in unison as they started moving erratically around me. "Move out!"

I closed my eyes and calmed my breathing down as I tuned out everyone around me.

"Spirit Guide Naphirie?"

I asked in my mind.

"*What do you wish to destroy or revive, oracle?*"

Naphirie inquired.

"Please remove the contaminated Victim blood from Tellus, Outer Earth, and Erda."

I asked.

"*It is done. Is there anything else you wish to destroy or revive oracle?*"

She asked.

"Yes. Revive the shaman academy on Erda and protect it from all evil. Make my powers surface so I can protect all three planets from evil. And lastly... show me the Nexus so I can protect it and lead the army on all planets and the army of the shamanic dead to victory against evil. Release my goddess powers now!"

I asked.

"*It is done!*"

Naphirie spoke.

"Thank you Naphirie. That is all for now."

I said.

"*Until next time, oracle.*"

Naphirie fell silent in my mind.

So many times, I have been left for dead by Orion, Timbrax, Claus, Victim, and others. I was about to make a decision with irreversible consequences.

With a burst of energy, a brilliant pale blue-violet light erupted from my body, casting an ethereal glow in all directions. My brain throbbed with an intense, fiery sensation. As I hit the ground, my body trembled and my lungs burned with each panting breath.

"MEL!" Sixus shouted as he rushed over to my side. He helped me up to my feet. His eyes were wide with fear. "What have you done?"

"I'm sorry," I whispered, feeling the wetness of the tears on my cheeks. "Was it not my duty to ensure the protection of the three planets?"

"They're gonna come back." Solas shook his head. "You know it!"

"I know," I nodded sadly. "If they kill me," I said to them. "Promise me you'll destroy my body at all costs."

"Why?" Sixus asked.

"Because," I said in a whisper, "I know where the Nexus is hidden now, Sixus."

"No." Sixus shook his head as he realized where it was.

Or where he thought it was.

I flashed an image of it somewhere in space in his mind.

I pushed my way past him as I ran up the steps. A vampire hunter opened the door, and I ran inside. I ran through the main lobby and up the hallway, and stopped in front of my dorm room. The doors slid open, and I ran inside. Sixus and Solas and Cy were on my heels as they ran after me. I allowed the tears to escape my eyes as Sixus pulled me into a tight hug. Solas and Cy both hugged me as I sobbed uncontrollably.

"I'm going to die!" The sound of my sobs echoed through the room. "There's no coming back from this!"

"I'll go to hell and back for you, Mel," Sixus whispered. "I'll revive you with the Holistic sword for all of eternity if I have to damn it!"

"Are everyone's shields up?" Solas asked in a whisper.

"Yeah," Solas nodded as he felt everyone's blocks. "They won't be back tonight, at least."

"Will someone turn that fucking alarm off?" I shouted. A moment later, the institute fell silent. "Thank you!"

Everyone released me, and I walked out of the open French doors and stood on the balcony. Twilight was falling, and the wind blew my hair.

Sixus pressed the intercom button on the wall, and I glanced back at him.

"Before everyone turns in for the evening," he said. "It has been an honor-"

He blinked back tears and cleared his throat, trying to hide his emotions.

"Fuck it," he forced a dry laugh. "Your queen is about to surrender to the enemy in order to protect Tellus, Outer Earth, and Erda," his breath caught in his throat as he cleared it again. "I will lead the war against Orion, Claus, Victim, and the Victim Commander Timbrax in her place until she returns to us... alive." he paused. "May the dragons protect her and all of us... we die with honor!"

"Queen Melfina!" A female voice shouted from below me. I walked to the railing and gazed down. My eyes widened as everyone who was alive and, on our side, stood and gazed up at me. "You survived and won the Flight

Games!" a vampire hunter shouted. "You will return alive and lead us to victory over the enemy!"

"All hail Queen Melfina!" They shouted as Sixus, Cy, and Solas stood beside me.

"Everyone believes in you, Mel," Sixus whispered to me. "Now show our enemies why you are the badass oracle who is gonna destroy them all!"

"All hail your Goddess Queen Melfina!" Solas shouted.

"All hail our Goddess Queen Melfina!" the crowd shouted in unison as they kneeled before me.

"Rise!" I shouted, and they stood at once, gazing up at me. "Victory will be ours!"

The crowd cheered, and I nodded.

"Dismissed!" Sixus shouted and everyone entered the institute as we walked back inside.

"I love you, mom," Cy said as she hugged me tightly. I returned her hug and kissed her on the top of her head. "Don't get yourself killed, okay?"

"If I do," I released her as she gazed down at me. "Your dad will revive me with the Holistic sword."

"I hope not," Cy frowned. "I'll keep the Aeon Dra deity on standby, just in case."

She hugged Sixus and Solas before she turned and walked towards the door. They slid open, and she stepped out and went to her room next door. The doors closed, and I felt the exhaustion hit me.

"Can we," I asked them. "Go on one last fly together, please?"

"Sure," Sixus gave me a sad smile. "But only around the institute, okay?"

I nodded in agreement as we walked back out onto the balcony. We climbed on the marble ledge and flexed our backs. Our dragon wings exploded out of our backs and Cy ran past us, leaping into the air. She laughed as we leaped off the ledge and our dragon wings flapped faster to catch her. The few Crux vampires and Abel, the half-breed gargoyle shifter, flew with us.

I took in the institute one last time. The lights made it look beautiful. We flew around the dragon sanctuary, and the dragons all flew out and flew around us. They roared as they merged their powers together, causing many massive fireworks to blow up over our heads. There was a burning sensation on my back. I knew it was another symbol. It hasn't become visible to me yet. On my left inner wrist, I felt another one. I moved the sleeve up and saw vampire fangs glowing in a red color.

Laughing, I twirled around as the magical elements floated down all around us. My three guardians flew up to me and I kissed the top of their noses and kissed Cy on the head again before she flew back to Sixus' side.

"Do not get yourself killed, oracle!"

Xemret yelled in my mind.

"And remember! Dragons do not go down without a fight!"

Norlos added.

"I will *never* stop fighting!" I shouted at them.

I watched as the dragons all flew back inside of the hole and returned to the safety of the sanctuary. We flew back to the institute, and everyone landed on the lawn. I hugged everyone before they went inside. Varric, A.J. and Nell all approached me. They hugged me and Nell placed golden bracelets on my ankles, hiding them beneath my socks and pants so they wouldn't be noticeable. I instantly felt my shamanic powers being locked away.

Zyra appeared and touched my forehead. I felt her locking my vampire powers away. She nodded before vanishing.

I was back to being a Half-Draconian. At least for a little while, until Timbrax figures it out.

"I'm sorry, my queen," A.J. kneeled before me. "For doubting you."

"Rise," I whispered, and she stood looking me in the eye. "Take care of my family and everyone on all three planets, okay?"

"Yes, my queen." They bowed their heads and looked up. They turned and escorted Cy up the steps. Varric held open the door, and they entered. He followed them and it shut behind them.

"Are you two coming to bed?" I asked as I leaped up onto the balcony. They joined me and we all entered the room. Sixus closed the French doors and shot a thick layer of ice to seal it shut. He did the same to the main door, and Solas gave him a confused look.

"You've never fucked a Half-Draconian before, have you?" Sixus smirked at Solas.

"No?" Solas threw him another look. "You'll never go back to any mundane pussy after you do."

Solas was about to object when I sensed danger approaching.

A loud explosion hit the balcony, sending thick layers of ice flying towards us. We fell as the alarms sounded once more. The ice melted from the other side of the door, and it flew open. The vampire hunters and the shamans rushed into the room with Cy.

My head had collided with the floor, and I was slightly dazed. Someone was pulling me up by the arm and my vision was blurry.

"We're under attack!" Sixus shouted over the roar of the alarms. "Get the princess and the queen to safety!"

"No," I shoved the hands away. "I'm not leaving you!"

"Mel, look at me," Sixus shouted as he placed his hands on my cheeks. I felt his panic from his end of the bond. It was for me and Cy. "I will always love you," he smiled sadly. "I will always choose you and our daughter!" He kissed me and I returned his kiss before he broke it.

Orion entered the room, and Sixus formed two icicles in his fists before flicking them towards him.

Orion slapped them away as he walked up to Sixus. He formed a thick lightning bolt in his fist before bringing it down into Sixus' chest.

"SIXUS!" With a scream of terror, I observed his body shaking violently, anticipating the moment when Orion would drop the lightning bolt. The sight of blood pooling from Sixus' chest and mouth made him collapse onto the floor. I witnessed the moment his eyes lost their spark and his body became completely motionless.

"The dragon king is dead!" Orion shouted as Victim leaped onto the balcony. He walked past me and stood on the terrace. "Your kingdom has fallen to me again, Melfi."

"SIXUS!" Overwhelmed with urgency, I dashed towards him, sinking to my knees, and gently extracted the still lightning bolt from his chest. With a sudden jolt, it slipped from my grasp and made a loud clattering sound as it hit the floor. The moment I pulled him close, a cold sensation washed over me, as if his body were draining the warmth from mine. It all came rushing back to me - the deep bond we had forged over the past year and a half. The mate bond! It was a deep, unspoken connection that resonated through every fiber of our beings. The excruciating pain made me feel like I was dying, each second dragging on like an eternity.

Barely Breathing started playing, and I broke down.

My mate was dead.

"Mel!" In a swift motion, Solas seized my arm, causing me to involuntarily release Sixus's lifeless body, which fell limply to the ground. Tugging me urgently, he led the way towards the radiant blue portal, its glow growing brighter with each step. "We have to go!"

"Leaving him is not an option for me!" I shouted.

Upon entering the room, Timbrax cast a quick glance at the surroundings before his attention shifted to me. His expression was unreadable as I entered the light.

I had to be sedated once I arrived at the academy.

My life would never be the same.

I had just lost everything.

NINE

The ringing of a large bell startled me awake. My eyes shot open, and I sat up in bed. I took in my surroundings and recognized nothing.

"Where the fuck am I?" I whispered to myself as I shoved the hot blanket off my body and leaped to my feet.

"Nyxie," a familiar male called me. I turned and saw him climb out of bed and walk up to me. "You've been suffering from terrible nightmares, remember?"

"No?" I gave him a confused look. "Who the hell are you again?"

"Evan," he gave me a strange look. "Your husband, remember?"

"No?" I shook my head. "I don't know where I am!"

"The Sovereign Academy of Shamans," Evan replied. "Just a reminder, you have a book signing today at a local bookstore to promote your books." he said, making sure I didn't forget.

"What books?" I asked, unable to comprehend any of this shit. "I never penned a single damn book!"

"Your medication needs to be adjusted by the doctors, babe." Evan moved his hand, and he put me in a white fancy dress with matching short white boots with a thick heel on them.

With a flick of the switch, the bathroom was instantly illuminated, revealing its clean and tidy appearance. My reflection in the mirror held my attention as I studied the way the light played on my features, mesmerized by the sight. As I glanced at my reflection, I couldn't deny that there was something noticeably different about my looks. My face was still mine, but something was different. With my hair pulled back in a chic high ponytail and flawless makeup, I felt confident and put-together. I looked absolutely stunning!

Evan's entrance was swift and stylish as he ran into the room, his black tuxedo and polished dress shoes making a statement. With his hair spiked up, he exuded a cool and unconventional vibe. "We need to hurry if we want to make it to the bookstore in two hours." he said, checking his watch.

"Is mom ready yet?" From the bedroom, a voice, unmistakably feminine and recognizable, asked. "Dad, we really need to leave now or else we'll be late!" she warned.

"I have a daughter?" With Evan's firm grip on my arm, I questioned him as he forcefully led me out of the bathroom. Standing tall in a beautiful short pink dress and long matching boots, the teenage girl exuded a sense of fashion and grace. In a tight bun, her hair was expertly tied up, perfectly complementing her impeccable makeup. Her beauty was simply breathtaking, with her flawless complexion and graceful presence. Her eyes, a striking shade of pale blue, instantly caught my attention. "I apologize for forgetting, but could you please remind me of your name?"

"Cyandra," she reminded me. "That's the name you gave me." As she tilted her head, Cy's eyes locked onto mine with a perplexed expression. "Dad, did mom forget to take her pills yesterday?" she asked, concern evident in her voice.

With a shrug, he replied, "I guess," his nonchalant demeanor not revealing his true thoughts. "Okay," he said. "Take these before we leave." Evan manifested four white pills into my hand and I gazed at him.

With a smile that didn't reach my eyes, I pretended to drop the pills into my mouth and swallowed, hiding my true emotions. I hid them under my tongue. "Let's go." Upon seeing Cy and Evan hastily left the room, I immediately rushed to the bathroom, where I swiftly disposed of the pills by spitting them into the sink and then turning on the faucet. As I turned it off, I grabbed a washcloth that was conveniently nearby and used it to clean my mouth. I made a turn, intending to exit the room, but my path was unexpectedly blocked by Evan, who stood there, his gaze fixed on me.

With a perplexed look in his eyes, Evan watched as I brushed past him and made my way through the room. Lingering in my mouth was the bitter taste of the pills that I could still detect. I could sense that something was off, a nagging intuition that demanded my attention and investigation. I couldn't recall the names of the two women and one man, but all three were impeccably dressed. Stepping down the steps, the silence on the ground level greeted us. The sheer size of this place was overwhelming. Instantly, I recognized this place, as if I had seen it in a dream.

"Grab the door, Varric," Evan instructed, and Varric swiftly made his way to it. He pulled it open, and we walked towards it. The moment I stepped outside, the chilly morning air nipped at my face, awakening my senses. "Let's go."

While making our way down the steps, a sudden jolt of surprise hit me when I caught sight of the paparazzi stationed outside the gates, their cameras clicking away as Evan expertly shielded me and led me into the limousine that awaited us. Once everyone had climbed inside, the driver closed the door with a resounding thud. The sound of the limo's engine roared as it jolted forward, but they didn't let that stop them from capturing the moment in pictures. The lights in the sitting area cast a soft, pale glow.

"Have you noticed how the paparazzi are getting more daring lately?" Varric sighed heavily. "You're a celebrity, Nyx."

"If they ask you about the movie deal," one woman said, her gaze fixed on me. "Inform them that the selection process for the actors is underway, and that's all the information they require for now, alright?"

"Absolutely," I said, forcing a smile that didn't quite reach my eyes. "I just wish I could remember every detail of this moment."

As Evan handed me the books, I could feel the smooth texture of their covers under my fingertips. The covers were adorned with intricate dragon designs, each one more mesmerizing than the last.

"Did I actually write these?" With a quick glance upward, I asked them. As they nodded, my eyes instinctively dropped to the books. With curiosity, I opened the first book and swiftly scanned its contents with my eyes, eager to discover its secrets.

A sudden surge of clarity washed over me, and I was captivated by a powerful vision.

Throughout the epic romantasy series, I had the privilege of witnessing Melfina Aeon Dra and Sixus Westin's remarkable journey unfold.

In an instant, it was gone.

I couldn't put the first book down, so I forced myself to set it aside and immediately picked up book two, unable to resist the urge to keep reading. I skimmed through it in a rush, and a sense of familiarity washed over me, as if I had read it all before.

My mind was filled with a fresh, captivating vision.

Amidst the chaos of the Flight Games, my attention was captivated by the intense battle between Sixus and Melfina, their lives hanging in the balance, while the formidable presence of the Victim Commander provided unwavering support. The setting changed, and now they were immersed in a mystical world guided by the shamans. The sound of Orion's thunderbolt meeting Sixus' flesh echoed through the air, sealing his fate. Melfina and Cy were whisked away to Erda through the magical portal, leaving behind their previous reality.

Slowly, it dissipated into nothingness.

With the book closed, I became aware of the pain slowly seeping into my consciousness.

"The barrier shielding her memories is starting to crumble." In a hushed tone, Varric informed Solas. "What is our next course of action?"

"It's real?" I whispered as I gazed up at them as they sat across from me. Their faces grew solum, and I knew I was right.

With a click, Cy activated my cell, and the melodic sounds of Let Go immediately began to play.

The realization hit that Sixus was gone for good. As soon as I heard the melody of this song, I was immediately transported back to that exact moment. The realization sank in - Sixus had breathed his last breath, leaving behind an eerie silence. It was a miracle that I had survived, and I couldn't quite comprehend it. I should be dead as well. Yet I wasn't.

"Sixus!" I let out a gasp when Cy wrapped their arms around me in a tight hug. "My mate is dead!" I cried out, my voice filled with anguish. My memories resurfaced as the wall slowly crumbled away. "Please," I sobbed, tears streaming down my face. "Let me out." Cy removed herself and was crying too. "I need to see him!" I exclaimed; my voice filled with urgency.

"We'll take you back to Tellus tomorrow," Solas whispered to me, his words barely audible. "If I understand correctly, you required some form of written proof or documentation for the events that occurred. Is that correct?" With a nod, I accepted the tissue from him, feeling the delicate texture against my skin as I used it to wipe my face and Cy's. "Sinergy became a part of you, lending her expertise to your writing process and aiding in the publication of your books."

"Your books took the world by storm and became a bestselling series," Varric remarked, astonished. "As your fame skyrockets, you're jetting off to international book signings and have secured a significant movie deal."

"Take these back to Tellus," Solas said, his voice filled with tenderness. "As the oracle, Melfina, these records will chronicle everything that took place on Tellus."

"Shit," Varric muttered quietly to himself. "This is the place," he said, pointing to their destination with a satisfied smile.

A.J.'s hand moved gracefully, ensuring that Cy's makeup and mine were perfectly in place. "Pull it together, my queen," she whispered, her voice barely audible. "The line of your adoring fans stretches out before you, their copies of your books clutched tightly in their hands, eager for your signature."

As I looked down, my gaze landed on the book titles, series names, and the author's name that I had meticulously penned beneath.

Rebels Flame and Flight Games.

The Oracle of Aeon Dra Saga

Isabella Tredway

"This actually sounds," I said softly, my voice tinged with sorrow as I offered them a sad smile. "Like some epic shit I would definitely write about."

I stepped out of the car, wearing a smile that felt anything but genuine, as the driver opened the door.

"It's her!" A male exclaimed, his voice filled with excitement and disbelief. "Isabella has arrived!"

Walking towards the doors with my entourage, I was met with a thrilling chorus of screams from the crowd. We were safely rushed inside by a guard who held the door open for us.

"I hope you weren't too bothered by the crowd, Mrs. Tredway?" I was approached by a woman who extended her hand for a handshake. "Your fizzy beverage is prepared and chilled, all set for you."

"Thank you so much." As I withdrew my hand, I smiled warmly and spoke. "I can't function without my dose of caffeine."

Varric and the girls brought me to my table and assisted in setting it up. Cy's task was to aid Nell and A.J. in live streaming the event using their cells.

With each sip from the plastic cup, I relished the refreshing coolness of the iced pop as it smoothly went down my throat. Someone came by with a box of pastries that were made recently. I received a frosted pink one with gratitude. With each bite, the flavors of strawberries burst in my mouth, creating a delightful experience as I chewed and swallowed.

It took me less than five bites to complete my snack. I cleaned my hands with hand sanitizer while Varric diligently removed any excess crumbs from the table. In an effort to get through the day without shedding any tears, I plugged in my ear pods and listened to rock music.

With a two-hour delay, the doors finally opened, and I eagerly interacted with my fans, signing autographs and capturing moments in photographs. I was unaware of how fast time was passing, and now there was just one man standing alone in the dwindling line.

"To whom should I address this?" While he slid his copies of each book towards me, I posed a question. His scent instantly caught my attention. The combination of cranberries, snow, and an element of mortality. A sudden instinctual response made me aware of the danger that surrounded me. His attire included a sleeveless T-shirt in black. His arms, full of muscle, were prominently visible. Black jeans and red tennis shoes were part of his outfit. As he removed his sunglasses, I noticed his eyes. The eyes are white in color and feature red rings surrounding the outer edges. The eyes that had entranced me with their beauty, a stunning shade of blue, were no longer present.

"*Your husband, the charismatic and well-respected Sixus Westin.*"

He conveyed his thoughts that aligned with mine.

As I autographed both books, I could feel my hand trembling, forcing me to focus on maintaining a steady grip. As I closed the covers, he eagerly snatched them from my hands, promptly putting the glasses on his face.

I could hear the familiar melody of Magnetic playing in the background as I slowly rose to my feet. It felt as if time had frozen, and I found myself in a state of utter shock.

"*I'll see you back home, Mel.*"

I could hear Sixus' voice inside my head, his words resonating with a commanding presence.

Only Cy and I were aware of his presence; no one else seemed to notice him. Walking casually out of the building, he nonchalantly glanced over his shoulder as we hurriedly ran after him. As we stepped outside, we scanned the area but couldn't locate him anywhere.

"Was that dad?" she asked, her voice filled with anticipation and hope. Cy asked me.

"Yeah." I said, my words coming out in short, gasping breaths. The transformation was swift and unsettling; Timbrax had turned him into a Varacolaci, a being cursed to roam the darkness as an undead vampire.

Solas and the others swiftly guided us behind the building, shielding us from whatever threat approached. The emptiness of the surroundings was eerie; it seemed like the whole world had disappeared. Varric opened his green portal, and as we raced through it, the sensation of being pulled and stretched filled the air. The moment we emerged on the other side, the grandeur of the academy greeted us.

My eyes locked with Solas and the other shaman as I uttered, "You knew," realizing that they were already in the know. "And you didn't bother mentioning that Sixus is a goddamn Varacolaci, did you?"

"The protection wards keep them out," Solas replied, his hand nervously running through his thick, dark hair. "Mel, take comfort in the knowledge that you and your daughter are shielded from danger within the walls of the academy."

"I have a plan," I said confidently, locking eyes with each of them. "Make sure to collect six tubes containing Cy's blood and promptly bring them to Mixie Lightborn on Erda." I caught them off guard, and their shocked expressions locked onto my face. "Her older sister is Zuni Sword," I scoffed, my tone dripping with sarcasm. "As a scientist on Outer Earth, she possesses the ability to create a cure for Sixus by harnessing the pure Half-Draconian blood of his daughter."

"Let's go!" Nell's response was accompanied by her guiding A.J. and Cy up the hallway and into a different room.

"Are you even sure this is going to work?" Varric asked skeptically, raising an eyebrow. He stressed, "Remember, we only have one chance to nail this. Let's make it count."

"I know that, Varric," I scoffed, unable to hide my annoyance at his lack of understanding. "But it's the only thing I can think of doing, besides using the Holistic sword he owns, by the way."

"Is there anything casual I can dress in?" Making a face, I glanced down at myself.

With the snap of his fingers, Solas conjured up a fashionable outfit for me - a tight black T-shirt, complemented by black skinny jeans and sleek Converse boots. My hand instinctively moved to my hair, and I could feel its strands slipping through my fingers. My hair, dyed jet black and perfectly straight, framed my face with a bold and edgy look. With a wave of his hand, Varric materialized a massive mirror that unveiled my reflection in vivid detail. To enhance my features, I opted for a dramatic look with red eyeshadow, black eyeliner, and a bold red lipstick. I nodded briefly at him, and in response, he effortlessly made it disappear.

"I need to meet with the other shamans," Solas said to me, his words echoing in the silence of the room. "Do you think you can handle being alone for a bit?" he asked, worried.

"Yeah." A bittersweet smile crossed my face as he handed me my copies of my books. "I'll be fine."

They turned and walked up the hallway, their figures gradually blending into the shadows until they were no longer visible. I let out a deep sigh as I made my way towards the door, feeling a mix of anticipation and uncertainty. As I pushed open the creaking wooden door, a flood of brilliant sunlight greeted me, temporarily blinding my vision. It felt like a ghost town, with not a single person to be seen. Moving closer to the gate with every step down the sturdy cement stairs, a sense of anticipation welled up inside me. I closed it behind me and crossed the street before any cars could come. The sight of the park ahead lured me in, and I eagerly stepped onto the perfectly manicured lawn. I located an empty bench, its surface smooth and inviting, and sank onto it, clutching my books tightly.

Inhaling deeply, I gathered my strength and opened the astral thread behind me; the sensation sending tingles down my spine. With a backward lean and a rush of adrenaline, I dove through the portal, and as it closed behind me, I was immediately immersed in a boundless expanse of blue. Breaking through the wall, I found myself on the lush lawn of the institute grounds on Tellus. The air was alive with the sweet melodies of birds chirping. The sight that greeted me was one of destruction and despair, causing my eyes to widen in shock at the aftermath of the last attack.

As the institute continued to smolder, slowly extinguishing itself, the air was filled with the lingering smell of smoke. Despite the impact, it remained completely undamaged. The absence of the front doors was noticeable, blown off and scattered across the floor. When I looked to the right, I was surprised to find the oracle dormitory completely untouched, as if frozen in time. As I turned to the left, a sigh of relief escaped my lips as I took in the sight of the undisturbed dragon sanctuary.

With a single leap, I ascended onto the balcony and unleashed a mighty kick, obliterating the right door and sending sparks and smoke into the air. The moment I entered my dorm room, my eyes were drawn to the horrifying scene before me - Sixus blood, a deep red stain on the floor. With the books safely on my desk, my eyes were immediately drawn to the disturbing sight of blood on the floor once more. The alarms had been deactivated, but the flashing emergency lights served as a reminder of the chaos that had ensued.

As soon as my intuition kicked in, I could sense the presence of imminent danger. I hadn't even taken a step towards the door when an icy coldness washed over me, making it impossible to move. With a slow and deliberate motion, I stood up and flicked my wrists, instantly igniting two pale blue flames in the palm of my hands. As I spun around, I flung them towards the figure, feeling the rush of adrenaline coursing through my veins. With a swift motion, Sixus froze them in place. Descending rapidly, their fiery blaze diminished, leaving only the sound of crackling embers as they hit the floor.

Sixus stepped into the room, stopping abruptly and standing mere inches from where I was standing. I dragged my eyes upwards, taking my time to meet his powerful gaze, which seemed to hold a world of secrets.

"I didn't expect you to come back alone, Mel," he said, his voice barely a whisper, yet filled with an unsettling intensity. "You look hot as fuck in that outfit."

"I half-expected to return and discover your lifeless body lying on the floor." With a hint of snark, I commented. "Imagine my astonishment when I returned, only to discover that you and the Victim Commander had formed an unbreakable bond."

"We're far from best friends, Mel," Sixus said, a mischievous smirk playing on his lips. In the blink of an eye, a red thread shot out from his body, forcefully connecting with mine before swiftly disappearing. Once again, I could feel his presence inside me. His rage was palpable, and I couldn't help but make a face in response. "But you already know that… don't you?" he said with a knowing smirk.

"Why not utilize the Holistic sword on yourself to return to your original state?" I inquired.

"I don't have it," he shrugged nonchalantly. "The tumultuous scene revealed the unfortunate truth that the Valistik sword and Venin dagger were inadvertently abandoned with my lifeless body, swiftly claimed by the vampire hunters prior to their own evacuation."

"Damn it," I sighed, frustration evident in my voice. "Did you decide to team up with Orion and his gang of asshole Victim or what?"

"Of course," he said with a smug grin. "Not."

"I don't believe that shit," I scoffed, crossing my arms. "Seriously, dude, you're an evil vampire!"

I could feel his eyes piercing into mine as he took hold of my wrist, pulling me closer into his chest with a sense of urgency. His hand was as frigid as the touch of death itself. The familiar warmth that had once filled his body was now absent.

"You aren't afraid of me?" he asked, his voice filled with a mix of surprise and curiosity.

"No," I whispered under my breath as he let go of me. "The pain of losing you, Sixus, left my heart in ruins."

"My heart may not beat ever again," he whispered. "Mel, my love for you remains as strong as it was when destiny brought us together."

The battle within him had become too intense to continue fighting. With a slight bow of his head, he pressed his lips against mine in a soft and affectionate kiss. His lips were freezing, sending a shiver down her spine when they touched. I closed my eyes and was immediately enveloped in the sweet taste of his kiss. With a low growl, he passionately intensified his kisses.

His hand shot out, and in an instant, the entire outside perimeter turned into a frozen, icy landscape.

As he tenderly placed me on the bed, our bodies intertwined, and the sound of fabric tearing filled the air as our passion escalated. The frigid air in the room hit my skin like a blast, causing me to catch my breath. I felt his hard cock slide deeply into me, sending waves of pleasure through my body. Before I could even gasp, he tapped into his supernatural speed, igniting a series of orgasms that left me breathless and trembling.

"SIXUS!" My fingers tangled in his hair, and in that moment, his name slipped from my lips with a gasp. "FUCK. ME!"

"I plan on it," Sixus affirmed, his voice filled with determination. He kissed me, the gentle touch of his lips sending shivers down my spine, before finally pulling back. The sensation of his tongue on the side of my neck was quickly replaced by the sharp pain of his fangs sinking into my skin.

His endorphins kicked in, and I let out a moan of pure delight, savoring the moment. As he fed on me, I could hear the disturbing sound of him sucking down my blood. He hadn't eaten in days, and his empty stomach was a painful reminder of how starving he felt. The hunger was agonizing, as he had endured days without blood and his body screamed for nourishment.

With each bite, I was overwhelmed by a sense of pure bliss.

"Get the fuck off her!" Timbrax shouted angrily, his voice filled with urgency. As Timbrax snarled, he aggressively yanked Sixus away from me. "Are you deliberately trying to kill her harm, you fucking idiot?"

The moment Sixus got up, the piercing shrieks and the distinct smell of blood permeated the room as the vampires engaged in a fierce fight. The room quickly turned into a fiery inferno as Timbrax melted all the ice, making it nearly unbearable. Taking the fight outside, they moved from the balcony to the lawn, their heated words carrying through the open spaces.

As if in a delirious haze, I saw a captivating vision materialize before my eyes.

Startled by a sudden, brilliant blue flash, both vampires were unceremoniously ejected from the protective magical seal.

"They'll be back," Solas said, his voice filled with urgency as he rushed to my side. With a gentle yet firm grip, he picked me up and effortlessly carried me into the bathroom, his footsteps echoing on the tile floor. With a gentle push, he

moved the curtain aside and turned on the water, its soothing sound filling the room before he carefully placed me inside. "Clean yourself up!" he shouted; his voice filled with urgency.

The unfolding vision captivated me, each moment adding another layer of detail to the incredible sight.

"I got her!" With her vampire speed, Zara efficiently washed my hair, got me dried off, and helped me put on my double-sided uniform and boots. With precision, she placed my weapons on my body and tossed Solas the Holistic sword. "This is yours to wield until we successfully restore the dragon king to his rightful place!"

After the surge of endorphins faded away, I regained my composure.

The moment Zara hit play on my cell, the familiar melody of "Barely Breathing" erupted from the tiny speaker, amplifying through the loudspeaker. Together, we ventured out onto the balcony, where they and the shaman stood beside me and Cy.

With the disappearance of the magic seal, they stepped out and were immediately hit by a gust of wind. Sixus donned the extra set of clothes from Erda that belonged to Timbrax, relishing in the scent of a distant land that clung to the fabric.

With a powerful leap, both men cleared the wall, and I couldn't help but flex my back in awe. In a burst of fiery energy, my dragon wings erupted, sending me soaring through the sky before I gracefully landed on the ledge. As I brandished the Valistik sword, I propelled myself into the air, feeling a surge of adrenaline rush through my veins.

As I flipped through the air, I effortlessly landed in a crouching position before swiftly getting back on my feet. With determination, the vampire hunters emerged from around the institute, their weapons glinting in the moonlight. As they approached the vampires, their weapons were ready, aimed directly at their targets. The sound of gunshots reverberated through the space as they fired.

They decided to forgo acid bullets and used a substitute that posed no acidic threat. The air was filled with the scent of blood as the two vampires crumbled to the ground, their bodies limp and unresponsive.

"What did you add to that?" With a question on my lips, I used the tip of my boot to kick Sixus in the arm. Despite everything, he remained unmoved. As he snored, the noise reverberated through the area, catching the ears of everyone present. It was impossible to ignore his loud snoring when he slept. It's probably the reason why I hardly got any sleep!

"Fifty bottles of sleeping medication," Tork answered, her words hanging in the air as the hunters swiftly moved in, restraining both men with silver handcuffs. As soon as it made contact, a fiery sensation coursed through my wrists. "Being Varacolaci, they won't take long to wake up - give them twenty minutes, tops."

"Put them in a solitary, high-security cell," I ordered, my command leaving no room for negotiation. "To prevent their powers from being unleashed, they would place magical seals around them and secure brackets on their wrists and ankles."

"Yes, my queen!" With a flurry of movement, the vampire hunters raced around the building, leaving no trace behind.

I couldn't help but laugh lightly, knowing that they would be pissed when they realized they were going to be sharing a cell. "I wonder who will strike first in this deadly confrontation."

Twenty minutes would reveal the answer to me, wouldn't it?

TEN

As the vision progressed, more intricate details were revealed, captivating her gaze.

Having regained full control over the institute and the Kingdom of Eozadion, I could now make decisions without any hindrance. Thankfully, the vampire hunters' quick thinking prevented a high number of casualties. During Sixus' absence, Solas was crowned as the temporary king until Sixus could regain his position.

The moment I walked into the cell, the bright lights overhead flooded the room, making the men on their metal cots shield their eyes.

"Are you enjoying casa de Melfina gentlemen?" With them in front of me, I asked my question, trying to gauge their reaction.

"Oh, yeah." With a hint of annoyance, Sixus rolled his eyes in response. "In this dismal cell you've confined me to, it's truly a remarkable experience."

"I want my own cell," Timbrax spat, the intensity of his words filling the air. "I'm gonna kill his ass!"

"Why did you turn him, Brax?" I asked, my voice filled with curiosity. "Does the solitude of being a Varacolaci on Team Orion ever get to you?"

"Hardley," Timbrax scoffed, his voice dripping with disdain for the incredulous claim. "I didn't want you falsely accusing me of his murder when I had no involvement in it!"

Utilizing his vampire speed, Exley effortlessly retrieved the Holistic sword from Solas and made his way into the room. As his blade met Sixus' ribs, a metallic scent filled the air, mixed with the gasp of pain that escaped Sixus' lips. As the bright blue light flashed, our vision was overwhelmed, only to gradually fade away.

I shielded my eyes with my arm, trying to block out the blinding sunlight. As I slowly lowered it, my eyes locked onto Sixus, taking in every detail. His eyes met mine, and in that moment, I witnessed the pallor in his face fade away as a rosy hue returned. His eyes, a stunning shade of blue, sparkled once again.

"Mel?" With a touch of sadness in his voice, Sixus ran his fingers along the cold metal shackles and whispered my name. In a sudden motion, he froze and

snapped off the shackles, rising to his feet. "I'm back." he said, his voice echoing through the empty room.

"Sixus!" I hugged him tightly, savoring the feeling of his arms around me, and the way he held me close. Taking a deep breath, his scent wafted into my nostrils, leaving a lingering impression in my mind. There it was. The scent of cranberry wafted through the air, blending with the crisp freshness of the snow. Listening closely, I could hear his heart beating faster and faster as I placed my ear to his chest.

My mate. The love of my life was back, and my heart skipped a beat.

"It's time to go," Sixus whispered, his warm breath tickling my hair as he kissed me tenderly on the top of my head. His hand closed around mine, and together we walked towards the door, our footsteps echoing in the hallway. "Later loser."

"You think you've escaped this without any harm, don't you, Sixus?" The sound of Timbrax's sinister laughter filled the air, instantly bringing us to a standstill. His head swiveled, and Sixus narrowed his eyes, directing his gaze at him. "In your veins also courses the blood of the Stregoni Benefici."

The air was filled with tension as Exley boldly sniffed Sixus' scent, provoking a snarl from Sixus.

"Sixus," Exley whispered, his voice barely audible. "Are you now a Tribrid?" he asked, intrigued by the possibility of her transformation.

I followed closely behind Sixus as he stormed out of the cell, the sound of our hurried footsteps echoing through the corridor. Exley wasted no time in leaving the cell. The metallic click of the door closing echoing in her ears. The long hallway stretched before us as we walked, the echoing sound of my boots filling the silence. With precision, Exley returned the Holistic sword to its sheath and passed it to Sixus, who acknowledged the gesture with a brief thank you. They then proceeded to trot up the steps and exit through the metal door.

As if in a hurry, Sixus swiftly pulled me around the corner and onto the inviting, grassy lawn. With a single motion, he swept me off my feet and propelled us both onto the balcony, the rush of adrenaline filling the air. As soon as he landed, he hurriedly carried me inside and carefully set me down on the solid ground.

"I'm sorry, Mel," Sixus said softly, his breath lingering on my neck as he gently inspected it. The once-open wound on my neck was now in the process of *healing, as the skin around the bite mark began to knit back together.* "I never meant to hurt you," he said, his voice filled with remorse.

As the doors swung open, Cy raced into the room, the sound of her footsteps mingling with the hurried steps of the shamans.

"Dad!" Cy rushed over to us, her footsteps echoing through the room, and he embraced his daughter tightly, showering her with affectionate kisses on the cheek. He pulled me into the hug, and as we held each other, I could feel his warmth and the steady rhythm of his heartbeat. Her desperate plea filled the room. "Please, promise me you'll never leave me again!"

As time passed, the vision faded into obscurity, becoming nothing more than a fleeting image.

I jolted awake, immediately absorbing the details of my surroundings. I occupied my dorm room at the prestigious institute. Without warning, I flung the searing hot comforter off my body and swiftly stood up. Donning my mecha pilot boots, I took a moment to appreciate the practicality of my double-sided uniform.

"Was it all just a dream?"

I thought.

Startled at the sound of glass being broken behind me. The hairs on the back of my neck stood on end, a clear indication that danger was approaching. I spun around and launched them with all my might, aiming straight at Sixus. With his vampire speed, he effortlessly dodged their attacks, standing inches away from me. The presence of cranberries, snow, and death combined. His complexion appeared lifeless, with a deathly white tone, and his eyes were circled by red rings, giving them a haunting quality. He was still cursed to be a Varacolaci, a creature of the night.

My face fell with disappointment, and he was quick to notice the change.

"Don't give me that look, Mel," Sixus whispered softly. The bond between us allowed me to feel his annoyance. I had completely overlooked the fact that our souls were forever connected. "I thought you'd be happy to see me." he said, the hurt evident in his voice.

As my words caught in my throat, I exclaimed, "I'm-"

As I pondered the ideal response, I nonchalantly shrugged, conveying my indifference.

"A bag of mixed emotions right now, Sixus," I confessed, my voice filled with uncertainty. The words escaped my lips in a hushed tone. "I never expected... this." I said, my voice trailing off.

"You were delirious from my endorphins," Sixus chuckled lightly, the sound of his laughter adding a playful tone to his words. "Before putting your ass to bed, I had to give you a shower and change your clothes."

"That was you?" I exclaimed, my eyes widening in disbelief.

"You thought I was Solas, didn't you?" he asked, his voice tinged with annoyance as Sixus rolled his eyes and sighed. "He kept you hidden from me all this time, and worse, he still has our daughter, Mel."

"So, are you contemplating my death?" I asked, steering the discussion in a different direction. "Or do I have to eliminate you?" I coldly stated.

"Cutting right to the chase, as usual," Sixus smirked, his voice laced with a touch of superiority. "Mel, I need you to disclose the whereabouts of the Nexus."

The block went up in an instant, eliciting a weary sigh from him.

His words hung in the air, a question that revealed his doubt: "Mel, you don't trust me, do you?" He asked.

"Fuck no," I shook my head adamantly. "Not as long as your... this." With a sweeping motion of my hands, I indicated his entire presence and then singled him out with a pointed finger. "So," I whispered, barely audible. "Looks like we're back to our classic dynamic of mortal enemies." I sighed.

"We don't have to," he said, his gaze fixed on me, his voice filled with a mix of determination and uncertainty. "By joining forces, we can assert control over all three planets."

"Taking orders doesn't appear to be your strong suit, does it?" A wave of anger washed over him as Timbrax's voice came from behind. "Didn't I make it clear to you that you should avoid getting too close to her?" he reminded, his voice tinged with annoyance.

Turning around, Sixus' face twisted into a snarl as he came face to face with him. The moment I lowered the block, a wave of his rage washed over me, tangible and palpable.

"I don't take orders from you," Sixus snarled, his voice dripping with defiance. "You think I work for you or any of your lackeys? Fuck off, Victim Commander!" he snapped.

"I created you and her," Timbrax spat at him, his words filled with a mix of pride and disdain. "So, you listen to me," he shouted, frustration evident in his voice. "You stubborn ass dragon!"

"I'm beating your ass!" Sixus snarled.

"Before you do that," I said, causing him to quickly glance over his shoulder in my direction. "Could you please unbind your soul from mine before you leave?" I asked, my voice filled with annoyance.

He clenched his fists, feeling the cold rush through his fingers as he formed two icicles, ready to unleash his power. He unbound his soul from mine before turning his attention back towards Timbrax. In a daring move, he leaped at Timbrax, who gracefully dodged him by flipping out onto the balcony. Timbrax stood on the ledge, emanating an aura of toughness.

With a smug grin, Timbrax pointed out, "You missed," his voice laced with a hint of superiority. "Fucking dragon!" he exclaimed, his voice filled with anger. With a sudden flip downwards, he sent Sixus into a frenzy of screams as he hurriedly exited and leaped gracefully over the balcony.

Rolling my eyes in annoyance, I walked over to the desk. Balancing my two books, I stepped onto the balcony and instantly inhaled the crisp, salty fragrance of the sea. I leaped down, rolling before standing. While heading towards the oracle dormitory, I witnessed their ongoing power struggle, each trying to outdo the other.

I pulled open the heavy metal door and walked down the stone spiral staircase. Pushing open the door to the scrying room, I entered the living room and walked up the hallway. I walked over to the bookshelf that lined the wall before me. I took each book and carefully placed them on the shelf I could reach. There had to be over one hundred books here! After putting the last book on the shelf, I was satisfied.

I turned and walked out of the room, up the hallway, through the living room and up the steps. I walked out of the dormitory and closed the door behind me. They were still going at it! In a frowning manner, I made my way back to the balcony. I leaped up and walked into the room. I picked up my cell and pressed the side bar. The screen lit up, and I clicked a random rock playlist. Music started blaring and the two men didn't seem to give a fuck.

My Monster was playing.

And still nothing.

I walked out of the room after shutting off the music. As I flexed my back, my dragon wings exploded out of the back of my trench coat. I climbed onto the ledge and kicked off. My dragon wings caught the wind, and I flew higher and higher.

This caught their attention as Sixus flexed his back muscles and his dragon wings exploded out of his back. They were red, and he kicked off the ground and flapped them, catching up to me quickly.

"You know I can't allow you to leave, don't you, Mel?" Sixus shouted to me over the roar of the wind.

"So, you joined Orion?" I gave him a look of disappointment. "I'm just flying Sixus."

"It was the only way for them to spare our kingdom, Mel," Sixus replied. "They used me to draw you out of hiding and it worked!"

I stopped flying and landed. Sixus followed my lead and stood in front of me. I felt him rebinding his soul to me, and he could feel my emotions. I was a wreck right now.

"So," I sighed, meeting his gaze. "I'm your prisoner?"

"If you stay with me," Sixus said softly, his voice filled with warmth. With a reassuring smile, he whispered, "I'll protect you."

"Safe from what, Sixus?" I scoffed. "Look around you!" I moved my hands around the institute. It was a deserted wasteland. "My enemies won't stop until we're all dead!"

"And you," he whispered, his breath cold against my ear. "You're determined to stop them, aren't you?"

"There was a point in time," I whispered, feeling the weight of the past in my voice. "Where you wanted to stop them standing by my side, Sixus."

"There's nowhere you can go, Mel," Sixus' voice sent a shiver down her spine, devoid of any warmth or emotion. "Where you'll be hidden from my sight."

"Well, I guess it's official. We're back to being mortal enemies," I sighed. With a touch of sorrow, I mustered a smile for him. "Good times, right?" I asked, my voice filled with nostalgia.

"Are you my enemy, Mel?" With a raised eyebrow, Sixus directed his question towards me. "The thought of killing you would crush my heart."

"You don't have a heart," I muttered under my breath, my voice filled with bitterness and resentment. "I have a responsibility to our daughter, our people, and, above all, the dragons."

"You need to feed," he replied, his tone suddenly serious, avoiding further discussion. "While Timbrax's blood is harmful to you, mine won't pose any risk." he clarified.

"I'll starve," I exclaimed, pulling a disgusted expression. "I'm not letting you-"

"Drink it!" Looking down at me, Sixus snarled menacingly. "Mel, our priority is to achieve a perfect equilibrium among all the elements of your Tribrid body."

With a gentle tug, I brought his head closer to mine, and the sensation of his neck against my tongue sent shivers down my spine. With a swift motion, my sharp fangs punctured his skin, and I could feel his warm blood flowing into my mouth. It had a satisfying taste, with a perfect balance of flavors that danced on the palate. I drank until I could taste the sweetness on my tongue, feeling completely satisfied. As I retracted my fangs, I could taste the metallic tang of his blood in my mouth, and I quickly wiped the crimson stain off my chin with the back of my hand.

"How do you feel?" he inquired, eager to understand her emotions. His whisper came out in a soft, intimate tone, his intense gaze never leaving me.

"Fine," I replied nonchalantly, shrugging my shoulders. "Sixus, the Xeonada Empire is at your disposal, allowing you to govern it in any way you see fit."

"The Kingdom of Eozadion," Sixus replied, his words carrying a sense of mystery and intrigue. "Is yours, Mel."

"Let's go!" With a booming voice, Timbrax shouted to Sixus, his words carrying across the distance. "Without the vampire hunters aiding her," he laughed, his voice filled with amusement. "The absence of an army makes her kingdom susceptible to swift and effortless defeat!"

"I'll meet you back at The Xeonada Empire!" Sixus exclaimed, the sound of his voice echoing through the silent dorm room.

I watched in awe as Timbrax opened the astral thread, its shimmering blue color dancing before my eyes. He entered the space, and the thread closed behind him, sealing off the outside world.

With a swift movement, Sixus turned back to face me, his eyes filled with curiosity. I could feel the chill of his icy hand against my cheek, a physical manifestation of the impending loneliness I was about to face.

"I will always choose you, Mel," Sixus whispered softly, his words lingering in the air before he gently pressed his lips against mine. Before he brought it to an end, I closed my eyes and responded to his kiss wholeheartedly. My eyelids lifted, and there he was, leaning over me, his eyes filled with affection. "Embrace your new title as the queen of the dragons and pour all your energy into it, without any hesitation or reservations."

"I never thought I would lose you to the darkness, Sixus," I said, my laughter devoid of any joy. "I should be the one embracing it instead of you."

"Mel," Sixus said, his tone filled with hesitation as he retracted his outstretched hand and retreated a few feet away. "Our paths have diverged, and we now stand on opposite sides of this brutal conflict."

"I will tirelessly search for a cure, determined to reunite us, Sixus." I carefully dabbed at the tears that fell from my eyes, making sure not to smudge my makeup. "I will never abandon you!" With unwavering determination, I declared passionately, my voice filling the room.

"I'll see you on the battlefield," Sixus spat out with venom, his voice dripping with bitterness as he leaped high in the air. "See you later, Mel!" he shouted, his voice echoing through the empty institute grounds

With his supernatural speed, he raced through the skies towards the Xeonada Empire; the wind rushing past him. In an instant, a powerful gust of wind emerged, chilling me to the bone and causing my eyes to widen in disbelief as ice rapidly encased everything in sight. The entire empire had been transformed into a majestic ice palace under his command. He couldn't escape the remaining workload that awaited him. The bridge he formed from ice led directly to the entrance of the institute, ending just before the gates.

As I flicked my wrists, an enormous flamethrower appeared, crackling with fiery energy. With a single gesture, I shattered the ice bridge, watching as it teetered for a moment before plunging into the churning sea. I constructed a bridge of flames that stretched towards my end, effectively cutting off any possibility of him recreating his bridge.

With a sudden flash of blue light, the shamans appeared, leading Cy by their side. Their eyes widened in amazement as they took in the scene before them, marveling at the splendor of the Xeonada Empire.

Sixus worked his magic, turning my kingdom into a magnificent empire of ice. A frown creased my face. "Before he did that, we swapped kingdoms."

"So," Varric tore his gaze away from the majestic ice kingdom in front of him, its beauty stretching across the sea. "I'm guessing you're the new dragon queen?" he said, eyeing me curiously.

"I am," I sighed heavily, the weight of my words hanging in the air. "Orion, Claus, Victim, and my two husbands are formidable opponents, and I am left to fight them without any army at my side."

"You have an army," Solas said with a warm smile, his voice filled with reassurance. With a slow pivot, I came face to face with the shaman who had just departed, their gaze piercing through me. "Keep in mind," he cautioned, "the dead are beyond death's reach."

As a cold front swept across the sea, they disappeared from sight. The snow began to fall, and I sighed as I watched it, rolling my eyes at the inconvenience it would bring. "Guess we'd better get the heaters turned on," I exclaimed, feeling the cold seeping into my bones.

"I know where they are," Cy said confidently, a glint of determination in his eyes. "We managed to send the undisclosed item to the designated individual." With a playful wink, she and the girls sprinted up the steps, and Nell wasted no time in pulling open the door. They hurriedly entered, leaving me standing there, pondering my next course of action.

"We need to get you inside, my queen," Varric said urgently, his grip firm as he and Solas guided me up the steps. Varric pulled open the door, and a rush of warmth greeted me as I stepped inside the cozy building. As they stepped inside, the door clicked shut, sealing us in. "In case you were wondering, we've got your back. Your laptop is all set up in your dorm room for you to keep writing book three."

"Gotta write the important events for history," I said with a forced smile, feeling the weight of the responsibility. "Being the fucking oracle, I have an uncanny ability to foresee and guide us through our journey."

"Get some rest." Solas nodded at me. "We'll get everything back up and running." he assured her, making sure I understood the goal was to have the students return to the institute.

I embraced Varric tightly, conveying my appreciation, and he responded with an uncomfortable pat on the back. After setting him free, I couldn't resist the urge to kiss Solas, savoring the taste of his lips against mine. Before I could pull away, he eagerly reciprocated my kiss, leaving me breathless.

"I love you." I whispered to Solas; my voice filled with affection.

"I love you too," he said, his voice filled with the same affectionate tone. As Solas smiled at me, I couldn't help but sense a tinge of sadness behind it.

While I walked up the hallway, the sound of my shoes echoing off the silent walls created a creepy ambiance. As I reached my door and paused, the doors smoothly slid apart, revealing what lay beyond. As I entered, the heavy doors closed with a resounding thud behind me. There were people in my life who loved me wholeheartedly and would always have my back in any situation.

With a swift motion, I threw my hand out and witnessed the astral thread materialize right before me, as if it had been waiting all along. I entered, and it shut behind me. I closed my eyes, and as I exhaled, I could feel the weight of the world lifting off my shoulders. Startled awake, I could feel the comforting embrace of someone's arms around me, indicating that I must have dozed off. I slowly opened my eyes, and as I looked up. His gaze locked with mine, and I could see the unmistakable spark of desire and love in his eyes as our lips met in a passionate kiss.

Leader of the Broken Hearts started playing from his cell that was in his pocket.

"Your status as my enemy doesn't matter to me at all!"

Sixus snarled in my mind.

"I'm constantly thinking about you, Mel, and I can't help it!"

"Together we're stronger," I said through kisses. "I'm your heaven to your hell."

The moment I made contact, he flinched, as if my touch had caused him pain. With his heavy forehead resting against mine, I felt the weight of his exhaustion as I tenderly touched his thick, soft hair.

"You should leave," Sixus whispered, his voice laced with a hint of danger, as I sensed his pain through our bond. "It's becoming clear to me why Timbrax finds it incredibly challenging to be in your company, given the intensity you exude."

As I removed my hand and climbed to my feet, a sob threatened to escape, but I held it back. As he stood up, I turned my gaze away from him.

Statues That Cried Blood started playing next.

As I turned, Sixus' hand guided me, his touch firm yet gentle, until I was facing him. He felt my sorrow. My pain. And he caused it all. Well, the latest part of it, at least.

"Mel?" he called out, his voice echoing through the empty room. Solas's voice beckoned me from beyond the astral thread, pulling me towards him. "She's not here!" he said, frustration evident in his tone.

Right as I was about to reply, the astral thread shimmered into existence, and Timbrax stepped through its ethereal portal. As soon as he saw me, his lips curled into a snarl and his eyes narrowed with hostility.

"Remove her immediately!" With a commanding tone, Timbrax placed his order.

"Leave me alone!" As his rage grew, Sixus spat vehemently. I felt his rage fuming from his end of the bond. With a rebellious spirit, he declared, "I do what I want!" as he stood his ground.

As I ran through the wall, I felt a jolt of surprise before stumbling back into my dorm room. Solas wasted no time and grabbed me forcefully as Timbrax opened the astral thread, his glare filled with a mixture of anger and frustration.

"Avoid the astral thread at all costs!" Timbrax's voice urgently advised. His mouth twisted in disgust as he spat, the saliva landing with a splat on the floor. "Just so we're clear, this is *my* turf!" He declared with authority. As it closed behind him, my heart raced with a surge of adrenaline.

"Hold still," Solas murmured in a soothing voice as he gently inserted the needle into my skin. The pain was sharp and intense, radiating from the silver tip that had made contact with me. He removed it with a quick flick of his wrist and nonchalantly tossed it into the trashcan. "With the antidote now fortified, let's observe their futile attempt to savor your blood."

The gears of the plan to revert Sixus to his Half-Draconian self were set in motion, ready to bring about a profound change. Once this happened, the possibility of going back was completely eliminated. With every fiber of my being, I was set on getting my mate back, and I wouldn't rest until I succeeded. I am prepared to give up everything, even my own life, to achieve this. They understood that sacrifices were necessary to move forward. It felt like the weight of the world was resting on their shoulders, with everything at stake.

And I wouldn't have it any other way.

ELEVEN

With renewed energy, the institute resumed its operations, buzzing with productivity. Zara had returned, accompanied by the vampire hunters, and she returned to me the Venin dagger, Holistic sword, and Valistik sword that I had lent her. They felt an overwhelming sense of guilt for leaving me alone in my time of need. Not only that, but Zara couldn't help but blame herself for Sixus' transformation into a Varacolaci, intensifying her anguish. She couldn't be blamed for what happened.

Zuni was engrossed in her work, determined to discover a long-term cure for Sixus. In a desperate move, Abel resorted to using Sixus' frozen blood on the floor as a stopgap measure, enabling me to administer a temporary cure to him.

It seemed as though Sixus, and I had traded spots, as if our roles had been completely reversed. As I crept towards the Xeonada Empire, I caught a glimpse of him engaged in a brutal fight with Victim in the arena. With a chilling touch, he froze them in their tracks before mercilessly smashing their bodies into tiny ice fragments, leaving a chilling scene on the sandy ground.

The deafening blast of the horn filled the tunnel as I crouched in the shadows, my heart pounding in my chest. The match was officially over, and the silence that followed was palpable.

"Your winner!" Orion's shout pierced through the silence of the stands, reaching the ears of the Victim. With a flourish, the announcer proclaimed, "Presenting the one and only Dragon King Sixus Westin!"

The sound of boos filled the air as the Victim received a harsh reception, while Sixus remained apathetic.

"I'm craving something that will push me to my limits," he proclaimed. With excitement in his voice, Sixus shouted and pointed towards the constellation of Orion, his eyes filled with wonder. "I need someone who can survive longer than a mere five seconds after the match begins!"

"Your next challenger has arrived!" Orion's voice boomed through the arena. Orion laughed, his deep and hearty laughter echoing through the arena. With a cheer of "Good luck, dragon king!"

"Bring him out immediately!" he exclaimed angrily. Sixus cracked his neck muscles, relieving the stiffness that had built up. The bond between us transmitted his rage so strongly that I could physically feel it.

"Prepare yourself, because we're about to witness something truly special!" As Orion raised his voice, the noise of the restless crowd gradually subsided, giving way to an eerie silence. "Bring out the next challenger!"

The anticipation in the air was palpable as the crowd eagerly awaited the arrival of the next contender.

Startled by the blaring horn, Sixus quickly glanced around, trying to locate my whereabouts. Right as he was about to open his mouth, the sound of "Forgotten" blasted through the loudspeakers, filling the arena.

The moment he realized it was me, his eyes widened, reflecting a mix of shock and disbelief.

Utilizing the services of Timbrax and Orion, I had successfully negotiated a match with Sixus, which I had meticulously planned. It was obvious that they wouldn't turn down the offer. As he watched the show, he couldn't help but be in awe of the extraordinary talent on display. The crowd held their breath, anxiously awaiting the brutal clash that would decide the victor.

"Remember what I taught you," Timbrax's voice echoed from behind me. "Melfina, unleash your fury and kick his ass!"

"Firelash Power!" Surrounded by a burst of fiery energy, I shouted, my voice echoing through the air. I transformed into Hell's Guardian. "I will," I said with determination in my voice. With a quick turn, I flashed him a mischievous smirk and effortlessly slipped into my poker face, hiding any hint of what I was truly thinking. As I walked out of the tunnel, I couldn't help but feel a surge of pride, my head held high.

"Anyone but *her*!" he exclaimed; his voice filled with frustration. The moment Timbrax revealed himself, Sixus' lips curled back in a fierce snarl. With a swift motion, I unsheathed the Valistik sword and positioned myself in a defensive stance, prepared for whatever was to come. With a swift movement, Timbrax removed his sheath from around his shoulder and tossed it to Sixus, who caught it with a satisfied grin. Securing the strap over his shoulder, he smoothly withdrew the sword from its hiding place behind his back.

With my vampire speed coursing through me, I unleashed a swift and deadly swing of my sword towards his head. I lunged forward, slashing through the air where Sixus had just been standing, but he had already evaded my attack. I didn't hold back as I snarled at him, leaving no doubt about my intentions.

The sound of his fist connecting with the sand resonated through the air as he molded a substantial icicle, swiftly embedding it into the ground and encasing the fighting circle within a sturdy dome. My gaze lifted, and in an instant, memories of us trapped in a frozen orb rushed back to me before I forcefully banished them from my thoughts.

"There's no water in here, Mel," Sixus smirked as a sudden chill filled the air. A visible sign of the cold. My breath appeared before me, making me shiver involuntarily. Sixus assured, "I promise I won't allow the water to overwhelm you."

"Stop fucking around and fight me already, Sixus!" As I shouted, the sound of my voice reverberated and echoed throughout the dome.

"Why?" Sixus questioned, his brow furrowed in deep thought. With a commanding gesture, he sheathed the sword behind his back and approached me with determined steps. Taking the Valistik sword from my hand with a tender gesture, he smoothly inserted it into the sheath attached to my left side. He pulled me into an embrace, his touch simultaneously comforting and possessive, his hand caressing the small of my back and resting on my ass. "You look hot as fuck."

"Would you like to take this back to the castle?"

I asked in my mind.

Opening the astral thread, Sixus let out a snarl before swiftly picking me up and leaping through it, his arms securely around me. We ended up in my former bedroom, and as the door closed, a rush of nostalgia washed over me.

With a smug expression, Sixus leaned over me, his words dripping with desire as he whispered, "I've been restless, yearning for the moment when I can have you in my bed."

"Fuck me already," I said, my fingers tangling in his hair, urging him to fulfill my desire. "Or don't."

"What the fuck are you two doing?" The room fell silent as Timbrax burst in. A snarl ripped through the air the moment he caught sight of Sixus and I.

"Call the match," Sixus murmured softly, his eyes fixed on me with a mix of intensity and concern. "It was a draw."

"Rumors are spreading that a heated conflict is taking place between you two in the ice dome!" Timbrax's snarl echoed through the room, filling it with a sense of danger. "Go back into the fray and eliminate each other without mercy!"

"Let's go," I said with a mischievous smirk. "If we're not there, we won't be able to give them the show they're expecting, right?"

Sixus threw out his hand, and together we leaped through the rush of wind in our ears. Back in the dome, I felt a sense of relief as the astral thread closed behind us.

With a swift motion, I grasped the hilt of the Venin dagger and forcefully pulled it out of its sheath. Holding it in front of my face, I hurried towards him, my heart pounding in my chest. The moment I plunged it into his left side, he stood there, seemingly unfazed by the pain. After yanking the blade out, I tasted his blood on the blade, the metallic tang lingering on my tongue before I sheathed it.

As Sixus sank to one knee, I followed suit, mirroring his gesture of respect and submission. My outfit grew damp and sticky as the blood slowly seeped into the fabric, a visible reminder of the damage I had inflicted.

With a swift motion, he yanked me towards him, sinking his fangs into my neck, the sensation of his gulping down my blood sending shivers down my spine. Instantly, I could feel his endorphins flooding his body. As he forcefully extracted his fangs, he lost his balance and toppled forward.

With a fading voice, he whispered, "You," as he started to lose consciousness. "Win."

As he lost consciousness, I loosened my grip and let him drop to the ground, his face making a hard landing. As I stood up, the dome that had enclosed me seemed to liquify and disappear, leaving me feeling exposed and vulnerable.

Timbrax took a moment to assess the situation, his mind racing as he considered his next move. There he was, Sixus, sprawled unconscious on the ground, while I remained frozen in place, unable to look away.

As the match came to an end, the blaring sound of the horn filled the air.

"Ladies and gentlemen, put your hands together for our champion!" Orion proclaimed. As the music abruptly ended, Orion's shout filled the silence. As they chanted the name of the undefeated Hell's Guardian, the crowd erupted into a cacophony of split boos and cheers, creating an electric atmosphere.

Amidst the resounding boos from the crowd, Timbrax made his entrance into the ring, triumphantly lifting my hand before setting me free.

Racing out of the arena with my vampire speed, I found solace in the cool embrace of the tunnel's shadows. Timbrax walked up to me, his heavy footsteps echoing with each step.

"Go!" he commanded, his hand swiftly extending as he conjured the shimmering astral thread in front of me. Without warning, the outfit dissipated into nothingness. Just as I was about to hit the ground, Solas came to my rescue and caught me in the nick of time.

"Did he satisfy his craving by consuming your blood?" Solas asked, his voice filled with curiosity.

"Yeah," I murmured, my breaths coming out in short, labored puffs as exhaustion took hold. "I need to go to I.O.A." I muttered under my breath, trying to remember the way.

Glancing down, Solas noticed the crimson blood trickling down my leg.

I closed my eyes and instantly plunged into a void of complete darkness.

***

I felt a soothing warmth spread through my body as my wounds were being healed, and then someone skillfully wrapped fresh bandages around me. As my eyes flew open, I let out a gasp of surprise. In the hospital bed, the soft hum of medical equipment surrounded me, and I could feel the coolness of the mask against my face. The sound of snapping cords filled the air, and in that instant, everything froze as if time had stopped. As I was being lifted, I could feel the strong and secure embrace of someone's arms.

"I got you, Mel," Sixus whispered to me, his voice filled with determination. "Out of all the options in the world, my unwavering choice will forever be you."

I closed my eyes, and darkness consumed me once again.

***

A heated argument between two males echoed through the vicinity, their raised voices reverberating with tension and hostility. As I woke up, my eyelids flickered open and closed, still heavy with sleep. I didn't have the strength to keep my eyes open any longer.

"By bringing her here, do you have any concept of the consequences?" Timbrax spat, the sound echoing in the empty void of the astral thread.

"She's my wife!" he shouted, his voice filled with desperation and anger. Sixus snarled. "The consequences of not keeping her with me at all times are dire. She may not survive!"

"Your dragon bond," Timbrax sighed heavily, his voice filled with exhaustion. "Despite its weakness, it compels you to protect your mate at all costs, doesn't it?"

"*Six...us?*"

I thought.

With the opening of the astral thread, a rush of footsteps reached my ears, indicating the arrival of two people by my side. The touch on my right cheek sent a jolt of icy sensation through my body, leaving me startled.

"I'm here, Mel," Sixus whispered softly as I felt the weight of someone sitting on the bed beside me. "I need you to live, okay?" he pleaded, his voice filled with desperation.

"I'm cold," I whispered, my breath visible in the frosty air. "Would you mind helping me get warm?"

The left side of the bed dipped slightly, and an immediate sensation of warmth coursed through my entire body.

"I'm sending her back," Timbrax murmured quietly, his voice barely reaching my ears as I nestled against him. The bond between us was tinged with jealousy, emanating strongly from Sixus' side. "You fucking idiot!" he shouted. "She's inexplicably attracted to the scorching heat!"

I heard the astral thread unfurl, and soon after, I felt the gentle touch of hands carefully guiding me onto a plush bed in a room that radiated warmth. They walked through it, and in an instant, it vanished into thin air, leaving me in disbelief.

As I fell into a deep slumber, my mind became a blank canvas, devoid of dreams.

"I feel like I'm being smothered. I can't even take a single breath!"
I thought.

In an instant, my eyes shot open, and I was confronted by Largo Croix. His hands were wrapped tightly around my throat, his gaze fixated on me as I gasped for air.

His words were filled with venom as he shouted, "Tribrid bitch, you deserve to die!" Largo laughed like a madman.

I urgently clutched his hands, desperately trying to pry them away from me. His strength was overpowering.

"SIXUS!"
I yelled in my mind.

In an instant, the astral thread emerged, and the sudden movement of someone rushing out filled the air with a sense of urgency. Suddenly, Largo's hands released me, and I felt the jarring force of someone slamming them onto the floor.

"Keep your hands off my mate, you worthless piece of shit!" he yelled angrily. With a fierce snarl, Sixus made his displeasure known. The sound of his boots skidding across the floor echoed through the room as he tightly gripped two thick icicles in his fists. With a defensive stance, he positioned his body protectively in front of me.

The words echoed in the air, filled with an accusing tone, "Something's changed in you, dragon king!" Largo scoffed as he sniffed the air. "You possess the powers of three supernatural beings, just like your female counterpart!"

Sixus snarled, causing my eyes to widen in shock. With a quick motion of his wrists, the icicles were unleashed, whizzing past him as he sprinted forward. Bursting with energy, Largo dashed past Sixus, shattering the closed French doors into countless splinters of wood and shards of glass. With a daring leap off the balcony, he disappeared into the mysterious embrace of the night.

With the blaring of alarms and the sudden illumination of lights, the institute was instantly transformed into a state of alert. As my eyes adjusted, the bright lights temporarily blinded me, and Sixus cast a quick glance over his shoulder.

I quickly threw off the hot comforter and jumped to my feet, embracing him tightly. As I closed my eyes, his intoxicating scent filled my nostrils with each deep inhale. The scent of cranberries mixed with the pristine snow was intoxicating. There was no lingering smell of death in the air.

My voice barely above a whisper, I said, "You came," the words carrying a mix of emotions. My voice sounded bruised. "You-"

With a swift motion, the doors slid open, and my eyes landed on Solas as he stormed into the room, accompanied by the shaman and a multitude of vampire hunters. As soon as they saw him, they immediately pointed their weapons in his direction.

"Step away from the queen," Tork's voice rang out, filled with an icy intensity. "I will *not* hesitate to shoot you, dragon king!"

"No," I whispered, feeling the loss as he gently released me from his protective embrace. "Don't shoot him!"

"It's okay, Mel," Sixus reassured me with a sympathetic smile, his hands rising in surrender as he turned to face them. "I'll surrender myself into your custody." he said, his voice filled with resignation.

"Cuff him!" Tork ordered, her voice filled with authority and urgency.

Velzy walked over and secured his hands behind his back, the silver handcuffs digging into his skin. The sensation of burning intensified as dark red circles materialized on my skin, specifically on my wrists.

"I hope you find your cell unbearably hot," Velzy hissed, her breath hot against his ear. "Just the way you like it!"

"Wait!" I yelled, my voice raspy and raw. As I ran towards him, my heart pounding, I crashed into his chest and pressed my lips against his in a quick kiss. Velzy abruptly pulled him away, leaving me standing alone after our brief kiss as the hunters followed them out the door.

"I love you," Sixus whispered softly, his voice filled with adoration. "Always."

Solas quickly sprang into action, his movements precise and calculated. Pointing at the door, he instructed Varric to take care of the repairs without delay. With a sudden motion, he grabbed me and effortlessly lifted me in his arms, swiftly making his way out of the room. "We're relocating you to a more secure area." he said reassuringly.

"The oracle dormitory?" I asked, my voice filled with curiosity. As he walked up the hallway, I whispered softly under my breath. With Varric joining us, he swiftly went ahead and opened the door, the sound of it creaking filling the air. Solas walked past him, the sound of his trotting footsteps resonating as he descended down the steps. "You got it." he replied with a confident nod.

Leaping down the steps, Varric's heart raced as he made a beeline for the door. Just as Solas entered, he forcefully swung the door open and swiftly made his way down the twisting stone steps. Every step he took in his boots created a resounding echo that filled the silent walls. After landing in the living room, he made his way into the bedroom and was immediately struck by the comforting scent of fresh laundry. With gentle hands, he carefully covered me up with the soft, thick comforter, ensuring I was snug and comfortable.

In an effort to calm myself down, I took deep breaths. As I stood there, I sensed Sixus' fear, a protective worry that he held solely for my well-being.

"He's so selfless."

I thought.

As the door swung open, Velzy appeared, her eyes fixed on me in silence.

"Melfina," Velzy replied, her voice filled with urgency. "He wants to see you." Before I leaped to my feet and walked up to her, I hastily shoved the comforter off my body. Solas snapped his fingers, and in an instant, I transformed into a fully geared mecha pilot, donning a double-sided uniform, sturdy boots, and two protective jackets. I took extra precautions by strapping my weapons tightly against my body, leaving no room for error. Not only did he do my hair in the adorable cat ear pigtails style, but he also skillfully did my makeup. "Come with me," she whispered, his voice filled with reverence. "My queen."

While rushing out of the room, I quickly nodded my thanks to Solas, who stood at the doorway. As we walked up the long hallway, the sound of our footsteps echoed against the walls. As we ascended the spiral stone steps, the sound of our footsteps echoed through the air. The cool night air stung my face as we hurriedly dashed across the lawn, our footsteps echoing in the silence.

As we turned the corner, she revealed the metal door, its cold surface gleaming under the dim light. As we descended the metal steps, the sound of my boots sticking to the metal echoed through the stairwell. I followed her up the long hallway, the sound of our footsteps echoing against the walls. Rows of cells stretched along the walls on both sides, creating a symmetrical and imposing sight. Near the back, she paused and carefully pulled open a door on the right.

Stepping inside his cell, I found him sitting with his back pressed against the cold cement wall. The cuffs around his wrists were secured to the long chains, which hung ominously from the wall. As he glanced up at me, I felt a wave of relief wash over me upon seeing his mesmerizing blue eyes. Sitting beside him on the metal cot were the copies of my books I signed for him, neatly arranged.

"Sixus!" As he stood up, I hurriedly made my way towards him, the urgency in my steps matching the desperation in my voice. I threw my arms around him, and he hugged me tightly. "Are you okay?"

"Yeah." His nostrils flared as he deeply breathed in my scent, his face filled with a mix of curiosity and desire. "The vampire hunters are taking me to the arena, where I will stand before the mighty dragons, waiting to pass judgment."

"What?" I asked, looking up at him in disbelief. "There's no guarantee you'll make it out alive!" I cautioned, emphasizing the peril that awaited inside. "You can die!"

"So can you." His words were barely audible as he whispered in my ear. "You are my mate." he whispered, his voice filled with love and devotion.

"Time's up!" The room was filled with the sound of Tork's voice, which reverberated as she stood by the door. "We're escorting the prisoner towards the arena, the sound of shackles clinking echoing through the hallway."

"No," I exclaimed, my voice drowned out by Velzy's forceful grip as she pulled me away from him. "You can't kill him down there!"

Without uttering a single word, she forcefully dragged me up the hallway, my frantic kicks and screams echoing through the air. With a firm grip, she tugged me up the stairs and swiftly led me out the door.

A black transport van idled nearby, ready to transport Sixus to the arena. Sixus found himself surrounded by the vampire hunters, who quickly chained him and escorted him to the back of the van, while I observed from a distance. He was shackled by the constraints of his own kingdom, feeling like a prisoner in his own land.

"This is bullshit!" I shouted at them; frustration evident in my tone. "He's the ruler of this fucking kingdom!"

"Pull yourself together, Mel."

Sixus said in my mind.

With my composure restored, I confidently threw my hand out. I couldn't resist the allure of the astral thread opening, so I leaped inside, ready to be transported to the arena. Behind me, the astral thread closed, sealing off the outside world. As the bright lights illuminated the arena, I stood on the balcony overlooking the arena dirt while I stood where the royals were to be seated.

A putrid odor, reminiscent of death, invaded my senses as the astral thread opened up right beside me. Ignoring Timbrax, I shifted my focus elsewhere as Sixus was about to be executed.

"They're going to kill him, you know?" He said, keeping his gaze fixed forward. "Your gonna die too."

"I've died twice already," I replied, my voice trembling with the haunting memories of my near-death encounters. "Our survival is crucial, Timbrax." I said, my voice tinged with determination.

"The oracle needs to survive," Timbrax scoffed, rolling his eyes in disbelief. "Fuck him!" he muttered under her breath.

"Fuck you!" With a spat, I forcefully tore my gaze away from the sand, taking in the sight of the metal poles and chains. "I'm determined to rescue my mate from the clutches of death!"

"What was your strategy for accomplishing it?" In a hushed tone, Timbrax posed his question.

"What do you mean?" I asked, confused.

With a hint of anticipation, he posed his inquiry. "Can you turn Sixus into a Tribrid like yourself?"

"How would I know?" I scoffed. I nonchalantly shrugged my shoulders, my words trailing off as if unsure of what I was saying. "Driven by the urgency to save him, I acted swiftly and without hesitation."

"Right," Timbrax chuckled to himself, the sound of his laughter filling the air. "See you on the other side, Melfina." As soon as he stepped back into the astral thread, it blinked out of existence. It was just me, with no one else in sight.

I couldn't gauge the passage of time as I remained rooted in that spot, unsure of how long I stood here. As I heard footsteps approaching, I turned and saw Cy and the shaman walking towards me, their footsteps echoing in the silence. They dressed up in elegant suits and glamorous dresses, ready for the evening ahead.

Tears stained down Cy's cheeks, and their eyes were red and swollen. As she hugged me tightly, I reciprocated with an equally tight embrace, planting a tender kiss on the top of her head. She released me from her grip and settled down in the seat next to me.

The arena buzzed with excitement as dragon knights, mecha pilots, assassins, and vampire hunters filled its ranks. Tork and Velzy were dragging Sixus towards the first metal pole, their muscles straining with effort. As I watched, my heart raced in my chest, the sound of each beat echoing in my ears. They grabbed hold of his ankles, pulling him down, and wrapped their hands around his neck. As they approached the tunnel, the deafening roar of three mechas filled the air, their weapons ominously aimed at Sixus below.

"You're up Mel."

Sixus said in my mind.

"I love you."

"I love you too, Sixus."

I replied.

As the dragons flew over and landed on the ground, the link fell into an eerie silence. The rumble reverberated through the stadium, making my heart race.

"We are here to witness the trial of King Sixus Westin!" I shouted loudly. "May the dragons keep you in their fiery embrace!" I whispered, my voice trailing off in a soft, reverent tone.

"We have found King Sixus Westin... completely exonerated of all accusations!"

A dragon spoke in my mind.

A sense of justice finally prevailing.

The dragons' roars of victory echoed throughout the kingdom.

"The dragons declared King Sixus Westin innocent of all charges!" As everyone gazed at me, my shout echoed through the arena. In a commanding tone, my words filled the arena, leaving no room for hesitation. "Release the king!"

The moment I leaped off the ledge, I felt a surge of power, causing me to instinctively flex my back. As my dragon wings burst out of my jackets, I felt the rush of air against my scales. We fell to the ground, feeling the rough grass beneath us. They diligently worked on freeing him from the cold, unforgiving metal chains that bound his wrists, feet, and neck. The hunters joined them, the key clinking in their hands.

Above my head, a deafening explosion shattered the silence, and an immense wall of fiery orange surged towards us. I defended myself by thrusting my hands forward, conjuring a blazing wall of fire that pushed the threat back towards them.

"Hurry!" I exclaimed; my voice filled with urgency. I shouted to Cy and the others. "It's getting harder to keep my hold on it!"

Cy froze the shackles on Sixus' wrists, feeling the cold metal against her fingertips before crushing them in her hands. She repeated the same action on his neck and ankles, leaving a trail of metal.

"Quick, remove the princess from the arena!" With a loud voice, Sixus shouted to the hunters, his words carrying through the air.

They urgently seized Cy and hurriedly propelled her towards the dark tunnel.

As Timbrax leaped towards me, the intense heat from the flames he broke through filled the air. With a sudden jerk, he seized me by the neck, causing my hands to drop helplessly to my sides. The vibrant blue flames flickered and vanished. With a swift movement of his hand, he sank his sharp fangs into my neck, causing a sharp, piercing pain. His body immediately flooded with endorphins, filling me with a rush of euphoria.

"MEL!" Sixus called out, his voice filled with urgency. As Sixus screamed my name, I could sense his rage and panic reverberating through our bond. "Don't harm her!" he pleaded; his voice filled with desperation.

"She has the cure!" Timbrax let out a fierce snarl, his teeth bared menacingly. "The oracle plays a crucial role in Victim's quest for control over Tellus!"

As I looked at Sixus, his handsome face contorted into a determined expression right before everything went black, and I entered a state of complete darkness.

TWELVE

In an instant, my eyes flew open, and I sat upright, startled. As I woke up, I lay uncomfortably on a metal cot, wrapped in the warmth of the blankets. As I took in my surroundings, a feeling of déjà vu washed over me - I was in a cell I had been in before. My wrists were held in place by the chains attached to the wall behind me, their cold metal biting into my skin. The pain in my wrists was excruciating. When I glanced out the window, the sight of countless stars twinkling against the black sky mesmerized me. Once again, I found myself aboard a Victim ship.

The sound of the door unlocking and opening caught my attention, causing me to quickly turn my head. The moment Timbrax stepped into my cell, the air grew heavy and suffocating, the sound of the door closing amplifying my sense of isolation. As he stood before me, I couldn't help but look up and meet his gaze.

"Why am I back here?" I asked, my voice dripping with attitude.

"You know why," Timbrax smirked, his tone dripping with slyness, before his face suddenly turned grave. "Once you provide me with the details I require, you'll be free to go home to your stupid dragon mate."

"What details are you interested in learning?" As I climbed to my feet and looked up at him, I asked in a curious tone.

"What was your method for curing Sixus?" He asked. "Victim saw him transform back into his former self, and they know you were the one behind his transformation."

"I told you," I responded, my tone laced with exasperation. "My blood is constantly evolving and changing."

"So?" Timbrax asked, a hint of skepticism lacing his words. "If I understand correctly, the cure resides within *your* blood?"

"Yes and no," I replied, my voice wavering between uncertainty and conviction. "The cure, originally intended for Sixus alone, was now faced with the daunting task of treating an entire vampire army of Victim."

"Why only him?" he wondered, his voice filled with frustration. Timbrax's eyes narrowed as he demanded an answer from me.

"Because he's my mate," I replied firmly, my eyes never leaving his. "I have no concern for whether the Victim live or die."

"I'm sure the cure can work on Victim too, Melfina," Timbrax murmured as he gently unlocked my chains. The cot shook violently as they fell onto it, causing a loud clatter. After pocketing the key, he gestured towards the door, silently urging me to follow. I felt a powerful connection as he rebounded his soul to mine, saving me from Victim's attack. As he opened the door, a rush of voices and footsteps greeted him in the bustling hallway. As he walked up the hallway, I trailed behind him, the sound of our footsteps echoing. His voice carried an urgent tone as he spoke, "Stay with me, alright?"

As we entered the room, I couldn't help but cringe when my eyes landed on the chair they had prepared for me. Orion, Claus, Tasia, Largo, and Viz sat at a table, their laughter echoing across the room. The moment they saw me, they fell silent, and Orion stood and approached us as we walked to where the chair was. As I glanced at it, I noticed that it still had my old, dry blood stained on it.

"Melfi," he asked. "Do we need to use it on you?" Orion's voice broke through the silence, pulling me out of my reverie.

"What?" I exclaimed; my voice filled with disbelief. His words hit me like a punch in the gut, causing me to blink in surprise. "No."

"She said." Timbrax frowned at Orion, his brows furrowing with disapproval. "The dragon king's transformation back to his former self relies on the power of her blood."

"Really?" Orion arched an eyebrow at me. "Shall we put it to the test?" he said, a mischievous glint in his eyes.

"It's not gonna work on Victim," I scoffed, rolling my eyes. "Drinking it would be fatal for them."

"The lying Tribrid bitch!" Largo's laughter echoed with a sinister undertone.

"If I'm lying," I replied, my voice laced with a hint of defiance. "Largo, why don't you be the first to volunteer and taste it?"

"Fuck off!" Largo sneered, his lip curling with contempt.

"I think," Timbrax replied with a smirk, making his opinion clear. "Largo needs to get his ass over here and indulge in the Tribrid's blood."

Largo's expression turned grave as he locked eyes with Orion and Timbrax.

"I'll even sit in the chair for you," I said with a sweet smile as I gracefully took a seat. "Largo," I said, my voice dripping with disdain, "I can practically taste the fear emanating from you."

"I'm not scared of your bitch ass!" Largo snapped, his footsteps echoed loudly as he stomped towards me in a furious stride. "I'd go so far as to taste your repulsive blood just to emphasize my point!" His face contorted with rage; he clenched his trembling fist as he approached me.

Timbrax swiftly intercepted the swing, catching him off guard and causing him to stumble backwards, ultimately landing on his back and sliding across the room. He struck his head on the table where the others were seated, causing a loud thud.

"I made it clear that I would not tolerate any harm inflicted on my wife." Timbrax stood firmly by my side, his fingers crooked with a menacing intent, poised to rip Largo apart. "Do that shit again and I'm ripping your fucking head off and sending it out into space in flames!"

As I gazed up at Timbrax, my eyes widened in surprise, taking in his towering height. His rage was palpable, seeping through our bond. I had forgotten just how deadly and merciless he could be.

"Stop looking at me like that!"

Timbrax snapped in my mind.

I averted my gaze to the ground, trying to avoid any obstacles in my path as I looked forward. He still held the title of Victim Commander; despite all the challenges he had faced. I needed to constantly replay it in my mind as a reminder.

Timbrax wrinkled his nose and growled, a sign that he detected a familiar scent in the air. The familiar scent immediately triggered my nose. The scent of cranberries mixed with snow and death.

"No?" Slowly turning my head, I whispered as Sixus entered the room, my breath catching in my throat. He walked over to me, his footsteps echoing in the silence. His eyes were eerie, with a ghostly white color and red rings circling the edges. And there was complete silence. Not even a faint pulse could be heard. Sixus had transformed back into a Varacolaci, his fangs gleaming in the shitty dim lighting.

"I commend you for *trying*," Sixus said, his sigh heavy with disappointment. "Mel," he said with a smirk. "Your little plan failed."

"I don't understand?" I whispered to myself, barely audible in the quiet room. "Abel injected me with your blood to transform you back into a Half-Draconian Sixus?"

"It wasn't enough," Sixus replied with a hint of disappointment in his voice. "Furthermore, it was infected, emitting a putrid odor and displaying visible signs of decay."

"I told you so," he exclaimed triumphantly. As he climbed to his feet, Largo's laughter filled the air. "You stupid Tribrid bitch!" He spat; his voice filled with venom. "The dragon king is on our side, not hers."

I forcefully pushed past Sixus and Timbrax, feeling their resistance as I sprinted out of the room. I leaped up on the cold, metallic beams and settled onto a sturdy pipe, finding support as I leaned my back against another one. With my mecha pilot boots securely stuck, I could rest easy knowing I wouldn't fall off even if I dozed off up here.

"Where did she disappear to?" From below me, Tasia's voice echoed as she asked her question. "Is she trying to escape again?"

"I don't think so," Sixus replied, his voice echoing through the empty hallway. "She's hiding from us." he whispered, the tension palpable in his voice.

"Where are you at, Mel?"

Sixus asked in my mind.

I kept my mind empty, devoid of any thoughts or distractions. Through the bond, he could sense the depth of my pain.

As I listened, I could hear a faint rustling below me, and suddenly, Sixus appeared on the same metal pipe. As he sat down in front of me, I kept my gaze fixed ahead, refusing to acknowledge his presence.

"I understand," he said softly, his voice filled with gentleness. "You're disappointed, aren't you?"

I remained quiet, captivated by the faint hum of the ship resonating beneath me.

"It worked temporarily," Sixus said, his voice invading my personal space. He pulled me into his lap and held me tightly as he sat where I was. "You should be happy."

"Well, I'm not," I whispered, my eyes fixated on him, taking in every detail. "Can I go home now?" I pleaded; my voice filled with exhaustion.

"You're staying with me," Sixus whispered, his frigid breath tickling my neck. I gasped as his stiff lips caught me off guard, sending a chill down my spine. "Forever."

His sharp fangs pierced my neck, and I could feel the warm trickle of blood flowing down my skin. Almost instantly, I could feel the rush of endorphins coursing through my veins. I fell into a state of pure bliss and heard the menacing snarl of Timbrax before everything went dark.

***

As I awoke, a wave of dizziness and disorientation washed over me. I heard Timbrax and Sixus in a heated argument outside of my cell. Slowly, I sat up and ran my fingers over my neck, feeling the stiffness and soreness. It felt sore and tender, as if it had been through a beating. As I pulled my hand back, I was horrified to discover my entire palm was covered in blood. The air was thick. As I sniffed it, the unexpected blend of cranberries, snow, and my scent took me aback.

"You can't continue to drain her like that, you fucking idiot!" Timbrax spat, the sound echoing in the empty alleyway.

"Her blood," Sixus spat, the venom in his voice palpable. "It's *so* addicting!"

"And that's precisely why you must quit consuming it!" Timbrax spat, the sound echoing through the empty hallway. "You know I'm right, you fucking dragon!"

I tossed the white blanket off my hot body, feeling the cool air against my skin. As my hand made contact with the wall behind me, the astral thread unfurled, revealing itself. As I fell backwards, I slipped inside it, feeling the other side close behind me. As I fell through the other end, the sensation of weightlessness quickly gave way to a jarring impact as I landed on the familiar floor of my dorm room back at the institute.

As the doors slid open, I pushed myself up with a burst of energy.

"Mom!" she called out, her voice filled with urgency. Cy sprinted to my side, with the shaman and vampire hunters quickly following suit. "She's hurt!" she exclaimed, as she noticed the blood on her hands.

I urgently asked, "Can you please get me to I.O.A.?" I whispered; my voice is barely audible in the quiet room. "Your dad... has transformed into a Varacolaci once more."

I fell unconscious.

***

"Where are you, Mel?"

Sixus asked in my mind.

"Sixus?"

I replied.

"I thought you loved me?"

He went on.

"I do."

I replied.

"You left me."

His voice trembled with pain.

As his scent filled my nose, I heard the astral thread open, like a whisper in the wind. As I opened my eyes, the sterile scent of disinfectant filled the air, and I found myself lying in a hospital bed. Leaning over, he sank his fangs into my neck, causing a sharp, piercing pain. As I reached over, another sharp, shooting pain surged through my body, making it difficult to find the button to alert someone. Frantically, I found it and pressed the tiny red button, hoping for a response. As I struggled to stay awake, I released it with a sigh.

"Get off her!" Solas shouted, desperation evident in his voice. Solas yanked Sixus off of me and slammed him against the wall. The alarms blared loudly, causing me to gasp in surprise.

"Code Blue!"

The computerized female voice echoed above me, its repetitive message playing on a loop.

"Attention all medical staff," the urgent announcement echoed through the halls. "Report to I.O.A. immediately!"

Suddenly, I heard someone leaping through the astral thread, and it closed with a soft hum of electricity.

A flurry of doctors and nurses entered the room, their hurried footsteps echoing against the sterile walls. As the medicine entered my vein, a gentle wave of relaxation washed over me, and I surrendered to a profound and restful sleep.

***

The moment I opened my eyes, I realized I was lying in the comfortable bed of the oracle dormitory, feeling completely at ease. As I sat up, I could feel the weight of exhaustion settling into my bones, but I couldn't help but feel grateful for being alive.

"Mel, how are you feeling?" he asked with concern. As Solas entered the room, his footsteps echoed against the wooden floor as he made his way towards me.

"Fine," I muttered as I peeled the warm comforter off my body, rising to my feet at a sluggish pace. "What happened?"

"Oh, you know," Solas shrugged nonchalantly, his voice tinged with indifference. "Sixus was relentless in his sneaky attempts to drink your blood at every opportunity."

"Is he Vamping Out without taking a sip of my blood?" I asked, eagerly awaiting his response.

Solas nodded as he pondered his next words. "Mel," he said urgently. "We need to abort the mission."

"Are you kidding me?" I scoffed, rolling my eyes at his ridiculous statement. "Solas," I whispered, my voice filled with determination, "I'm on the verge of bringing him back."

"At the cost of you nearly dying every time, Melfina," Solas said, his voice growing stern, a tone I had never heard from him before. "Theres no cure other than him getting stabbed by that Holistic sword which he is currently in possession of."

"This is complete bullshit!" I shouted as I forcefully slipped my feet into my boots. I could taste the bitterness of my spit lingering in my mouth. Once I zipped them up, I stood up. I stormed past him, and Varric moved out of my way as I ran through the living room and up the spiral stone steps. I pushed open the heavy metal door open and found the royals standing on the lawn waiting for me.

"Fuck. Me!" I murmured under my breath, forcing a fake grin onto my face as I approached the royals. "Gentlemen," I said with a polite smile, "Is there anything I can assist you with?"

Prince Feran's firm and resolute voice signaled that the moment had arrived. Urgently, the prince urged me to prepare her army, his voice brimming with urgency. "The time has arrived to strike Orion and Victim."

"At once, my lord." I curtsied gracefully in my imaginary ball gown as I rose to my feet. As Solas approached me, I turned to see the shaman following closely behind him. "Before we get this party started, there's something I need you to do for me."

"And what's that?" Solas asked, his voice filled with curiosity.

"I need you," I said in a low, solemn tone. "To construct a barrier, shielding myself from the flood of memories and emotions associated with both Sixus and Timbrax."

Solas gave me a look as though I had just asked him to kill me.

I said confidently, my voice echoing through the room, "If I'm going to lead our army to victory against Orion, Victim, Sixus, Timbrax, and Claus, I need to be the lethal weapon Timbrax trained me to be."

"Once I do this..." Solas leaned in close, his warm breath tickling my ear as he whispered, his voice barely audible. "There's no going back."

"Just do it!" I exclaimed; my voice filled with determination. "Keep everything else within arm's reach, just in case I need to call on my other powers."

With a snap of his fingers, Solas jolted me out of my daze, and I blinked rapidly, trying to make sense of my surroundings.

"Your majesty," Tork said, her voice barely audible over the shooting of guns and the rustling of armor. "We await your command," the vampire hunters, dragon knights, assassins, and mecha pilots said in perfect unison, their voices reverberating through the empty open air.

"March into the formidable Xeonada Empire!" Without a second thought, I let out a loud shout from deep within my voice. "Burn it to the ground!" The army cheered behind me in approval. "And the Stettarenth Empire!" I added. "Mount Up!"

Everyone hurriedly ran to their designated areas, creating a flurry of movement. I had the mecha pilots and assassins embark on a journey to the Stettarenth Empire, a land filled with grandeur and opulence. Tasia found herself trapped in the vast emptiness of space. By the time she returned home, all that would remain would be a charred, smoky mess.

"What about the innocent people living their mom?" Cy asked as she walked beside me. "You can't harm them!" she exclaimed; her voice filled with desperation.

"Move them to the other kingdoms," I commanded, my voice firm and authoritative. "Hurry, bring them to safety!"

"Get Cy to safety within the walls of the institute!" I shouted at the top of my lungs, trying to get A.J. and Nell's attention. "Protect the institute!" I shouted, my voice filled with determination.

"Yes, Your Majesty!" they exclaimed, bowing deeply. As they grabbed her, their voices merged into a synchronized chant, propelling her up the steps and into the building. Someone held the door open, and I watched as they were safely inside.

As I raced towards the flight field, I ran down the well-manicured lawn and swiftly passed through the gate. As we approached the field, the guardians were already there, lined up on both sides, their horses saddled and ready.

Xemret stood before me, his presence towering and commanding. As I sat down, I forcefully slammed my boots into the footholds, feeling the impact reverberate through my legs. As they clicked into place, a satisfying sound echoed in the air. I reached into the satchel and retrieved the flight goggles. As I grabbed them, I eagerly opened my purple ear pod box and was greeted by the sleek, shiny headphones inside. I inserted both pieces into my ears, feeling them snugly fit, and closed the device before tossing it into the bag.

I pulled out my cell and felt the smooth, sleek surface beneath my fingertips as I pressed the sidebar. As the screen illuminated, I eagerly tapped on the music app and selected the battlefield playlist. I carefully tucked the cell inside my shirt, feeling its weight against my chest, and then pulled the flight goggles down over my eyes. The earbuds were snugly fit, pushing the pods deep into my ears. The loud blast of rock music filled the air, fueling my excitement to go.

"Ready oracle?"

Xemret asked in my mind.

"Let's do this, Xemret!"

I yelled in my mind.

Xemret's sudden movement jolted me, causing my stomach to lurch before settling back into place once I regained my composure. With determination, I set my sights on the mighty Xeonada Empire. Solas and Varric flew on either side of me, like loyal wingmen, ready to support and protect.

The moment had arrived for all the training I had diligently undertaken. In order to take advantage of the enemy's vulnerability, we had to strike while they were floating in space. With a limited window of time, I had grown weary of being their constant target.

As the wind whipped against my face, I could feel its sharp sting, reminding me of my own existence. My rage burned inside me, overpowering my senses, and I couldn't recall the reason for my intense anger.

"The Xeonada Empire is quickly coming into view, oracle!"

Xemret growled in my mind.

"Blast it to shit!"

I yelled in my mind.

"I hear and obey, my queen!"

Xemret snarled in my mind.

Xemret unleashed a colossal fireball from his mouth, engulfing everything in its scorching heat. Houses were reduced to rubble as a massive, fiery orange explosion erupted. Beneath us, a deafening explosion erupted, launching Victim into the air and engulfing them in a horrifying blaze. The blaring alarms immediately caught the attention of the enemy, warning them of the sudden attack.

"Sucks to be you, doesn't it, Sixus?"

I thought.

"What are you up to, Mel?"

Sixus inquired in my mind.

Looking around in confusion, I scanned the area but couldn't spot him amidst the chaos of dragon knights unleashing their elemental powers, causing buildings to explode.

"Why the fuck are you in my head?"

I demanded.

"Why the hell are you blowing up my kingdom?"

He demanded.

"Mortal enemies, remember?"

I thought.

"I thought we moved past that after I married you, Mel?"

Sixus asked.

I ignored him.

I could sense his rage emanating through our bond. How did I become entangled with the enemy? I couldn't make any sense of this at all; it was completely baffling.

To my left, I heard the distinct hum of the astral thread opening, instantly recognizable. Just as I turned around, Sixus burst out from it with an unexpected leap. As he collided with me, the impact was so forceful that my boots instantly released from the footholds. He wrapped his arms around me. I could feel myself falling deeper into his embrace. As we slammed into the ground, he turned and absorbed the full impact. As I pushed his arms away, the air filled with swirling rubble and dust, making me cough.

"The fuck you do that for?" I demanded; my voice filled with frustration.

"I-"

In a rush, I stood up and took in the sights of the surrounding area. The place I was at no longer buzzed with the vibrant energy of the city. It was littered with dead bodies. I knew every nook and cranny of my kingdom, as familiar as the lines on my own palm. As he leaped to his feet, the ground beneath him transformed into a sheet of ice, causing me to lose my footing and fall backwards. He caught me off guard and twirled me around, forcing me to meet his gaze. He looked down at me with a smirk, igniting my anger.

Why did he have to look hot as fuck?

"Did you hit your head? Your thoughts are all jumbled up." As Sixus took my arm, I felt the chill of the ice beneath my feet. He walked with such grace, as if he were gliding on ice skates. "You can't kill me, remember?"

"Why the hell not?" I demanded; my voice filled with defiance.

He rolled his eyes, clearly annoyed, and said, "Remember how our souls are bound to each other?" Sixus scoffed. "Plus, I have the Holistic sword to heal your wounds or revive you from the dead."

"I don't remember any of this shit." I shook my head in disbelief. "We're seriously married?"

"Look at your finger," Sixus smirked. I looked at my left hand and saw that I was wearing a wedding ring. I observed his finger and noticed he wore a matching one. "Mel, your sexy Tribrid ass is mine."

Suddenly, Largo Croix emerged from the shadows and plunged a metal pole into my abdomen. I was forcefully slammed into a wall, getting stuck in-between.

As I fought to remove the long piece of pipe stuck in my body, intense pain surged through me. The pain was excruciating. Blood trickled from my mouth, inciting Sixus' snarl while Largo's laughter echoed as he retreated to the shadows.

"Mel, I'm sorry," Sixus said, pulling the pipe out of me. I slumped against the wall as my head hung low. I had a deep wound that was gushing blood. "This is gonna hurt."

His head-butt caused me to lose consciousness.

I was on the brink of death because of my mate.

I was all alone with no one to lend a hand.

THIRTEEN

I woke up with a throbbing headache. I opened my eyes and gently applied pressure to my injury. It hurt like hell. I rose from the wall and darkness had descended. My flight goggles and ear pods were taken off and placed in my jacket pocket by someone. Someone turned my cell off.

As darkness fell, I could hear explosions in the vicinity. My nose wrinkled at the scent of burning chemicals and singed flesh. I had to escape from here. The sound of someone nearing me has jolted me awake. My nose detected a mixture of cranberries, snow, and death before Sixus emerged from my right.

"You should have that wound examined," he whispered. "Act swiftly to prevent infection and potential fatality."

"Please, just use the Holistic sword on me," I pleaded. "You can heal my wound."

"I could," Sixus replied, rubbing his chin thoughtfully. "However, I have no desire to."

"In that case, I'm fucked," I exclaimed with anger. "I'm out!"

"Where are you headed?" As he lifted me up, he asked, while securing my right arm around his shoulder. I winced in pain and slapped him in the chest, glaring up at him. He didn't care as he kept moving on.

"I can't imagine a place worse than this." I quietly said. "You're aware that you're the absolute worst, right?"

From his end of the bond, I could feel his amusement. And it really pissed me off. Sixus led me into a partially destroyed building caused by an explosion. He pressed me against a wall, causing me to drift in and out of consciousness. My time is running out.

"I'll help you this once," Sixus whispered, his voice barely audible as he unsheathed the Holistic sword. "From that moment on, any assistance would come at a cost." As the sword pierced through me, a blinding flash of bright blue light erupted, leaving us momentarily disoriented. After putting it back in the sheath, he turned and prepared to walk away, leaving me alone to fend for myself. As the block Solas had erected crumbled away, a flood of memories rushed back to me, overwhelming my thoughts. Tears streamed down my face, causing Sixus to freeze in his steps. He muttered a curse and retraced his steps, his footsteps echoing against the pavement as he approached me by the wall. "Don't cry, Mel." he said, his voice filled with gentle reassurance.

"Sixus, I can't bring myself to harm you." I managed to say through my tears. "Kill me."

"I can't," he said, his smile masking the sadness in his eyes. "I won't." he said firmly, his voice filled with determination.

"Why?" I asked, my voice filled with confusion. As I gazed up into his beautiful blue eyes.

"I can't even begin to describe how much I love you, Mel," he confessed, his non-beating heart overflowing with emotion. Sixus moved into my space and placed his icy hands on my cheeks. He moved in closer, his lips meeting mine in a gentle, lingering kiss. I closed my eyes, savoring the soft touch of his lips before he gently pulled away. In a soft, heartfelt tone, he vowed, "Mel, you will always be my first choice."

"Don't." I blinked back the tears, feeling a lump forming in my throat. "Please don't leave me alone, Sixus!"

"I will find you in hell if I have to," Sixus whispered. "There's no place on Tellus, Erda, or Outer Earth you can get away from me, Mel."

"I never want to," I sobbed, my voice trembling with despair. "You are the rhythm that pulses through my veins."

"Can I tell you something?" he whispered into my ear. "You can save me without a cure from someone else."

"How?" I asked.

"You are my cure." He nuzzled his nose to my neck.

"Where's my dragon?" I asked.

"What?" he asked, arching an eyebrow.

"My sexy dragon mate?" I demanded. "I want him to fuck me."

Sixus' eyes glowed a bright blue, and he snarled protectively. And I knew my dragon mate was in full control of himself.

"There he is," I smirked seductively at him. "Now help me destroy the Xeonada Empire and you can fuck me all night when we return to the institute."

"This isn't a trick, is it?" he asked.

I slipped my hand down his pants and found his cock. Upon slowly massaging it, his body responded to me instantly. I removed it and smirked at him.

Without saying a word, he formed a thick icicle on his hand and slammed it against the ground. Everything instantly froze all around us.

"Everyone!" I shouted. "Get to high ground!" I paused. "Your dragon king is back on our side!"

Sixus picked me up and ran out of the building as it crumbled behind us. He leaped into the air and landed on Xemet's back. He slammed his boots into the footholds and held me tightly as he gripped the horn.

Xemet roared loudly, and all the dragons roared in unison. They formed flamethrowers and fireballs in their mouths and exploded more buildings.

Sixus and I threw our hands out and our white and pale blue flames merged as we shot it out towards our castle. It exploded on impact, and our task was complete.

"Let's go home!" Sixus shouted.

I snuggled into his body as he pulled me tighter against his chest.

Xemet turned around and led the way back to the institute.

This time, I didn't feel bad about burning my kingdom down to the ground as I drifted off to sleep.

***

I awoke to someone laying me down in bed. My eyes met his beautiful blue eyes.

"Sixus!" I pulled him on top of me and he was taken aback by my need to hold him in my arms at this very moment. "Please stay with me forever."

"Baby," Sixus gave me a sad smile. "The moment I married you... I vowed to stay with you for the rest of my life."

"Please just," I gushed. "Stay in your Half-Draconian form for me?"

"I will," he nodded. "For Cy and you and everyone who is depending on us."

"I need to shower." As he helped me up to my feet, I distanced myself from him. "I don't need the scent of my blood bringing out that one percent Varacolaci in you, do I?"

"Not at all," he smirked as we tossed our jackets on the back of the seat and placed our weapons on the desk, along with our cells and my headphones. We removed our boots, and we stripped out of our blood-soaked uniforms. We tossed them into the laundry basket and entered the bathroom. Upon pulling the curtain back, we entered before he closed it behind him. I turned the knobs on, and the water sprayed onto us. "I really missed you, Mel."

We got clean, and I shut the water off. He opened the curtain, and we stepped out and dried ourselves off before getting dressed in normal clothing. I brushed my hair out, and the doors slid open. Cy entered the room and ran into her father's arms. She hugged him tightly, and he returned her hug before she broke it and stepped back.

"Can I sleep in here tonight?" she asked, glancing between the two of us.

"Yeah," Sixus smiled, and she rushed to the other bed and crawled under the comforter and laid her head on the pillow. "Good night, Cy."

"Goodnight, dad," she said. "Night mom."

"Night." I softly whispered. "Sweet dreams."

She closed her eyes and fell asleep quickly. The doors slid open and a few of the vampire hunters and the shaman entered and took up positions around the room as the doors closed. Sixus and I exchanged glances with each other before we crawled beneath the comforter and got comfortable. Sixus pulled me securely into his arms and held me tightly against his body. We closed our eyes and listened to each other breathing.

"I'll take a raincheck on that offer, Mel."

Sixus said in my mind.

"Oh, I know you will, baby."

In my mind, I thought.

By closing my eyes, I peacefully drifted off to sleep.

I witnessed something intriguing. It was real and not a vision.

As I neared the door, the sound of angry voices engaged in a heated argument reached my ears. I was in a Victim ship. I hid behind a wall and peeked my head into the room. Timbrax stood close with his back facing me. The others were seated at the table across the room in a state of confusion and rage.

"How the hell did she sneak attack us?" Tasia asked. "Fucking bitch destroyed my kingdom for no reason!"

By bitch, I was pretty sure Tasia was talking about me.

"We sent that mate of hers to kill her." Orion frowned. "And he turned his back on us!"

"I thought you had full control over him, Victim Commander?" Orion demanded.

"I do," Timbrax snarled. His rage was evident as it poured through his end of the bond. "He owns that damn Holistic sword and can heal himself, remember?"

"I thought the vampire in him was in full control?" Tasia asked.

"He is," Timbrax agreed. "The oracle can somehow manipulate him through their mate bond."

"Is that how I could get through to Sixus' Half-Draconian side?"

I thought.

Timbrax's body suddenly stiffened as he slowly turned his head and met my gaze. My eyes widened in surprise as he turned and walked out of the room. He took in his surroundings and saw no one.

"Something wrong, Victim Commander?" Orion called from the other room.

"We're not alone," Timbrax spoke in a quiet voice as the others rose to their feet and walked out of the room. "Someone is here... watching us."

"I don't see anyone?" Tasia whispered as she gazed around.

"Have you checked the astral thread?" Orion asked.

"I'm on it," Timbrax snarled as he threw his hand out and the blue portal opened. He leaped through it and was gone for a long moment. The others just stood there silently gazing through it, not moving. Timbrax emerged a moment later, and it closed behind him. "There was nobody there."

"Did you check on the dragons?" Orion asked. "And everyone else associated with them?"

"I already did that," Timbrax grunted. "Every single one of them were asleep or busy doing something to even notice my presence."

"Was it the spirits, perhaps?" Claus inquired.

"I don't fuck with ghosts!" Timbrax spat. "That's *your* department, shaman!"

"Everyone go to bed," Orion yawned. "We'll continue this discussion tomorrow."

I watched as they all stood and walked out of the room and up the long hallway and turned a corner. Only Timbrax stood there with annoyance in his bond.

He opened the astral thread and stepped inside. It closed behind him. He sat down, leaning his back against the icy wall.

"I know you're there Melfina," Timbrax spoke in a gentle voice. "How is it you are fast asleep yet able to be here with me in the astral thread at the same time?"

"That's a good question, Brax," I said. "I was about to ask you how I'm able to do this?"

"I dun know," he shrugged. "It has to be a shaman's ability because you never did this during the Flight Games or before it, either."

"I need to wake up!" I said as the panic rose in me. "But I'm asleep Brax!"

"Calm your ass down," Timbrax frowned. "Just wake up already, Melfina."

"You make it sound so easy!" I screeched in a high-pitched voice. "I'm trying and it's not working!"

"Your soul is out of your body," Timbrax replied calmly. "I can see you just fine, Melfina."

"That means," I whispered to myself. "That Claus can see me too, can't he?"

"Obviously," Timbrax grunted. "He's playing stupid just like I am."

"Why did I come here?" I asked him.

"You came to see me?" Timbrax asked. "Didn't you?"

"I," I paused, lost in thought. "Don't know?"

"Sit with me," he whispered. I cautiously walked over and sat down beside him, but I kept at least ten feet between us. "What's on your mind, gorgeous?"

I gave him a strange look when he called me Zyra's former nickname, which made him smirk. He gazed at me and moved in, kissing me. I could feel his stiff lips against mine. Returning his kiss, I closed my eyes before he broke it. I opened my eyes, and he just stared at me.

"You did good today," he whispered as he gently touched my cheek. "I'm sorry I have to do this to you."

Before I could reply, I felt my soul slam back into my body. I gasped as my eyes shot open and I sat up in bed. My breathing was heavy, and my heart raced in my chest.

"You okay, Mel?" Sixus murmured, half asleep.

"Yeah," I forced a smile. "Go back to sleep, Sixus."

He was snoring within seconds.

Too freaked out to sleep, I kicked the hot comforter off my body and climbed over his body, landing on the floor. Getting dressed and pinning my hair up in the cat ear pigtails, I used my vampire speed to put my weapons on my body and place my cell and ear pods in the charging station.

"I don't suggest you do that again, Melfina," Solas whispered from behind me. In a sudden motion, I whirled around to face him. "That was dangerous, and he could've killed you or, even worse, taken over your body."

"I didn't do it on purpose," I replied, confused. "I was asleep."

"You astral projected," Solas replied. "It's actually a quite common experience that happens to mortal on earth." He glanced at Sixus, who was snoring loudly, then back at me. "No wonder why you can't get any sleep."

"I got him," Varric replied from outside on the balcony. "I'm about ready to place a breathing strip on his nose to shut him up!"

Solas and I walked towards the door, and they slid open. We stepped out into the hallway and Zuni stood there accompanied by Lox.

"I got it," Zuni gushed. "We gotta get it into his system quickly!" We turned and ran back towards the door. They slid open, and she rushed past me. She pulled a thick syringe out. After removing the lid, she flicked it twice. She jabbed it into the side of Sixus' neck and injected the whitish liquid into his body before she removed it. She placed the lid back on and pocketed it. "He should return to his normal self when he wakes up."

"Thank you, Zuni!" I said as I gave her and Lox a quick hug before releasing them. "Get outta here while it's peaceful."

I heard growling coming from behind me and saw Zuni's eyes widen at someone behind me. Slowly, I turned around and found Sixus snarling at her and Lox as he stood there. Thinking fast, I balled my hand into a tight fist and pulled it back. I threw it forward, punching him hard in the throat, making him choke as he gasped for air as he fell to one knee.

"GO!" I choked as Lox grabbed Zuni by the arm and touched his Dragon Stone in his pocket. The bright green light flashed, and they disappeared through it as it vanished. "What the hell is wrong with you, Sixus?"

My throat hurt, as did Solas's. He threw me and Sixus both a look as he rubbed his neck.

"What did you do to me?" Sixus demanded as he cleared his throat. "My blood feels like it's on fucking fire!"

I took a step into his space as he growled down at me. As I shoved him, a smirk formed on my face, and I quickly made my way out of the open French doors onto the balcony. I leaped on the marble railing and flexed my back. My dragon wings exploded out of my back, and I leaped high into the air. My wings flapped, and I soared higher and higher.

"Trying to get away from me, are you, Mel?"

Sixus spat in my mind.

I heard him chasing me as he quickly caught up to me. I turned my head and found him gazing back at me with a smirk on his sexy face. We flew over the sea, and I could feel his adrenaline pumping with excitement as his dragon was enjoying the night flight with his mate.

"This is something I missed!" He shouted over the roar of the wind as we circled our way back to the institute.

"I know!" In response, I shouted back. My intuition kicked in, alerting me of an emerging danger. "Watch out!" I slammed Sixus hard with my right shoulder, sending him flying out of the way. A massive orange fireball slammed into me, sending me flying downwards towards the frigid water below.

Ice appeared below me, catching my fall like a slide. It curved as I slid down it at a fast pace. It did a spiral and ended, sending me flying high into the air. Sixus caught me in his arms as he flapped his dragon wings to get away from Timbrax. Sixus reached the institute and landed on the balcony. He raced inside and set me down on the floor. My heart was racing as I took deep breaths to calm myself down.

"Secure the perimeter," Sixus commanded the vampire hunters as they raced into the room. "The Victim Commander is back and attacked Melfina."

"At once my king," Velzy nodded curtly to him. "And welcome back." She turned and raced out of the room with the others. Thankfully, Cy stayed sleeping.

"Mel," Sixus' voice was kind as he gently touched my cheeks, forcing me to look into his mesmerizing blue eyes. "I got you."

A loud explosion rocked the institute, sending us flying to the floor. A fire had broken out from outside. The sounding of the alarms prompted Cy to swiftly get out of bed and get dressed.

"Erda is under attack!" I shouted to Sixus.

"The vampire hunters and shaman need to return to protect their kingdoms!"

"Go!" Sixus shouted to Solas and the vampire hunters. "We'll keep Tellus protected!"

"We'll be back!" Solas shouted as he and the shaman leaped through the green portal and disappeared. I ran out of the room and stood on the balcony. Timbrax leaped through the astral thread, and it disappeared behind him.

"You've lost your army, Melfi," Orion said as he leaped over the wall and stood on the lawn with Tasia, Viz, and Largo. "Surrender oracle!"

I was about to say something snarky when I heard Cy coughing. I slowly turned and my eyes widened in horror. Her veins were poking out of her skin, and they looked black.

"Mom," she whispered. "I don't feel so good." She dropped, and Sixus caught her. She was unconscious.

"What the hell have you done, Orion?" Sixus snarled.

"I unleashed a new virus upon all the remaining kingdoms," Orion declared. "Within seventy-two hours, everyone will turn into a Victim."

The Victim Commander emerged out of the astral thread and stood before me on the lawn as I gazed down at him. He looked up and locked eyes with me. I saw no emotion whatsoever in them.

"Deal with her Sixus," Timbrax shouted. "Or I will!"

"Sixus?" I turned, and he stabbed me with an icicle on the side of my neck. I dropped to the ground as blood seeped out of my wound. He picked me up and sank his sharp fangs into my skin as he drank my blood in a mad frenzy. I felt his endorphins kick in as he removed his fangs. He carelessly tossed me to the ground as he slowly rose to his feet. "Why are you doing this?"

"I'm embracing the darkness I was denied my entire life, Mel," Sixus declared as his eyes transformed from the beautiful blue to the white eyes with red rings around the edges. He was a Varacolaci again. "I suggest you do the same... or I *will* kill you."

I watched as he unbound his soul from me and pulled out the Holistic sword. He stabbed me with it and the bright blue light flashed before it disappeared. I squeezed my eyes shut and opened them, only to find them gone.

And Sixus had gone with them.

This was bad.

It was a fucking never-ending nightmare I couldn't seem to wake up from.

Because this nightmare was real.

I looked at Cy and thankfully Sixus had stabbed her with the Holistic sword sparing his daughter's life and mine.

For the moment, at least.

FOURTEEN

Cy and I had the daunting task of pulling the blood from all the thousands of humans in the institute and the remaining four kingdoms. Thankfully, the dragons had used their magic and transformed into their human forms in order to help us pull the toxic blood from their bodies.

Despite our exhaustion, we couldn't take a break. So many lives were on the line. I had to push the thought of Sixus returning to the life of a Varacolaci out of my mind. I hadn't realized he had rebounded himself to me until I heard his voice taunting me in my mind.

"You can't save them all, you know?"

Sixus said.

I ignored him and placed the barrier up, shutting his ass up.

I heard the astral thread open behind me and I turned, ready to fight Sixus or Timbrax. Thankfully, it was Setha and the vampire hunters returning. They assessed the situation and snapped into action, relieving Cy and me from our duties as they took over and cleaned the toxic blood from the mundane. As we jumped onto the balcony, the sound of our footsteps echoed through the open French doors, filling my dorm room.

"Melfina," Zara called me over to her as Cy crawled into bed and covered herself up. She closed her eyes and drifted off to sleep quickly. I was so proud of my daughter. She wasn't even ruling the kingdom yet, and she was doing what Sixus would've been doing to help protect our people and those of the other kingdoms. "You need to go back in time and retrieve Sixus blood before he became a Varacolaci."

"Can't one of you vampires do it?" I asked. "I can accidentally alter the current timeline if I ran into myself."

"It's a risk I need you to take," Zara sighed heavily. "It has to be you since no one will notice you, you know?"

"If the shamans show up," I said. "Lie to them to buy me some time and protect everyone for me, please?"

I was hesitant and torn because on one hand Zara was right. The state of turmoil made me afraid to leave my daughter and my kingdom. I finally nodded in agreement. I had to save Sixus.

"Setha is going with you," Zara whispered. "She will get you sent back to two years right before you arrived back on Tellus." She paused. "You won't run into yourself here and all you have to do is get a sample of Sixus blood, your blood, his brother and daughter's and your mothers and his mother's blood and have them saved in lots of viles so we can have access to them in our current timeline."

"What do I do if I run into anyone?" I asked, biting my lower lip nervously.

"Act casual," she said. "Use the earth name Olivia and get the hell out of there as quickly as possible, got it?"

"Got it." I forced a smile as Setha arrived. Zara used her vampire speed and threw me in the shower, washing me up quickly before drying me off, getting me dressed in a clean double-sided uniform, putting my weapons on my body, put my boots on, and my two jackets. She did my hair in the cat ear pigtails and did my makeup. I was ready. Exley stepped over and gave me a quick hug before releasing me. He wasn't the hugging type. I gave him a sad smile before Zara touched my third eye. She locked my vampire and shaman powers away so the dragons would only smell the Half-Draconian in my blood. "See you when you get back, mom."

I nodded and gave her a quick hug before releasing her. I nodded to Setha, and she threw her hand out, opening the astral thread. We leaped inside and I ran through it, emerging on the front lawn of the institute. It shut behind me and Setha stayed in the thread to keep her scent hidden. I didn't have time to take it all in. The astral thread has reopened, or so I heard. I turned and leaped through it and emerged outside of the dragon sanctuary. It shut behind me once more.

"Sorry about that," Setha said. "Get moving!"

I took a deep breath and walked to the door. I pulled one heavy glass door open and stepped inside. The muggy heat hit me instantly. I walked past the nursery and walked by the little playground where Cy had first leaped on me, knocking my ass down. I felt a tugging on the bottom of my trench coat. Confused, I stopped walking and glanced over my shoulder. I found Cy in her little pink dragon form, biting my jacket. I couldn't help but notice her eyes, bright and almond-shaped, shining in a captivating purple color under the dim fluorescent lighting.

"You don't have time for this, Mel!"
I thought.
"Play with me Mel!"
Cy said in my mind excitedly.

I noticed she was wagging her tail, and I figured I could play one round of fetch with her and get the hell outta here.

"Get your favorite ball," I whispered. "I really gotta go, Cy."

"Cy?"

She thought, releasing my jacket and gazing up at me.

"I mean," I caught myself. "Tandenth."

She scrambled off and returned with her purple ball. I took it and tossed it as far as I could so that way, I could get outta here. She turned and ran through the grass and disappeared. I turned to leave when she returned with the ball in her mouth. She made a joyful sound deep in her throat and wagged her tail. I took the soggy ball and tossed it again. This time, she didn't chase it. She leaped into my arms, and I hugged her as she nuzzled her head into my neck.

"Daddy's home!"
Cy exclaimed in my mind.

Sixus scent struck my nose, and it was rapidly approaching me. Cranberries mixed with snow. His footsteps stopped mere inches behind me. I heard his protective growl and knew he was about to rip my head off.

Slowly, I turned around to face him. His attire consisted of an emerald dragon knight uniform and red mecha pilot boots. His mesmerizing blue eyes captivated my gaze as I stared at him.

"How did you get in here?" Sixus asked in an icy voice.

"The door was unlocked," I replied calmly as Tandenth leaped out of my arms and into her father's arms. He held her tightly as she gazed up at him, then back at me excitedly. "I was just leaving."

"You aren't supposed to arrive for another month," Sixus said as I walked past him. "Don't walk away from me when I'm talking to you, candidate!"

I hauled ass and pushed open the heavy glass door and ran. I heard him chasing me down. He shoved open the door and snarled. I flexed my back muscles, and my pale blue dragon wings exploded out of my back. I leaped high into the air and started flying away from him.

"You can fly?"
Sixus asked in my mind.

The next thing I knew, he removed his jacket and shirt as his white dragon wings exploded out of his back. He leaped high into the air and grabbed me in a tight bearhug sending us both crashing to the ground.

"Fuck!" I gasped as instant pain shot up throughout my body. He rolled me over and I was lying on my back. He pinned me to the ground with his body weight. "Get off me!"

"Tell me what you're doing here!" Sixus snarled. "I know exactly who you are, Princess Melfina Aeon Dra!"

"You want the truth?" I spat.

"Indeed, I do!" he snarled with his face inches away from mine. "I don't-"

"I'm here to save you!" With a scream, I fought back the tears that so desperately wanted to escape from my eyes. "I'm from the future, and I need to save *you*!"

"If you're lying-"

"Release her Sixus!" His mother Queen Pyssyno stood with Cy in her arms and my mother Nymmylth beside her. "She speaks the truth!"

Sixus narrowed his eyes at me as he climbed to his feet and pulled me to mine. He kept his hand wrapped around my wrist as he pulled me to where our mother's stood.

"MOM!" I yanked my arm back to me as I ran into her open arms. She hugged me tightly, and I sobbed uncontrollably.

"It's okay, my sweet girl," she whispered as she gently kissed me on the forehead, hugging me tightly. "Your safe... if only for a little while."

"This woman is from the future?" Sixus asked his mother, giving me a skeptical look.

Nymmylth moved her hand and gently touched a pressure point behind my right ear. I felt myself fall into her chest as I closed my eyes.

"Well," Nymmylth demanded. "Take her to your dorm room, my king."

I felt Sixus pick me up gently in his arms as he leaped high into the air. He flapped his massive dragon wings. I rested my heavy head against his peck. The warmth radiating off his skin helped me fall asleep in his arms.

I awoke to whispering nearby. I kept my eyes closed and my mind blank, so they thought I was still asleep.

"Her uniform is upgraded from ours," Sixus whispered to someone. "Mel is defiantly my mate, mother." He laughed in amazement. "I felt a bond with her instantly."

"Tandenth could read her mind," Pyssyno whispered. "She came back to the past to save our kingdom and you from the evil that has taken over my son."

"She's traumatized," Sixus sighed heavily. "I caused her so much pain, mother."

"So, fix it while she's here," Pyssyno replied bluntly. "The bond of mated dragons runs deep, and you are hurting her by whatever it is your future self is doing to her, my son."

I opened my eyes and sat up. I found myself lying in Sixus' bed. They hadn't moved the other bed in yet. They reentered the room and Pyssyno rushed past me like I didn't exist. The doors slid open, and she exited the room as they shut behind her.

I shoved the hot comforter off my body and scrambled to my feet. I walked over to the desk and found my weapons, cell, ear pods, my jackets, and boots over there.

"Thank you, my king," I said with my back to him. "I must be going."

"I need you, Mel," Sixus whispered, making me stop and slowly turn to face him. "Stay with me tonight... please?"

"I can't." To prevent the lump from resurfacing, I cleared my throat. "I've already accidentally made alterations to your timeline, as it is."

"Let me take your pain away." Sixus gently grabbed me by the arm and led me towards the door. They slid open, and he stepped out into the hallway and walked towards one of the glass tubes. "I never showed you what else these tubes can do, did I?"

"No?" I replied cautiously.

The door flew open, and he stepped inside and pulled me into his body. The door slammed shut and locked into place. He reached up and pressed a white button I hadn't noticed before. Purple Lust Dust sprayed down on us, and he inhaled deeply. I did too. There was no point in holding my breath. The dust always wins in the end.

Sixus' eyes darkened as he gazed at me. I moved in and kissed him fiercely as I closed my eyes. He returned my kiss just as hungrily. He slipped his tongue into my mouth and searched wildly for mine. I gave it to him eagerly and willingly. I was his woman, damn it!

He pulled away and lifted me up. He reached up and froze my wrists against the glass, keeping me hanging up there.

"What are you doing?" I breathed as I gazed down at him.

"You'll find out," Sixus smirked up at me as he yanked my pants and panties down. He placed his head in between the fabric and my skin. "Won't you?"

He grabbed my bare ass and placed his mouth deep into my pussy, licking furiously as he tasted me for the first time.

"FUCK!" I screamed. "SIXUS!"

"Feel good Mel?"

Sixus asked in my mind.

"FUCK. ME!"

I replied in my mind.

Sixus removed himself and dipped three fingers into my pussy and twirled them variously around, making me have an organism in seconds. With enthusiasm, he removed his fingers and eagerly pressed his mouth against my pussy, slurping up my juices. He growled as he removed himself and pulled my panties and pants back up. He slammed his fists against the ice, and it crumbled. I fell, and he caught me as the door flew open after he pressed the button.

He pushed me out and joined me and led me back to his dorm room. The doors slid open, and he pulled me inside. They closed behind me, and he threw his hand out and froze it in a thick layer of ice. He crossed the room and closed the French doors and froze them into place as well before turning back to face me.

"Wait," I whispered as I walked to the desk and grabbed my cell. I pressed the sidebar, and the screen lit up. I clicked on the music app and clicked a random playlist. Barley Breathing started playing as I set it on the desk.

He grabbed me and tossed me onto his bed. I pulled him down and crushed my lips against his. He returned my kiss, and we removed our clothes in seconds. Sixus climbed on top of me and shoved his hot cock deep into my pussy. I moaned in delight as he started pounding himself deeper and harder into me.

"Ready?" He breathed as I nodded. With one last thrust, he cummed deep into me. He rolled off me and we lay there panting.

Magnetic started playing, and he kissed me on the shoulder as I gazed up at him.

"I miss you so much," I whispered as I blinked back the tears. "Thank you for this."

"Take this," he breathed as he removed his necklace and placed it around my neck. He saw the wedding ring on my finger and looked up at me. "Did I marry you?"

"Yes," I nodded sadly. "Orion killed our twins."

"We can have another one once you fix whatever is happening in your timeline," he said. "Just know... that I love you unconditionally, Mel."

"I love you too," I whispered. "I will *always* choose you, Sixus."

His eyes widened in surprise, as he knew I meant what I said. With reluctance, I got out of bed and headed towards the bathroom. I walked inside and pulled back the curtain. I stepped inside the shower and turned the knobs. The water sprayed down on me, and Sixus soon joined me before closing the curtain. We washed up, and he turned the water off.

I pulled the curtain back, and we stepped out. Grabbing clean towels, we dried ourselves off and got dressed. Once I brushed out my hair, I re-pinned it up. With my boots on, I quickly zipped them up. Once I had reattached my weapons to my body, I deactivated the music and carefully stored away both the device and my ear pods. I put on both jackets and found copies of my books lying on the desk. I guess Setha had brought him Sixus copies from my timeline to put in the oracle dormitory.

He slammed the ice on the French doors, and the ice crumbled to the floor. He crossed the room and slammed his fists against the main door. The ice crumbled to the floor there, too.

"Tande told me what you need for us," Sixus said as he walked back over to me. "You'll have what you need from all of us waiting for you back in I.O.A. in your timeline, Mel."

"Thank you Sixus," I gave him a hug, and he returned it. "I'll return you to this form you're in now."

"What are those books?" Sixus asked, arching an eyebrow at me.

"The documents from the oracle." I gave him a sad smile. "You have one coming in this year, you know?"

"Really?" He acted surprised. "Tell the oracle thank you for their documentations."

"The pen name on the books isn't her real name," I added. "She's famous on Erda as an author, so she hides her real identity from the world."

"That's interesting to know," he smirked as he released me. "I will always choose you, Mel."

"You'd better." I took a few steps away from him as I heard the familiar humming of the astral thread open. Sixus' eyes widened when he saw Setha's eyes. "Setha won't hurt you, I promise."

"What is she?" He asked.

"A Varacolaci Vampire," I replied as I stepped inside the thread. "That's what you turned into, and I promise to bring you back to me, Sixus."

It closed behind me before he could ask any more questions. We leaped out and stood back in my dorm room in my present timeline. The thread closed behind us and Zara leaped to her feet when she saw us.

"You did it, mom!" She smiled as she gave me a hug before removing herself. "We have many samples of their blood that are pure for Abel and Zuni to use to heal Sixus."

"Thank the dragons," I sighed in relief. "How are things going here?" I looked over at Cy and she was snoring, sound asleep.

"Everyone who was poisoned in the four remaining kingdoms has been cleansed," Zara sighed wearily. "And there have been minimal alterations to our present timeline." She winked.

"You said minimal alterations?" I asked slowly. "What alterations have been made here?"

"You'll see," she smiled warmly at me. "How are you feeling, by the way?"

"Fine," I shrugged. "Why do you ask?"

"You gonna tell her?" Setha asked, laughing excitedly. "Or should I?"

"Tell me what?" I demanded, as annoyance crept into my voice. "I really don't have time for this shit, you know?"

Setha threw her hand out, and the astral thread opened. As I looked at her, she motioned with her head, showing that I should follow her. I leaped through it and emerged, standing in the nursery at the dragon sanctuary. I was clueless about what the hell I was doing back in this room. My hatred grew after all the family deaths that had occurred recently. Zara, Cy, and Setha stood behind me.

Rolled my eyes at them, I started walking up the long row. I gazed at all the different colored eggs that lined the section, sitting on individual pillars with bright lights beaming hot warmth into each egg.

All the eggs looked the same when I reached the end of the row... normal. I frowned as I turned. The light turned on, beaming brightly onto a white and blue egg. A bright pale blue flame surrounded it in a protective form. My eyes widened as I reached out and gently ran my fingers down the tiny scales of the thick shell. The egg moved slightly as the ladies surrounded me. I removed my hand and gazed at them. They wore smiles and had tears in their eyes as they gazed at me, then at the egg.

"Mom," Cy ran into my arms and hugged me tightly. I wrapped my arms around her. "You and dad are having another baby!"

"How is this possible?" I asked. "He's not-"

My eyes widened when I remembered fucking Sixus in the past as a Half-Draconian.

"Sixus from the past," Zara smiled. "Felt terrible for what he turned into here." She paused. "So, his gift to you is a pure Half-Draconian baby."

Tears rolled down my cheeks as I gazed at my baby.

Hope had been restored.

I had to ensure that this baby survived at all costs.

Cy moved away from me, and then Zara pressed her index finger against my forehead, freeing the vampire and the shaman, and then she dropped her hand. My Tribrid status was restored.

When the shield was lowered, Sixus immediately sensed a shift had occurred.

"I'll see you soon, Mel."

Sixus spoke in my mind.

"He's coming," I whispered as I placed the shield back into place, and they grew into protect mode. "Protect this baby with your lives."

"This baby is going to be a world changer like her big sister and her parents," Setha snarled. "You dragons are ruthless with protecting your family, just like us vampires."

"I'm not such an easy target, Sixus."
I replied in my mind.
"I'm waiting for you. Come and get me!"
I added.
Silence filled the link, signaling Sixus' imminent arrival.

FIFTEEN

I stood alone in the nursery with Heartache playing over the loudspeaker, quietly of course. I was preparing the babies for battle before they even hatched.

An aroma reminiscent of cranberries, snow, and death wafted into the room. An instant later, Sixus slowly approached me, stopping beside me at the end of the first row.

"Of all the places you could be around here," Sixus spoke quietly, not to disturb the dragon eggs. "I didn't expect to find you in the nursery, Mel."

"I saved all those lives and cleanse the virus from the water supply in the four remaining kingdoms," I said as I glanced over at him. His eyes were white with red rings around the edges. He was still a Varacolaci. "Kill me if that's why you're here."

"Claus needs you alive, remember?" He arched an eyebrow my way. I turned and stood facing him. He could see and feel my exhaustion. I only had one hour of sleep since arriving back from the past. His gaze shifted to my neck. "Where did you get that necklace?"

"This?" I lifted the thick golden chain with my thumb before allowing it to fall back down against my body. It was a dragon head. His mother had given it to him as a birthday present last year. "You gave it to me, remember?"

"When?" he demanded as he reached down and held it in his hand. "I don't remember giving it to you?"

"You can have it back," I sighed wearily as I removed it. "It belongs to you."

"No," he whispered, stopping me. He took the chain and placed it back around my neck. "You can keep a part of me with you."

"Thank you Sixus," I whispered as I suddenly felt dizzy. Swaying to the left, I accidentally hit the pillar with my baby's egg on it, making it wobble and rock. Sixus caught me with one hand and touched the pillar and steadied the egg. It stopped rocking. I glanced at it and the blue flame was gone. Sixus didn't seem to notice anything odd about the egg. To him, it was just another egg. "I guess I need to sleep or something."

He was about to reply when the egg shook, catching his attention.

"I gotta go," I said as I tried to shake his hand off of me. "Let's move this conversation outside, okay?"

"Wait," he held a hand up to me as he never took his gaze off of the egg. "This egg... is new, isn't it?"

"Didn't notice," I shrugged as I took deep breaths to keep my heart beating at a steady pace. "Let's go."

"Whose kid is this?" he asked himself as he moved his hand back. A moment later, the pale blue flame shot out, surrounding the egg protectively. My eyes widened as he gazed at the egg, then slowly dragged his eyes to me. "It's... *yours?*"

"Sixus," I spoke cautiously as I ran in front of the egg. "Please don't do this."

"Did you fuck Solas?" Sixus snarled as I felt his rage flowing through his end of the bond.

"Of course *not*!" I spat as my rage flared throughout my entire body. "It's yours, you asshat!"

"Mine?" Sixus scoffed, not believing me. He shoved me, sending me flying into the wall. I slammed into it and fell to the floor. The impact of my head hitting the ground caused a slight, pulsating throb. "I'm killing it!"

"NO!" I screamed as I staggered to my feet. I rushed over to the pillar and bumped into it again. The egg rocked and fell to the right. Sixus, tapping into his vampire speed, grabbed it before it hit the ground. The blue flame shot out and went up his arms, engulfing his entire body in fire.

Sixus screamed in pain as the flame fizzled out. A moment later, he started laughing as he rose to his feet. He turned and held the egg in both hands. I screamed and my blue flame shot out of my mouth and surrounded him in a circle that rose, transforming into a birdcage. He tried stepping out, but the flames shot towards him.

"Let me out of here Mel!" Sixus shouted as his rage fueled hotter than before. "NOW!"

"Fuck you!" I snarled. "It's over Sixus!"

Without giving him a chance to reply, the egg's shell split open and fragmented, falling onto the floor. The blue flames shot towards Sixus, exploding, causing the room to be blinding in the flame's light before it died out.

I closed my eyes and slowly opened them to find Sixus lying on the ground, motionless. He assumed a fetal position, with his back facing up, his arms clenching, his stomach, and his head bent down.

I dragged the Venin dagger out and walked cautiously towards him. I raised the dagger high above my head and was about to bring it down when he rolled over and showed me what was in his hands. He was holding a newborn baby girl. His beautiful blue eyes were gazing up at me in shock.

I dropped the Venin dagger; it clattered twice before stopping. As he slowly sat up, I sank to my knees beside him. I grabbed the dagger and put it back in the sheath. Lowering myself, I reached down and picked the tiny baby up in my arms. She whimpered, and I hugged her and wrapped my warm trench coat around her shivering little body.

"It's okay," I whispered. "Mommy and daddy are here, little one."

Sixus was still in a state of shock as he gently touched my back and placed his other hand on the baby's cheek as he gently stroked his index finger against her skin. She quieted down and opened her eyes. They were the same beautiful blue eyes as his and Cy's. Her dark hair was thick, her tiny face was a balanced mixture of mine and Sixus' faces. She was going to be gorgeous when she grew up.

"She brought me back to you, Mel," Sixus whispered as he gave me a sad smile. "Our daughter saved my life."

I heard many footsteps rushing towards us. We both turned our heads and saw Cy, Zara, Tork, and Velzy run to our sides.

"Dad!" Cy hugged him as he removed his arms from me and our baby and wrapped them around his eldest daughter. "Your back!"

"I am." He kissed her on the cheek as she wiped the tears from her eyes after she released him. She gazed down at her sister with so much pride in her eyes to see she was alive. "Can I hold her?"

We rose to our feet and Zara unfolded a small fluffy pink baby blanket and carefully wrapped the newborn baby in it before cautiously handing her over to Cy, who hugged her sister and kissed her on the cheek as we walked out of the room.

Sixus used his ice powers and collected the broken shell pieces and held them. When we exited the room, he walked over to where the tiny dragons were sleeping or playing. He tossed the shell pieces into the grass and the tiny dragons ran over to it and sniffed it before eating the shell pieces.

I gazed at them in amazement before turning back around. Sixus took my hand in his and interlaced our fingers together as we walked towards the door. Velzy held it open for us and the night air struck my hot, sticky skin, cooling it off instantly. I welcomed it as I breathed in the fresh air.

Sixus surprised me when he released my hand and picked me up in his arms. I rested my heavy head against his chest as I gazed up at him. He was staring down at me, and I could feel his love for all three of us flowing through his end of the bond.

The baby whimpered again, and Cy handed her carefully back to me. I pulled my trench coat across her tiny body, shielding her head from the chilly breeze that was blowing. My intuition alerted me that danger was near. Everyone stopped walking, and they formed a protective circle around my little family.

The astral thread opened, and Timbrax stood inside, gazing at us. His eyes fell on me, and I kept my jacket pulled up tightly. He gazed at Sixus and narrowed his eyes at him.

Sixus snarled as Cy grabbed onto his arm tightly.

"I see you've reverted to your former self dragon king," Timbrax replied. "We're coming for your heads!" As he was about to close the thread, the baby let out a small whimper, causing him to stop and glance back at me. The thread disappeared moments later, and I knew we were in trouble.

Mitrik appeared through the astral thread, and we raced through it, emerging in I.O.A. Abel was there and I carefully opened the jacket, revealing the tiny newborn in my arms. With caution, he picked her up, and Cy insisted on joining him. He permitted her to depart, and they hastened towards one of the hospital rooms.

I was so eager to go with them, but I had to have a deep conversation with Sixus. I had complete trust in Abel taking care of my baby. When I felt a new thread forming in my body, I knew it belonged to my baby as it disappeared. The feeling was mutual between me and Sixus as we locked eyes.

"This is real?"

I thought.

"Now, my baby and I are connected."

"Mel, you're an extraordinary woman," Sixus murmured as he helped me settle on the ledge of one of the expansive windows. He stood in between my legs as he placed his hands on my waist to keep me steady. "You time traveled back two years and brought me back to you."

"Our daughters need their father," I whispered as I placed my hands behind his neck, drawing him into me. "And I needed my husband back to keep me from going insane."

"I will never allow that darkness to corrupt me ever again, Mel," Sixus whispered. "It's not something to take lightly."

As he said those words, the rest of the darkness that remained within his body I absorbed into mine, leaving him completely full of his radiant light. I was clearly unbalanced now and Sixus had to bring me back before the darkness could overpower me like it had before the Flight Games. months ago.

"Come back to me," Sixus whispered as I slowly met his gaze. He placed his hands gently on my cheeks, stroking them with his thumbs. "I will always choose you, Mel."

Hearing those words broke me. I felt his love and the warmth of his light flowing into my body as he gently kissed me. Returning his kiss, I closed my eyes before he broke it. I felt the light balancing the darkness out as I opened my eyes.

"Thank you Sixus," I gave him a sad smile. "I'm okay now."

I was until I wasn't. With the weight of exhaustion, my soul was forcibly extracted from my body. I watched myself collapse against his chest.

"Mel?" Sixus caught me, and I was unresponsive. "Somebody help!"

"Sixus," I said. "I'm right here!"

I observed him moving my unconscious body out of the room, and I was thrown upward into space. Glancing around, I noticed how bright the stars were. I could actually feel them pulsating all around me.

"The fuck is happening to me?"

I thought.

I felt a force pulling me downwards, and now I was in the astral thread. Timbrax was already there, sitting with his back leaned up against the icy wall. If he felt my presence, he didn't react to me as I cautiously moved over to him.

"Did you see anything that was out-of-place out there in space?" Timbrax asked, keeping his gaze fixed forward.

"Only stars," I whispered as I gave him a strange look. "How am I back here and out of my body again?"

"This is part of your new shamanic powers," Timbrax shrugged. "To return to your body, just follow that blue string that's connected to your body, and you'll be back in no time."

"Are you done with Sixus?" I demanded, changing the subject. "I had to go to insane lengths to restore him back to his Half-Draconian form, you know?"

"Oh, I'm done with him," Timbrax laughed lightly. "It was fun screwing with you was why I did it."

"That's fucked up!" I spat as my rage flared within me. "You can't do that to people you love!"

Timbrax climbed to his feet and turned to face me. His expression was unreadable.

"It's not like you can hurt me when you're astral projecting yourself, Melfina," he scoffed. "Your harmless in this state."

"Don't call me weak." As I balled my hand into a fist, I pulled it back. I threw it forward and struck him in the jaw. "Cause I'm not you jackass!"

"Damn." Timbrax narrowed his eyes at me as he rubbed the side of his jaw. He lowered his hand, and I saw a bruise forming on his pale skin. "That hurt like hell."

I was flung back down and flew into my body. In an instant, my eyes shot open, and I gasped. I took in my surroundings and lay in a hospital bed in a room in I.O.A. Sixus was sitting in the chair beside me and Abel was standing in front of a computer.

"MEL!" Sixus leaped to his feet, and I sat up with a jolt as he wrapped me in a tight hug. "I thought you were in a coma!"

"I accidentally astral projected again," I whispered. Timbrax and I found ourselves in the astral thread.

Sixus body stiffened as he slowly released me, and he gazed at me intently. I felt his rage through his end of the bond. Thankfully, Timbrax had unbound himself from me. I don't know when it happened, though.

"What did he want?" Abel asked, so Sixus didn't have to.

"He asked me if I saw anything out there," I said. "Before I was flung into the astral thread where he was waiting for me, I was thrown into space."

"You didn't tell him anything, did you?" Sixus asked quietly.

"No," I shook my head. "I punched him in the jaw and gave him a bruise before I was flung back into my body and woke up."

"Astral projecting is dangerous, Melfina," Abel said. "I would recommend you stop doing it because you run the risk of getting possessed by something and you won't be able to get back into your body."

"I'm not doing it on purpose." I threw a quick glance at him. "Believe me, I am not."

"It's okay." Sixus forced a smile as I felt his anxiety calming down through his end of the bond. "We need to name our daughter Mel."

"Oh," I had completely forgotten to give her a name since all the chaos was happening around me consistently. "I forgot about that part."

A name flashed in my mind.

"HAMANI."

It vanished, and Sixus saw it as well.

"Hamani is a beautiful name," he smiled at me. "It means Ice breath."

"I guess she's an ice welder like you and Cy," I gave him a small smile. "At least she has a name now."

"Your flame is rare, Mel," Sixus replied. "It's a 1 out of 99 shot that our children will ever wield your powers."

"I want to monitor you for the remainder of the night, Melfina," Abel said as he placed a liquid into my IV with a needle. I felt it seep into my vein and I felt exhausted. Sixus gently lay me down and covered me up with the blanket. "It's important to get some sleep... remember, you just had a baby."

I closed my eyes, and my breathing changed as I lay there.

"She's sleeping, right?" Sixus whispered as he climbed to his feet.

"I believe so," Abel agreed. "Whatever is going on with her," he sighed heavily. "Solas is the only one who can help her with it."

I heard footsteps approach as someone entered my room.

"Speaking of the devil," Sixus murmured. "Here he is now."

"You're the one who kept embracing that dark shit," Solas replied, with a hint of annoyance in his voice. "What do you want?"

"What the hell is your problem?" Sixus snarled as I felt his rage through his end of the bond. "Melfina keeps fucking with the timelines and it's your fault!"

"I didn't tell her to go back in time and save your ass," Solas spat. I felt his rage through his end of the bond, too. "That was all those vampires doing... not *mine*!"

"Stop," I said in a quiet voice, making them stare at me as I opened my eyes and stared at them. "What's happening to me, Solas?"

"The shamanic powers are seeking the Nexus on their own, Mel." Solas walked over to my bedside and gazed down at me. "We can't stop it... that's why we weren't here when you went back in time and returned with a baby."

"I had to bring Sixus back at all costs," I replied. "My-"

I gasped as I felt my soul leaving my body. Solas snapped into action by placing a purple beaded necklace around my neck and my soul slammed back into my body, causing me to gasp again.

"Why does that keep happening to her?" Sixus demanded as his fear crept into my bond.

"When Melfina went back in time and made those slight alterations," Solas frowned down at me. "She found the key to unlocking the Nexus unintentionally."

"That's why her soul keeps astral projecting." Abel put two and two together. "Being the Shamanic Universal Queen and the oracle of Tellus is causing her to seek the most powerful-"

Solas put a finger to his lips, and Abel shut up immediately.

"I have to stay by your side at all times, Mel," Solas grew even more serious as he gazed at the others. "We can't allow the enemy to get the Nexus."

"You knew the actual location this entire time, didn't you?" I whispered.

"Of course I do," Solas replied cockily, like Sixus liked to do. "I've always known the location, Melfina."

"You're the one who keeps blocking it from her," Sixus figured it out. "No wonder why you're always gone or quiet around here."

"I'm keeping the Victim Commander and his allies thrown off," Solas rubbed his tired eyes. "It's exhausting and I'm constantly utilizing more energy than I can get back."

The cool, computerized female voice spoke above our heads.

"Pilot Melfina is now released from I.O.A. Have a great day!"

The cords fell away from my body and the needle pushed itself out of my arm, falling into a tiny white box and throwing itself away. As I sat up, I quickly discarded the hot blanket from my body. I saw the three men exchange worried expressions with each other. Able wasn't able to keep me in here after all.

With a quick motion, I got up, quickly putting on my boots and zipping them up. Standing up, I walked silently past them and exited the room. I walked up the long hallway and stopped in front of the long window and saw Hamani sleeping peacefully in her tiny plastic bin hooked up with too many machines. She was born prematurely, so she needed to be monitored Twenty-four-seven.

Explode was playing quietly in the nursery and I saw Cy sleeping in a chair as she curled up beside her sister. It surprised me that rock music wasn't bothering the newborn. She was my daughter, and I smiled sadly as I gazed down at her.

"She's beautiful," Solas said in a quiet voice as he and Sixus both stood on either side of me and gazed at the baby. "To ensure Hamani has a future... protect the Nexus with your life, Melfina." He placed a finger on my forehead where my third eye was located, and he locked the location away once more.

I watched as A.J. and Nell both entered the nursery and took up positions beside both of my daughters. I nodded a quick thank you as Varric stood beside Sixus. He kept giving him strange looks like he could turn back into a Varacolaci at any moment. Thankfully, this time he was back to himself.

Sixus suddenly dropped to the floor, and I glanced at him, then up at Varric.

"His ass needs to sleep," Varric said as he lifted Sixus up by the armpits and drug him up the hallway towards my dorm room. "Get her too Solas."

Solas placed a hand on my cheek as I turned and faced him. "Time to sleep, Mel," He moved in and kissed me. I moved away, and I felt tired as he sucked all my energy out of my body. He picked me up, and I fell into a deep sleep.

As much as I wanted to kick his ass for forcing me to sleep when I wanted to protect my family and my kingdom. I needed to sleep.

I'd kick Solas's ass tomorrow.

SIXTEEN

Sixus awakened me, snoring loudly. My eyes shot open, and I sat up in bed. The light turned on by motion and I shoved the hot comforter off my body and climbed over his body. I was relieved to see him sleeping. Being a Varacolaci for weeks had exhausted his body.

Solas cleared his throat from behind me, and I turned to look at him. He gazed at me with his arms crossed and his feet spread apart, with his head tilted to the side as he gazed at me.

"Wanna sleep in my bed?" he asked, glancing at Sixus, who was dead to the world. "Completely slipped my mind that sleeping with that loud dragon snoring is impossible."

"I'm awake," I replied. "I'll take a quick shower and strategies." Upon activating my vampire speed, I swiftly raced to the bathroom, only to find Timbrax standing there, gripping my throat tightly and lifting me off the ground, depriving me of air.

"SOLAS! SIXUS!"

I screamed in my mind.

I heard two sets of footsteps rushing into the bathroom.

"Let her go, Timbrax!" Sixus snarled.

"No," Timbrax replied bluntly. "We've wasted enough time waiting on the Tribrid to give us the location of the Nexus."

"I keep wiping her memory," Solas replied calmly. "She will never give it to you!"

"You are suppressing it with this, aren't you?" Timbrax asked as he placed his other hand on the beaded necklace around my neck. He yanked it and black beads fell to the floor, clattering loudly as they rolled around his feet. "If you don't do as I say," Timbrax narrowed his eyes at me. "I will *kill* your newborn baby!"

"I'll do it!"

I screamed in my mind.

"NO!" Sixus shouted as the astral thread appeared behind Timbrax. He slowly stepped inside as it closed behind him. He dropped me and I fell to the floor.

"Give me the key, Melfina," Timbrax crouched down before me. "And this will all be over."

"The key isn't-"

I caught myself and shut up.

"You won't get any information out of me." I replied defiantly.

"You must enjoy being tortured, don't you?" Timbrax asked as he yanked me up by my hair. The pain was intense, but I didn't flinch. He exited the thread, dragging me by my hair behind him as he walked over to my cell. He pulled open the door and tossed my ass inside. With a shove, he guided me towards the metal cot, resulting in me slamming my head into the wall and feeling dazed. I could feel the tight grip of the metal shackles around my wrists. "This time, I'm the one responsible for your torture."

I stood and walked up to him. He gazed down at me and head-butted me, sending me flying backwards onto the cot.

"That's for punching me last night!" he snarled as he walked towards the door. He pulled it open and stepped out. He slammed it and locked it before walking away.

"Dragons don't break Mel!"

Sixus spoke in my mind.

"We're stubborn and we don't die!"

He added.

"I refuse to bread!"

I replied.

"I love you Sixus!"

I added.

Both Sixus and Solas unbound their souls from me. I could feel it. They had to protect Tellus, Erda, and Outer Earth.

Zyra, Nyxie, and Sinergy appeared before me. I gazed at them, and they all had one mission in mind. To protect the Nexus.

I threw my hand out and took a deep breath.

"Spirit Form Accord!" I said as all three spirits glowed and shot into my hand in different colors balls of light. One red, purple, and blue. I thrust my hand into my chest, and I was under their control.

The door unlocked and was yanked open as Timbrax entered the room. He used the tiny key and unlocked my shackles. They dropped to the bed, and I slowly stood, keeping my head down.

Timbrax sensed the shift of energy in the room, and he snarled at who was in control of my body.

"Let's go," Zyra's voice came out of my body. "I can take your punishment."

"Let's see if you can survive," Timbrax snarled. "I will kill you again Z!"

"You can't kill what's already dead, Timbrax," I smirked. "And trust me, I'm as dead as they come."

"I know what to do with you!" Timbrax chuckled as he opened the astral thread. He grabbed me by the arm and tossed my ass inside. I flew in and fell out, slamming into a thick wall of ice. My back hurt like hell as I dragged myself up. Timbrax emerged, and the thread closed behind him. "RUN!"

I turned and ran. I slipped on the ice and fell, striking my chin against the thick sheet of ice below me.

"Looks like Sixus turned your kingdom into an ice wasteland, Melfina," Timbrax laughed as he flicked his wrists. Two orange flames sat in his palms as he flicked them towards me. I rolled to the right and his flames blasted the broken cement wall behind me, causing it to explode. Fragments of concrete flew around me. "Victim attack!"

"Firelash Power!" I shouted as I transformed into Hell's Guardian. As I screamed, a massive flamethrower erupted from my mouth, causing Timbrax to roll quickly to his left and avoid it. I leaped over the ice wall and melted the ice around me as I ran. Leaping behind a tall wall that was in the shadows was where I hid.

Vendetta Started playing over a loudspeaker from somewhere nearby.

"Timbrax is taunting me."

I thought.

"Peekaboo, bitch!" Largo laughed maniacally as he poked his head down from the wall I was hiding under. With the Venin dagger in hand, I pierced the underside of his neck. The blade passed through his mouth, nose, and eyes. Using my vampire speed, I yanked it down, pulled it out, and rapidly fled from him. As I stopped running near my ruined castle, the sound of Largo's anguished screams faded away.

"You are far too predictable, Melfina," Timbrax spoke from behind me. I spun around with the Venin dagger raised in a defensive stance before me. "I want you to rebuild it, so we have-"

"No," I replied, cutting him off. "Let it decompose until it becomes part of the ground!"

Enemy started playing, catching Timbrax off guard.

I kicked off the ground and flew into him, knocking him down onto his back. I positioned the dagger over his non-beating heart. He held his hands on my ass as I straddled him. He lay there looking at me, waiting to see what I would do.

"How can I possibly kill the man I love?"

I thought.

"I won't hesitate to kill you, Melfina," Timbrax whispered. "Do. It!"

"It's impossible!" I blinked back the tears. "I love you, you fucking asshole!"

Timbrax leaned his body up and crushed his lips against mine, catching me off guard.

Dreamstate started playing next.

Timbrax reached across my body and grabbed the dagger. He placed it back in the sheath and kissed me harder.

"I can't kill you ether!"

He snarled in my mind.

My powers erupted from my body, reconstructing the Xeonada Empire without me even trying. We were back in my bedroom. Timbrax growled protectively deep in his throat as he carried me over to my bed in my bedroom. He lay me down, and the outfit disappeared.

"How did you do that?" He whispered as he lay on top of me.

"I," I glanced around in confusion. "Don't know?"

Like That played next.

This song was fitting in my current situation. I was laying beneath him on my bed!

"I love you, Melfina," Timbrax whispered in my ear. "That's why I can't be with you."

I shoved him off of me and I rose to my feet. As I walked over, I flung open the doors to my closet. I turned to find Timbrax standing inches behind me.

"What do you want from me, Brax?" I asked in a quiet voice. "I don't know where the Nexus is!"

"Melfina, I want you," he said as he placed an icy hand on my cheek. "Can't you see that I'm doing all of this for *you*?"

"I don't want this, Brax." I shook my head. "Stop fucking with my emotions and my heart!"

"You think I'm fucking with you?" Timbrax looked shocked. He rebounded his soul to mine, and I could feel his emotions. "I promise you, I'm *not*!"

"Then why did you kill our unborn baby?" I whispered.

"Can one truly love something that was once a piece of myself?" He slumped his shoulders in defeat. "I took you away from Sixus... I'm not deserving of you."

"Isn't that my decision to make Timbrax?" I whispered. "You sold me out to save yourself."

"I vowed to protect you," he whispered as he kneeled before me. He shoved me roughly against the wall and pulled my pants and panties down. He flung us through the astral thread, closing it behind him. Removing his belt, he pulled down his pants and silk boxers. He slammed his cock deep int my pussy. The extreme cold made me gasp, but he used his vampire speed to enter me quickly, causing me to experience multiple orgasms before he pulled out. "And love you until my dying breath."

"I forgot how good you fuck me Brax," I breathed, still feeling honey. "Fuck me all night in our bed?"

He used his vampire speed and pulled up my panties and pants and his own boxer shorts, pants and fixed his belt before he took my hand and lead me out of the astral thread. Orion was holding an unconscious nearly dead Exrah in his arms, making me stop dead in my tracks upon seeing her.

Claus held out his hand and the three spirits flew out of my body at once, causing me to gasp at how forceful it was. They disappeared, and I felt something was off. Something was very wrong here.

"What's happening?" I asked as all three men stood there silently watching me.

"Didn't they tell you?" Claus asked calmly. "There are consequences to your actions of going back in time and altering our current timeline."

"I watched Exrah die." I pointed my index finger at her. "What's-"

"We swapped her out with a Victim to make it look like she was dead," Timbrax replied calmly. "Claus revived these two as they were killed, and it wasn't their time to die yet."

I glanced down and saw Zyra and Nyxie, both alive, laying on the floor before me unconscious.

"You're going to return to the institute," Timbrax replied as he picked up the two girls' bodies and tossed them through the astral thread. Orion tossed Ezrah's body in as well. "Everyone will leave you and you will pray for death by the end of this, Melfina."

Claus, with a flick of his wrist, used his dark shamanic powers to send me flying backwards through the astral thread. I flew through the other side and landed on my back on the lawn of the institute, and it closed behind me. I slowly rolled to my side and found the three girls lying beside me. All alive and unconscious.

Sixus, Solas, Cy, and Zara all ran out of the door. They trotted down the steps and ran over to the three fallen women.

"Their alive!" Zara shouted to them. "Get them to I.O.A. quickly!"

They all picked up a girl and stood. They turned and raced up the steps. Varric held the door open, and they all ran through the door. He looked at me and nodded curtly before entering the building. As the door closed, I found myself lying on the lawn alone. Gradually, I stood up and brushed off the dust from my body. I couldn't shake the feeling that this wasn't right.

Little did I know just how right I was.

***

Prior to going to I.O. A., I showered and freshened up. I caught my balance as the door opened and closed behind me, flinging myself out of the tube.

"Mel," Solas walked up to me and hugged me before releasing me. "Nyxie is doing great," he smiled. "We're taking her back home to rest."

"That's great." I formed a smile. "Please make sure she rests up and gets back out there to kick ass, okay?"

He nodded as he entered her hospital room. I saw the blue light flash before it disappeared. I stood in the doorway and found the room to be completely empty. As I made my way up the hallway, I spotted Zara leaving another room.

"Mom's back!" She hugged me and released me as well, mirroring Solas's movements moments ago. "We're taking her home to the Dark Region to rest."

"That's wonderful," I forced a smile. "Take care of her, okay?"

"We will," she gave me a nervous smile. "Thank you." As she ran into the room, I watched and heard the astral thread close before it fell silent. Upon peeking inside the room, I discovered that it, too, was completely empty. To my surprise, all the vampire hunters had disappeared when I turned around. I was the only one in the eerie corridor.

As I walked up the hallway, Sixus accidentally bumped into me.

"Mel," he grabbed my shoulders to steady me as I was falling. "I just wanted to thank you for bringing Exrah home." He smiled warmly at me. "Orion held her captive, and Victim were feeding on her."

"I'm glad she's okay," I forced a smile. "Everyone left, I guess."

"They returned to Erda," Sixus went on. "Can you take charge of things while I ensure Exrah gets healthy?" he asked.

"Of course," I forced a smile. "No problem."

He kissed me on the cheek before he turned and ran up the hallway, leaving me even more confused. I turned and walked up the hallway, heading back towards my dorm room. I noticed mecha pilots had been carrying my belongings out of the room.

"What are you guys doing?" I asked.

"Sixus asked for your things to be moved to the oracle dormitory," a male first year replied. "He's moving Exrah in there so he can monitor her when she gets out of I.O.A."

I forced a smile and turned around once more. I wasn't sure what the fuck was going on around here! Abel exited a room holding Hamani. He handed her off to me and explained how she was healthy, and I could bring her to my room. He was in a hurry to get home. Just like everyone else had been.

I turned and walked towards a glass tube. The door flung open, and I stepped inside. It closed behind me. I turned and crossed my legs and hugged Hamani close to my chest as I wrapped my trench coat around her to keep her warm. She was sleeping peacefully in my arms.

The cool, computerized female voice spoke from above my head.

"Prepare to descend in 5... 4... 3... 2... 1... GO!"

The floor dropped beneath my feet, and I slid down the tube being thrown around. I covered Hamani's head with my other hand. The door shot open, and I experienced being flung out. I landed on my feet and walked up to the main area. With a forceful shove of my shoulder, I swung open the heavy door and made my way down the cement steps. I walked across the lawn and pulled open the door leading to the oracle dormitory. Stepping inside, I closed it and walked down the spiral stone steps. I entered the living room and crossed into my bedroom. I found all my things on the couch in the front room and on my bed.

Laying Hamani down in her pink bassinet, I tapped into my vampire speed and put my things away in record time. I put Hamani's things in her bedroom. I was glad the shamans had updated everything down here to be more accommodating to Erda and current up-to-date era technology.

Following the bath and feeding, I settled Hamani beside me on the bed to sleep. I took off both my jackets and boots. Settling into bed, I tightly hugged my daughter.

Hamani was all I had left.

Twinkle Together was playing quietly on my cell and I silently cried after I placed the block up to keep Cy and Sixus' ends of their bonds quiet. They hadn't even come to check on me or my baby!

This was what Timbrax and Claus were talking about when they said I had changed the timeline.

Everyone was alive.

All at the cost of my happiness.

SEVENTEEN

The attacks by Victim had ceased, and everything had changed drastically around here. Sixus had been at Exrah's beck and call after her release from I.O.A. He moved her into my former dorm room and he and Cy had been all about Exrah and her comfort. I didn't wanna feel jealous, but that was my husband and my daughter!

Everyone believed that my position wasn't necessary in the dragon knights, so I demoted myself back to a lowly Private First Class. Nobody seemed to notice. I was now a single parent, so I took care of Hamani and brought her to my classes with me. Thankfully, she was a delightful baby and slept through my classes, allowing me to do my work in peace.

Sixus had neglected his duties of paperwork since the Flight Games. So, I created my office next to his and tackled the five tall stacks of manilla folders that were piled high to the ceiling. I used my stamp and signed the documents. To get things done, I tapped into my vampire speed and was on the final document.

The familiar scent of cranberries mixed with snow reached my nose, and I knew Sixus was approaching. I didn't bother to look up when he entered the room.

"What happened to my office?" he asked with confusion in his voice.

"This is my office," I replied without looking up. I pointed my pen to the left. "Your office is over there."

"Right," he said as he walked away. A moment later, he returned and stood beside my desk. "What happened to all the paperwork?"

"Just finished it," I replied as I placed my signature on the last piece of paper and quickly stamped it with my seal before closing the folder and handing it to him. "I have a royal meeting to attend in an hour."

I dropped the pen into a metal cup on my desk and stood stretching my muscles before stepping to the side and picking up the car seat with Hamani sleeping peacefully inside it. She had a pacifier in her mouth and was covered in the pink blanket Zara had given her when she was born.

He looked surprised to see Hamani when her scent struck his nose. I placed her car seat down on the desk as I walked over to the couch and picked up her diaper bag, tossing it across my shoulder. I turned to get her when I saw him stroking her little cheek with the back of his finger.

"I'm sorry daddy's been busy, Hamani," he whispered to our daughter. "I'll find time for you and mommy soon, I promise."

Fade Away was playing on my cell as I walked over and picked it up and placed it in my jacket pocket, still playing. I walked around him and took the handle of the car seat and picked it up. I turned and headed for the door.

"Mel," Sixus called after me, making me stop dead in my tracks. "Exrah volunteered to be our repairer."

"Great," I replied with fake enthusiasm in my voice. "Have fun with that."

"I thought you'd be happy?" he asked as he walked over to where I was standing. As I lowered the block, he and Cy could perceive my emotions. I was all over the place. I was confused, pissed, suicidal, on the verge of having a nervous breakdown. It had been two fucking months! He ignored me and our daughter! I quickly placed the block back up and stormed out of the office.

Sixus chased after me as I walked through the main lobby and pushed open the heavy door. Trotting down the steps, I walked towards the dormitory. I pulled open the door and trotted down the spiral stone steps and into the living room. I placed the car seat down on the couch, and Sixus trotted down the steps and walked over to me.

"Why didn't you tell me you needed me, Mel?" Sixus whispered.

"I shouldn't have to!" I hissed through my teeth. "You wanna divorce me fine!"

"I don't want to," he shook his head. "What happened to us, Mel?"

"Exrah!" I screamed, making Hamani cry. I took off her blanket and disconnected the straps. With great care, I removed them and pulled her out of the car seat. I held her and rocked her, trying to soothe her as tears escaped my eyes. "None of this is the life we wanted, Sixus."

"I'm sorry Mel," Sixus shook his head. "It's like someone has control over me or something, you know?"

"I gotta get ready," I replied as I turned and entered my bedroom. I set Hamani on the bed, and Sixus followed me. He walked over and picked her up. She fell silent quickly as he gently rocked our daughter in his arms. He held her until she fell back asleep. He lay her down on the bed and I didn't know what to say to him. "Thanks."

"I thought you were going to a royal meeting?" he asked, arching an eyebrow my way. "You aren't getting dressed."

"I lied." While giving him a sad smile, I walked over to Hamani and picked her up. As I turned and walked out of the room, he followed me closely. I strapped her in and placed her back in her car seat before covering her back up with the blanket. As I grabbed the handle, picking up the diaper bag and swinging it across my head and left shoulder, I glanced at him. "I'm going home Sixus."

"To the Xeonada Empire?" Sixus asked with shock in his voice as he followed me up the steps. I shoved open the heavy door and stepped outside.

"Yeah," I nodded. "Home."

"How long has this been going on for Mel?" Sixus asked.

"For the past two months," I shrugged. "Hamani enjoys the fresh air."

"What the hell happened to us?" he repeated his question.

"I time traveled back in time," I replied. "By saving your life… I altered our current timeline by fucking it up."

"Then undo it," Sixus replied bluntly. "You're the oracle, damn it!"

"If I do," I shook my head. "Then I lose you and we lose Hamani."

The astral thread appeared, and Timbrax stood there, gazing back at us silently.

"Are you ready for death yet, Melfina?" Timbrax asked. "I told you; you wouldn't like the outcome of this."

"It gets worse, doesn't it?" I asked.

"Oh, yeah," Timbrax laughed lightly. "We both end up alone and miserable together as we watch the world burn to the ground!"

"Change it back," I sighed as I gazed down at Hamani. "Please?"

"On one condition," Timbrax replied. "Sixus will return to being a Varacolaci. Zyra and Nyxie remain dead," he smirked. "And you find that damn Nexus and get to keep Hamani."

"What will happen to Exrah?" I asked. "You keep her ass away from my family!"

"Done," Timbrax agreed, snapping his fingers. I felt the shift in my reality as it gradually changed back to its original state. "This baby is all you get to keep from the altered timeline, Melfina."

"Hamani is worth it," I whispered as she opened her eyes and looked at me. I saw the beautiful bright blue in them. The scent of cranberries mixed with snow and death struck my nose, and I turned to see Sixus gazing at the baby intently. "You stay the hell away from my baby!"

"Cute kid," Sixus smirked as he took a step towards me. I stood my ground as I held the car seat handle in my arm tightly. He dabbed the necklace around my neck with his index finger. I glanced down and was surprised to see the dragon necklace was still around my neck. "How can you possibly keep our daughters alive and win a war against me and the Victim Commander Mel?"

The blue portal appeared, and Solas returned with the three shamans. With urgency, they ran to my side and without hesitation; the girls snatched the car seat and diaper bag from my arm and shoulder, bolting up the steps. Cy opened the door, and they raced inside.

The astral thread opened, and Zara stepped out, followed by the vampire hunters. Setha closed it behind her as they stood beside me.

"I made a mistake," Zara whispered to me as I glanced at her. "I'm so sorry, mom."

"It's okay." I gave her a sad smile. "Protect your sisters Zara."

I watched as Sixus dropped his hand and slowly backed away from me. His eyes were those of Varacolaci, white with red rings around the edges. He turned and walked over to Timbrax and stood beside him.

"What will you do now, Mel?" Sixus asked. "You've lost everything you've ever loved."

"No, I haven't," I shook my head. "I will get you back, Sixus."

"Good luck with that," Sixus smirked as he rebounded his soul to me. "See you later, Mel."

I watched as he turned and disappeared through the astral thread. It shut, and both men were gone.

"Get the queen inside quickly!" Tork shouted as Solas snapped into action. He took my hand and guided me up the steps. He guided me inside, and I was overwhelmed with exhaustion and shock. I hadn't even realized

I was in my dorm room until he sat me down on the bed. Timbrax had returned it to a previous version with all of my belongings in it.

"Are you okay, Mel?" Solas asked in a gentle voice, bringing me back to reality.

"Is Hamani alright?" I asked, not caring about my wellbeing. "She was just born-"

"The baby is fine," he gave me a sad smile. "We're running out of time."

The doors slid open, and Cy entered, carrying Hamani in her arms with the shaman and Zara behind her. She carefully handed her sister over to me and I held her tightly as she slept, completely unaware of the danger of going on around her. I lay down with my back facing the wall and held Hamani in my arms as I closed my eyes.

"You," Solas spoke to someone standing in the room. "Do you have any idea what you've done, Zara?"

"I wanted to see my mom!" she cried, making my eyes shoot open. "I'm sorry, dad number three!"

Dad number three?

I thought.

"The Nexus will be unleashed when they come for her." Despite his composure, Solas' words struck us to the core. "You've just destroyed three fucking planets thanks to your selfishness, Zara."

"Come here," I whispered as I sat up and opened my eyes. Zara sat down beside me, and I hugged her tightly as she sobbed uncontrollably. "I don't blame you for what happened." With sadness, I gave her a smile. "My desire to bring Sixus back was so strong that I was willing to pay any price."

Setha entered the room accompanied by Darby, Tork, Rhydian, and Velzy. Zara removed herself from me and Setha placed a hand on my left shoulder. I felt her absorbing my darkness until I had balanced out. She removed her hand and fell unconscious. Rhydian caught her, and I climbed to my feet and gazed out the open French doors. I saw the Xeonada Empire still lay in wreckage after my army had destroyed it.

"The vampire needs to feed Melfina," Velzy said. "And those tubes of blood you fought to collect from the failed mission," she paused as I looked at her. "We still have them all intact."

"What?" I asked as the shock filled me. "Get the samples to Zuni and Abel."

"Already on it, my queen," Tork replied. "We need to inject you three with your blood." Velzy pulled out three syringes and Tork took one. She stepped over to me and injected me on one side of my neck and the metal burned like hell as she removed it. I felt the cool liquid seep into my vein, and I felt better. Velzy stuck Cy and removed it as well.

I noticed an imminent danger as my intuition alerted me. I walked over and carefully picked up Hamani and placed her carefully back into her car seat and buckled her in before I covered her up with her blanket. Turning around, I was taken aback by the sight of a castle being built right before my eyes. The castle was made of pure ice. Before the ice bridge flew and slammed into the end of the ground where the water's edge met the institute, he built the surrounding kingdom.

Sixus moved across the bridge as if he was wearing ice skates, gracefully sliding down and locking eyes with me.

"Use this on him." Velzy mouthed as she slipped the third needle into my jacket pocket.

I nodded curtly as I held the car seat in my hands. Cy carried the diaper bag over her shoulder, and we walked out of the open French doors and stood on the balcony. He formed an ice slice, and Cy carefully took the car seat from my hands and held it as she stood sliding down the slide. She landed and stayed beside it, waiting for me. I walked up to it and sat down. Nodding, Solas confirmed as I glanced over my shoulder. I turned back and slid down. I flew down at a rapid speed and I flew off. Sixus leaped high into the air and caught me landing and placing me down beside him on the ground.

He took me by the hand, and it was as cold as death. Cy walked up to us, and she walked ahead of us, leaping up onto the bridge. She moved her feet like she was ice skates and disappeared ahead of us. He leaped up, and we both landed on the bridge. I wasn't as graceful as he and Cy were being a Pyro-Lancer.

I slipped, and he held me up with both hands by the waist. He turned his head and blew out ice, creating an army made of ice. They stood blocking the bridge so nobody could get across it after us. He picked me up in his arms and he slid up the bridge as I placed my arms around his neck.

"You don't need to be afraid of me," Sixus whispered down to me. "I'm still me Mel."

"Right." I forced a smile as I tried to calm my racing heart. He could sense my anxiety through the bond. Our souls were still bound to each other. He hopped off the end of the bridge and his ice army blocked the bridge, so there was no going back now. "Sorry."

Cy was standing there, holding the car seat in both hands as Sixus set me down on the ground. It would melt where I stood and when I walked over to Cy, it reformed like I hadn't stood there at all. Ice was weird shit. I didn't understand it at all as a power!

We walked up the steps and an ice guard held open the door for us. We entered the castle, and it was absolutely freezing in here!

"You know where your room is, Cy," Sixus said to her. "Keep your sister in her crib in your room, okay?"

"Yes, father," Cy nodded as an ice maiden escorted her and Hamani up the steps to their room.

"You must be starving, Mel," Sixus said. "Let's get you something to eat."

"I'm not hungry," I said. "I just wanna sleep."

"Of course," He forced a smile as I felt his irritation through the bond. "Guess I'll take you to our bedroom."

"If you got something to say," I started. "Say it!"

"You don't wanna hear what I have to say to you, Mel," Sixus scoffed as he turned and gazed at me. "Trust me."

"What?" I asked as I walked up to him. As I slipped my hand inside my jacket pocket, I gripped the thin needle. After pressing my thumb against the lid, I effortlessly slid it off and flicked the tube twice with my middle finger, creating a subtle clicking noise. I had to inject him with his blood to turn him back into a Half-Draconian. "You gonna tell me I'm weak?"

"No?" he arched an eyebrow as I felt his confusion through his end of the bond.

"You love Exrah-"

"I HATE THAT BITCH!" Sixus screamed, as his rage flew out of control. While he was distracted, I utilized my vampire speed to stab him in the neck and squeeze the red plasma into his vein. He snarled as he slowly turned his gaze and met mine. I injected him with the last of it before he shoved me backward.

As I lost my balance, I fell backwards, feeling the cold ice against my skin as my head slammed against it.

As soon as it happened, darkness consumed me, and I lost consciousness.

***

I awoke laying on a metal cot. Slowly, I sat up and discovered that I was shackled to the wall in a cell made of ice, which didn't come as a surprise to me. The door swung open, and Sixus stepped into the cell. He stopped before me. His eyes were still white with red rings around the edges. The disappointment flowed through the bond from my end.

"I haven't punished you since last year," Sixus sighed heavily. "Stay down here-"

"I need my baby," I panicked. "She's only one day old!"

"You should've thought about that before stabbing me," Sixus said in an icy voice. "I froze her and Cy in ice to keep them here with me."

"Let them go," I whispered. "I'll be your prisoner!"

"You already are," he whispered as his icy breath struck my face. "And so are they."

"What do you want from me, Sixus?" I cried out.

"Give me the location of the Nexus," he replied. "And I'll *think* about it."

"I can't remember." I shook my head. "Release our daughters!"

"Motivation," he said. "Be a good girl and I will let you come out of your cell."

"Fuck you!" I spat as I shook my head. "Put me in an eternal sleep!"

"I advise against that," Sixus replied. "Your heart will stop beating."

I lay down and covered myself up with the thick black comforter, and rested my head on the pillow.

Sixus sighed heavily as he walked towards the door and stepped out. He closed it and looked at it and walked away.

Once it fell silent, I blocked out his end of the bond.

"Spirit Guide *Naphirie?*"

I silently asked within my thoughts.

"Tell me, Oracle, would you prefer destruction or resurrection?"
She inquired.
"I request access to the 5D in order to find the Nexus."
I asked.
"I am now deploying the oracle to the 5D to locate the Nexus."
She answered.

The link fell silent, and I removed the block before I felt my soul be flung from my body as I lay unconscious in a coma.

The door to my cell broke off the hinges, and Sixus rushed into the room. He crouched down beside me and brushed his fingers against my neck. My pulse was present, but difficult to notice.

"Mel?" He touched my cheek. "What have I done?" His emotions were creeping to the surface, and he sobbed tears of ice. "Baby," he whispered. "I LOVE YOU!" He leaned forward and kissed me.

"Come back to me, Mel."
Sixus uttered those words in my thoughts.
"Our daughters need you... I need you... three worlds need you!"
His voice echoed loudly in my thoughts.

Sixus magic seal shot out of his body and merged with mine. They intertwined together and slammed back into our bodies. The force sent Sixus flying backwards, causing him to hit his back on the wall. He groaned as he slowly opened his eyes and gazed at my body. His eyes were back to the beautiful blue once more. He scrambled to his feet and rushed to my side. But by the time he made it to where I was, my body vanished.

"MEL!" Sixus shouted.

I felt his panic through the bond.

At least he was back to being a Half-Draconian again.

The long-awaited moment had arrived - the cure had finally proven its effectiveness.

EIGHTEEN

I took in my surroundings and realized I was in space. The stars twinkled all around me and I could feel them all pulsating around me like they were alive.

"Is this the 5D?"

I thought.

"Mel!" Sixus' voice spoke from directly behind me. Stunned, I spun around to find him floating in space with me. "I can't believe it worked?"

"Sixus?" I asked. "How did you find me?"

"I entered the 5D after you did," he shrugged. "I wasn't sure I'd find you in here."

"Your eyes," I pointed my index finger towards them. "They're so blue."

"I have something to tell you Mel," he grew nervous. "Don't get pissed, okay?"

"What is it?" I demanded.

"I've been altering my appearance to look like a Varacolaci," he whispered. "Showed me a trick after he revived me with the Holistic sword-"

I shoved him hard in the chest, making him fly backwards a bit. He flew back and was in my face now.

"Your such an asshole!" I hugged him tightly. "You must have some seriously strong shamanic abilities to pull that shit off."

"My parents trained me to blend in with my surroundings well," he agreed. "I'm sorry I deceived you." he whispered, his voice laced with guilt and sadness.

"Who is with the girls?" I asked, releasing him. "Get your ass back there now!"

"Okay," he breathed, giving me a quick kiss on my forehead before moving back. "Be careful in here."

He vanished, and I was alone.

Out of nowhere, I experienced a force that slammed my soul downwards, and I was returned to my body. My eyes shot open, and I gasped in surprise. I sat up and was lying on a metal cot with my wrists shackled. The metal burned my skin.

Timbrax stood before me, and I took in my surroundings. I was in a cell on the Victim ship. "I snatched your body while Sixus was knocked out in his ice castle," Timbrax smirked, announcing his actions. "What did you see?"

"Stars," I whispered. "Something thrust me back into my body, so I couldn't see anything past that." I paused. "I wasn't able to see anything past that since somebody made me come back."

"He didn't hurt you, did he?" Timbrax asked. His question totally caught me off guard as I threw him a strange look. "If he did, so help me-"

"No," I shook my head. "Since when do you give a shit about anything that goes on in my life, Brax?"

"Since always?" He threw me a confused look. "Especially since-"

He cut his words, shaking his head.

"What?" I asked gazing up at him. "You can tell me anything, remember?"

The door to my cell opened, and Orion entered the room. I felt the annoyance coming from Timbrax's end of the bond. He must have rebounded his soul to mine when I was in the 5D.

"Did you tell her the good news, Victim Commander?" Orion inquired with a genuine smile upon his face.

"I was about to," Timbrax rolled his eyes. "Before you barged in here."

"You found the Nexus?" I asked. "I should've known-"

"No," Timbrax frowned. "It's something... else."

"I'm exhausted," I sighed. "I need to eat and go to bed."

"Here's their pizza," Tasia gazed at me, then at my stomach. She handed it to Orion, who tossed it to Timbrax. He caught it and sat down beside me on the cot. He opened the box, and I grabbed an enormous slice of peperoni and took a bite. The flavors popped in my mouth, and I chewed it and swallowed. "Congratulations."

She turned and walked out of the room, followed by Orion, who closed the door behind them. I could hear them arguing outside instantly.

"The fucking Victim Commander knocked her up again!" Tasia shouted.

My eyes widened, and my head shot towards Timbrax, who sat quietly beside me. I set the half-eaten piece of pizza back in the box and wiped my hands on a paper napkin.

I heard pissed off footsteps marching towards the cell. The scent of cranberries mixed with snow and death reached my nose before I sensed the rage coming from Sixus' end of the bond. He entered the cell, and I saw his white eyes with red rings around the edges. He snarled at Timbrax, who slowly rose to his feet.

The two vampires started fighting, and Timbrax tossed the box of pizza onto the floor. Orion walked in and casually stepped over to me. He fished out a tiny key and unlocked my shackles. They dropped to the cot, and he pocketed the key. He grabbed me by the wrist, and I stood up. He led me out of the room, closing the door behind him and locking it.

"What are you doing?" I asked.

"They can keep their fight in there," Orion replied as he pocketed the key and pulled me up the hallway and into another room. He closed the door behind him. "Lay on the bed, Melfi."

I glanced around the room. It looked like an operating room. I cautiously walked over to the bed and lay down. Claus fastened my wrists to the metal table, and they stung me once more. He also fastened my feet.

Something was very wrong.

"SIXUS! BRAX!"

I screamed in my mind.

"MEL!"

Sixus yelled.

Claus placed a gas mask over my nose and mouth, and I held my breath, so I didn't breathe in whatever gas was in there. My lungs burned, and I gasped, sucking in the white gas. It was sleeping gas. I closed my eyes and blacked out.

***

I awoke to pain in my lower abdomen. My eyes fluttered open, and I saw Orion holding a black and pale blue egg in his hands. Blood dripped down his arms as he laughed triumphantly.

"We don't need you after all, Melfi," Orion said looking at me. "I have your Tribrid child!"

"NO!" I screamed as my pale blue flame exploded out of my body and melted the metal straps on my wrists and ankles.

With a powerful kick, the door was sent flying across the room and came crashing down with a noisy clatter. Timbrax and Sixus both raced inside. Sixus yanked out the Holistic sword and stabbed himself with it. The bright blue light flashed and temporarily blinded us before it disappeared. It healed my wound. But it started bleeding again. Sixus rushed to my side and touched my stomach. The ice flew into my skin through layers, and I screamed in pain before blacking out again.

***

I awoke feeling groggy. I could hear two males in the middle of a heated argument in my mind.

"That bastard killed my baby!"

Timbrax snarled.

"The unborn baby returned the power back into Mel's body!"

Sixus retorted.

"I'm gonna fucking kill them all!"

Timbrax screamed.

I fell back asleep and slipped back into a coma like state as my soul flew out of my body. I floated in space and Solas stood before me.

"That was a close one, wasn't it Mel?" He spoke.

"Aren't you gonna chastise me or something?" I asked. "I had sex with Timbrax in the astral thread before he altered the timeline."

"And that's why you were pregnant with his child," Solas nodded. "This baby's death will alter his perception and make him switch sides; you know?"

"Like one of these football bandwagon team jumpers?" I asked.

"Exactly," he nodded curtly. "I'm just here to make sure you haven't found the Nexus, Mel."

"I'm so sick and tired of hearing about this fucking Nexus!" I spat. "I don't see it out here in fucking space!"

"Good," Solas smirked. "It signifies that I am accomplishing my tasks effectively."

Something slammed me back into my body forcefully and I gasped as my eyes opened wide. I sat up and Sixus leaped to his feet from the chair he was sitting in. He was holding Hamani in his arms as he rocked her to sleep.

I reached out my hands, and he handed me our baby. I kissed her on the head, and she snuggled her head into my breasts. She searched for my boob, and Sixus quickly handed me a premed bottle. I popped the nipple into her tiny mouth, and she started sucking on it, drinking the formula.

"How are you feeling, Mel?" Sixus asked as he pressed a kiss upon my forehead. Concern flashed in his captivating blue eyes.

"My baby's dead," I whispered. "I'm worried about Brax."

"He's in the astral thread losing his everlasting mind," Sixus sighed heavily. "Nothing can calm him down, Mel."

"Shift," I mouthed to him. Sixus snapped his fingers and returned to being a Varacolaci. Timbrax had purposefully wiped his own memory of revealing that skill to Sixus. "Brax?"

The astral thread opened, and He stepped out. It closed behind him. He saw me holding Hamani, and I carefully handed her off to Sixus, who took her and exited the room.

"I couldn't save her," Timbrax whispered as he walked around the bed and sat down beside me. "I'm sorry we lost another child, Melfina."

As I comforted Brax, I tenderly placed my hand on his head, relishing the feel of his thick, dark hair between my fingers. "I'm here for you."

Sink or Swim played on his cell, and I gave him a sad smile.

"Why do you love me?" he asked.

"You're my Morally Grey husband," I replied bluntly. "I need a bad boy in my life."

He laughed lightly before growing serious once more.

"I'm gonna kill Orion and Claus," he whispered. "I won't allow them to hurt you, gorgeous."

"You know," I gave him a smile as I lightly laughed. "Sixus made an ice castle and knights made of ice if you wanna go make some friends."

"Time to make some new acquaintances," Timbrax stood and opened the astral thread as he threw out his hand. "Light em up!" He leaped through it, and it disappeared behind him.

The computerized female voice spoke from above my head.

I.O.A. has released Pilot Melfina. Have a great day!

The cords fell away from my body, and the needle pushed itself out of my arm. I watched it fall into a tiny white box that closed itself and tossed itself into a trashcan. Getting up, I tossed the hot blanket off my body and rose to my feet. Taking a seat, I slid my feet into the boots. After zipping them up, I stood. I walked out of the room and up the silent hallway.

I followed the scent of my newborn baby. The scent took me to the tranquility room. The doors slid open, and I stepped into the peaceful room that looked like a beautiful park back on Erda. Startled by the voices nearby, I hastily concealed myself behind an imposing stone statue of a mecha, its rough texture pressing against my back as the doors sealed shut.

"Sixus," Varric sighed, his annoyance evident in his voice. "Let Melfina know that there is no difference between you and Solas; you are essentially one person."

"Just like she and Nyx are the same person," Nell added, a hint of a smile playing on her lips. "Hey, dude, when do you think your ability to deceive her will reach its limit?"

"Who knows, Nell," Sixus replied, his voice carrying a faint trace of anger. "It was never intended for our two worlds to intertwine in such a way."

I discreetly adjusted my body to better tune in to their voices. With my shamanic abilities and training, I had honed my stealth skills to a level beyond ordinary comprehension. During the Flight Games, Sinergy's entry into my body brought a rush of Nyxie's memories flooding into my mind. No one else knew about it, as I decided not to tell a soul.

"Does she still have no idea where the Nexus is?" While Sixus cradled Hamani and patted her on the back, Varric posed a question, curious about the scene unfolding before him. "If she ever uncovers the secret, the consequences would be catastrophic - three planets would face annihilation."

"She won't," Sixus sighed, his voice heavy with resignation. "Not as long as all of us continue to erase her memories."

"We should get some sleep," A.J. yawned. "I'm exhausted."

"Get to bed," Sixus agreed. "I'll meet up with you all in the morning, got it?"

The three shamans nodded and walked up the path. I held my breath as they walked past the statue. The doors slid open, and they exited the room. Once the doors closed, I saw Sixus walking up the path, and I quietly exhaled as he stopped beside the sculpture. He kept his gaze fixed on the door as he patted our baby on her back.

"Come out, Mel," Sixus smirked. "I smelled your scent the moment you entered the tranquility room."

"Well, it seems I overestimated my stealthiness." I stood up, my face contorting into a frown. Our eyes locked as I looked up at him, and I could see a mixture of curiosity and concern in his expression. "You're an asshole."

"I know your scent anywhere, Mel," Sixus smirked as I stepped before him and faced him. "And so does Hamani."

"I'll stop searching for the Nexus," I whispered. "Timbrax is destroying your ice kingdom, by the way."

"Seriously?" Sixus arched an eyebrow. "I can always rebuild it just to piss him off later."

I smirked as we walked together out of the room. The doors slid open, and we walked up the hallway. Our boots clicked off the silent walls. He handed Hamani to me, and I held her tightly against my body. The doors to my dorm room opened, and we entered. They closed behind us. She closed her eyes and fell asleep quickly. I walked over to her crib that was across the room and carefully lay her down, covering her up with her pink blanket.

"We make beautiful babies, don't we?" Sixus whispered as he stood beside me.

"Yeah," I gave him a sad smile. "Too bad three of them are dead."

"I'm sorry I kept fucking with your mind," he sighed. "I'm terrified of losing you, Mel."

"What happened to us, Sixus?" I asked.

"After Claus ended your existence," Sixus whispered solemnly. "In the wake of Solas' suicide on Erda, I unexpectedly assumed his position, now overseeing the shamans on Erda Mel."

"I figured as much," I sighed heavily as I rested my heavy head against his chest. "That's why Claus is still hellbent on killing me, isn't it?"

"Yup," Sixus sighed. "Their souls are a part of us now, Mel."

"When I went back and time traveled," I started. "That nearly exposed the Nexus's location, didn't it?"

"Yeah," he agreed. "After I figured out what was going on after reading your books, I snapped into action and altered events here."

Sixus quickly shifted back into his Varacolaci form, and I turned in time to see Timbrax leap into the room from the astral thread. He had unbound his soul from us when I was in I.O.A. My intuition let me know he was back to being my enemy.

"That was fun," Timbrax sighed as Sixus turned to face him with an annoyed look on his face. "You need to create more ice soldiers so I can kill em."

"Maybe another time," Sixus replied bluntly. "For now, you need to go back to the Victim ship and deal with your asshole brother-in-law."

"Last I checked," Timbrax narrowed his eyes at him. "*I'm* your Victim Commander, remember?"

"Like I listen to your ass." Sixus rolled his eyes at him. "Melfina needs to rest after losing *another* child, don't you think?"

"She *did* rest," Timbrax snarled. "She's coming back with me, got it?"

"Her baby needs her here," Sixus pointed out. "Half-Draconian's need to bond with their mothers-"

"Bullshit!" Timbrax snapped, taking a step towards him. "Her mother gave birth to her, then left after five minutes to return here."

"She didn't bond with me at all?" I whispered to myself.

"Hey," Sixus snapped his fingers in front of me to snap me out of my thoughts. "Pull it together, Mel."

I winced as the marking on my wrist throbbed with a sharp, stinging sensation. As I lifted my jacket sleeve, I glimpsed its iridescent, blue-violet shimmer. The institute quaked violently, causing objects to rattle and walls to creak.

I could sense a tremendous power building up inside, struggling to unleash itself. It was a constant battle, trying to keep it contained within the confines of my mind.

"Fuck!" Sixus snarled as he ran over and placed his hands on my shoulders. "Don't!" He snarled, and I snapped out of the power struggle. The ground stopped shaking and everything fell silent and still.

"What the fuck was that?" Timbrax demanded.

"She's unstable," Sixus scoffed, glancing back at him. "Leave. NOW!"

"I'll be back!" Timbrax spat as he stepped inside the astral thread. "You know something... and I'm gonna figure it out!" It closed behind him.

We sighed in relief.

"Thank the dragons," Sixus whispered as he dropped the Varacolaci glamor. "You gotta gain control over your shamanic abilities, Mel."

I nodded as he hugged me tightly.

That power nearly destroyed the institute.

I wondered what else it could destroy.

Sadly, I was on the verge of uncovering the truth.

NINETEEN

I awoke to hear Hamani crying. My eyes shot open, and I sat up. Sixus groaned from beside me as the light turned on by motion. He buried his head beneath the pillow and fell back asleep. I slapped him hard on the shoulder and kicked off the hot comforter. Once I climbed over his body, I stood on the floor. I turned, shocked to find Timbrax holding Hamani in his arms. He was feeding her as she fell silent and drank the formula from the bottle.

"What are you doing?" As I walked over to him, I whispered. I reached for Hamani, but he pulled back, shaking his head at me.

"I didn't get to do this for any of my kids," he whispered back. He glanced over my shoulder and found Sixus sleeping. He arched an eyebrow at him, then looked back at me. "You turned him back into a Half-Draconian?"

"Yeah," I shrugged. I had to keep Sixus' secret hidden from Brax. "He needs to parent his daughters too, you know?"

"I guess," Timbrax mumbled as he handed Hamani to me. "Wake your ass up and parent your kid's dragon!" Hamani squirmed at him, raising his voice, and I threw him a look, telling him to shut the hell up. "Sorry."

"You know," Sixus growled as he shoved the comforter off his body and climbed to his feet. He narrowed his eyes at Timbrax, who didn't seem to give any fucks. "You need to get your ass back to that Victim ship and stay your ass there!"

"I was in the astral thread," Timbrax snapped. "As soon as I heard your baby crying, I came over, changed her diaper, and was feeding her when Melfina woke up!"

"Thank you?" Sixus said as he carefully took Hamani from my arms and removed the bottle from her mouth as she finished it. Placing it on my desk, Sixus gently patted her back as he turned her to burp her.

"Don't look at me like that," Timbrax rolled his eyes at us. "I'm not gonna hurt your baby, you got that?"

"That's good to know," Sixus murmured under his breath, not taking his eyes off Timbrax. "What do you want now?"

"I don't feel so good," I said as I suddenly felt sick. "I need a mouth guard."

"You can't keep the plasma down in those things, remember?" Timbrax reminded me as he held his arm out to me. "Drink my blood."

"Your blood is poison to her, remember?" Sixus reminded him. "She's not drinking that toxic shit!"

Alarms sounded around the institute, and Sixus and I snapped into action. The doors opened and Cy rushed into the room with the shaman, Zara, Tork, Darby, Velzy and Rhydian and Exley with them. Sixus handed Hamani off to Cy, and she and the shaman females both ran out of the room, accompanied by Darby.

I tapped into my vampire speed, as did Sixus. We got dressed and had our weapons strapped onto our bodies, and I even pinned my hair up before Timbrax attacked us.

"She needs to feed!" Velzy shouted to Rhydian as she and Tork pulled their weapons and started shooting at Timbrax, who flipped backwards and out onto the balcony.

"I got her!" Exley called as he grabbed me by the arm and led me into the bathroom. He removed his trench coat and thrust his arm towards me. "Drink it!"

I grabbed it and sank my sharp fangs into his flesh. He grimaced but stayed still as I gulped his blood down. Satisfied, I removed my fangs, dropping his arm.

"Thanks," I said as I wiped his blood from my jaw with the back of my hand. "I'm feeling-"

As if struck by lightning, my chest constricted and a powerful surge of energy pulsated through me. A sense of unease hung in the air - something was definitely wrong.

"Get Sixus!" I ordered. "Hurry!"

Exley nodded as he raced out of the room. A black magic seal appeared and surrounded me. I slammed into the wall of the ball of darkness, but it didn't budge.

"I've grown tired of your little games, Universal Shamanic Queen," Claus said as he stood before me. "You are going to lead me to the location of the Nexus now!"

He used his powers, and a hand formed inside of the ball I was stuck in. It reached out and grabbed me by the throat. With fingers crooked, it choked the air out of me. He walked out of the bathroom and past Sixus, who caught sight of me. He walked out of the French doors and stood beside Timbrax, who held the astral thread open.

"Everyone hold your fire!" Sixus shouted and the vampire hunters held their weapons pointed towards Claus and Timbrax, who used me as a shield. "Let her go Claus!"

"I'm disappointed in you, Shamanic King of Light," Claus replied, glaring at Sixus. "You weren't meant to commit suicide, were you?"

"You weren't supposed to kill my wife ether," Sixus spat. "But here we are, aren't we?"

"I'm going to kill her again," Claus smirked. "Once she revealed the location of the Nexus to me... I have no more use for her."

"Stop it!" Timbrax snarled as he glanced over at Claus. "You've made your fucking point!"

"You've grown soft on us Victim Commander," Orion spoke from beside Claus. "You get to have your fun toying with her emotions before we kill her, remember?"

"Sixus. I will always choose you!"

I yelled in my mind.

"MEL!" Sixus snarled as his shamanic powers shot out of his body. He formed a thick icicle in his fist and flicked it towards the black energy ball. It stuck and froze the black ball. The hand gripping my throat froze, and I felt the coldness instantly. Sixus leaped forward, punching it. It shattered on impact. I gasped as I fell. He caught me and walked quickly backwards into the room. "Shoot them!"

Tork, Exley, Velzy, and Zara aimed at the three men, and they ran into the astral thread. It closed behind them.

"Are you alright Mel?" Sixus breathed as he gazed down at me with deep concern in his beautiful blue eyes.

"What's wrong with me, Sixus?" I asked. "That power is terrifying!"

"Whatever you do," he whispered in my ear. "Do *not* let it out!" I nodded as he pressed a kiss on my forehead. He held me as we turned to face the others. Varric wore a look of concern on his face as he gazed at me. "Don't say a damn thing," Sixus ordered, giving him a warning look. "We keep the Nexus protected at all costs, got it?"

I felt the energy tugging inside of me. Sixus felt it and he drew a magic seal in the air, and it flew onto my collarbone. The energy stilled within my body, and I breathed in relief.

"We're not trained to deal with shamanic activities," Tork shouted as Velzy and Rhydian ran out onto the balcony and leaped off. A moment later, the alarm fell silent. "This is out of our jurisdiction, Sixus."

"I know," he agreed. "Your job is to shoot Victim, and we kill them once they turn into demons. Got it?"

My intuition kicked in, alerting me that danger was near. I turned and ran out of Sixus' protective arms. I ran to the balcony and flexed my back muscles. My pale blue dragon wings exploded out, and I climbed onto the cement railing. I kicked off it and flapped my wings.

"Mel!" Sixus called after me. I ignored him as I headed towards the dragon mountain. Or at least the cave that was near it.

"What do you think you're doing?"

Sixus shouted in my mind.

"Leading Claus away from our girls!"

I replied in my mind.

I flew onto a mountain and caught my breath. A moment later, I felt someone kick me hard in the back, sending me flying into a large bolder. Pain shot through my left side as I struggled to climb to my feet. I snarled as I turned my head and saw Claus, Largo, Timbrax, and Orion standing there.

"Let's play you Tribrid bitch!" Largo laughed as his red eyes narrowed at me. "You are so dead for that shit you pulled!"

"And here I thought stabbing you would've shut you the fuck up," I spat as I stood. "Guess I gotta stab you again!"

"You know the location of the Nexus," Claus replied calmly. "Just tell me where it is so I can kill you mercifully."

"Go to hell!" I spat as I yanked the Valistik sword out and stood in a defensive stance. "I ain't telling you a damn thing!"

Largo ran towards me, and I ran the blade through his abdomen. He pushed himself straight through it as he reached me. The hilt of the blade was touching his skin. He laughed maniacally as Timbrax walked over and yanked him off the sword, tossing him behind him. Largo's blood dripped off the blade onto the dirt beneath our feet.

I made a face in pure disgust as I watched Largo heal himself. He climbed back to his feet and Orion put his arm out, keeping him where he stood.

"We've thrown everything we can at you," Timbrax whispered. "All of this was meant to break you down!"

"Oh, you broke me down," I laughed dryly as he handed me a red cloth. I took it and wiped Largo's disgusting blood off my blade before tossing it at him. He glanced down at it as it fell to the dirt before meeting my gaze again. "Especially after you killed my babies!"

The sound of the astral thread opening behind me made Timbrax's eyes shift. He growled protectively deep in his throat as the scent of cranberries mixed with snow and death struck my nose.

"Do you know?" Sixus spoke in a low voice as the astral thread closed. "Shifting from one form to another on a dime is damn difficult!" he murmured.

I spun around to face him. His eyes were back to being white with red rings around the edges. He gazed down at me with annoyance in his eyes before he shifted his gaze back up to Timbrax.

"Then stop fucking shifting into your other forms, you stupid jackass!" Timbrax snarled. "We've worked far too hard for our plans to fall apart now!"

The look on my face made everyone around me take notice.

"How could I have been so fucking stupid?"

I thought.

"You know," Largo laughed. "For being the oracle... you sure are an idiot, aren't you, Melfina?"

"She knows nothing," Orion grumbled. "Both Sixus and the Victim Commander have been wiping her mind, causing her to be defective to us."

"We made her *think* she was purifying Sixus blood," Claus spoke up. "When in reality all she was doing was contaminating it even further for us by injecting him with the Victim Commander's blood."

"All of you can fuck off and die in a hole!" I spat as I stormed off and sat on a large bolder, keeping my back towards them.

As if by magic, a vivid and ethereal vision unfolded in the depths of my mind, leaving me spellbound.

Timbrax would consistently manifest from the astral thread whenever I utilized Sixus' blood, deftly replacing the tubes carrying Sixus' blood with his own lethal Varacolaci blood before promptly dissolving into the astral realm.

The vivid vision disappeared in an instant.

"I'm surprised you let her keep that Half-Draconian baby," Largo laughed maniacally. "I say we kill it!"

"You touch my kid," Sixus spoke in a scary, calm voice. "And I'll freeze your fucking body and send it out into space in a thousand tiny pieces!"

"Damn," Largo laughed again. "I propose we appoint the dragon king as the new Victim Commander, replacing Timbrax," he said, pausing for effect. "He's way more mentally unstable than you!"

"And I will burn you for all eternity," Timbrax spat. "Fuck off Largo!"

Sixus walked over and stood beside me. I kept my gaze fixed downwards. I still couldn't wrap my mind around the fact that all of them had been fucking with me mentally, emotionally, and physically this entire time.

"Did Solas really commit suicide?" I asked in a quiet voice.

"Yeah," Sixus replied. "He passed his powers onto me just as Nyxie did for you, Mel."

"So," I went on. "You've been a Varacolaci this entire time, haven't you?"

"I have," he nodded in agreement. "This darkness is addicting," he laughed in amazement. "How do you deny yourself of such power?"

"When it's all I've known for most of my life," I shrugged. "You end up hating it and yearn for the light."

"What the hell are we doing?" Largo shouted to us. "I'm ready to kill more dragon knights!"

"We're waiting!" Sixus shouted to him.

"For what?" Timbrax demanded as he stormed his way over towards us. "I told you, we've wasted enough time, damn it!"

They started arguing and fighting. I sighed heavily and slid off the rock. I walked over towards the edge of the mountain and just stared up at the stars.

"You sense it, don't you?" Claus asked as he walked over to me.

"It's out there," I nudged my head towards space. "I can find it in the Aeon Dra."

"So, find it," Claus ordered. "Deploy your mecha and pinpoint the location of the Nexus."

"On it Bossman." I waved him off. As I kicked off the mountain and flew back towards the institute.

"If you pull anything, Mel," Sixus shouted over the roar of the wind as he quickly caught up to me. "I *will* kill our daughter!"

"You know what?" I shouted at him. "I'm tired of your shit!"

He placed a hand on my shoulder, and I snarled, shrugging him off. I threw my hand out and opened the astral thread. I flew through it, as did he. It closed behind us, and I flew through the other side. The hanger where the mechas were held was where I ended up. A moment later, Sixus joined me. He stood in his Half-Draconian form.

I trotted up the metal steps leading to the platform. My boots echoed off the silent walls. I stood in front of the Aeon Dra. I stepped through the thick green gel door and fell inside. The thick black cords wrapped themselves around my body and the lights turned on.

The cool, computerized female voice spoke from inside the deity.

"Pilot Melfina has been given clearance to leave by I.O.A."

The voice fell silent.

The Aeon Dra moved towards the platform and stood ready to go.

The voice spoke again.

"Ready to launch in 5... 4... 3... 2... 1... GO!"

The doors were open, and Sixus shot out the Aeon Dra at G Force speed. I flew through space, and I calmed my racing heart down by taking deep breaths. The Flight Games still left me feeling traumatized by being out here.

"Mel," Sixus' voice spoke through the intercom. "Can you hear me?"

"Yeah," I replied. "You're coming in clear."

"Good," Sixus replied. "I want you-"

"You can fuck off!" I replied. I pressed the off button, and the speaker fell silent.

"Mel, what the hell are you doing?"

Sixus yelled in my mind.

I ignored him by placing the block up. His end fell silent, and I breathed a sigh of relief. I only had a moment to do what needed to be done.

"Spirit Guide Naphirie?"

I thought.

"What would you like to destroy or revive oracle?"

Naphirie asked in my mind.

"*I want you to go back to the point of time right before Claus killed Nyxie. Keep Sixus from being killed and turned into a Varacolaci.*"

I asked.

"*It is done. Is there anything else you would like to destroy or revive oracle?*" Naphirie asked.

"Make sure Solas kills Claus before he can find and activate the Nexus! That is all Naphirie."

I spoke.

"*It is done. Until next time, oracle.*"

Naphirie fell silent.

I closed my eyes and when I opened them, I was standing on the lawn of the institute, holding the shamanic dagger in my hand. Sixus and the others looked around with confusion on their faces.

Nyxie stood with Solas and the shamans. They knew exactly what was going to happen if they didn't protect their queen from the Dark Shamanic Prince.

Claus aimed his dark magic seal towards Nyxie. I used my vampire speed and shoved her out of the way, making her fly into Solas who caught her pulling her tightly into his body. The giant black birdcage surround me instead as it lifted me higher into the air.

I saw the thick metal spikes peeking out from the inside of the bars. I prepared myself for the pain as soon as the spikes flew towards me. They slammed into my body, and I screamed in pain as they flew back into the metal bars.

"MEL!" Sixus shouted as he froze the metal, and it shattered into tiny ice crystals below us. I fell backwards as he caught me. My dagger clattered to the ground.

"You were supposed to kill the Shamanic Queen of Light!" Timbrax snarled. "Not my wife!"

"I don't understand?" As his magic seal shot back into his body, Claus found himself confused. "I aimed for *her*!" He pointed his index finger towards Nyxie.

"Retreat!" Orion shouted. "The plan got fucked up, Claus!"

"Not you!" Solas growled as he leaped at Claus, knocking him down to the ground. He raised his dagger and brought it down, piercing him in the heart. "That's for killing my wife, you fucking Spellbinder!"

"You think you've won Shamanic King of Light?" Claus laughed maniacally. "To activate the Nexus, we need the blood of a royal Half-Draconian, vampire, and a shaman!"

"What?" Solas asked as he yanked the dagger out of his chest. He scrambled to his feet and ran back to the shamans. He pulled Nyxie back into his body.

"The Tribrid is going to unleash hell upon three planets!" Claus went on. "All I needed was her... blood to unlock the... door."

He took one final breath and died. I watched as his soul exited his body. Using a Dybbuk box, Nyxie captured and stored his soul and Phyre's souls. She slammed the doors shut and sealed it with hot wax and shamanic symbols to keep them inside.

"We're taking his body back to earth to burn it," Solas said as Varric moved over and picked up the corpse. His green light flashed, and they ran into it. "Keep her safe, Sixus!" Solas turned and raced into the light before it disappeared, and they were gone.

I noticed Timbrax, and the others were gone, leaving us to deal with the aftermath of the dead. I touched my stomach and moved my hand back, revealing scarlet blood.

"You're gonna be okay, Mel," Sixus whispered as he picked me up in his arms. "I promise."

Ignoring his misguided opinion, I closed my eyes and instantly plunged into a void of absolute darkness.

The future seemed dark and uncertain.

And I was the one responsible for all of it.

TWENTY

I awoke laying in my bed in my dorm room. I turned my head and found Sixus sitting in the wooden chair, lost in thought. He felt my gaze and lifted his head. His beautiful blue eyes met mine, and I sat up and pulled him into a tight hug. I ignored the pain that throbbed in my limbs.

"Baby," Sixus held me tightly, and I shook my head. I didn't wanna look at him. The thought of him turning back into a Varacolaci scared the shit outta me. "I'm not... that guy in the alternative timeline."

"You died protecting me," I whispered. "In order to transform you back into your current form, I had to go back in time by two years and obtain a sample of your blood." I sighed lightly. "Timbrax's sinister plan involved gradually replacing your blood with his own, leaving you craving the darkness. I had no choice but to return and protect you from this fate, Sixus."

"No wonder why you're so terrified," he held me as I started trembling. "The shamans need to talk to you, Mel."

I shoved the hot comforter off my body, and I stood. Sixus slipped my feet into my boots and zipped them up before standing.

The doors slid open, and the four shamans walked right up to me. The doors closed, and I waited for them to yell at me.

"You," Solas spoke gently. "Saved us?"

"I went against the Shamanic code," I said. "But I was not about to let Claus win!"

"At least she admits to her mistakes," Varric murmured under his breath. "She's on the right track."

"You saw what the Nexus is, didn't you?" Solas asked me.

"Almost?" I shrugged.

"What does it matter?" Sixus asked. "Claus is dead."

"The Victim Commander," Solas replied casually. "Is going to be the one to force the Tribrid to open the door to the Nexus."

"Can Nyxie seal my powers?" I asked them. "I'd give them to her, but she'd have to kill me-"

Without a word, Nyxie's hand moved with precision as she grabbed her dagger and mercilessly thrust it into my chest.

A surge of shock overcame me as she delved into my body, retrieving my powers. I watched as the pale blue light entered her body, disappearing without a trace.

"What the fuck are you doing?" As Sixus growled, he forcefully pressed a thick layer of ice into my chest, sealing the wound with a chilling sensation.

"Taking back what belongs to us," Solas replied, the sound of his dagger piercing Sixus' neck echoing through the room. With a swift motion, he unleashed his powers, feeling them surge into his body as a dazzling blue light flickered and faded away. "Let's go!" he said, his voice filled with excitement.

He opened the blue portal, and they ran into it. A moment later, it vanished.

Sixus pulled the Holistic sword out and stabbed me in the arm. The bright blue light flashed before it disappeared.

"Mel," Sixus placed the Holistic sword back in the sheath and pulled me into his arms. "Talk to me, babe."

"I'm kicking her ass," I spat as I shook my head. "I'm guessing I'm not a Tribrid anymore."

"That's a blessing in disguise," Sixus said as he helped me up to my feet as he stood. "Fuck those shamans!"

When I glanced at my desk, I was taken aback to find the two books I had written resting on it. I tilted my head and Sixus turned and noticed them as well.

"I'm curious about what else managed to survive in our timeline," he asked me. "Aren't you?"

"There were four babies," I whispered. "Did any of them survive?"

"Don't know?" Sixus shrugged. "Wanna look in the dragon sanctuary and find out?"

I threw my hand out, and the astral thread opened. We leaped through it and ended up in the nursery of the dragon sanctuary. We cautiously walked up the first row, not expecting to find anything. I was right. All the eggs were normal. I couldn't help but feel disappointed. Sixus gave me a sad smile and hugged me with one arm.

"I was hoping," I sighed heavily. "That at least one of our babies survived."

Two of the eggs at the end of the row lit up with my pale blue flame. Sixus and I both stood there in shock as they cracked open and the magic seals from our shamanic abilities shot back into our bodies. We fell to the gourd, and I ended up falling on top of him. He held me protectively in his arms as he sat up. Slowly climbing to our feet, we raced out of the room and up the hallway. He shoved open one of the heavy glass doors and we ran outside, stopping dead in our tracks when we saw Varric and A.J. standing before us. Something was different about their energy.

"What happened?" I asked them. "Why are you guys back here?"

"We just came to tell you both that Nyxie and Solas were killed when we returned to earth," Varric casually said. "We're devastated."

"Utterly," A.J. placed a hand over her chest. "Devastated."

"Do you know who killed them?" I asked.

"We have an idea," Varric and A.J. exchanged glances with each other before they pulled their other hands out from behind their backs. My eyes widened in shock as each one held up the corpse of Nyx and Solas by the hair before them. Their T-shirts were soaked in blood, which dripped onto the ground beneath them. "Us."

"What the fuck?" I whispered, as my shock turned to rage. "Why?"

"We grew tired of being second best to these two," Varric sighed as they tossed their corpses to the ground with such disrespect for their slayed royals. "So, we killed them and absorbed their powers."

"You're looking at the new shamanic power couple," A.J. smirked at me as she flipped her long, dark hair across her shoulder. "But your powers seem to have vanished." She sighed heavily. "So, we came to collect them, too."

"So, it was you two this whole time?" I said, a mix of surprise and realization in my voice. "You've been the Spellbinders, manipulating the timelines and cleverly shifting blame onto Claus to divert our attention."

"You are sluggish, aren't you, Tribrid?" As she examined her perfectly manicured fingernails, painted a vibrant shade of red, A.J. asked. "Indeed, Varric and I, the mischievous Spellbinders, have been orchestrating this elaborate wild goose chase for our own entertainment."

"Enough talk," Varric spat as he stepped on Solas's body and stood before Sixus. "Let's kill them and take their powers, A.J."

"I've been waiting to kill this bitch," A.J. laughed as she too stepped on Nyxie's corpse and stood before me as she pulled out her dagger. "You popped my shoulder out of place, and I really hate being hurt in fights!"

As Sixus and I drew our daggers, my blade ignited with a pale blue flame, lending an ethereal glow to the weapon. With A.J. charging towards me, I swiftly flipped over her head, landing a powerful kick to her back that sent her flying forward.

In a swift motion, she flipped, abruptly stopping herself in mid-air, and then swiftly resumed her charge towards me. The sound of her slashing the air above my head echoed through the room as I quickly leaned back to avoid getting hit.

"Why won't you fucking die?" A.J. screamed as her rage boiled to the surface.

"I did," I replied as I stood back up. "Twice."

"I died once myself," Sixus chuckled to himself, pissing off Varric. "Surprise, bitch!" Sixus formed thick icicles in his fist and threw them at him.

In an attempt to ward it off, Varric swung his left arm, but the ice quickly seized his arm, turning it into a frozen statue. Varric's pained screams filled the air as he brought his frantic sprint to a sudden halt, allowing Sixus to unleash his awe-inspiring dragon speed. As Sixus balled his hand into a fist, he unleashed a devastating blow, instantly shattering Varric's arm complex.

Varric winced in pain as his blood dripped from his arm, causing tiny shards of ice to scatter onto the ground. With seconds ticking away, Sixus sprang into action, desperately trying to save Varric's life. Thinking on his feet, he quickly placed thick layers of ice into the wound, creating a makeshift clot that would hopefully keep him alive until he could reach medical attention in I.O.A.

"VARRIC!" A.J.'s scream pierced the air, causing her to quickly dash to his side. As my dagger connected with the left side of her face, I could feel the resistance of skin and bone, leaving a trail of blood in its wake. Her flesh sizzled and her scream reverberated in the air as my flame scorched her. In a frenzy, she rolled around in the dirt, her screams echoing through the air. "It fucking burns!"

Picking her up, Orion swiftly flew back in the direction from which he had come. A.J.'s screams persisted until they gradually vanished into silence.

Varric reached for his dagger with his one arm that was still intact when Sixus kicked it away. He bent down and pocketed it just as the hunters ran up the hill to meet us.

"The fuck happened here?" Velzy asked looking at the dead shaman royals laying on the ground.

"Varric Rake and A.J. Battle murdered them," I said as I put my dagger back into the sheath in unison with Sixus. "Orion took A.J. before you got here."

"What do we do with him?" Tork asked as she pulled Varric up by the back of his shirt collar.

"Get him medical attention," Sixus replied. "We'll figure out what to do after that."

"Let's go." Tork grabbed him by his good arm and dragged him down the hill with a group of vampire hunters. "See you back at the institute."

"What are we going to do about them?" Velzy asked, looking at the bodies. "We can't just leave them like this."

"Have the vampires drain them of their blood," Sixus said. "We'll talk to Nell and see if she's not on Varric and A.J.'s side and go from there."

Velzy and Rhydian both picked up their corpses and carried them down the hill, leaving Sixus and me to deal with the aftermath of the pointless bloodshed.

***

After the surprise attack on us, Sixus went to deal with Varric, following our conversation with Nell. Thankfully, she wasn't in on their plans. She was mourning the loss of her shaman royals.

I showered and changed into a clean double-sided uniform and just finished pinning my hair up when the doors opened and Sixus entered my dorm room.

"Judging by the pissy look on your face," I said. "It didn't go well with Varric, did it?"

"Not at all." Sixus shook his head, sighing heavily. I could feel his rage pouring through his end of the bond. "He's obsessed with bringing out the fucking Nexus."

"We should let the shamans punish him back on Erda," I sighed. "The murders occurred down there, anyway."

"As of right now," Sixus frowned. "We're the only shaman rulers representing both Erda and Tellus Mel."

"So, what do we do then?" I asked.

"We have him put to death in the arena," Sixus replied. "And have Nell broadcast it live to the shamans on Erda."

"The punishment fits the crime," I agreed. "I didn't expect to watch more murders in the arena."

"We'll catch Orion, A.J., Timbrax, Tasia, Largo and Victim." Sixus gave me a sad smile. "You don't have to dress up just in case they decide to make an appearance to rescue Varric from death."

"They are responsible for deaths here, Sixus," I whispered. "I hope the dragons kill them all for killing our babies!"

"The murders of royal dragons is punishable by death," Sixus agreed. "And that's exactly what they are all going to receive."

The doors slid open and Velzy entered, accompanied by Cy and Nell. "The prisoner wants a word with Melfina," Velzy frowned. "I don't think it's a good idea, Sixus."

"I'll go with her," Sixus said. "I don't trust that one armed fuck after the shit he pulled earlier."

"He wants to speak to her *alone*," Velzy added. "He said it's important."

"Take me to the prisoner then," I said as I tapped into my vampire speed and put my weapons on my body and my two jackets. "I'm prepared for anything now."

"Are you?" Sixus asked, keeping his face unreadable. His emotions I felt. He experienced feelings of anger and anxiety, knowing that Varric was planning to kill me, and he could not reach me.

"I have to be." I pulled him by the collar of his shirt and inhaled his scent. Cranberries mixed with snow. It was intoxicating. "You trained me, remember?"

Sixus bent his head and crushed his lips against mine. He growled protectively deep in his throat as I closed my eyes and returned his kiss before breaking it. I slowly opened my eyes and released him. I regained my composure before following Velzy. The doors opened, and we stepped out into the hallway. We walked in silence as we entered the main area. It was completely empty. Rhydian was holding the door open for us as we reached him. I stepped outside and found a large group of vampire hunters standing there.

I trotted down the steps, and Velzy led the way around the building. A male hunter held open the door for us. We walked down the staircase, my metal boots sticking to the steps as we descended downwards. We stopped at the first cell. She unlocked it and pulled open the door. I glanced at her and she nodded curtly at me. I took a deep breath before stepping inside. She closed the door behind me.

Varric sat on the cot with his one arm shackled to the wall. They shackled his legs to prevent him from moving.

"I didn't think you'd come." He raised his head and met my gaze evenly. "You know you're gonna kill everyone, don't you?"

I stayed near the door, not wanting to get any closer to him. That's when I saw it. The dark energy had overpowered his light essence. I turned to leave when his words stopped me.

"I met your father when you were living on earth two years ago," he said, making me turn and look at him. "He's the one who told us about you and your Half-Draconian powers."

"What did you just say?" I asked, as I turned around and walked closer to him.

"He told us to monitor you," Varric smirked. "I got A.J. to help me, and Solas and Nyx didn't suspect a thing."

"Why are you telling me this?" I demanded.

"I'm getting ready to be killed in the arena for all of this shit," Varric shrugged. "We met with the Victim Commander back then, too."

"What?" I asked.

"Did you know that Timbrax and A.J. are *actually* married?" He chuckled, his voice dripping with amusement, saying, "You aren't special to him, you know?"

"Shut up!" I spat as my rage boiled over. "I don't wanna hear any more of this shit!"

"He used you in order to turn you into a Tribrid," Varric smirked. "There's one more person your father brought into the fold."

"Who?" I demanded.

"Someone who travels to Outer Earth and earth," he laughed. "By the time you figure out who they are... it'll be too late."

"I hope the dragons burn your eyes and tongue off," I spat as I turned to leave. "Or *I'll* do it for them!" I pounded my fist on the door and Velzy opened it. I stepped out, and she shut it.

"Are you okay?" Velzy asked as she led me up the steps. I pushed my way past her and breathed in the fresh air.

Sixus and the others stood there waiting for me. I ran into his arms, and he pulled me tightly into his body. He had heard everything since he was also an oracle. I felt his rage boiling over with my own.

"Transport the prisoner to the arena," Sixus ordered the hunters. "Execution by the dragons is imminent."

"Yes, King Sixus." Tork turned and looked at the hunters she led. "Transport the prisoner to the arena for execution!"

I watched as they turned and headed back down the steps I had just come up from. All of this shit happened right under my nose, and I was still pissed, hurt, and frustrated at myself for allowing it. They waited two years to put their plan into motion and each had a part to play in it.

Setha held out her hand and the astral thread appeared. We leaped through it and emerged standing in the arena of the royal balcony.

"I would like to stay here and become your new repairer," Nell said to Sixus and I. "I need to stay and guard the new Universal Shamanic Queen Melfina and King Sixus and Princess Cy with my life on Tellus."

"It would be our honor to have you as our new repairer Eleanor Nightingale," I smiled as I gave her a hug. "I offer my deepest condolences for the loss of your former king and queen." I said sympathetically.

"Thank you, Mel," Nell manifested a box of tissues and took one and dabbed at her eyes with it. Nell expressed her grief, saying, "My best friend was killed, and I miss her so much."

I released her as she and Cy pulled out a cell phone and got it ready for the execution to be livestreamed for the shaman on Erda to watch. The arena filled up with mecha pilots, assassins, and dragon knights sitting in their designated seats. The hunters brought Varric into the center of the arena, shackling his legs, arm and neck so he was stuck to the tall, thick metal pole. They turned and walked off, disappearing into the tunnel.

Nell's cell was poised in her hand as Sixus gave the signal, and with a quick press of the record button, the livestream commenced. "We are gathered here today," Sixus shouted, his voice echoing through the silent crowd. "To witness the public execution of the Shaman Guardian Varric Rake!" he paused briefly, the anticipation in the air palpable. "In a horrifying act, he and the shaman Angelina Battle plotted the assassination of the Shaman King of Light Evan Reigns, the Shamanic Queen of Light Nyxie Reigns, myself, my daughter, my wife Melfina, and all of you gathered here today!"

The crowd erupted into loud boos as Sixus quieted them down.

"Does the prisoner have any last words before being executed by the dragons?" Sixus shouted. Varric flipped him off with his hand behind his back, staying silent. "Bring in the dragons!" Sixus shouted. "And may the dragons have mercy on your soul... because we sure the fuck don't!"

From high above, the dragons swooped down, their massive bodies thudding against the earth as they landed. The sheer force of the impact reverberated through the entire arena. Surrounding him, they let out menacing growls that reverberated through the air.

TRIBRID NEXUS

As one, the dragons telepathically transmitted a single word into our minds, leaving us in awe.

"Guilty!"

The menacing sound of their growls filled the air.

Their mouths opened, and I could see the fiery glow illuminating their faces, while the heat engulfed me before they let it out. The dragon's fiery breaths converged into a powerful conflagration. Above the crackling flames, I distinctly heard Varric's voice, shouting something instead of pleading for his life.

"The Tribrid will destroy the worlds!" Varric shouted. "You can't stop the Nexus from killing you all!"

As the dragons closed their mouths, they ascended into the air, their powerful wings carrying them swiftly towards the dragon sanctuary.

My heart sank as I turned and saw Varric's body, the smell of burned flesh filling the air. The stench of singed flesh overwhelmed my nostrils, causing me to recoil in disgust. The moment unfolded before my eyes: the release of the blue shamanic seal, its speedy trajectory towards Sixus, and then the sudden appearance of an astral thread. Timbrax, with unwavering courage, leaped in front of it, bearing the full force of its collision.

"Sorry," Timbrax's voice dripped with bitterness as he turned to face us, his figure silhouetted against the stone ledge. "Was that meant for *you*?"

The sound of his evil laughter filled the air as he leaped back through the astral thread. With a final click, Nell ended the livestream just as the thread closed behind him, effectively cutting off the feed.

"We have a major problem on our hands," Nell said, and we turned to look at her. "The Shamanic King of Light and Shamanic Queen of Light's powers are in the bodies of our enemies."

"Fuck!" Sixus shouted as the crowd leaped to their feet and quickly exited the arena to return to the institute.

The shamans and Timbrax and this mystery person from Outer Earth had a plan to destroy me this entire time.

I had to intervene urgently to prevent the complete annihilation of three planets.

TWENTY-ONE

With Sixus finally asleep and the vampire hunters posted at the institute, I took a detour to The Sovereign Academy of Shamans. Making sure the bodies of the royals and Varric were given to the shamans for a ceremonial burial was a matter I held great significance to. Nell stayed behind, eager to assist them in getting everything ready.

Exiting through the gates, I was met with heartfelt thanks from them. The academy was alive with energy, despite the late hour, as she walked through its doors after midnight. A tan scroll, its contents a mystery, was carefully bound with a strip of worn leather and placed in my hands by Nell. She emphasized the significance of reading the text written on it when I eventually came back to Tellus. Before leaving, I took a moment to thank her as she hastily retreated indoors. I walked to the park that Nyxie had frequented, and as I crossed the street, I could feel the coolness of the breeze on my skin.

By extending my hand, I caused the astral thread to open. I leaped through it, and it shut behind me. I ran out of the wall and stood on the rubble of the Xeonada Empire. It was deathly silent as I sat on a pile of stone which used to be my castle.

My intuition alerted me that danger was near. The stench of death struck my nose before I turned to find Timbrax standing there. He appeared to be alone. But I wasn't trusting his ass. I stood and hopped down, landing on the ground. I started walking away from him when his words stopped me in my tracks.

"Varric told you, didn't he?" Timbrax called after me.

"Who gives a shit, right?" I murmured under my breath as I kept walking.

Timbrax leaped into the air, landing in front of me. I stopped walking and gave him a warning look. He didn't seem to give a fuck.

"I do," he replied. "And you do too, even if you don't wanna admit it."

"What does it matter?" I sighed in annoyance and asked, "Didn't you do what you were ordered to do?"

He didn't reply.

"Goodbye Brax," I said, as I walked past him. "I'm done here."

He threw open the astral thread, and I leaped through it, as did he. It closed behind him. I leaped through it and landed on the balcony of the institute. It closed behind me.

I walked into the dorm room and found Sixus pacing the floor anxiously. When he noticed me, he stopped and walked up to me.

"Did he hurt you?" Sixus demanded.

"No," I shook my head. "He confirmed everything Varric said before he died, but that's about it."

"Good," Sixus sighed as relief filled his end of the bond. "I'm still killing his ass for fucking with us."

"Yeah," I gave him a sad smile. Timbrax crushed my heart once again because I knew who he was. The very essence of his being. A damn Varacolaci. "Guess I'm just always going to be everyone's second choice."

"Baby," Sixus pulled me into a tight hug as I sobbed uncontrollably. "You are and *always* have been my *first* choice."

"Do you still love Exrah?" I whispered, making his body tense up as he gazed down at me. "If you do-"

"I love *you*," Sixus spoke, and I felt his truth through his end of the bond. "I will *always* choose you, Mel." As I grabbed the collar of his shirt, I forcefully pulled him towards me and eagerly kissed him with intensity. He growled protectively deep in his throat and returned my kiss just as fiercely. "You know," Sixus said through kisses. "I kinda wanna fuck you in the tube just to see how it feels."

I brook the kiss and burst out into laughter. He laughed, smirking at me. We removed our jackets and tossed them onto the back of the chair. He took me by the hand and pulled me towards the door. They slid open, and we stepped out into the hallway. He walked us towards the first tube and the door shot open. He stepped inside and pulled me in just as the door closed. Extending his arm, he located the button. When he pressed it, the tube became filled with purple Lust Dust.

"Holy shit," he breathed as he inhaled the dust into his lungs. "It actually worked!"

"And here I thought you knew everything about this place," I winked as I sucked in air. "We need this."

Magnetic started playing in the tube and I did not know who was near my cell, but right now, I gave zero fucks about it.

I saw his beautiful blue eyes darken and felt his horniness for me from his end of the bond. He lifted me up and placed my hands above my head and froze them in place against the glass. He pulled my pants and panties down before placing my legs across his neck. Grabbing me by the ass, he thrust his mouth into my pussy. Moaning in delight, I squeezed my legs tighter around his neck. He inserted his tongue and licked my clit vigorously.

"FUCK!" I moaned. "SUXIS!"

"Feel good Mel?"

Sixus asked in my mind.

"Fuck yeah!" I moaned. "I'm gonna cum!"

"Cum in my mouth, babe!"

Sixus said in my mind.

I released it and he lapped it until I was dry.

I was panting as he removed his head and set my body straight. He slammed his fist against the ice, and it shattered the glass, falling into tiny shards on the floor. I fell, and he caught me as he stepped out. He carried me back to my dorm room with my ass hanging out. The doors slid open, and he entered. The doors slid closed, and he threw his hand out. Thick layers of ice flew out, sealing it shut. He did the same, sealing the French doors in a thick layer of ice before carrying me over to the bed.

We removed our double-sided uniforms and boots quickly and were naked in seconds. Sixus turned me around and shoved his hot, long cock into my pussy from behind as he cradled me by the throat. The music drowned out everything except for the sound of bare skin slapping against each other.

"You feel so fucking good, Mel," Sixus growled as he fucked me. "Your pussy is all I ever want and all I ever will fuck you, hear me?"

"Yeah." I breathed as he slipped his long index finger into my mouth. I sucked it, making him moan even louder. My pale blue flames exploded out of my body, as did his ice. I melted the ice on both doors, and I burned the comforter on the bed. He threw his hand out and put the fire out before he slipped his other index finger between my lips and vigorously fingered, fucked me.

Never Again started playing, and it was fitting for us.

"I'm gonna cum," Sixus whispered in my ear. With one final thrust of his hips, hot sticky cum filled me as he removed his finger. We collapsed onto the bed, panting and sweating. He shoved the destroyed sheets onto the floor, which was soaking wet. "You burned the bed up, Mel."

"My bad," I breathed with a small smirk on my face. "Good thing we got another one over there."

Sixus laughed lightly as he turned me around to face him. He kissed me tenderly before breaking it. Walking across the room to pull the bed over, I admired his muscles, still glistening in the light with beads of sweat.

I walked over to my cell and turned the music off. The room fell silent, and I placed it on the charger. My intuition alerted me that danger was approaching. With lightning speed, I and Sixus got dressed in a clean double-sided uniform, quickly sliding into our mecha pilot boots, zipping up both jackets, and securing our weapons onto our bodies.

The French doors burst in with glass and wood splintering around us. I shielded myself with my jacket and shoved the sides back as pieces of wood and glass shards fell to the floor.

Timbrax stood on the balcony snarling at me. I screamed and my pale blue flame powered up before shooting out like a flamethrower, hitting Timbrax directly.

"Really?" He rolled his eyes as I closed my mouth, and the flame cut off. "You can't burn a Pyro Lancer with that thing."

"What the fuck do you want?" Sixus growled, narrowing his eyes at him.

"I came," he spoke calmly. "To get her." He pointed his index finger towards me.

"Not happening." Sixus shook his head. "Now get the hell out of here!"

"I don't have the patience for your shit, Sixus," Timbrax snarled. "Melfina is coming with me now!"

"I'm exhausted," I yawned. "You know I'm a bitch when I don't get my sleep."

"She ain't lying there," Sixus murmured under his breath. "You've caused enough fuckery around here for all of eternity."

Sixus and Timbrax began arguing, and I found myself distracted by something outside. I walked past Timbrax and stood on the balcony, gazing up at the stars. I noticed a blinking pale blue one that stood out to me. It sat between Erda and Outer Earth.

"What do you see, Melfina?" Timbrax asked as he walked over and stood beside me, gazing up at the sky.

"Just stars," I replied, shifting my gaze to the right to throw him off course. "Nothing but an endless sea of stars in the sky."

"She doesn't see shit!" Sixus growled as he ran out and pulled me away from the view. I blinked and was out of the trancelike state instantly. "You need to sleep, Mel."

Timbrax tapped into his vampire speed and held the twin's dragon eggs, one in each hand.

"You both know I'm not fucking around!" Timbrax snarled. "One will live, and one will *die*!"

"Not on my watch, you asshole!" Viz shouted as she snatched both eggs out of his hands and ran behind Sixus. With the doors sliding open, the vampire hunters stormed inside, brandishing their weapons at Timbrax's head and chest.

From an unknown location outside, the black magic seal emerged and enveloped me in a sphere before forcefully ejecting me outside. The force of the throw caught me off guard, sending me flying backwards. I fell on my ass as the ball came to an abrupt halt in the middle of the lawn. The ball transformed into a giant birdcage, and I scrambled to my feet.

"Mel!" Sixus shouted as he and the others leaped off the balcony and towards the cage. "I'm coming!"

"Stay where you are!" A.J.'s voice shouted from my right. I glanced over and found her walking casually towards the cage with a slight cocky smirk on her face. "The Tribrid and I will have a match to the death inside of that cage."

"Death matches happen in the arena, you stupid bitch!" I called down to her. "Everyone knows that."

"Then we'll move the fight to the arena!" she shot back. "Your gonna die in the end of it all and I will take your powers and become the new Universal Shamanic Queen!"

"I'll meet you at the arena, babe!" Sixus shouted up to me.

"I'll keep her company in there," Timbrax said to Sixus. "She'll be fine." Timbrax leaped through the black energy and walked over to me.

I sat down on the floor, and he followed my movement. The birdcage transformed back into an energy ball levitated and drifted away from the institute. I glanced back over my shoulder and found Sixus gazing up at me before I turned back forward.

"This is gonna take a while," Timbrax sighed as he glanced at me. "Lay down and take a nap."

I turned my back towards him as I lay on my right side and used my arm as a pillow. I closed my eyes, and I felt Timbrax pick me up and hold me in his arms. Confused, I opened my eyes and looked up at him. He gazed down at me, and I closed my eyes.

"I told you," he murmured. "This would never work between us, Melfina."

"Which is why you should sign those damn divorce papers," I replied. "Your married to Angelina, anyway."

"But I don't love *her*," Timbrax admitted. "I'm in love with *you*, Melfina."

"I've heard that one before from you, haven't I?"

I thought.

Timbrax gently kissed me, and my body jumped at his touch as it surprised me. Keeping my eyes closed, I returned his kiss before he slipped something metal into my mouth with his tongue. My eyes shot open, and he pulled back. I spit it out into the palm of my hand, and it was my wedding ring.

"Put it back on your finger," he whispered. "You've always belonged to me, Melfina."

"Sixus-"

"Damn dragon already knows I'm madly in love with you Melfina," he gave me a sad smile. "You never asked for anything from me other than for my love and that's what I will offer you, gorgeous."

"Then why did you leave me?" I whispered. "All you do is play these fucked up games with my emotions and my heart-"

"I'm afraid," he admitted, letting his walls down temporarily. "I have to keep my heart and my emotions for you in check if I am to lead Victim to victory over you."

"Yeah." I closed my eyes as I laid my heavy head against his chest. I inhaled his scent of death. I had grown used to it. But it still made my skin crawl occasionally. "Promise me you won't kill Sixus or turn him into a Varacolaci again."

"That," he laughed lightly. "*Never* should've happened."

"He was about to take your job from you, and you couldn't handle it," I smirked. "He's just a total badass, you know?"

"*I'm* a total badass," he corrected me. I heard the annoyance in his voice. "Fuck that dragon!"

"I already did tonight."

I thought to myself, hiding the smile that wanted to creep up my lips.

"Oh, don't think I don't know you did," he scoffed. "His disgusting scent is all over you!"

"He's my mate," I said as sleep overpowered me. "I love him, and our bond is unbreakable."

My sleep was devoid of dreams.

***

Someone abruptly woke me up by dumping a bucket of cold water on my face. I was shocked awake as I started coughing and spitting up water. My eyes shot open, and I heard A.J.'s maniacal laughter from before me.

"Wake up, bitch!" A.J. spat down at me as I climbed to my feet. When I took in my surroundings, I realized Victim had filled the arena. They were shouting down at us. I felt the vibrations of their voices through my body. "Let's get this over with!"

"Welcome Victim!" Timbrax shouted as the crowd grew silent. "The oracle is fighting for her survival against the Shamanic Queen of Light!" he paused as Victim murmured amongst themselves. "The Shamanic Queen of Light will absorb the powers of the oracle if she dies!"

I had grown used to being in the arena before and during the Flight Games. But there was an eerie feeling that hung in the air. I had a bad feeling in the pit of my stomach, and my intuition alerted me to the danger that surrounded me. I turned and found Sixus and Timbrax standing outside of the circle. They stood fifteen feet apart from one another.

"Dragons don't go down without a fight!"

Sixus spoke in my mind.

"Kill that shaman bitch, Mel!"
Sixus added.

I nodded curtly at him and turned back to face my opponent. I observed that her flawless skin had been covered in red and black charred marks on the left side of her face.

The horn sounded, and the match was on. Dreamstate started playing over the loudspeaker and I pulled my dagger out, holding it in front of me in a defensive stance.

A.J. ran towards me and I could predict her every move. My oracle abilities were on high alert, as she was the current threat who was trying to kill me.

She brought her dagger down, trying to slam it into my chest. I blocked it with my dagger and the metal clanked as she shoved off me. Her rage was on full display and that's what made her so easy to predict. She wasn't in full control of herself.

I flipped backwards and kicked her in the jaw with my metal boot, causing her to stumble backwards as I landed on my feet and spun around to face her. This just pissed her ass off even more once she regained her balance.

"Enough games, Tribrid!" A.J. shouted as she prepared for another attack. "Let's end this shit!"

Below The Belt played next, and I was ready for her attack.

A.J. kicked off the sand and flew towards me. As she landed on me, I was knocked onto my back. As she knocked the air out of me, she proceeded to place her dagger in her mouth and tightly wrap her hands around my neck. She strangled me, squeezing the air out of my body.

"I'm gonna kill you!" A.J. laughed evilly. "And then I'll be the only Shamanic Queen of Light to rule over earth and Tellus!" She paused, shooting a glare down at me. "And I'm gonna fuck your sexy dragon mate!"

Feel Me Now played next in the lineup. And that was all the motivation I needed to kill her ass after her last comment.

I reached over and grabbed a handful of sand and turned my head as I tossed it into her eyes.

A.J. screamed in shock as she scrambled off of me as she tried to rub the sand out of her eyes.

I leaped to my feet and grabbed my dagger. I ran and crouched down, thrusting the dagger through her chest, piercing her heart. And I had Nyxie's dagger and stabbed the blade through the bottom of her jaw the same way I did Largo in the alternate timeline.

A.J. gurgled blood as it gushed out of her wounds. I yanked the daggers out and she fell backwards. Her wide eyes shifted over towards me, and I licked her blood off of both blades before I placed them into their sheaths. The metal stung my tongue, but it was worth it to kill this bitch.

The horn sounded, and the match was over.

"Your winner!" Timbrax shouted. "Is the oracle!"

Loud boos erupted from the crowd of Victim sitting in the stands.

Forgotten started playing.

In that moment, I turned to look at A.J., her final breaths escaping her lips, the weight of the moment sinking in. I reached into her chest, causing her to grimace in pain, as I felt the softness of her flesh beneath my touch. Extracting Nyxie's powers along with my own, I skillfully pulled them out, separating them from their origin. As the two luminous orbs, one shimmering in pink and the other pulsating in purple, found their place within my chest, I could sense an instant enhancement in my physical power. Her blood dripped slowly off my fingertips, creating a mesmerizing pattern of crimson on the sandy surface beneath me.

Lowering myself, I grabbed her dagger and secured it in her leather strap. I stood and Timbrax and Sixus both entered the circle. Timbrax grabbed my arm and raised it high in the air in victory. More books erupted from the Victim before he dropped it.

Timbrax threw his palm out and the blue shamanic seal that belonged to Solas shot out and flew into Sixus body.

Sixus arched an eyebrow his way in confusion.

"I'm dead, remember?" Timbrax rolled his eyes at him. "I gave you Evan's powers."

I ran into Sixus' open arms as he pulled me tightly into his body. He inhaled my scent deeply before I rested my heavy head on his chest.

"I knew you'd whoop her ass, Mel." Sixus gave me a sad smile. "I'm proud of you for getting Nyxie's shamanic powers back into your body."

Glancing around, I noticed Victim had never left as the music abruptly cut off. They were still sitting in the arena.

And that uneasy feeling I had sitting in the pit of my stomach. Was still there. It never left.

"Something's wrong Sixus."

I said in my mind.

"I feel it too, Mel."

Sixus replied.

Just as we were about to exit the circle, a powerful force pulled us apart and we formed a perfect triangle as we levitated in mid-air. The blue-violet light shot out of my body and into Sixus'. The blue light shot out of his body and flew into Timbrax's. And the red light flew out of Timbrax's body and straight into mine.

"What the fuck is happening?" Sixus shouted over the sound of the power surging between the three of us.

"The Nexus!" Timbrax shouted back. "I realized it takes a Half-Draconian, a vampire, and a shaman to activate the gateway!"

"Is that why you turned us all into Tribrid's?" Sixus shouted to him. "That's why you had the fucking Spellbinders send us through different timelines in order to activate the Tribrid in all three of us, isn't it?"

"You catch on quick, Sixus!" "Timbrax smirked. "Unleashing hell on all three planets is possible with Melfina as the key!"

As I was shifted into the middle, panic rose in me, and I left the place I was in open. I wondered who would take that place. I had my answer. The black and blue dragon egg that was my and Timbrax's child flew into the spot, flying downwards.

"SIXUS!" I screamed as the black light merged with the red and blue ones, completing the triangle once more. "I will *always* choose you!"

"MELFINA!" Sixus shouted my name.

The power I struggled to contain finally released itself in a mighty explosion, causing the triangle to be broken. Sand flew up all around us and I felt a shift in my energy before I embraced this new power, I had just unleashed upon Tellus.

"Mel!" Sixus shouted as he slowly climbed to his feet. His eyes were wide with fear as he stared at me. I felt his panic through his end of the bond. "What have you done?"

Timbrax picked up the dragon egg and walked casually over to where I was standing in the center of the arena. He placed a hand around my waist, pulling me tightly into his body.

"MEL! I LOVE YOU!"

Sixus spoke in my mind.

That was the last thing I heard before Timbrax sank his sharp fangs into my soft skin. His endorphins kicked in and I blacked out.

TWENTY-TWO
-SIXUS-

I had Frudi's egg cracked and had her placed in I.O.A. to be under twenty-four-hour protection. She was born prematurely and needed to be placed on oxygen.

"Dad!" Cy's voice drew me from my thoughts as I turned from the glass window, watching Frudi to look at her. She held the black and pale blue dragon egg in her hands. She handed it to me, and I just gazed down at it in shock.

"Did Mel abandon their baby?"

I thought in my mind.

The egg cracked, and the shells fell to the floor around my feet. I was now holding Xeyva who was also a newborn baby that looked like a good mix of both Mel and Timbrax's features. Her dark hair was thick on the crown of her head. Xeyva slowly opened her eyes and gazed up at me. Her eyes were white with red rings around the edges, with a speckle of gray flakes in the iris. Xeyva turned her tiny head and bit my hand.

"Ow!" I snarled as Setha rushed over and took Xeyva from my hands and handed her off to Abel, who took her into the room to be with her twin sister. "Xeyva bit me!"

"What did you expect?" Setha smirked at me. "Xeyva is part vampire, you know?" She walked back over to me and bit me on the side of the neck. I snarled as her endorphins kicked in, causing me to feel relaxed.

"Relax. The bite of a newborn vampire baby is stronger than any normal vampire. I'm just sucking out the endorphins, okay?"

Setha spoke in my mind.

A moment later, she removed herself and I leaned up against the glass as Exley and Zara approached us. Exley grabbed the Holistic sword and stabbed me in the right leg. The bright blue light flashed, blinding us temporarily before it vanished. He placed the sword back in the sheath before stepping back.

"Thank you," I breathed, grateful to be feeling better quickly. "Did they abandon Xeyva?"

"No," Zara shook her head. "Xeyva and Frudi are twins and Frudi brought her here using her dragon abilities."

"They are some powerful babies." Sixus shook his head as he watched Abel place Xeyva beside Fruci in a larger white bin so they could bond. The girls instantly lay by their twin and fell into a peaceful sleep. I smiled sadly, knowing Mel wouldn't wanna miss this moment of her baby's bonding. "I really wish the powerful shamans were alive because they could have provided valuable assistance in dealing with this Nexus problem."

"Err," Setha gave me a look. "Aren't *you* a powerful shaman who has knowledge of how to stop the Nexus from destroying three planets or something?"

"Huh," I frowned at the obvious. "Guess I forgot I absorbed Solas' powers."

"Dad, you can be an idiot sometimes," Setha replied straightforwardly. "Did you *really* graduate from this institution?"

"I don't like your tone," I replied, narrowing my eyes at her. "And I'm not your father!" I spat as I walked up the long hallway and stood in front of the dorm room I shared with Mel last year. The doors slid open, and I entered the room. They closed behind me. I had to temper my rage. I shouldn't have taken my anger out on Setha. She did nothing to deserve it.

The astral thread opened behind me. Spinning around, I watched as Setha stepped out and it shut behind her.

"I'm sorry, Setha," I sighed as I did my best to temper my rage. "I'm still having a hard time adjusting to being the father of a bunch of vampires, you know?"

"I'm not like my father, you know?" she whispered. "But thank you for apologizing."

I nodded curtly at her as I turned and walked over to the desk. When I saw the tarot deck, a thought suddenly came to me. I spun around, and she was still standing there staring at me silently.

"You, Velzy, and Zora are Nitan Westfall's daughters, aren't you?" I asked her.

"That's right," she nodded. "But Timbrax got jealous of my dad knocking up Zyra more than him, so he changed the timeline and made me be his daughter."

"Make alterations," I ordered her. "Make yourself be siblings with Velzy, Exley, and Zora again."

"Is there a point to all this?" Setha asked, giving me a look.

"Yes," I replied as I turned and grabbed my weapons and placed them on my body. "Piss off Timbrax more than he already is now."

"That's easy to do, you know?" Setha shook her head.

"I know," I smirked. "He'll be back, and the war will start between Victim and us." I exited the room through the open French doors and stood on the balcony.

"Melfina is still neutral," Setha said from behind me. "I hope you sway her to stay on the side of the light, Sixus."

I pressed a button hidden beneath the marble railing. "Dragon Knights!" I called into the speaker. "Mount up!"

"What's happening, dad?" Cy asked as she rushed into the room and stood beside me.

"We're getting your mother back," I replied. "My mate is returning to me at all costs."

***

-MELFINA-

My eyes shot open, and I lay on a stone slab. Someone had shackled my wrists and ankles down. The metal burned my skin, and I lifted my head to find Timbrax standing with Orion as they spoke away from me. Timbrax noticed I was awake, and he walked over to me.

"Your awake," he stated the obvious as he gazed up at me. "That's good."

"What's happening?" I asked as the panic rose within me.

Timbrax pressed a button on a metal box that was located beside the stone I was lying on. It lifted the stone until I was half laying and half standing. It rotated and stopped. I noticed I was facing the end of a hill that dropped into the sea. I turned my head and Timbrax saw the fear in my eyes.

"You should be used to pain by now, Melfina," Timbrax replied. "The faster you help us get the Nexus open, the faster you can rule by my side on earth."

"Victim Commander!" Orion called. "A word, please?"

"Be right back," Timbrax said. "This shouldn't take long." He turned and walked away. I had little time, so I had to act fast. I blocked Timbrax out even though I wasn't bound to him at the moment.

"Spirit Guide Naphirie?"

I asked in my mind.

"What would you like to destroy or revive oracle?"

Naphirie asked in my mind.

"Make me be the commander of the army of the dead shaman once I open the Nexus."

I replied.

"It is done."

Naphirie replied.

"Is there anything else you wish to destroy or revive, oracle?"

Naphirie asked.

"No. Thank you Naphirie."

I spoke.

The link fell silent.

I heard footsteps approaching me. I turned my head and found Timbrax standing in front of the controller box.

"There are weird symbols on here!" He shouted to Orion. "I don't understand them!"

"Are they shamanic symbols?" I asked.

"I don't know?" He snapped, giving me a major attitude, and I rolled my eyes and turned my head and gazed forward. He sighed in aggravation and kept pressing the symbols. "We need one of those fucking shamans to help us!"

"Aren't you a shaman?" Orion shouted. "Fix that shit Victim Commander!"

"I don't have the patience for this shit!" Timbrax murmured under his breath.

As I closed my eyes, I felt a needle being inserted into the left side of my neck, and a cold liquid was administered into my vein.

"What the fuck are you doing?" Timbrax snarled as my eyes shot open. I saw Largo removing the needle from my body. The burning of the metal tip faded, and I inhaled as it took effect instantly.

"Giving her the injection," Largo scoffed with rage in his voice. "The Nexus needs to be activated by the Tribrid already!"

"I don't remember authorizing you to inject her, Largo!" Timbrax spat. "We don't have a lot of time here, damn it!"

"Orion ordered me to inject her," Largo spat. "So, I did it Victim Commander!" The two vampires started fighting, and they stepped behind me as they started throwing punches and kicks. They had completely forgotten about me. For the moment, at least.

I was feeling disoriented and dizzy. I noticed movement before me. Viz placed her index finger against her lips and I knew the enemy hadn't noticed her yet, or at all. She crept over and burned the metal chains on my ankles and my wrists. When I slid down the slab of stone, she caught me.

"Can I become your guardian?"

Viz asked me in my mind.

"Yes."

I replied.

I felt and saw the thin red thread shoot out of her body and into mine before it disappeared. I could feel her bound to me. She placed my arm across her shoulder and held onto me as we moved closer towards the edge.

"Your scent is familiar," Orion spoke as he walked towards us. "Who are you Half-Draconian?"

Viz released me and transformed into her dragon form. She waited for me. I fell onto her back and grabbed onto her smooth scales. She bolted up into the air and my stomach leaped into my throat before she straightened out. She flapped her wings, and the cold air stung my eyes. I felt the blood running down my palms as I struggled to hold on to her back. Up here, I couldn't function properly because of the drugs I had been given! Viz soared over the sea, flapping her wings fiercely.

Orion flew after us. He swooped beneath Viz and caught her by the throat. She shot upwards, and I felt my hands slipping off of her back. I fell downward at a rapid speed. The water was rapidly approaching me, causing me to panic.

At the moment, right before I was about to plummet into the freezing waters below, someone swooped down and saved me.

My eyes met Sixus' as I glanced up and found him gazing down at me. I held onto him tightly as he pressed me into his body.

I turned and saw Viz slap Orion with her long, spiked tail, making him release her. She flapped her wings furiously and Sixus sat on her back as he held me.

"I got you Mel!" He shouted over the roar of the wind. "Your safe now!"

I shut my eyes and lost consciousness.

***

Lying in my bed, I woke up in my dorm room. I blinked twice before turning my head. Sixus sat in the wooden chair, staring back at me silently. His beautiful blue eyes bore into my soul, and I lowered the barrier to feel his emotions. He was relieved, pissed, filled with love, and wanted to protect me from Timbrax and Orion and Victim at all costs.

"War is coming to our doorstep, Mel," Sixus whispered as he kept his gaze even with mine. "I need to know that you're on my side, babe."

"Of course I'm on your side," I said as I sat up and kicked the hot comforter off my body. I leaped to my feet, feeling much better after getting some sleep. "They couldn't figure out the markings on the control panel last night."

"Good." Sixus sighed in relief as he climbed to his feet. "There's something I wanna show you after you shower."

Utilizing my vampire speed, I undressed prior to showering. I got dressed in a clean double-sided uniform and pinned my hair up and put my mecha pilot boots on before zipping them up. I pinned my hair up and put my weapons on my body before putting on my two jackets.

Sixus took me by the hand and interlaced our fingers together as we walked towards the door. They slid open, and we stepped out into the hallway. We walked up it with our boots echoing off the silent walls. We paused in front of the window that held the babies. I glanced inside and my eyes widened when I saw Frudi and Xeyva lying beside each other in a plastic bassinet.

"Xeyva bit me last night after she was born." Sixus frowned as he gazed at her. "Little biter."

I gave him a side eye glance, and he smirked. I smiled as we gazed at Frudi. She was our first baby together.

"Is Cy okay with having sisters?" I asked.

"Of course she is." Sixus arched an eyebrow my way. "She is already overprotective of them both."

There was a quick flash of a vision that I had witnessed.

I saw my father standing with Timbrax, Tasia, Orion, Largo, Feron, Varric, A.J., the contact from Erda/Outer Earth, and Exrah on Erda in the park across the street from the academy.

It vanished.

Sixus and I both exchanged glances with each other as the realization struck us. The babies were fine.

"Cy!" We said in unison as we turned and found Exrah holding both Cy and Viz with two guns pointed towards their heads.

"You?" I asked as the shock was on my face. "You are the contact who had access to Tellus, Erda, and Outer Earth."

"They warned me you are slow oracle," Exrah scowled. "You truly are an idiot!"

"Let them go," I said with my hands out in front of me, showing her, I was unarmed. "They have nothing to do with this."

"Mom!" Cy cried with terror in her eyes.

"Shut up Tande!" Exrah screamed as rage filled her eyes. "I told you that woman is *not* your mother!"

"Take me in their place," I said as I slowly made my way over to her. "I'll open the Nexus."

"Wise choice," Exrah replied as she shoved Cy forward. She stumbled and ran into Sixus' protective arms. He hugged her tightly as tears fell from her eyes. She was in shock as she stared at her birth mother. "This one is coming with us," she added as she moved us towards a glass tube. "Orion wants his daughter."

"This is low," Sixus snarled, narrowing his eyes at her. "What happened to you, Exrah?"

"Your Half-Draconian freaks shouldn't exist!" she screamed. "I saw an opportunity to get revenge on you, Sixus," she smirked. "And I gratefully embraced the opportunity!"

Her mind was preoccupied. I glanced at Viz and she turned and punched Exrah in the nose.

Exrah screamed as she grabbed for her face. Viz escaped as she raced over to Sixus' side. He grabbed her and pulled her tightly into his arms. Right as I was planning to move, Exrah slammed me in the temple, pistol-whipped me.

In an instant, my senses faded away, and I drifted into a state of complete unconsciousness.

***

Upon waking up, I was greeted with a pounding headache. A bright light was blinding my face, so I didn't bother opening my eyes. My wrists were burning. I knew I was in shackles. I lay on the metal cot and just wanted to sleep.

Upon hearing a door unlock, someone entered the room. Footsteps approached me and I kept my breathing steady and slow. I felt an icy hand dab the side of my face, startling me. My eyes shot open, and I sat up with a jolt. Timbrax looked at me, keeping his expression unreadable. I felt relief through his end of the bond.

"You have a concussion," he said in a quiet voice. "You shouldn't be sleeping." I slapped his hand away, and he stood, keeping his gaze fixed on me. "Now you know all the players on the playing field, Melfina."

"Does Sixus still have ties to any of this?" I whispered.

"In the beginning, we brought Sixus into the fold," Timbrax agreed. "But once your father saw he had fallen in love with you... we had to kick him out and treat him as our enemy, like you, Melfina, because the plan had been compromised."

I stayed silent, relieved Sixus wasn't full my enemy as he had started out to be last year.

"As long as my soul is bound to yours," Timbrax went on. "Exrah can't kill you."

Someone entered my cell, and my eyes widened when I saw them. He stood behind Timbrax and Timbrax didn't seem fazed by his presence.

"Did you miss me, Melfi?" He spoke with a muffled voice behind his black mask.

"Dad?" I whispered. "Your... *alive*?"

"Orion sent me back to the Victim ship," he said. "He made it look as if he had killed me."

"But" I shook my head. "He ripped your heart out of your body and Timbrax melted it in the palm of his hand."

"I am Victim," my dad replied. "You have disappointed me, Melfi."

"Always good to know I'm the family disappointment, father," I replied with so much hate in my voice. "You should be used to that by now."

"Get her back under your control Victim Commander!" My father growled through his black mask.

"As you wish, Lord Aeon Dra," Timbrax nodded curtly as my father exited the room, closing the door behind him. I felt him unbind himself from me, and I knew another round of torture was in my future. "Sorry about this... it's just business, Melfina."

"No problem," I replied in a bitter voice. "Do your worst Victim Commander."

"My worst?" Timbrax arched an eyebrow my way. "Have it your way, then."

Timbrax yanked the Venin dagger out and pressed my cheeks open forcefully. My tongue rolled out for him to torture first. He grabbed the blade and slid it deep into my mouth. The taste of my blood filled my mouth instantly. I didn't even scream this time around. But the burning from the blade stung the shit out of my mouth. Timbrax removed the blade and dropped his hand. I watched as he licked both sides clean of my blood as he gazed at me the entire time.

"Why didn't you scream?" He demanded. "I know that fucking hurt you, Melfina."

I smirked and laughed, keeping my gaze fixed on him. He didn't know how used I was to being tortured. My father had ensured that I experienced daily torture at night by our guards. Probably preparing me for this moment.

"That was fun."

I grew serious.

"Do you know why my father and all of Tellus are afraid of me, Brax?"

I asked him in my mind.

He gazed silently at me.

"Dad would send guards in to torture me and once they were done... I'd kill them and play with their corpses and have tea parties and concerts with my dead guards!"

His eyes widened as he realized I was telling him the truth.

"My father kept me hidden away, not because he was afraid Tellus would harm me. It was because I would kill everyone on Tellus."

I was the grim reaper in the flesh.

"If my mother hadn't been from the Kingdom of Eozadion, I would be pure evil. That tiny spark of light had been the only reason my father hadn't killed me. He knew he could use me to destroy Tellus in the future."

"You demented bitch." My sudden change in demeanor took Timbrax aback. He realized I was more psychotic than him. It came from my dragon side of the family, no doubt.

"That was fun."

I thought.

"Let's play something a bit more deadly, Brax."

The Victim Commander wanted me at my worst.
He was about to get it.

TWENTY-THREE

By the time Timbrax was done with me, I was nothing more than a bloody mess. And the worst part? I laughed in his face the entire time, which only pissed him off even more. I heard him screaming at my father outside of my cell.

"How the fuck did you raise someone as psychotic as her?" Timbrax demanded. "The more I tortured her ass, the more she seemed to enjoy it!"

"I told you Victim Commander," my father spat. "My daughter is not to be taken lightly!"

"She pretended to be normal around everyone!" Timbrax spat.

"No," my father replied. "Melfina is good at hiding her true personality from the world."

"You should've let me kill her ass two years ago back on earth!" Timbrax snarled.

"I needed her to tap into her powers," my father argued. "Only then could I put my plan into motion."

I felt my wounds being healed. Even my tongue. The fact that Sixus had used the Holistic sword on himself was known to me. I was on the verge of dying and I was pretty sure Exley had to use the sword on him again.

"You scared the shit outta them with your dragon form, didn't you, Mel?"

Sixus chuckled in my mind.

"I... guess I did, didn't I?"

I replied.

"Mundane, don't understand us dragons... they think we're psychotic, bloodthirsty untamable creatures... you're perfectly normal. Nothing's wrong with you at all, Mel."

He added.

"That's good to know."

I thought.

The link fell silent between Sixus and me before I heard my father shouting again.

"Clean up that mess!" my father screamed. "The scent of her blood is exciting, Victim!"

I heard footsteps approaching. The door to my cell was unlocked, and it opened. Timbrax entered, walking cautiously towards me. I just silently stared at him.

"Take a shower and clean yourself up," Timbrax spoke quietly. "Your being moved to another cell so they can clean this one up."

I climbed to my feet and lifted my wrists. My pale blue flame ignited and melted the metal, making two metal puddles near my feet.

Timbrax gave me a look, and I smiled. Walking past him, I stood in front of the door. Regaining his composure, he came towards me. Taking my arm gently, he led me out of the cell. He walked me up the hallway and pushed open the door to the bathroom. I entered the room, and he followed, closing the door behind him.

I stripped off my blood-soaked uniform, boots, and jackets and tossed them onto the floor. Unpinning my hair, I placed the pins on the banister of the sink and let my long hair cascade down my back before opening the door and stepping inside the shower.

Timbrax reached in and turned the knobs for me, and the water sprayed down onto my body before he closed the door.

Laughing nervously, Timbrax confessed, "I never expected to fear you," as he tried to hide his anxiety. "I'm defiantly signing those divorce papers now."

I didn't reply as I quickly washed the blood out of my hair and off my body. As I observed, the dried blood flow down the drain. Shutting the water off, I rang out my hair and pushed open the door. Timbrax handed me a long black towel, and I wrapped it around myself before stepping out. Timbrax had brought clothes from Erda for me to change into, and I noticed they belonged to Zyra.

I got dressed and repined my hair up. He grabbed my jackets and my uniform and boots and promised he would get them cleaned for me. He tossed them into a black trash bag and swung it across his shoulder. Opening the door, I stepped out, and he grabbed me by the arm once more. This time he led me up the long silent hallway, past my former cell and straight to his bedroom. The doors slid open, and we walked inside as they closed behind me.

"I'm ready to go to my cell now Brax," I replied as I gazed out of the window. Space was beautiful. But I got the same view from my dorm room back at the institute, too. "Please?"

"This *is* your new cell," Timbrax whispered, making me turn and gaze at him. "You're my responsibility, Melfina."

"Being stuck with you twenty-four hours is pure hell," I spat. "Fuck you!"

"You are free to go back to your dragon mate," Timbrax smirked. "After you open the Nexus, of course."

"Fine," I rolled my eyes. "Let's get this shit over with."

I walked past him when he caught me by the wrist, making me turn and hiss in his face. His smirk widened even more.

"There's that sexy vampire I married," he whispered into my ear. "Now feed!"

I turned, licking the side of his neck. I sank my sharp fangs deep into his neck. He growled protectively as he grabbed me by the ass, pressing my body deeper into his. Because of my intense starvation, I consumed his blood. I gave zero fucks it was tainted. Upon removing my fangs, he kissed me. I returned his kiss before he broke it.

Recipe For Disaster started playing loudly from his cell as he tapped into his vampire speed and turned his music on full blast.

We started making out as he threw me down onto his bed. He climbed on top of me and our hands roamed over each other's bodies. We removed our clothes in seconds. He slammed his hard, hot cock deep into my pussy and used his vampire speed, causing me to have multiple orgasms within seconds. I moaned into his mouth as he continued to fuck me for the remainder of the night until I grew exhausted.

He held me in his arms until I dozed off. He covered me up with his thick black comforter and got dressed before shutting off the music. Someone pounded loudly on the door, and he walked over and unlocked it. They slid open, and he stepped out as they shut behind him.

"Well?" Orion demanded.

"Well, what?" Timbrax spat with annoyance in his voice.

"Did you get her back under your control?" Orion asked, sighing heavily. "We are running out of time."

I shoved the comforter off my body. With the help of my vampire speed, I quickly got dressed. I placed my weapons on my body and put my trench coat on and my mecha pilot boots. I leaped up and hung upside down, and the doors opened.

Both men turned and looked in the room. They didn't see me. Timbrax snarled in annoyance when I dropped my head down and gazed at them. I flipped, landing on the floor. I spun around and faced them as I exited the room.

Timbrax gently pulled me into his body and bent his head down, kissing me. I closed my eyes and returned his kiss before he broke it. I opened my eyes and looked at Orion, who stared at us.

"Does that answer your question, Orion?" Timbrax asked. "My wife obeyed my orders as she drank my blood without the slightest bit of hesitation."

"I'll let my father know," Orion nodded to him. "Good job Victim Commander." He turned and walked up the hallway, disappearing into the large briefing room.

"You're an asshole," I shoved Timbrax away, punching him in the arm. "You don't love me at all."

"I'm not doing this with you, Melfina," Timbrax frowned. "Take another shower and get dressed in something clean."

"I don't have any clothes here?" I gave him a look. "I'm a prisoner, remember?"

"At least you know what you are," Timbrax murmured under his breath as he grabbed me by the arm and led me up the hallway. He pushed open the door to the bathroom and shoved me inside. I stumbled before catching my balance. "Get your ass showered and meet me in the briefing room in twenty minutes." He opened the door and stepped out, closing it behind him.

"Asshat!" I shouted as I undressed and placed my weapons on the banister.

"I heard that!" Timbrax spat from outside the door.

I opened the shower door and stepped inside, closing it behind me. Turning the knobs, water sprayed down onto my body, and I rewashed myself and my hair. I heard the door open, and someone entered the bathroom. The shower door flew open, and someone sprayed white smoke in my face. While inhaling, I coughed and ended up falling to the floor.

Before I blacked out into total darkness, I looked up and saw Exrah smirking down at me.

***

As soon as I woke up, I felt incredibly groggy. With slow motion, I opened my eyes and identified my environment. I found myself shackled to the large slab of stone again.

"She's waking up!" Largo shouted to someone. "Hurry and get the controls turned on!"

After my eyes focused and I took deep breaths of fresh air, I found Exrah standing at the control panel box with Tasia standing beside her. To my surprise, Tasia used her sunlight powers and made each symbol, and they all floated before me. I stared at them, wondering what they meant.

My shamanic seal shot out of my body and lit up each symbol in the correct order they needed to be in, in order to activate the Nexus.

"She's doing it!" Largo shouted excitedly.

I watched as Tasia grabbed each symbol and placed them over the controls as they flew back towards her and Exrah. There were over thirty symbols in all that remained dark.

"One more!" Largo shouted. "Fucking Tribrid bitch will destroy three planets at once!"

"NO!" I shouted as I closed my eyes and shook my head. "I won't finish the sequence!"

"The fuck you won't!" Largo punched me in the face, making my eyes water as they shot open. He held my head straight, making me look at the remaining symbols to activate the final one. "Finish it bitch!"

My magic seal shot out and lit up one that resembled a Gemini symbol. Largo released me and Tasia grabbed it, placing it onto the metal panel.

"We did it!" Exrah shouted, laughing evilly.

"NO!" I screamed as the magic seal shot out of my body and up towards the star that was between Erda and Outer Earth.

The ground trembled like an earthquake was happening. My body lifted, only being held down by the shackles. The immense pain made my entire body feel as though it were on fire. I screamed as it intensified with each passing second.

Timbrax, Orion, and my father came into my view, and I gazed at them. Timbrax stood there looking at the star I had stared at back at the institute before turning and looking at me.

"MEL!" Sixus shouted. I turned my head and saw him flying towards me, with the dragon knights on the backs of their guardians. The vampire hunters leap out of the astral thread standing near me. "I'm coming!"

Sixus leaped down, landing beside me to the right with Cy and Viz beside him. He took one look at my father and snarled. I could feel his rage through his end of the bond.

"Dragon knights!" Sixus shouted as he formed two thick icicles in his fists. "Attack!"

He flicked his wrists, and I heard Timbrax snarl, and it was on. They both fought beside me.

The pain was excruciating. Sixus, Cy, and Viz could all feel it. It was affecting them, yet they kept fighting around me.

Cy and Viz both grabbed onto the chains. Cy froze them and crushed the metal into tiny fragments. While Viz used her dragon flame and melted the one from my wrist and foot.

"Tande!" Exrah shouted. "Get over here now!"

"Fuck off, lady!" Cy shouted. "I'm staying with my *real* mom!"

"You stole my daughter from me, you Tribrid bitch!" Exrah shouted.

Before I could reply, my body shot up, and I was flung towards the glowing star. The fighting fell silent, and I directed my attention towards the star. I flew closer and closer until I floated before the star. I lifted my hand and threw it out before me. My blue-violet shamanic seal shot out, forming a bright door before me. With a gentle movement, I reached out and touched the doorknob. I turned it and opened it. I stepped inside and the door closed behind me.

That was the last thing I remembered before all hell broke loose on Tellus.

-SIXUS-

A loud explosion erupted from the heavens, sending a massive shockwave down onto us. The explosion caused everyone to scramble towards safety. I looked around and didn't see Mel anywhere.

"Where's Mel?" I shouted to Cy and Viz.

"She flew up there!" Cy shouted as she pointed her index finger towards the glowing door that appeared between Erda and Outer Earth.

"It's too late!" Timbrax shouted to me as I looked at him. "The Tribrid has opened the door, and she will destroy our worlds!"

"You son of a bitch!" I snarled as I formed thick icicles in my fists and flicked them towards his head. He dodged them easily as he ran towards me again.

"My stepmother was a bitch," Timbrax agreed as he crooked his fingers and brought his hand towards my face. I dodged it and kicked him in the gut, causing him to sink to one knee. "But so was yours, wasn't she?"

"Your so fucking dead!" I spat as my rage boiled over.

"I'm already dead, remember?" Timbrax laughed lightly.

Exrah tried shooting me with her weapon, but Cy used her dragon speed and shot ice at her, causing it to freeze instantly in her hand.

"Ah!" Exrah dropped the gun, which shattered on the ground on impact. She shook her hand, trying to keep it from turning into ice. "Tande!"

"You attempted to kill my parents," Cy snarled as she grabbed Exrah by the throat, lifting her off the ground. "You tried to kill *me*!"

"You're a bunch of fucking freaks!" Exrah screamed as Cy tightened her grip around her throat.

"It wasn't a pleasure meeting you, bitch!" Cy used her ice powers and Exrah screamed before being turned into an ice sculpture. Cy removed her hand and kicked her body, shattering it into a thousand million ice pieces onto the ground.

Timbrax saw what happened, and he backed off from me, leaning casually against the stone slab Melfina was just stuck to moments ago.

I noticed Tasia was staring at Viz. She never took her eyes off her. Viz finally noticed her staring, and she backed away from her.

"Who are you?" Tasia asked as she walked cautiously towards her.

"Nobody," Viz shook her head. "Forget you ever saw me."

"She's our daughter, Tasia," Orion replied from a distance. "I killed her and Dynastra revived her before I killed her!"

"What?" Tasia was shocked as she looked at Viz. "You're alive?"

"I'm Melfina's guardian," Vis replied. "I'm staying with my family at the institute."

"Come with me," Tasia begged. "I'm going back to my kingdom."

"Not interested," Viz spat. "Stay the hell out of my life, you walking corpse!"

Another blast came from above us and I gazed up to see the door had opened. A figure stepped out, surrounded by a bright pale blue-violet light. She descended towards us. The fighting stopped and Melfina was beside me.

Her appearance had changed. No longer was she wearing Erda clothing. She wore a black dress with a long slit running down one leg. Her hair was now teal and straight. Her makeup was dark.

"Mel?" I whispered her name, and she looked at me. I raised my hands in a defensive stance to show her I wasn't a threat. "Are you okay?"

She lifted her arms above her head and a powerful energy shot out of them. It formed a massive black spiral between all three planets.

"Holy shit!" I whispered looking at Timbrax. "She's gonna kill us all!"

-MELFINA-

I couldn't control myself. I heard Sixus shouting at me, but I was unresponsive to him.

"Nell!" Sixus shouted to the shaman. "Turn that shit off!"

"I'll try my best!" Nell shouted as she ran to the control panel with Cy and Viz by her side.

"Mel!" Sixus shouted to me. "Stop this!"

I flew into his space and balled my hand into a fist. I brought it back and thrust it forward, slamming him hard in the jaw. He flew backwards, catching his balance. He snarled at me as I felt my jaw throbbing where I had struck him.

Timbrax walked over to the metal panel and placed his hands on it. His orange flame caught the metal on fire and started melting it, causing sparks to fly as they ran from it before it exploded.

"The fuck you do that for?" Sixus shouted to him.

"I thought blowing it to shit would cause her to turn back to her lovely bitchy self!" he yelled over the roar of the flames. "Guess I was wrong!"

"You're a fucking idiot!" Sixus snarled. "You vampire bitch!"

Timbrax was about to say something fucked up when Cy intervened.

"Look!" she shouted as she gazed up at the sky.

The shaman army of the dead stood behind me. Nyxie, Solas, Varric, and Angelina stood amongst them.

"Good job, my daughter," my dad said, clapping slowly as he approached me. "Send them to me without delay, so that we may annihilate all the planets, transforming them into fiery ruins!"

I didn't move. Neither did my army.

"Are you stupid?" My father spat. "Send me the shaman army at once!"

"Victim!" Timbrax shouted as he flipped backwards, and the legion of vampires stood behind him. "Stand by!"

"Dragon knights!" Sixus shouted. "Prepare to-"

When I held out my hand, Sixus promptly stopped talking. My gaze fell upon my father. I snapped my fingers, and I sent Sixus, the vampire hunters, the dragon knights, and everyone who was associated with him, back to the institute unharmed. I sent the dragons back to the sanctuary. Returning to the Xeonada Empire, I restored it within seconds.

"Mel!"

Sixus spoke in my mind.

"Did you send us back here?"

He demanded.

I didn't reply.

I felt his panic mixed with fear as he tried reaching me.

The astral thread opened, and Timbrax emerged. I stood on the balcony outside of my bedroom, gazing down at him. He stood there, gazing up at me.

"Your father sent me to talk some sense into you, Melfina," Timbrax called up to me. "Give him the shaman army of the dead!"

"No." I replied, speaking in Sinergy's voice. "Only a shaman can lead the army."

"Of course," Timbrax smirked as he leaped up to the marble balcony. He crouched down before me, so we were eye level with each other. "Then hand the army over to me... I am a shaman to remember?"

"No." I replied.

"Did you just tell your Victim Commander no?" Timbrax asked.

"Fuck you." I replied.

"Then you give me no choice," Timbrax replied. "My Victim army will destroy everything you love!"

I smirked at him.

"I have one question for you," I said as he leaped into the astral thread. He turned and faced me. "Which army of the dead is going to win?" I smirked "Yours? Or mine?"

"Guess we'll find out, won't we?" Timbrax replied as the astral thread closed behind him.

"Sixus?"

I said in my mind.

Sinergy shifted to the back, allowing me to speak for the first time since she possessed my body.

"Mel?"

Sixus asked

The shock in his voice was evident.

"I started a war with Victim."

I spoke.

I felt the anxiety in my body growing. My intuition alerted me that danger was approaching.

"I figured as much," Sixus replied as he flew down, landing beside me on the balcony. His white dragon wings glistened in the moonlight. He gently placed a hand on my cheek and kissed me. I returned his kiss before he broke it. He rubbed my cheek with his thumb as he gazed into my eyes. "Take charge and lead your combined forces of the living and the dead to victory."

I gazed down and saw the shamans kneeling before Sixus and I before they rose to their feet below us.

"Show them no mercy!" I shouted.

"Here they come!" Sixus shouted as Timbrax appeared and headed straight for me with his sword aimed at my heart.

I was prepared for this moment.

One of us was going to die.

And it would not be me.

Victim or Tellus.

I chose Tellus!

TWENTY-FOUR

I yanked the shaman dagger and the Valistik sword out. The dagger transformed into a sword, and I crossed them before he brought his sword down before me. Metal clanked as I shoved him off. He flipped backwards, landing on the ground.

The war from the other timelines wasn't right. This war happening at this exact moment. Felt right. Pieces had to be ripped from the other timelines in order for this one to be what it is now. Lives had to be lost.

I stood beside Sixus and transported us back to the institute. He glanced around in confusion as I gazed at the Xeonada Empire. A loud explosion erupted from it as fire engulfed the kingdom. I watched as my castle came crashing to the ground again. Sixus turned and arched an eyebrow at me.

"I'm allowed to blow up my kingdom again, aren't I?" I asked.

"Do whatever the hell you want," He laughed. "As long as we aren't the target of your rage."

"Mom!" Cy called from the balcony behind us. I turned and looked up. "Darby and I will protect the twins in I.O.A.!"

"Go!" I shouted. She nodded and disappeared into the room.

Viz transformed into her dragon form and landed before me. The ground shook beneath my feet. Setha ran out and did a quick wardrobe change, dressing me in a clean double-sided uniform, mecha pilot boots, and my two jackets. Zara pinned my hair up, and I was ready to go after she placed my weapons back on my body. Sixus got dressed in a clean shirt and put his two jackets on.

Jumping up, I made my way across her scales. With a click, I secured my boots into the footholds and settled onto the saddle. Upon opening the satchel, I retrieved the flight goggles. I slipped them over my hair and drew them down across my eyes. I grabbed onto the horn with one hand, and Viz shot into the air. My stomach flew into my throat before it settled down.

Parasite started playing over the loudspeaker and I smirked as Sixus joined me in the air moments later, sitting on the back of Ivrem.

"Dragon knights!" I shouted down to them. "Mount up!"

They turned and ran towards the flight strip where their guardians were waiting for them.

"Hunters!" Zara shouted. "Kill Victim and show them no mercy!"

Sinergy appeared beside me. I threw my right hand out, as did Sixus, as Helios appeared before him.

"Spirit Form Accord!" we shouted in unison. The two spirits turned into bright orbs and flew into our palms. We thrust them into our bodies, and they took over, shifting our consciousness to the back.

I (Kinda) Wanna Die started playing as our guardians flapped their wings as we soared over the roaring sea below us.

I watched as the fire engulfed my fallen kingdom once more. I wondered how many Victims survived. The dragons flew around the institute, and they hovered in the air behind us.

The astral thread appeared before me, and Timbrax emerged, sitting on a flying motorcycle. Flashbacks of one blowing up and killing me during the Flight Games appeared before I blocked the memory out.

"I didn't expect for you to blow up your kingdom Melfina," Timbrax replied. "You killed a large amount of Victim pulling that shit!"

"Wars are catastrophic Victim Commander," I said in Sinergy's voice. "You should know that by now."

"Get the fuck out of her body!" Timbrax snarled. "She is not a puppet to be controlled!"

"Your love for her is evident," Sinergy went on. "Yet you deny your love and turned your back on her for what?"

"SHUT UP!" Timbrax screamed. "VICTIM! ATTACK!"

"Dragon knights!" I shouted as I returned to being in control of my body. "ATTACK!"

The dragons flew past Sixus and me and attacked Victim on their motorcycles, sending them plummeting into the freezing sea below us.

Nothing Ever After started playing.

I flicked my wrist, and my pale blue flame sat in my palm. I flicked it towards Timbrax's head. He slapped it away. It turned and flew back towards him, striking him on the side of the neck.

"Sone of a bitch!" Timbrax snarled as he slapped the flame, causing it to sizzle his skin.

"Did I burn you?" I asked innocently as I smirked.

He snarled and leaped off his motorcycle, landing on Viz. He screamed in fury as he ran towards me. Timbrax speared me like a pro wrestler, causing me to go flying off of Viz's back as my boots came unclicked.

I flexed my back muscles, and my dragon wings exploded out of the back of the jackets. I head-butted Timbrax, causing him to grab for his eyes. Turning to the right, he flew off me, plummeting into the fringed water below.

Turning, I flew upwards, flapping my wings. Viz swooped down, and I landed on the saddle on her back. Slamming my boots back into the footholds, I grabbed the horn, and we took off.

Viz swung her long-spiked tail towards fifteen Victim. She slammed it into their chests, sending them flying off of their bikes and into the water. I turned and noticed they were swimming towards the land. The institute!

"Fuck!" I shouted.

Viz turned around and powered up her flame. She opened her mouth and charred the Victims who were rising out of the water.

Sixus flew past me, freezing the Victim with his ice breath. The dragon knights hopped off the backs of their guardians and crushed the Victim with their weapons or elemental powers.

Sixus and I both unclipped our boots and stood. We leaped off our guardians' backs and landed on the front lawn of the institute.

The Fight Within started playing.

Timbrax flipped over the tall brick wall, soaking wet. Normally, seeing him dripping wet would be hella sexy. But he was the enemy. And I wanted nothing more than to kick his ass! He used his flames and dried himself off without burning his clothes. Hot steam emanated off of his skin as he drew his blade from behind his back. Snarling at me, he rushed towards me at full speed.

"Firelash Power!" I shouted as I transformed into Hell's Guardian. I yanked the Valistik sword out and ducked as he swung his sword where I was just standing. Balling my hand into a tight fist, I brought it back, then thrust it forward, punching him in the balls.

"Bitch!" Timbrax snarled as he sank to his knees, dropping his sword.

Forgotten played next.

I snatched up his sword and stabbed him in the stomach. Screaming, I pressed further and further until the hilt of the blade was against his body. Timbrax's face filled with shock as he gazed up at me, coming to terms with the fact that I had stabbed him.

"I'm sorry," I whispered as I yanked the blade out. He fell backwards, gazing up at the sky. "What was I supposed to do, Brax?"

Suicide (The Lovers) played next.

"I trained you well, Melfina," Timbrax coughed up blood. "I expected nothing less coming from you, gorgeous."

Feel Nothing (Reset) played after.

"I'm so sorry," I whispered as I picked up his head and kissed him one last time. "I love you so much, you fucking jerk!"

"I know," Timbrax gave me a sad smile as he gently touched my face. "At least you're pregnant with our second child."

My eyes widened in shock as his hand dropped to the ground. With one final breath, he lay still.

Twinkle Together played next.

With tears in my eyes, I watched as the outfit disappeared. I climbed to my feet and Sixus pulled me away from his body.

"I killed him!" In shock, I let out a scream.

Exley snatched the Holistic sword out of the sheath hanging off of Sixus' side and raced towards Timbrax's corpse. He stabbed him and the bright blue light flashed, temporarily blinding us. I shielded my eyes and when I removed them; I saw Timbrax gasp.

Exley reached down and helped Timbrax stand up. When his eyes met mine, they were a bright red with a black flame in his pupils. His skin displayed a tan complexion, and I could audibly perceive his heart beating in his chest as his wound was being healed.

They ran over to my side and Exley handed Sixus back the sword. Sixus put it away and Zara ran into her father's arms.

Timbrax hugged her tightly as she removed herself.

Enemy played next.

I ran into Timbrax's arms, and he hugged me tightly. I sobbed even harder, and he kissed me on the cheek before releasing me. Breathing in, I took in his scent. He smelled sweet with a mixture of fire.

Who Are You? played next.

Velzy ran over and tossed Timbrax his scarlet trench coat. He put it on, and I tossed him his sword.

"Hunters!" Timbrax snarled. "Kill Victim!"

"Victim!" Orion shouted, glaring at Timbrax, who switched sides once more. "Kill them all!"

"Shamanic army!" I shouted. "Attack!" The army of the dead appeared behind me and rushed towards Orion and Victim in waves. We stood there as we watched the hunters killed Victim transforming them into demons.

Panic played next.

I saw Orion, and I snarled at him. He narrowed his eyes at me as my father and Largo Croix stood beside him.

"Victim!" Orion shouted, causing them to look at him. "I'd like to introduce you to your new Victim Commander..." he smirked. "Nitan Westfall!"

"Oh, shit!" I whispered as Velzy, Exley, Zora, and Setha gazed at him as he leaped over the wall. His eyes were white with red rings around the edges. He was a Varacolaci. He held up Tasia's corpse and tossed it towards us. It landed before my feet.

"MOM!" Viz screamed as she kneeled down, and tears filled her eyes. "You killed her?"

"She was already dead," Nitan replied casually. He was eerily calm. "I'm vengeful as fuck right now, Timbrax."

"What do you want, Nitan?" Timbrax snarled. "An apology?"

"We're far past apologies, Timbrax," Nitan replied coldly. He drew his other hand out from behind his back and held out a black dragon egg with pale blue around it. A blue flame exploded outside of it. "This egg seems like a good choice, don't you think?"

"Don't!" I took a step forward when Sixus grabbed me, keeping me stuck. "He's gonna kill my baby!"

Unparalyzed played next.

"That baby is innocent, Nitan!" Timbrax spat.

"So was Zyra," Nitan replied. "Yet, you killed her unmercifully, didn't you?"

"I made a mistake," Timbrax shouted. "I'm sorry Nitan!"

"Apology," Nitan said. "Not accepted." He lifted his hands above his head, and I panicked.

Setha appeared and bit Timbrax on the side of his neck. He screamed in pain and died. She removed her fangs, and his eyes shot open, and I knew he was back as a Varacolaci. The stench of death rolled off of him.

Timbrax shot his hand out and opened the astral thread. He snatched the Holistic sword and leaped through it. He emerged in front of Nitan, snatching the egg while stabbing him with the sword.

Nitan screamed as the bright light flashed. Timbrax tossed him through the thread, and he fell laying before us. When he lifted his head, his eyes were back to neon green. Timbrax removed the scarlet trench coat and threw the sword and coat through, and they landed in front of Sixus' feet. Sixus quickly reached down and grabbed it. He stabbed Tasia's corpse in the arm and the bright blue light flashed, temporarily blinding us before it dissipated. He placed it back in the sheath.

The astral thread closed just as I heard Tasia gasp. She was alive. Sixus had revived her so Viz wouldn't be alone and pissed off, seeking revenge for her father, killing everyone she loved.

"MOM!" Viz cried as she ran into her arms. "I'm so sorry!"

"It's okay," Tasia said. "Mom's here, my precious baby girl."

My intuition alerted me that danger was coming.

"Isn't danger upon us now?"

I thought.

A loud explosion erupted from the sky. All eyes looked upwards, and the doorway glowed brighter and brighter.

The egg Timbrax had been holding shot out of his hands and flew into the open door before it slammed shut.

"Let's get outta here!" Orion shouted. They leaped over the wall and the remaining Victim fled along with them.

Timbrax leaped over the wall, and I tapped into my vampire speed and ran flipping over the wall. I landed in a crouching position and stood. The roar of the sea was all I heard. The coolness of the air stung my face. I experienced a hit of the smell of salt in my nose. Timbrax was gone.

I turned around to flip back over the wall when I stopped. Timbrax was leaning casually against the wall with his arms crossed over his chest as he gazed at me. I lowered my gaze briefly before I looked up and started heading towards the open gates when he stopped me.

"You shed tears for me when you killed me," Timbrax said in a quiet voice. "You still love me, don't you, Melfina?"

"Of course I do," I replied, shaking my head. "It doesn't matter. Seeing as you've returned as the Victim Commander, right?"

"That doesn't mean that I stopped loving you, Melfina," Timbrax whispered as he pushed himself off of the wall and walked towards me as he dropped his arms to his sides. He placed an icy hand on my cheek, and I gazed into his creepy eyes. "We're magnetic, remember?"

"Your such an asshole," I whispered, which made him smirk. "I'm going to get my baby."

The ground rumbled and Timbrax held me to keep me steady.

My intuition kept screaming at me that something was coming.

"Bring our daughter back to us," Timbrax whispered in my ear as he ran his tongue across my neck. I gasped as I pressed my body into his as he rebound his soul to mine. He released me. "Save the world Tribrid!"

I saw the dragons flying back towards the sanctuary in a hurry. The final one flew into the gigantic hole before a larger white dome formed around it and spread out towards the institute and the Kingdom of Eozadion. Alarms sounded around the institute.

"Oh, shit!" I said as the dome closed. I was denied entry into the institute, despite my best efforts.

Sixus pounded on the unbreakable glass standing near the gates. I ran over and touched it. He placed his hand against the glass and our hands touched. Sorta.

"This only happens when Tellus is in danger!" A shout erupted from Sixus. His voice muffled slightly. "We can't do anything until we clear the threat!"

"Sixus," I gave him a sad smile. "I'm the threat to Tellus, Erda, and Outer Earth!"

"Don't you even think about pulling any stupid shit, Mel!" Sixus snarled as he pounded his fist on the glass. Nothing happened.

"Protect our daughters Sixus!" I shouted as I dropped my hand and took a few steps back. "I will always choose you!"

"MEL!" Sixus shouted as I turned my back to him. His panic for me was evident through his end of the bond.

As my eyes lifted, I gazed at the door. I felt myself being lifted in the air. Slowly, I floated in front of the door. I placed my hand on the doorknob and turned it. It slowly opened and, once again, I stepped inside. The door slammed shut behind me.

I found a little girl sitting in the middle of the floor with her back turned towards me. White smoke floated around me, clouding my vision. The only way I could see her was because of the pale blue flame and her shamanic seal flowed around her body. Her magic seal was blue-violet mixed with crimson. Her long, dark hair was wavy and cascaded down her back.

"Hello?" I called out to her. I knew damn well that was a stupid move to make. Everyone who did this in horror movies ended up dead. "I'm bringing you home!"

The girl slowly stood and turned to face me. Her eyes were gray with a tint of blue and white speckles on her iris. Red rings surrounded the pupils. She was the perfect blend of Timbrax and me. She looked to be around the age of six. The same age Cy would be right now.

"Mommy?" she asked as I finally reached her. "I'm ready to go home now."

As I reached down, I scooped up the little girl in my arms. Blocking my path were a legion of dead shaman that I faced. I tightened my grip around my child as I gazed around the dead faces.

"I'm leaving," I said. "I'm bringing my daughter with me."

"You can't leave," Nixie said, stepping towards me. "This is your home now, Melfina."

"Then let my daughter leave!" I spat as the rage boiled over within me. "Please?"

"I'm afraid the child must stay," Nixie went on. "A Tribrid must stay in the gateway and be the gatekeeper."

"Then I'll be the new fucking gatekeeper!" I screamed.

"We have already selected the child. Melfina, it is your responsibility to prevent the worlds from obliteration." continuing, Nyxie stated, "You must keep the worlds from destruction, Melfina."

"How?" I asked. "I'm not exactly filled with the fucking knowledge of everyone's history!"

My daughter leaped out of my arms and walked back to the circle. She crouched down and the protective shell of the dragon egg built itself around her as she grew smaller and smaller until the egg became solid. The scales, black and pale blue, were in plain sight. The encirclement of it was once again by the pale blue flame. A protective dome created by the magic seal encompassed the egg.

Dynastra and Zyra both appeared, forming a perfect triangle around me, with Nyxie in between them.

"What's happening?" I asked as I glanced between the three of them.

"You are being elevated to the next stage in your transformation sequence," Zyra replied. "Everything will be just fine."

All three of them placed a hand on my head before I felt a new surge of power enter my body.

I screamed as a bright blue light slammed into my body, knocking me out completely.

TWENTY-FIVE

I awoke to someone holding me in their lap. I inhaled their scent. Death. My eyes slowly opened, and I looked up to find Timbrax gazing down at me. Memories of Dynastra, Nyx, and Zyra flashed through my mind, and I quickly scrambled off of his lap.

Timbrax slowly rose to his feet as fear rose within me.

I gazed up, and the door was gone! I turned and the glass domes were still covering the institute and the dragon sanctuary.

"FUCK!" I screamed, as I started pacing anxiously. "What happened to the door?"

"After your unconscious body was thrown out of it," Timbrax replied calmly, "It disappeared." He paused briefly. "I caught you and held you until you awoke."

"Those fucking shamans!" I yelled. "They won't give me back my baby!" I paused, panting. "They made her be the fucking gatekeeper!"

"I know," Timbrax replied bluntly. "Why do you think I didn't send the egg back through the astral thread earlier?"

"I thought you were gonna kill her!" I growled.

'We intended for that child to fulfill the role of the gatekeeper, Melfina." Timbrax continued, "You still have a job to do, remember?"

The ground rumbled beneath my feet again, and I stumbled. Timbrax caught me and pulled me tightly into his body as the rumbling stopped.

"Mel, you doing okay out there?"

Sixus asked in my mind.

"NO!"

I shouted.

"I know you lost your child, but you put that on the back burner to save three planets from being destroyed, Mel."

Sixus reminded me.

He was right. They both were.

"I trained you to be a lethal weapon for a reason, Melfina," Timbrax whispered as I gazed at him. "I was preparing you for this moment."

"Well," I forced a dry laugh as I raised my hands and let them drop down to my sides. "I'm sorry to tell you I'm the family disappointment, remember?"

Timbrax crooked his fingers and came at me.

I ducked, punching him hard in the gut, sending him flying backwards. He struck his back hard into the glass. Snarling, he came at me again.

"The fuck is your problem?" I spat as I flipped over his head, kicking him hard in the back. This time, he flipped and turned to face me.

"I didn't train you to be a whiny bitch!" Timbrax spat. "Now pull your head out of Sixus' ass and save three fucking planets. Goddamn it!"

"I didn't train her to be a whiny bitch either, you fucking prick!"

Sixus snapped in my mind.

"She sure as hell didn't get it from her asshole father!"

Timbrax spat.

"She didn't get it from her mother either!"

Sixus added.

Timbrax was arguing with Sixus in our minds, and he stopped fighting me.

I took a deep breath, clearing my mind. I had to contact Naphirie for her guidance.

"Spirit Guide Naphirie?"

I asked.

"What would you like to destroy or revive oracle?"

Naphirie asked in my mind.

"Show me what I need to do to save our planets from certain destruction, please?"

I asked.

"You must tap into the goddess energy that was granted upon you oracle."

Naphirie replied.

"The power of the Tribrid?"

I asked.

"Yes."

Naphirie replied.

"Only the Tribrid can enter the Nexus to destroy it from within."

Naphirie added.

"Can you show me where the Nexus is located?" I asked.

"You already know the answer to that question, oracle. Is there anything else?" Naphirie asked.

"No. Thank you, Spirit Guide Naphirie." I spoke.

"Until next time, oracle." Naphirie said in my mind.

"Where is the Nexus?" I said aloud to myself as I gazed up at the sky. Then a crazy thought struck me. "Brax?" I asked as I looked at him. "Take me to the Victim ship."

"You... wanna go there?" Timbrax arched an eyebrow curiously. "*Willingly?*"

"Yup," I nodded as I walked up to him. "So, let's go!"

Timbrax walked over to me, and I grabbed him. I licked the side of his neck before I sank my sharp fangs into his skin. He growled protectively deep in his throat as he wrapped his arms around me. Having consumed enough, I retracted my fangs. Just before I blacked out into total darkness, I looked up at him, his silhouette fading away.

***

When I woke up, I discovered I was lying in Timbrax's bed on the Victim ship. He was nowhere in sight. I leaped to my feet and walked to the door. They slid open, and I walked into the empty hallway. I followed the voices that were coming from the briefing room.

"And you're positive she's back under your control, Victim Commander?" Orion asked. "She's tricky to control, you know?"

"She is under my control, Orion," Timbrax grumbled. "Ask her yourself if you don't believe me."

When I stood in the doorway, everyone's attention shifted towards me.

"I need a mecha," I demanded. "I know the location of the Nexus."

"Who the fuck do you think you are, Tribrid bitch?" Largo laughed.

"I'll have a mecha prepared for you within the hour," Timbrax replied. "And watch your tone when you speak to my wife, you vampire fuck!"

"Accompany, her Victim Commander," Orion replied, making me look at him. "Just in case she tries to return to Tellus."

"Tellus, Erda, and Outer Earth are about to be blown to shit," I shrugged. "Why the fuck would I return to any of those dead planets, Orion?"

"I suppose you're right, Melfi," Orion agreed. "It's why we're up here in space."

"Exactly," I replied. "I'll be waiting on my mecha in the hangar." With each step I took up the metal steps, I could feel my boots sticking to the surface, creating a slight resistance. Upon entering the hangar, I walked across the metal grate. I leaned my arms on the metal bar as I gazed at the many mechas that lined the walls.

My father approached me. I ignored him.

"You volunteered to go into space?" he asked. "To search for the Nexus?"

"I did," I nodded curtly, keeping my gaze fixed before me. "You fucked up my life, dad."

"No Melfi," he shook his head, his voice muffled through the metal mask. "I improved it."

"By trying to kill me more than once?" I scoffed.

He grabbed me by the throat and held me over the bar like he had last year when Sixus saved my life. I gazed at him, unaffected. "You aren't afraid of death?" he asked.

"Why should I be?" I replied bluntly. "I've already died twice."

My father swung me back across the bars and placed me back down on my feet before he released me from his grasp. "Sixus and Timbrax have trained you well," he said. "I am proud of you, Melfi."

The sound of footsteps reached my ears. I turned and saw Timbrax walking towards me with an attitude on his face. I felt his annoyance coming from his end of the bond when he saw my father.

"The mecha is prepped and ready to go, Melfina," Timbrax said as he softly took hold of my arm. "Get your ass in there and lead me to the Nexus, got it?"

"Yeah," I said, stepping away from him. "Victim Commander." I turned and walked to the mecha at the far end of the aisle to the left. I pushed my way through the black gel door and fell inside, stumbling to catch my balance. The lights turned on and the thick black cords wrapped themselves around my body. It reminded me of the practice mecha's we used in I.O.A. before I became a certified mecha pilot. Timbrax joined me in the mecha a moment later.

"I hate flying!" Timbrax snarled as the thick black cords wrapped around his body. "Let's get this shit over with and get our asses back here, got it?"

"You good?" I asked, arching an eyebrow his way. "You seem prissier than usual."

He rolled his eyes at me but stayed silent. I felt his anxiety mixed with fear. But not for him. For me.

"This is Pilot Melfina Aeon Dra-Westin-DeRaps," I glanced at Timbrax as I added his name to my long list of surnames. "Requesting permission to leave the port."

"Permission granted," Orion spoke through the microphone. "Open that Nexus for us, Melfi."

"You got it, Orion," I said as I muted the channel. "Asshole."

"I heard that Melfi!"

Orion spoke in my mind.

I smirked, knowing I got under his skin just as easily as I did the other men in my life. The mecha started moving towards the launching strip. I stood there as it rocked into position. Timbrax looked freaked the fuck out.

The cool female computerized voice spoke from within the mecha.

"Prepare for launch in 5... 4... 3... 2... 1... GO!"

The mecha was flung towards the open doors and sent out into space at G Force speed. Timbrax snarled as he grabbed onto me to keep from being flung around. A moment later, the mecha slowed down and floated in space at a slow pace. Timbrax sighed in relief as he released me.

"Vampires aren't supposed to be out in fucking space!" Timbrax snarled. "Fucking Orion!"

"And dragons are?" I asked, giving him a look. "Get over it and stop whining like a little bitch!"

Timbrax laughed lightly. "Looks like I'm rubbing off on you," he shook his head. "We're a perfect match after all, aren't we, Melfina?"

"You're okay," I replied. "For a vampire."

Timbrax murmured something under his breath, and I felt his annoyance through his end of the bond.

"Where is the Nexus, Melfi?" Orion demanded through the speaker.

In order for him to hear me, I pressed the unmute button.

"I need you to reroute the mecha back to the Victim ship," I replied. "I'm going in the escape pod to get closer and not blow the Victim Commander to shit."

"Rerouting the coordinates back to the Victim ship now, Melfi," Orion replied. "Hurry and get in that escape pod."

"On it," I said as the cords fell away from my body, releasing me. I turned and walked over to the black escape pod. When I pushed the green button, the door suddenly shot open. I climbed inside and sat down. My hand felt around for the red button. I found it and pressed it, drawing my hand back inside as the door closed. It locked securely in place. Grabbing the seatbelt, I pulled the padded straps across my body and clicked them into place. I was ready to go. "Shoot the pod, Orion!"

"You're leaving me in here?" Timbrax panicked. "I can't fly this fucking robot!"

"You'll be fine." I rolled my eyes. "Orion placed it on autopilot for you, you big baby."

I felt Sixus' amusement through his end of the bond. And Timbrax rage through his end of the bond. Ice and fire never mixed. Unless it was Sixus and I fucking each other's brains out. Then we mixed well.

"Focus Mel."

Sixus spoke in my mind.

"Right. Sorry."

I replied.

"It's not like the fate of three fucking planets are depending on my ass to destroy the fucking Nexus or anything, right?"

I added.

I heard the door open, and I felt the pod crawling, getting pushed back. It spun around and forcefully propelled outwards. Clutching onto the metal handles that were secured to the straps, I maintained my grip. Even though it burned the shit outta my hands. I didn't give a fuck. Tightly shutting my eyes, I felt the circular escape pod spinning around in fast movements. I felt the pod finally slowing down until it floated in space. I opened my eyes and looked out the tiny circular glass window before me. The many twinkling stars glistened in the endless blackness.

"Damn it Melfina!"

Timbrax snarled in my mind.

"You nearly gave me a fucking heart attack!"

He added.

"You don't have a heart."

I replied, pointing out the obvious.

"At least you care somewhat about me, Brax."

I added.

"I never stopped caring about you, gorgeous."

Timbrax replied.

"I'm back in the Victim ship, by the way."

He added.

"Good."

I replied.

"Now stop being a little bitch, will ya?"

I added.

I felt him laughing lightly at my joke. But he was still worried about my safety, heightening his anxiety.

"Are you okay, Melfi?" Orion asked through the intercom.

I pushed the white button.

"I'm fine," I replied. "I'm entering the Nexus now." There was a brief pause. "You are gonna lose all communication with me after I destroy it."

"Destroy it?" Orion asked, with confusion in his voice. "You are supposed to locate it so father can control the shamanic army of the dead Melfi."

"Dad isn't a shaman," I pointed out bluntly. "Nor is he a Tribrid."

"Damn it, Melfi!" Orion shouted, clearly pissed off. "If you destroy the Nexus, I will-"

"Fuck off and die in a hole," I said to myself after I turned off the speaker completely. I disabled the location of the pod as well as the ability for him to bring me back to the Victim ship. "I know."

It would be a matter of time before Orion and Timbrax sent out mechas to bring the pod back. Then they would torture me until I gave them the location of the Nexus.

I sighed heavily as I placed the block up, keeping Timbrax out of my mind.

"Sixus?"

I thought.

"Mel?"

Sixus replied in my mind.

"You, okay?"

He asked.

"I'm getting ready to blow up the Nexus."

I spoke.

"I love you and our daughters."

I replied.

"You're talking as though you're not gonna be coming back, Mel."

Sixus said.

"That's cause I'm not Sixus."

I replied.

"I will always choose you, my sexy Half-Draconian mate."

I thought.

I blinked back the tears as I removed my hands from the handles. The burning ceased.

"Where is the Nexus, Mel?"

Sixus demanded.

"In space."

I replied.

"Where in space, Mel?"

Sixus asked.

"I can't tell you Sixus."

I spoke.

"Why not Mel?"

Sixus demanded.

"Because... you won't let me blow up the Nexus... and if I don't do this now, it will result in the destruction of three planets."

I said in my mind.

"You can escape back into the pod and come home to me and our family, Mel."

Sixus said in my mind.

"Just blow up the Nexus and return home, baby."

Sixus added.

"SIXUS I CAN'T!"

I screamed in my mind.

My emotions exploded as I started sobbing uncontrollably. He knew this situation differed from the previous missions we had been on. Different from the Flight Games ever were.

"Tell me where the fucking Nexus is, Mel!"

Sixus snarled in my mind.

"The Nexus."

I whispered.

"Is in ME Sixus."

I finished.

I felt his fear rise to the surface as he realized what I had to do. By myself, I made it to space. I had to destroy myself away from all three planets safely.

"Mel. Please don't do this!"

Sixus screamed in my mind.

"I FUCKING LOVE YOU!"

Sixus screamed.

I lowered the brick wall from Timbrax's bond, and he was losing his everlasting shit. Sixus was heard and felt in his mind. He felt his emotions. Timbrax realized what I was about to do. And neither man could handle it.

"Brax?"

I thought.

"I love you too."

I added.

"Gorgeous!"

Timbrax snarled.

"We'll find another way to do this!"

He screamed in my mind.

"There is no other way to do this!"

I screamed back.

"This is the only way to save Erda, Outer Earth, and Tellus!"

I added.

I heard the mecha's approaching the pod.

It was now or never.

I closed my eyes and slowed my breathing down.

I gathered my shamanic magic seal's energy and threw my arms out.

With a loud scream, there was an explosion all around me.

Then everything fell silent.

The Nexus had been annihilated.

Erda, Outer Earth, and Tellus were safe.

At the cost of my life.

TWENTY-SIX
-SIXUS-

I stood outside on the lawn of the institute with Cy, Viz, Tasia, and the assassins, dragon knights, mecha pilots, and vampire hunters. We kept our eyes fixed on the night sky. For a moment, nothing happened, and I prayed Melfina had changed her mind about blowing her ass up. Then I saw it. A bright explosion of blue-violet exploding outwards. Tellus rumbled violently beneath our feet and Cy clenched my arm to keep herself balanced. The power was massive, and I heard the thick layer of protective glass rattling above our heads.

I was prepared for it to shatter and spray down onto us at any moment. But it held up. With the fading of the bright colors, the ground stilled. The glass slowly descended back down and slid back into the earth. The fresh air and the coolness of the sea stung my face. Someone silenced the alarm, and everything fell quiet around us.

The bond that Melfina and I shared was something I searched for. I felt nothing. I glanced down at Cy and over at Viz. Surly, they could feel her bond. They were her fucking guardians, damn it!

"I don't feel mom anymore, dad," Cy whispered with tears in her eyes. "She sacrificed herself to save us."

"No," I shook my head in disbelief. "How am I still *alive*?" I asked the vampire hunters. "When the mate of a dragon dies, so does their mate!"

"We can't feel her presence," Zara whispered. "Not here, earth, or anywhere."

"Is she in the underworld, then?" I demanded, as I looked at Nell. She was a shaman. She could sense if Melfina was there or not.

"No," Nell shook her head. "I don't sense Melfina anywhere."

"None of this shit makes any fucking sense!" I screamed.

I turned and found Timbrax standing across the courtyard by the wall, glaring angrily at me. He unbound himself from me at that moment.

"You have some balls showing up here," I snarled, narrowing my eyes at him. "Melfina is dead because of YOU!"

"I didn't know she was going to commit suicide out in space, you fucking dragon!" Timbrax shouted. "I would've stopped her!"

Victim leaped over the walls and stood behind Timbrax, who took five steps forward, challenging me.

"Dragon knights! Assassins! Mecha Pilots! Shaman!" I shouted. "Mount up!"

"Hunters!" Tork shouted. "Attack!"

"Hunters!" Zara shouted, staring at her father. "Attack!"

I formed two thick icicles in my fists and flicked them towards Timbrax. He flicked his wrists, and two orange fireballs sat in his palms. He flicked them towards my icicles and melted them before they could pierce his chest.

I drew the shaman's dagger, and it transformed into a sword. Timbrax grabbed his sword from behind his back and we brought them forwards clanking them together. We knew each other and our moves like the back of our hands. We had to join forces to survive in the Flight Games. But that alliance was short-lived.

Someone turned on Mel's cell. Rock music started blaring from the speakers.

Barley Breathing started playing.

Both Timbrax and I stared at each other before we started fighting again.

"Fucking Victim Commander!" I snarled as I slashed the air before me.

"Fucking dragon!" Timbrax spat as he flipped backwards three times before he came at me again.

Victims were being slaughtered before transforming into demons. Nell and Cy were the only shamans we had available to us. They needed help.

"Sixus!" Nell shouted as she stabbed a demon, turning it into black ash before her feet. "Summon the shaman from earth!"

"Shamans!" I shouted as I gazed up at Erda. "I command you to aid us on Tellus to kill these demons!" I wasn't sure if my order would work. They never met me. I was the king of the dragons. Now I was the king of shamans too?

This Is The Hunt played next.

I saw a large group running down the blue violet floor that was slanted and glowing. It was the shamans. Upon hearing my call, they came!

Slashing demons, they leaped over the wall and turned to ash around us. They acknowledged me with a curt nod of their heads as they ran past me dressed in different colored uniforms.

Break My Fall played next.

Helios and Solas appeared before me. I knew it was go time. I threw my right hand out, palm facing forward.

"Spirit Form Acord!" I shouted in a powerful voice. Helios and Solas turned into bright blue balls, flying into my palm. I thrust their spirits into my body, and we were now one mind, body, and soul. Solas shifted himself to the front, bringing in full control of my body.

Timbrax snarled as he held his right hand out. Varric appeared before him.

"Spirit Form Acord!" He shouted. Varric's body turned into a bright green ball flying into his hand. Timbrax slammed his spirit into his body. Varric was in control.

"You betrayed me, Varric," I spoke in Solas's voice as I held the shaman blade in my right hand. "You killed me so mercilessly!"

"I grew tired of being second best to your ass!" Varric spat as we circled each other. "And Nyx *never* should've been our fucking queen!"

"Varric, even in death," I smirked. "You are still forced to obey your king."

"You are not my king!" Varric spat. "I killed you!"

"Kill the demons Victim Commander!" I ordered.

"I'm not-"

Timbrax pulled out his shaman dagger and started stabbing demons as they attacked him.

"What the fuck is happening?" Timbrax demanded. "I can't control my body!"

"What are you doing Victim Commander?" Orion demanded as he watched him kill his own allies.

"I can't control my body!" Timbrax snapped as he struggled to keep his blade from stabbing another demon. The tip touched his skin, and he turned into a dark pile of ash before his feet.

Last One Standing played next.

"Make it stop, you fucking dragon!" Timbrax snarled. "I'm fucking killing your ass for this!"

"You did this to yourself, you stupid vampire!" I laughed lightly as I turned and started attacking demons.

"Get this fucking shaman out of my body, Sixus!" Timbrax snarled as he kept slashing demons using his vampire speed.

"I wanna hear you say it!" I shouted to him as I kicked a Victim straight into Cy's dagger. He transformed into a demon and turned into a dark pile of ash before her feet.

It surprised me to see Viz and Tasia working together as a team. Tasia would flick her throwing stars at Victim and Viz would light their asses on fire as she blew her orange flame out of her mouth, burning them up. Cy would run over and stab them with her dagger, killing them instantly.

"Sixus!" Timbrax snarled as he made his way towards me. "Your fucking dead, you fucking dragon!"

"Gotta catch me first!" I laughed as I flexed my back muscles. My white dragon wings exploded out of the back of my trench coat. I ran towards him. Timbrax prepared himself for an attack. Instead, I ran towards him, leaping onto his head and kicking off, slamming the tip of my toes on his head as I soared higher and higher in the air. "Surprise bitch!"

"Get your ass down here, you fucking dragon!" Timbrax snarled as he flicked his wrists and shot orange fireballs at me.

I did a spiral in the air and laughed as I flicked my wrists and threw sharp icicles towards his head. He slapped them away with fireballs as he flipped backwards, landing on the lawn. With a snarl, he gazed up at me before tapping into his vampire speed and leaping onto the wall. He leaped off, trying to catch me. I threw my hand out, forming a thick sheet of ice in front of him. He slammed his face into it, falling into the frigid sea below with a loud splash.

His head shot out as he gasped for air. He caught me laughing at his stupid ass and he screamed in fury as he turned and swam back to shore.

"Fucking dragon!" Timbrax shouted once he pulled himself out of the water and climbed to his feet. He kicked a Victim off of a motorcycle and sat down. He revved the engine before flying it into the air. "I'm killing your ass!"

I turned and flew towards the dragon sanctuary. Timbrax followed me, of course. I changed course and headed towards the rubble of the Xeonada Empire. Again, he followed me.

Timbrax was hellbent on killing my ass.

The feeling was mutual. Asshole killed my mate! I would show him zero mercy for it! I flung more ice walls, thick icebergs forming out of the water in his path. He dodged them all. I don't know why I was going toward the Xeonada Empire. It's like I was being pulled there by some unseen force or something.

Timbrax startled me when he flew up beside me, also gazing at the rubble of the Xeonada Empire.

"You feel it too, don't you?" I shouted to him over the roar of the wind.

Timbrax nodded curtly, never taking his gaze off the rubble.

"You think her spirit is there waiting for us?" I asked as we grew closer to it.

"You're a fucking idiot!" Timbrax spat. "I'm calling a truce until we can figure this shit out. Got it?"

"Fine by me," I murmured. "Temporary truce it is."

I wondered what would await us in the Xeonada Empire.

Timbrax and I were about to find out.

***

-MELFINA-

My eyes shot open, and I gasped as I sat up. I found myself in the Victim ship. And from the sound of it, I was possibly alone. That is until I heard a familiar coughing coming from nearby.

Silently, I climbed to my feet and walked to the door. They slid open, and I stepped out into the hallway. As my mecha pilot boots stuck to the metal floor, I walked up it with each step I took. I approached the torture room; I entered the room and found my father standing before a large picture window gazing at explosions happening on Tellus. Seeing my reflection in the window, he spun around to face me.

"Melfi?" My father said my name as his voice trembled. "You... you're dead!"

"About that," I whispered as I slowly approached him. "I am the flame... Fire can't kill me, dad."

"What is it you want?" he asked, unable to hide the fear that was rising within him. "Power?"

"I have power, dad," I went on as I kept making my way over to him. "I don't want it, nor do I need it from *you*."

"Do you want to order Victim to do your bidding by your Victim Commander's side?" He went on trying to buy himself time for something. Hell, if I knew what. "This ship is yours, Melfi!"

"The only thing I ever wanted from you, dad," I went on standing in his space. "Was your love... and you refused to give me it!"

"Love?" He asked like it was a foreign word to him. "I gave you everything you could've ever wanted and more!"

"I needed your love, dad!" I screamed as my rage boiled over. "And you found every excuse in the world to *never* give me that!"

"Love is for the *weak*!" He snarled. "You wanted to be loved?" he shook his head. "You found it from that disgusting dragon, King Sixus Westin!"

"I'm killing you now, dad," I whispered as I saw the fear in his eyes. "You destroyed my life!"

"We can talk about this," he said as he hid a hand behind his back. He drew it forwards holding a dagger. "On second thought, I'll kill you instead!"

He thrust it towards my neck, and I blocked his right arm, bringing my knee up. I slammed it in his forehead, making him stagger backwards, hitting the back of his head against the window.

Nightmare started blasting from Timbrax's cell. It played over the loudspeaker.

I heard footsteps running towards me and I spun around fist balled into a tight fist. I threw it back then brought it forwards striking Largo Croix in the nose.

Largo stumbled backwards, snarling at me as blood dripped down his face. He licked it and popped his neck muscles.

"Fucking Tribrid bitch!" Largo spat. "The Victim Commander isn't here to save your ass from me killing you!"

"Who said I need saving?" I asked innocently as I grabbed a long metal pole. By forcefully yanking it, I removed it from both the ceiling and the floor. I thrust it deep into his stomach and ran, slamming him into the wall. The thick metal beam shot through the wall, and I bent it, stabbing the other end of it through his left leg and shoving it deeply through the wall. I walked out of the room and bent both sides of the metal, bending them into the metal wall. Walking back into the room, I gazed at Largo.

"Your fucking dead!" Largo snarled as he struggled to release himself from the wall. Dark blood seeped out of his wounds, dripping into a pool on the floor beneath his feet. "Fucking Tribrid bitch!"

"Don't you ever shut the fuck up?" I asked as I walked over to him, grabbing his head in my hands. I snapped it. Releasing it, his head slumped down in a fucked-up angle. "That's much better."

Turning, I faced my father again. I found him cowering beneath the window.

Madhouse played next.

I smirked sweetly at my dad. His eyes widened in fear as I walked casually up to him. This song was fitting.

He yanked out a throwing star and flicked it towards my head. I stopped it in midair as it levitated. I blinked and my pale blue flame ignited it, melting it in seconds before his very eyes. The metal fell, pooling into a shiny silver puddle before him. "Melfi," Zand cried out with his hands out before him. "I love you!"

"Kinda late for that, don't you think, Zand?" I replied in a scary, calm voice. As I pressed my hand against his face, a pale blue flame surged out, causing the metal to melt into his face. As the smell of burning flesh and metal mingled, Zand's screams of agony and terror pierced through the air.

"Melfina, I beg you to have mercy!" Zand yelled.

"You didn't show me or anyone you killed any mercy," I snarled. "Fuck off and die in a hole Zand!" I grabbed onto his head and placed a hand on his shoulder. With one swift motion, I pulled his head off his body. A sickening ripping sound erupted in the room as I held his head in my hand. His scream fell silent.

Throne played next.

Picking up his corpse in one arm, I opened the astral thread. I leaped through as it shut behind me. It opened in the Xeonada Empire. It shut behind me. I tossed his body and head down and picked up a large piece of broken marble. I slammed it in the dirt and tossed the dirt over my shoulder. Digging a grave in the family plot was my ultimate moment for my father.

I heard two familiar voices in the middle of a heated argument off in the distance. I tapped into my vampire speed and dug a shallow grave. Tossing my father's body inside, I quickly covered the grave with the dirt. Picking up the head, I threw my hand out and opened the astral thread. Leaping through it, it shut behind me as Sixus and Timbrax reached the gravesite.

"I smell fresh blood," Timbrax replied, sniffing the air. "It smells like an Aeon Dra."

"You don't think-"

Sixus let the words die on the tip of his tongue. He couldn't bear to say the words. The thought of him finding me dead would devastate him.

"Help me dig it up," Sixus ordered, as I heard him shoveling dirt with a piece of marble. "Now!"

"Don't fucking order me around, you fucking dragon!" Timbrax snarled.

I smirked. At least they're getting along. For now, anyway.

"JESUS FUCKING CHRIST!" Timbrax shouted, drawing me out of my thoughts. "Zand's head's gone!"

I felt relief from Sixus' end of the bond. He was glad it wasn't my body in the shallow grave.

"Help me rebury this shit," Sixus whispered. "He was your boss."

"Now how am I gonna get paid?" Timbrax grumbled.

"You can always come back and be Mel's bodyguard if she's alive." Sixus joked.

I leaped through the astral thread standing on dragon mountain. It shut behind me. I could hear the war raging nearby. As I looked up, I saw the two strips still leading to Erda and Outer Earth. I noticed Victim were trying to climb it to attack the innocent civilians on both planets. At the moment, none of them possessed weapons capable of killing them.

I dropped Zand's head on the ground. It fell on the dirt with a loud thud that echoed off the silent walls of the cave. Lifting both hands, I focused on the two strips. They disappeared into my body, causing Victim to plummet to their deaths on the ground below.

The scents of death and cranberries mixed with snow flew past me as I hid in the cave's darkness. I reached down and picked up Zand's head.

It hit me that both men were unintentionally following my scent! I had walls blocking everyone so nobody could sense me on any planet, in space, nowhere. Nyxie was leading me in my movements.

"It's time Mel."

Nyxie spoke in my mind.

"Now is the moment to give them a show they will never forget."

She added.

I took a deep breath and closed my eyes as I focused on my new look. I imagined everything in my mind's eye. Then I felt the shift in my body. My eyes shot open, and I ran towards the edge of the mountain. I leaped off and disappeared into the sky.

Sixus turned back and saw nothing. He turned and descended back behind the walls of the institute where the war was raging.

My music was still playing.

Magnetic is the song I changed to.

It was evident to me that Sixus was feeling confused on his end of the bond. I was giving him hints, damn it!

With a swift movement, I propelled my body towards the institute and descended, floating before everyone in my transformed state. The fighting ceased, and all eyes fell on me.

"What the hell is that?" Tork asked nobody in particular as she raised her weapon towards my head. "I'm gonna shoot!"

The shamans all kneeled before me as they placed their daggers on the floor before them. Timbrax was fighting his body but failed as he kneeled before me, placing his dagger on the ground before him as well.

"Wait!" Sixus shouted to everyone, holding his arm up with a fist. "Don't move!"

Undertow played next.

I held up Zand's severed head up high in the air so everyone could see it. Fresh blood dripped down onto the lawn below me.

Sixus shifted into his alien form and floated up towards me.

"Mel?" He whispered my name as he reached me. He placed a hand on my cheek, and I gazed up into his eyes. "You're alive?"

I lowered Zand's head and Sixus kissed me hungrily. I closed my eyes and returned his kiss. Our shamanic seals shot out, striking every demon and turning them into black dust instantly. I broke the kiss and opened my eyes and looked at him. He was back in his Half-Draconian form. As was I.

The shamans all stood and picked up their weapons.

Rise started playing next.

"NO!" Orion screamed. Sixus pulled me tightly into his arms as we dropped to the ground. I spun around to face him. Zand's head swung back and forth in my hand as I gripped it tightly by the hair. "You killed our father, Melfi!"

"I buried his body in the family plot," I replied coldly. "He tried to kill me, and I won."

"I'll be back!" Orion screamed.

"You've brought this war upon yourself, Orion!" I shouted. "The next head on my mantel will be yours," I paused, then turned my attention towards Timbrax. "And the Victim Commanders!"

Orion leaped into the air and fled, flying away. The Victim leaped over the wall and followed him on their motorcycles.

Timbrax stood there with a shocked expression on his face as he gazed at me. "You'd really kill me?" he asked.

"As long as you are my enemy Brax," I whispered. "Yes, I will."

Timbrax regained his composure and leaped over the wall, and disappeared through the astral thread.

I turned around and raised Zand's head high in the air once more and everyone erupted into loud cheers.

This war between Orion and I... just got personal.

TWENTY-SEVEN

The vampire hunters sent the shamans back home to Erda through the astral thread. They acknowledged Sixus and me as their new king and queen. Sixus had frozen Zand's head and placed it in a thick layer of ice to keep it preserved.

I had taken a shower and washed all the blood off of my body and my hair. Utilizing my vampire speed, I quickly dried off and changed into a fresh, double-sided uniform. I glanced at the desk and noticed the block of ice with my father's head in it was gone.

"That's weird?"

I thought.

The doors slid open, and I turned to find Sixus enter the room as I put my boots on and zipped them up before placing my weapons on my body, pinning up my hair, and putting on my two jackets.

"What's weird?" he asked as he approached me. The doors slid closed behind him.

"Zand's head's gone?" I pointed to the wet spot on the desk where the head had once sat. "Did you see anyone come in here while I was in the shower?"

"I was out patrolling the perimeter, babe." Sixus shrugged. "Didn't see anyone."

"Oh?" I stifled a yawn. "I'm sure it'll show up around here."

"Your exhausted," Sixus pointed out the obvious. "You should be sleeping."

"The enemy doesn't sleep," I pointed out. "I can't shake the feeling that something is off."

Barely Breathing started playing on my cell and Sixus and I exchanged confused glances with each other.

"Mel," Sixus said, looking out the open French doors and onto the balcony. "Move!" Sixus shoved me out of the way, sending me flying onto the bed. I struck the back of my head hard and I felt a throbbing pain.

I saw Timbrax get tossed onto the floor, rolling a few times before stopping at Sixus' feet.

"The fuck's happening around here?" I shouted to Sixus.

"Fucking dragon!" Timbrax snarled as he pushed himself to his feet. "I came to collect Zand's head."

"Your too late," Sixus replied bluntly. "Someone already stole it!"

"Fucking great!" Timbrax snarled. "Guess I hunt them down and kill em." Timbrax turned and headed for the balcony when I stopped him.

"It fucking hurt my soul when I killed you Brax," I said to him. "Why can't you just come back?"

"Staying away from you," Timbrax replied as he glanced over his shoulder at me. "Kills me inside Melfina."

"Aren't you already dead inside?" Sixus asked as I climbed to my feet and stood beside him.

King Of Misery played next.

"This song," Timbrax whispered to me. "Will tell you what I can't say myself to you." Timbrax threw his hand out and the astral thread appeared. He leaped through it, and it closed behind him.

I could hear the music playing outside on the lawn. Laughter and joy reached my ears. Sixus allowed the hunters to throw a victory party for everyone.

"You wanna go down there for a bit?" Sixus asked me. "Help clear your mind."

"Why not?" I gave him a sad smile. "Thank you for loving me, Sixus."

"You're my mate," Sixus whispered as he inhaled my scent deeply as he closed his eyes. "I will always choose you, Mel."

"I know," I whispered as he opened his eyes and gazed down at me. His beautiful blue eyes bore down into my soul. "That's why I love you so much."

I pulled his shirt, pulling his head towards me. I closed my eyes as I crushed my lips against his. He returned my kiss just as hungrily before he broke it, leaving us both breathless. I opened my eyes, and he gently touched my cheek with his hand.

"You are my world, baby," he whispered. "I love you, Mel."

The cries of babies coming from the nursery brought us back to reality. Upon our approach, the door slid open. As we entered the hallway, we made our way up. We reached the door, and it opened. We entered the room, and each took a baby. He changed Frudi, and I picked up Xeyva.

I changed her before picking up a prefilled blood bottle. I sat in the rocking chair as I popped the nipple into her mouth. She started sucking on it and I smiled down at her. I glanced up and found Sixus rocking Frudi in his arms after he fed and burped her. He gave Xeyva an I don't trust you look.

"I'm keeping Xeyva at a distance," he whispered. "She bites."

"She is part vampire," I whispered as I took the bottle from her mouth as she quickly drained it. I set it down on the desk and stood to burp her by patting her gently on the back. "She bit you, didn't she?"

"Oh yeah," he agreed as Frudi fell asleep. He walked over to the basinet and placed her inside, covering her up with the blanket. "Dragons hold grudges for all of eternity, Xeyva."

Xeyva burped and drifted off to sleep. I walked over and started to lay her down in the basinet beside Frudi when she tried biting Sixus in his right arm. He leaped out of the way, knocking the bottles on the floor. They clattered, and he scrambled to pick them up.

As the doors opened, I was taken aback to see the royal vampires enter and walk towards us.

"Why don't I like the looks on their faces," I whispered to Sixus as he stood. "What's up?"

"I owe you an apology, Melfina," Nitan said as he stood before me. "I was grieving Zyra's death and embraced the Varacolaci in me."

"It's okay." I gave him a sad smile. "I did the same thing, sort of last year."

"The babies aren't safe here," Nitan went on. "My preference is to leave the twins in the Light Region on earth under Queen Zara's care."

"Take that one," Sixus pushed me towards him. Setha carefully took Xeyva from my arms and I turned and gave Sixus a fucked-up look. "We can't risk Xeyva turning me or anyone else around here into a Varacolaci, Mel."

"Can't we keep Frudi with us?" I asked.

"I will keep Frudi and Xeyva safe," Zara stepped forward. Sixus turned and picked the sleeping baby up in his arms and pressed a kiss upon her forehead before handing her off to me. I kissed her forehead and reluctantly handed her over to Zara. "It's only a temporary situation."

The doors opened and Cy ran in. She kissed her sisters on their heads before placing tiny gold bracelets on both of their tiny wrists. Sixus and I both wrapped our arms around Cy as tears filled her eyes and my own.

"Zara will love and protect them," Nitan said, as Setha raised her hand and opened the astral thread. Zara took both babies into her arms and walked through. "Thank you, Zara."

It closed behind them.

We silently walked towards the doors. They opened, and we exited the nursery. There was no need to go into that room anymore. It was at that moment when I felt a slight shift in the timelines merging into our present one. Cy felt it too.

Nell rushed towards us and shoved Cy and me behind her as the vampire hunters rushed up the hallway and surrounded us.

"What's happening?" I asked nobody in particular.

"I'm gonna need you two to come with us," Velzy spoke to Setha and Nitan as she held her weapon towards their heads. "NOW!"

"Setha," Nitan replied as his glamor dropped. His eyes were white with red rings around the edges. He was a Varacolaci again. The stench of death stuck my nose as they both stood before us. "Kill them all."

"Get Cy and Sixus back to the room and send it down to the dragon knight dormitory quickly, Nell!" I spoke.

Nell grabbed both of them by the arms and drug them through the crowd and towards the dorm room. The doors slid closed behind them, and I heard the room shifting downwards.

I sighed in relief, knowing they were safe.

"Mel!"

Sixus screamed in my mind.

"What the fuck are you doing?"

He demanded.

"Protecting my family!"

I responded by shouting.

I shoved my way around through the back as Nitan and Setha both leaped through the astral thread, and it closed behind them.

In a hurry, I ran towards a glass tube. The door shot open, and I quickly stepped inside. The door closed, securing itself in place. I crossed my legs and crossed my arms over my chest and waited to descend.

Nothing happened.

"The fuck?" I kicked my boot against the glass, splintering it.

Setha entered the tube through the astral thread and punched me in the face, causing my vision to go black for a moment as my head struck the glass once more. With her vampire speed, she quickly snatched the Venin dagger. She stabbed me in the stomach, chest, neck, arms, legs, everywhere leaving me a bloodied mess. She placed the blade back before I blacked out into total darkness.

***

The moment I woke up, I realized that darkness had engulfed everything outside. As I lay in a bed, I heard movement nearby. I kept my eyes closed and my breathing even. I had to figure out where the hell I was. My head hurt and I had a pounding headache. The scent of fresh blood struck my nose. The scent was mine.

"You nearly killed her, Setha," Nitan spoke in a scary, calm voice. "I told you we need her alive."

"Can't we just kill her dad?" Setha scoffed. "The vampire hunters already placed a bounty over our heads."

"It's time to take her to Orion," Nitan went on. "Timbrax will denounce himself as king and the Dark Region will belong to us and our family will reign and start a war with the Light Region!"

"Brax?"

I thought.

"The Dark Region..."

Was all I could say.

I heard the familiar humming of the astral thread opening and someone exited as it shut behind them.

"You two double crossed me!" Timbrax snarled as he raced to the bed where I lay dying. He picked my body up in his arms and snarled at them. "This is *my* kingdom!"

"Not anymore," Nitan replied coldly. "You've abandoned it and your people to play Victim Commander on a planet that has nothing to do with us!"

"Melfina is your queen!" Timbrax snapped. "Your just pissy cause I killed Zyra!"

"This dragon bitch can die!" Nitan scoffed. "You killed Zyra for no fucking reason!"

My intuition kicked in and danger was upon us.

"Get your ass in the tube Victim Commander!" Setha ordered. "Or I'll kill Melfina!"

Timbrax snarled as he opened the astral thread and tossed me in. I landed on the lawn of the institute, rolling twice before I came to a stop. It closed with a soft whisper, making the astral thread disappear as if it had never existed.

"Mel!" Sixus shouted as he leaped off the balcony and ran towards me. He yanked out the Holistic sword and stabbed me with it. The bright blue light flashed, temporarily blinding us. It faded away, and I felt my wounds healing themselves. He put it away and pulled me up to my feet. "Are you alright?"

"Nitan and Setha," I shook my head. "They have Timbrax and are taking him to Orion."

"I say this with love." Sixus shook his head. "Not my problem."

"But it's *my* problem!" I spat. "Their gonna kill him!"

"Mel," Sixus groaned, making a face in annoyance. "This is a vampire problem!"

"Your right," I nodded in agreement. "It is a vampire problem!"

Sixus turned away, and I used that moment to my advantage.

"Firelash Power!" I shouted loudly, transforming into Hell's Guardian. As I flexed my back muscles, my pale blue dragon wings burst out from my back. I turned and kicked off the ground. My wings caught the air as I flapped them higher and higher.

"Damn it, Mel!" Sixus shouted up to me.

The astral thread opened and Setha leaped out, landing on me, causing me to fall back onto the institute lawn.

As she reached for the Venin dagger hanging from my waist, I felt the air being knocked out of me.

"I'm tired of being your portal opener!" Setha snarled down at me. "Die you Tribrid bitch!"

I saw a thick icicle fly towards us. It stabbed Setha in the left side of her neck. She snarled as she rose to her feet. She was about to attack Sixus when her body instantly froze into a solid ice sculpture.

A single gunshot rang out, shattering Setha's body into a million tiny pieces.

Still in a state of shock, I turned my head to find Velzy and Exley both lowering their weapons in unison. They both shot and killed their own sister!

"That loudmouth bitch," Exley replied. "Finally got what was coming to her."

"Mel!" Sixus rushed to my side and pulled me tightly into his arms as he pulled me away from the dead body. He swirled his hand and collected all of her body parts and placed them into an ice pouch. He tossed it to Velzy, and she placed it in her jacket pocket.

The astral thread opened and Timbrax and Nitan both spilled out of it. They landed on the lawn, rolling onto each other with crooked fingers. They leaped to their feet and Nitan looked for Setha. She was nowhere in sight.

"What did you do to Setha?" Nitan demanded as he stared at me.

"We killed her," Exley and Velzy spoke in unison. "She's dead, father."

They had the twin telepathy thing down to a tee.

"NO!" Nitan screamed. He growled, staring at me. "This is your fault!" He rushed towards me when Exley stepped forward taking the Holistic sword, he stabbed his father with it. The bright light flashed, blinding us before it vanished.

Nitan lay on the lawn beside Setha.

Setha?

Exley must have stabbed the bag of ice containing her body parts inside.

"Damn it, Exley!" Setha spat as she gazed at her brother. Her eyes were neon green like Nitan's eyes. "I'm kicking your ass for stabbing me!"

The commotion caused the vampire hunters to rush outside. They assessed the scene and hauled all of us up the steps and through the doors. We stood in the main lobby as Velzy and Exley both told Tork of what had happened.

"Take the dragon royals to their room," Tork ordered Velzy. "I'll deal with your father and sister."

My intuition alerted me that danger was upon us. I shoved my way back to the door and pushed it open. I stepped out and saw Orion. He held Viz up by the throat. Tasia was screaming at him to let her go. He didn't move as I slowly made my way down the steps and walked back onto the lawn.

"You killed our father," Orion shouted across the courtyard to me. "Now I'm killing her!"

"It was a pleasure to serve as your guardian, Melfina."

Viz spoke in my mind.

"NO!" I screamed as Sixus and the vampire hunters ran outside with Timbrax, who stood beside me, as did Sixus.

Orion stood there, waiting for something.

"Bring me my father's severed head Victim Commander!" Orion ordered.

My head shot towards Timbrax, and he snarled, shooting daggers at Orion.

Then a familiar scent struck my nose. Cranberries mixed with snow and death.

"No," I whispered as I gazed at Sixus. "Not you." I muttered under my breath, shaking my head in disbelief.

Sixus slowly turned his head and met my gaze evenly. His eyes were white with red rings around the edges. He was a Varacolaci once more.

"Surprise," Sixus spoke in a bitter voice as he slowly stepped forward, turning his gaze forward. "Bitch."

"SIXUS!" I screamed as I reached for him. Timbrax grabbed me, holding me in a bearhug. "Let me go, Brax!"

"Don't be stupid!" Timbrax growled in my ear. "Setha bit Sixus earlier tonight and he didn't tell you!"

"DAD!" Cy shouted, and Darby had to hold her back as well.

We stood there helplessly as Sixus tossed the circular ice cube to Orion. Catching it, he tossed it to the ground, causing it to shatter upon impact. He bent down and picked it up. He tossed it back to Sixus, who caught it.

"Let's go Victim Commander," Orion spoke, looking at Sixus. "We no longer require your assistance, Timbrax."

"Fucking dragon!" Timbrax threw his hand forward, opening the astral thread. I pushed him away and leaped through it before he could. It opened behind Sixus. I landed, and he turned around to face me.

"Deal with her Victim Commander," Orion said Bordley. "I'm bringing my daughter with us."

"Right." Sixus nodded curtly as Tasia ran over to Orion. He shoved her away, knocking her down to the ground. He kicked off the ground and flew away with Viz, who had gone unconscious from him, cutting off her oxygen. "I'm giving you one minute before I freeze that pretty little heart of yours, Mel."

"Do it," I dared him as I stood in his space. Bound by our mate bond, our souls were still connected to each other. I felt his rage mixed with a desire for me. "I didn't blow up the Nexus."

"Quit lying," Sixus snarled, narrowing his eyes at me. "If you weren't bound to me-"

"Orion!"

I screamed in my mind.

"I have the Nexus!"

"She's lying!"

Sixus snarled in my mind.

"Bet!"

I replied.

"Bring her to the ship!"

Orion ordered Sixus.

Sixus grabbed me by the arm, and I glanced across the lawn at everyone before Sixus punched me in the side of the temple, knocking me out.

***

I awoke to a pounding headache. My eyes slowly opened, and I lay on a familiar metal cot. My wrists burned like hell from the metal shackles. The door unlocked and opened. Sixus entered the room with Orion beside him. I sat up as they approached me.

Sixus crouched down before me and I gazed into his creepy eyes.

"Are you lying to me about the Nexus, Mel?" Sixus whispered.

"No," I replied, maintaining eye contact with him. "Victim Commander."

Sixus smirked as I used his new title. He searched my feelings for any sign of deception. He found none.

"The Tribrid speaks the truth," Sixus sighed as he stood up. "She knows the location of the Nexus."

"Release the prisoner from her cell," Orion ordered. "Bring her to the toucher chamber at once, Victim Commander."

Sixus placed his hands on the shackles and froze them. They snapped, cracking into tiny pieces. I slowly stood and grazed my wrists. They were stolen with thick red rings around them.

"Follow me, Mel," Sixus whispered as he turned and headed for the door. I followed him out of the room. Victim hissed at me as I passed them as he led the way. "This way."

I stopped walking as we neared the door. Sixus noticed and stopped walking. He slowly turned to face me. His expression unreadable as he searched my feelings.

Fear overwhelmed me.

He walked up to me, and I kept my gaze down. I pulled out my cell and pressed the side bar. The screen lit up, and I pressed the music app.

Falling Apart started playing quietly. I handed it to Sixus as well as my purple ear pod box.

"What's this for?" Sixus asked, arching an eyebrow as I met his gaze.

"Hold on to it for me until I come back." In response, I took a step back from him. "I will *always* choose you, Sixus."

I closed my eyes, and I felt myself levitating as my pale blue flames sat in my palms.

"Spirit Guide Naphirie?"

I asked in my mind.

"What would you like to destroy or revive oracle?"

Naphirie asked.

"Destroy... the Nexus... which is me."

I requested.

"It is done."

Naphirie said.

"MEL!" Sixus yelled.
I felt a powerful explosion from within myself.
Then the world fell into total darkness.

TWENTY-EIGHT
-TIMBRAX-

I stood outside of the institute, gazing up at the night sky. Dawn was quickly approaching, and there was no sign from Melfina.

That is until I saw a bright blue explosion coming from space.

I opened the astral thread and caught Melfina's unconscious body as she fell into my arms

"Good job, gorgeous," I whispered down to her. She was filthy after taking a direct blast like that. "Now we wait for that stupid dragon to come."

"Sir," Tork rushed to my side and took one look at Melfina. "I need to take her to up to I.O.A."

I handed her off to Mitrik, and he ran with her, leaping up to the balcony.

By opening the astral thread, I managed to land through it. My destination turned out to be the burning Victim ship. I found Vizzeirra and picked her up. Jumping through the thread, I arrived in I.O.A. Mitrik was there and I handed Viz to him. He took her and ran into a nearby room.

I entered a hospital room and found Melfina lying in a bed. She had machines hooked up to her and was wearing an oxygen mask. Her vitals were stable. That was a good sign. I walked over to her bedside and sat down in the chair beside her.

Abel entered the room, and I looked at him. "Melfina is in a coma," Abel signed. "I don't know if she's gonna wake up."

I nodded curtly as he turned and walked out of the room. My attention shifted back to her. "You'd better wake up soon," I said. "That dragon of yours is gonna go ballistic when he sees what he did to you."

Catching my attention was the familiar hum of the astral thread opening. The stench of cranberries mixed with snow and death made me wrinkle my nose. The thread closed as the footsteps stopped beside me. I didn't bother looking at him. He was staring at his wife. Our wife.

"How is she alive?" Sixus demanded.

"You know the answer to that question," I scoffed in annoyance. "You caused her to extinguish a part of herself."

"I-"

Sixus cut his words off. He knew I was right.

I stood, and he looked at Melfina with pain in his eyes. I snatched the Holistic sword and stabbed him in the leg. The bright blue light flashed temporarily, blinding me before it vanished. Sixus' eyes were back to the amazing blue that drew Melfina towards him like a moth to a flame.

"Mel," I heard him choke out her nickname as he gently cradled her head in his arms. "I did this to you."

I slipped the Holistic sword back in the sheath and moved to the side to give him more room. Maybe his scent will wake her up.

"She's in a coma," I whispered. "She destroyed a part of herself to bring you back home."

"Which part?" Sixus asked. I heard the pain in his voice.

"Not the dragon," I whispered. "She can never become Hell's Guardian again."

"The vampire?" Sixus couldn't hide the shock.

"I already took the weapons and the transformation pendants." I stopped briefly. "I need the Holistic sword."

Sixus unclipped the sword and tossed it at me. I caught it and clipped it onto my belt. It hung from my side.

"When she wakes up and realizes she has lost you, she's going to be devastated," Sixus said. "Thank you for protecting and loving her when I wasn't-"

I pulled him away from her and he looked like he was on the verge of a nervous breakdown. Honestly, so was I. The only difference was I was better at hiding it.

"She is still and always will be my wife," I snarled. "I love her just as much as you do. You got that?"

Sixus was about to say something stupid, judging by the look on his face. So, I head-butted his ass. Sixus went flying backwards, slamming into the bed Melfina was laying in.

He snarled as I smirked at him.

"Later, dragon," I said as I threw my hand out and opened the astral thread. I walked through it and turned to look at him. "Wake her ass up so she can kick my ass, got it?"

The thread closed, and I sighed heavily as I sat down.

Now the waiting game begins.

-SIXUS-

"Fucking vampire!" I spat as I did my best to temper my rage. I moved towards the chair and settled in by sitting down. The pain I caused my mate is something I could never forgive myself for. My actions resulted in my love being in a coma. "Please wake up Mel."

I pulled out Mel's cell and pressed the sidebar. The screen lit up. I clicked on the music app.

Lifeline started playing.

Someone hurried into the room. I turned and looked at them. It was Cy.

"Dad!" She rushed over and hugged me tightly. "I thought I lost you and mom forever!"

"I'm back, my baby girl," I hugged her tightly as I stood pressing a kiss on the top of her head. "Your Mom is in a coma, and I don't know if she's gonna wake up."

"Can she hear us if we talk to her?" Cy asked as she pulled away from me.

"I think so," I sighed inwards. "I'm sure she'd love to hear your voice, Cy."

"Mom," Cy said as she walked over to her bedside. The machines beeped in our ears and each breath she took fogged up the oxygen mask. "Don't stop fighting... Me and dad need you."

Battlefield played next.

"You need to get some sleep," Nell said to us as she entered the room. "Abel is taking great care of our queen."

"I'm not going anywhere." By shaking my head, I expressed my disagreement. "I'm staying by my wife's side until she wakes up."

"I'll be back later, dad," Cy yawned. "I love you both so much."

"We love you too, my baby girl," I gave her a sad smile as I hugged her goodnight. She wiped her tears, and Nell escorted her back to her room. "Night."

I pressed a button on the side of her bed, and it extended the bed out. Getting into bed, I positioned myself beside her. I took her hand in mine and gently brought it to my lips. I kissed it tenderly. Holding her hand brought me some comfort, but not much.

Virus played next.

The hum of the astral thread opening and someone stepping out caused me to stay alert. I was prepared to shoot icicles into their eyes if they touched Mel. The familiar scent of death reached my nose. I made a face at the stench. I knew who it was.

Timbrax.

"She's not waking up Sixus," he whispered as I turned my head to look at him. "We have to go with Plan B."

Break My Fall played next.

Releasing her hand, I rolled to my left and landed on my feet. I nudged my head towards the door so we could speak out in the hallway, so we didn't disturb her. I led the way out of her room and Timbrax followed. We stepped out into the brightly lit hall, and I slid her door mostly closed, leaving open a crack.

"Whatever your Plan B is," I whispered as I crossed my arms in front of my chest. "It's a hell no from me."

"You haven't even heard it yet," Timbrax replied pointedly. "Abel told me earlier tonight that Melfina isn't gonna remember anything when or if she wakes up Sixus."

"So?" I shook my head. "I'll show her visions of everything, and she'll regain her memories faster."

Timbrax was about to respond when the sound of alarms coming from Mel's room drew my attention back to her. Opening the door, we quickly raced into the room. I found her bed completely empty! I saw all the cords scattered across the bed. Melfina was gone!

"No!" I shouted as panic filled my entire body. "Mel!"

"Looks like she's decided for herself," Timbrax shook his head. "She's chosen to return to earth and live her life as a mundane to finish writing her next book."

"How do you know?" I demanded.

"I know my wife, you idiot," Timbrax rolled his eyes at me. "I'm freezing time on Tellus so we can monitor her movements from the shadows until it's time to bring her home."

Explode played next.

I picked up her cell and ear pods.

"I don't like this plan of yours," I frowned as Cy and Nell entered the room. They knew something was wrong when they saw Mel was missing. "We're going to Erda to bring you home, Mel."

-MELFINA-

My alarm went off, and I opened my eyes and grabbed my cell, pressing the off button. The sound fell silent, and I groaned as I sat up in bed. I had to be up at three in the morning to make a TV appearance and do a book signing right after.

The press and my growing fanbase really wanted the scoop of how close I was to finishing the next book. The only issue I was running into was that I had writer's block. I couldn't seem to find the right way to complete the story! I had three chapters to write, and I will complete the book. But something wasn't clicking.

I got out of bed and took a quick shower, got dressed and ran out the door dressed in a black pants suit with matching heels. My publicist Nell came with me as we walked down the steps of The Sovereign Academy of Shamans. We walked towards the gate, and I shoved it open. The metal stung my fingers slightly. I made a face as I continued to the waiting limo. I climbed into the backseat and Nell got in, sitting across from me. The driver closed the door and walked around to the front. A moment later, the vehicle pulled away from the curb and we headed to the studio.

"Are you excited, Nyxie?" Nell asked me. "It's a big day for you."

"I'm more anxious, honestly," I gave her a nervous smile. "I can't seem to finish the book, you know?"

"Your probably reaching burn out," Nell shrugged. "You need to take a break after you get this book edited, formatted, and set up for preorder, Nyx."

"I can't," I shook my head. "The story needs to be told, Nell."

The limousine came to a stop and my intuition alerted me that danger was approaching.

Nell opened her door, and we both scrambled out of the vehicle and rushed towards the buildings when it exploded. Two figures appeared before us and shielded us from their trench coats. As I crept my hands away, I glanced up at my savior. My eyes widened in surprise as I met his mesmerizing blue eyes. My heart was beating loudly in my ears.

"Are you alright?" he asked me with deep concern in his eyes. "Are you hurt at all, Nyx?"

I shook my head no. While Nell and I were quickly escorted into the studio, he and the other male turned and ran around the building.

The experience left me in a state of shock. I hoped to see my savior again so I could thank him for saving my life.

***

The TV appearance went smoothly after the attack on my life. I had the option to cancel the book signing, but I did it. They stepped up security and the signing went by quickly. A few fans were still in line. I needed to get through this, and my day was finally over.

As my other five pens ran out of ink, I grabbed a new one.

Someone set two books down on the table and I clicked the pen open.

"Hi," I said with cheerfulness in my voice as I grabbed the two books and opened them. "Who do I make these out to?" I asked as I glanced up.

"Hi," a familiar male voice spoke. It was him! The hot guy who saved my life earlier this morning! "You can make it out to the sexy dragon king."

With a smirk on my face, I wrote it in both books before signing each copy. I closed the covers and piled the books before sliding them back to him. I placed the pen back down on the table and stood.

"Thanks," he smirked as he grabbed the books. "I guess I'll see you around, Nyx."

"Wait," I called as he turned to leave. "Can we have dinner tonight?" I asked.

"Sure," he smirked. "I'm Evan Reigns by the way."

"They'll take care of the cleanup," Nell said, as she had already grabbed my belongings and started shoving me and Evan towards the doors. "You two have a great time, Nyxie."

"Yeah," I smiled nervously as Even held open the door and we stepped out into the cool night air. "Can we go to your place, Evan?"

"You wanna come home with me?" Evan arched an eyebrow in surprise. "You just met me."

"I know," I shrugged. "But I feel a strong connection to you."

"Absolutely," Evan smiled at me. "Follow me." The lime green Charger stood before us, its glossy exterior reflecting the surrounding city lights as he clicked the key fob to unlock the doors. With a swift movement, he opened the passenger door, and I wasted no time in taking my seat before he sealed it shut. With a firm grip, he walked around the front and swung open the driver's door, touching the smooth handle in his hand.

He casually flung the books into the backseat, the sound of their pages rustling echoing through the car. Taking a seat, he closed it firmly; the sound echoing in the empty vehicle. As he pulled out his keys, I could hear the soft jingle of metal. With a sense of satisfaction, he selected a key and inserted it into the ignition; the click echoing in the quiet car as he turned it. With a quick acceleration, he pulled away from the curb, the engine roaring to life and commanding attention. Every time he accelerated, my heart couldn't help but race in response.

Cutting the engine, he pulled over near a park, and the peaceful ambiance of chirping crickets and rustling leaves engulfed him. Removing the keys, he swiftly stowed them in his pocket while we exited the vehicle. Reached into the backseat and grabbed the two books. As we closed the car doors, he reached for the keys and locked them, sealing his vehicle. Walking hand in hand, we explored the park, admiring the vibrant colors of the flowers and listening to the waterfall nearby. As his icy hand clasped mine, a chill ran through my body, causing me to tremble slightly. He wore a smirk on his face as he guided me towards a tree in close proximity.

"Please don't tell me you live in the park?" I gave him a disappointed look. "That would just suck."

"No," he laughed lightly as he pulled out a gold pendulum with a dragon face on it. He handed it to me, and I gave him a strange look as I held it in my hand. "Close your eyes and count to thirteen."

"Are you planning on mugging me?" I asked. He rolled his eyes, and I humored him. I closed my eyes, and he held onto my waist. I took a couple of deep breaths and calmed my racing heart. "One... two... three... four... five... six... seven... eight... nine... ten... eleven... twelve... thirteen."

"Open your eyes," Evan whispered as he released me. I slowly opened my eyes and gasped in shock. We were standing on the lawn of the institute. "Welcome home Mel."

I dropped the pendulum, and he caught it, placing it in his pocket. I took in my surroundings and looked up. Erda was sitting in the sky next to Outer

Earth and the moon. The dragon sanctuary was to the left. I turned around and saw the Xeonada Empire laying in ruins across the massive sea.

I ran leaping up onto the balcony. He joined me as I shoved open the French doors leading to my dorm room. He took my cell and the next thing I knew, a song played.

Tell Me.

All my memories of what had happened came flooding back at that moment. He caught me by the arm and held me until I was okay.

"Sixus?" I asked as I turned and faced him. "Are you really back?"

"I am." Sixus gave me a sad smile. "It's been a while, Mel. I missed you."

With a firm grip on the collar of his black T-shirt, I pulled him towards me, bringing our faces close together. I closed my eyes and crushed my lips against his. He returned my kiss just as hungrily. Instead of pulling away, he grabbed me and laid me on the bed. We undressed in seconds, tossing our Erda clothing around the room.

Sixus plunged his long, hot cock deep into my pussy, making me moan in delight as waves of eustacy rolled over me.

"Fuck!" I gasped as he smirked down at me.

The slapping of bare skin was barely audible over the rock music blasting from my cell.

"I'm gonna cum!" Sixus gasped. With one final thrust of his rocking hips, I felt the host, sticky cum, flow inside of me. Sixus collapsed beside me on the bed. Both of us panting. "Fuck!" he moaned, kissing me on the lips before breaking it. "I fucking love you, Mel."

"I love you Sixus," I gave him a small smile. "My sexy dragon king."

"Let's take a shower," he said as he climbed to his feet. He held out his hand, and I took it. I stood on the floor beside him. "My scent is all over you."

My attempt to tap into my vampire speed but was unsuccessful. I thought that was weird, but I dismissed it as I crossed the room and opened the closet. I grabbed a clean double-sided uniform and pulled it off the hanger before grabbing my undergarments and heading into the bathroom. Sixus joined me and we placed our clothes on the banister. He pulled back the curtain and turned the water on. We stepped inside and washed ourselves up before he turned it off. He shoved the curtain open, and we stepped out. Handing me a towel, I dried myself off before getting dressed.

I walked out of the bathroom, tossing the towel into the laundry basket with my dirty clothes. Prior to zipping them up, I slipped on my socks and mecha pilot boots. I brushed my hair out and put it in a ponytail. I grabbed my jackets and put them on. Picking up the shaman dagger, I clipped it on my uniform and looked for the Valistik sword and Venin dagger.

"Where are my other weapons?" I asked, turning to face Sixus.

"Gone," Sixus replied as he finished clipping his dagger onto his uniform. "Timbrax took them back."

"Why?" I asked, not understanding what would compel him to do something like that.

"When you blew up the Nexus on the Victim ship," Sixus sighed heavily. "You blew up a piece of yourself along with it, Mel."

"What?" I asked as I thought about it. "I'm able to access the Half-Draconian easily," I went on. Sixus gave me a look, and it hit me like a ton of bricks. "The vampire is gone, isn't it?"

"You got it," Sixus nodded curtly. "You've lost the ability to transform into Hell's Guardian or use the weapons, Mel."

"Why didn't Timbrax tell me this was gonna happen?" I asked. "He fed me the information through my dream state."

"Timbrax wanted you to lose your vampire abilities, Mel," Sixus whispered quietly. "You are no longer a Tribrid."

"That's," I said, unable to hide my disappointment. "Pretty fucked up of him to do to me."

"I'm sorry." Sixus walked over to me and hugged me tightly. "I thought you'd be happy not to drink blood anymore."

"I expressed my anger through a sigh as I moved away from him." "But now I feel empty without that missing part of myself, Sixus."

"Fly with me to the dragon sanctuary?" Sixus asked, changing the subject. "There's something I need to show you." I followed him out the open French doors and we stood on the balcony.

"Wait for me!" Cy said as she entered the room. She raced towards us and hugged us both. I hugged her tightly before she released me. "I'm glad you're back, mom."

"Me too," I gave her a sad smile. "Let's fly as a family."

In a flawless formation, we stood in line. As our back muscles flexed, our dragon wings burst out of the backs of our trench coats. We climbed onto the marble balcony. I took a deep breath, and we kicked off, our wings flapping as they caught the wind. Flying towards the dragon sanctuary, we flew together. The wind struck my skin, and I felt free flying up here. The dragon sanctuary loomed ahead. Flying faster, we reached it, and we descended, dropping to our feet on the ground.

"You missed that, didn't ya?" Sixus asked me with a mischievous smirk on his sexy face.

"I did," I laughed lightly as he pulled open one of the heavy glass doors for me. I stepped inside and the humid air struck my face. It smelled like dragons in here.

"Haven't I seen everything there is to see in here?" I asked as he and Cy entered and walked excitedly ahead of me. They didn't reply. I rolled my eyes and followed them up the long stone floor.

"Not everything, mom," Cy exclaimed excitedly as she took my hand and pulled me to the left. A hidden door I hadn't noticed before loomed before us. "It's in here."

Sixus pressed a four-digit code, and the red light turned green. As he pulled open the thick metal door, he heard a clicking sound. He nudged his head for me to go inside. I cautiously walked in with him and Cy following me in. The door closed behind us. A bright pale blue flame and a white one sat on two large stone pillars. They illuminated the dark room as we approached them.

"What is this place?" I asked as my voice echoed off the silent stone walls. I stood before the pale blue flame that seemed to flicker brighter as it sensed my presence.

"That flame," Sixus spoke as I glanced at him to my right. "Belonged to your mother."

"Really?" I asked as I looked at it again.

"Now," he said. "It belongs to you, Mel."

Like a moth drawn to the flame, I reached out and touched it. It didn't burn me. Instead, it shot into my body, knocking me onto the floor.

A moment later, I felt the flame engulf my entire body. I felt like I was being burned alive from the inside out.

I screamed in pain before blacking out into total darkness.

TWENTY-NINE

I awoke laying in my bed in my dorm room. I found Sixus standing over me as he gazed down into my eyes.

"What the hell happened?" I asked as I slowly sat up.

"You're a full Half-Draconian now that you absorbed your mother's powers Mel," Sixus smirked at me as I slowly climbed to my feet. "I couldn't allow you to harness her powers until you became a Half-Draconian again."

"But I don't feel any different?" I said as I examined myself. "I fell the same."

"Just wait until you kill Victim," Sixus smirked. "You're the strongest Half-Draconian on all of Tellus."

"Did I surpass *you*?" I asked, arching an eyebrow. "I have my doubts, Sixus."

"I got my powers too!" Cy exclaimed excitedly from behind Sixus.

"You weren't supposed to get them until you turned twenty, Cy," Sixus shot her a look. "But your mother and I may die in this war, and we need you to rule in our place just in case you know what I mean?"

My intuition alerted me that danger was approaching.

I gazed out the open French doors and saw a male and a female I'd never seen before approaching the institute by flying without wings. I walked out to the balcony and Cy and Sixus both joined me.

Sixus sniffed the air and snarled. "Demigods!"

We climbed onto the ledge and leaped down. Cy ran back inside to safety.

They both dropped onto the lawn before us and walked towards us with purpose.

"Who's in charge of this place?" The female demanded as they stopped ten feet before us. She was beautiful. Her oval face framed her shimmering brown eyes beautifully, while her high cheekbones and perfectly proportioned nose added to her captivating features. The gentle breeze tugged at her long, dark hair, creating a mesmerizing sight. With a slender, athletic frame, she possessed both grace and power in equal measure.

"We are," Sixus replied in an icy voice. "What is your business here, Demigods?"

"We were sent to retrieve the rare element from the dragon who was keeping it safe for us," said the female, as she looked at us. "Lead us to them and we'll be gone once they give it back to us."

"Well, I hate to break it to ya," Sixus said, forcing a smile at our unwanted guests. "But someone killed that dragon last year."

"You remind me of a Half-Breed gargoyle I met once," the female shook her head. "He was a cocky asshat just like you are Half-Draconian."

"I heard you talking about me!" Abel called down from the balcony as he leaped down and walked casually up to us. "It's good to see you again, Brooke and Trunks."

With his towering height and well-defined muscles, Trunks made quite an impression, and his short, pale purple hair added a touch of intrigue to his overall look. His eyes, a striking shade of blue, had an irresistible pull. With an attractive oval face, his features were perfectly proportioned. He didn't share Brooke's high level of energy and remained composed.

"You know them?" Sixus asked, giving him a look. "Their trying to steal a powerful elemental from us."

"Their old friends of mine," Abel replied. "They only show up when an unknown threat is upon us."

"We can handle the Victim problem Abel," Sixus scoffed. "They want the blue flame's power back."

"This is a demigod problem now," Brooke replied bluntly. "So hand over the blue flame and we'll be gone Half-Draconian."

"After the dragon died," Trunks asked. "The flame should have been released from their body and returned to the vault with the other elementals, right?"

"It was," Sixus agreed. "It's gone."

"Did someone steal it?" Brooke demanded.

"Not exactly," Sixus replied. "The dragon's offspring recently received the power."

"If it's an egg," Trunks went on. "Hand it over and we'll protect it."

"It's not an egg," Sixus scoffed. "And you aren't taking it off, Tellus!"

"I will go through every dragon and those eggs in that sanctuary," Brooke said, narrowing her eyes at Sixus. "I *won't* ask you again, Half-Draconian!"

"Stop!" I shouted, making them look at me. "The blue flame is in me."

"Mel!" Sixus snarled, giving me the side eye. "Their gonna take you with them!"

"*You?*" Brooke asked, exchanging shocked glances with Trunks. "Your mother was the dragon who welded the blue flame?"

"Yeah," I said as Sixus pulled me tightly into his body. He wasn't letting me go without a fight. "I'm the oracle of Tellus."

"Of course it would be in a Half-Draconian," Brooke rolled her eyes in annoyance. "We'll be taking her with us-"

"Like hell you are!" Sixus snarled protectively, deep in his throat. "The oracle is the only one who holds the knowledge and is leading us in the war against Victim!"

"What's taking you guys so long?" An unfamilure female voice demanded from behind them. I looked up to find her accompanied by a teenage girl walking furiously towards us. Her face grew with surprise when she saw Abel. I looked at him and his face wore a similar expression. "Abel?"

"Tuffara?" Abel walked up to her. "I thought you were dead?"

"I faked my death," she replied. "To become a Slayer like my mother wanted me to be."

"Dad!" The girl threw her arms around her father.

"Hey Wren," Abel hugged his daughter tightly. "I missed you both so much, you know?"

Wren's words hung in the air as she pulled away from her father, her voice tinged with gratitude and independence. "Mom's been my protector," she said, a sense of safety evident in her voice. With her radiant smile and graceful demeanor, she was a sight to behold. Her oval face, adorned with captivating blueish green eyes, mirrored Abel's own features. She embodied the perfect fusion of the two, effortlessly blending their distinct characteristics. Her slender yet toned physique and tall stature made her instantly noticeable. Framing her face, a curtain of long, dark hair added to her already striking appearance. "We miss you too." she replied, her words filled with genuine affection.

"We need to get the blue flame and get the hell out of here now," Tuffara said to Brooke and Trunks. "The Supernal's are coming!"

"It's a complicated situation, Tuffara," Brooke nudged her head towards me. "It appears that the dragon, who was entrusted to protect the blue flame, has died and transferred her powers to her daughter."

"Fuck!" Tuffara looked at Abel. "You've been protecting these Half-Draconian's haven't you?"

"Myself and others from earth and Outer Earth are yes," Abel agreed. "Our three planets are in danger and these two are leading the charge of protecting us all from destruction, Tuffara."

"Alright, new plan," Tuffara said to Brooke and Trunks. "We protect the Half-Draconian royals and do not allow the Supernal's to get their hands on the blue flame, got it?"

The astral thread opened, and Zara stepped out, holding my twins. She handed Frudi to Sixus and gave me Xeyva. Cy leaped down and ran over to us and hugged her baby sisters. The vampire hunters and the royals returned. As did Nell before the astral thread closed.

"Chaos," Tuffara gave him a warm smile when she saw the vampire hunter. "It's been a long time, hasn't it?"

"It has," Chaos returned her smile as he walked over to her and gave her and Wren a hug. "I'm glad you are all doing well."

"I wish we came under better circumstances," Tuffara replied. "The Supernal's are on their way here to destroy this planet to get their hands on the blue flame."

"I'll fight them all," I said, making the others look at me. "They aren't getting their hands on my powers."

"No offense," Brooke said to me. "But you look... Mid."

"Yeah," I replied. "I get that a lot."

Zara showed them visions of my entire journey up to this point. They all looked at me again and were left stunned.

"Then we'll take the babies with us," Tuffara said. "We'll keep them safe in the Slayer's secured location."

Sixus was about to lose his shit when I placed a hand on his shoulder, making him look at me.

"Ethier they take the babies," I whispered. "Or they take me."

"Your sure we can trust them?" Sixus asked Abel and Chaos. "We can't separate Half-Draconian twins or they'll die."

"They were good to Lyric and Zyra when they were alive," Chaos replied. "I trust them completely."

"Tuffara is my wife," Abel said to us. "She keeps her word." he paused. "As do the Slayers."

"The twins are gonna need a caretaker," I said, looking around at the others. "Would anyone like to stay with them?"

"It will be my honor to protect the royal babies." Chaos bowed his head slightly to me and Sixus. "I am getting too old to be on the field fighting."

"I'll go too," Viz said as she stepped forward. "My father is trying to kill me and they need a Half-Draconian to aid them, right?"

"Thank you both," I said, hugging them quickly before releasing them. They each took a baby after we said our goodbyes to them. Mitrik held open the astral thread for them and they rushed through with Tuffara before it closed behind them.

"I didn't wanna let Viz go," Tasia gave me a sad smile. "But it's better knowing she's safe than to let Orion kill her again."

"Yeah," I gave her a sad smile. "At least you got your kingdom back, right?"

"Yeah," Tasia laughed lightly. "Thank you for protecting Vizzeirra for me. I am in your debt, Melfina."

The astral thread opened and Tuffara emerged with Wren as it shut behind them.

"They are all safe," Tuffara said to us. "You are the sole target of the Supernal's now, Melfina."

My eyes widened in surprise when I saw Nyxie, Solas, A.J., and Varric standing with Zyra behind the Slayers.

"Aren't they?" I asked nobody in particular, as the words died on the tip of my tongue.

"We were dead," Solas smirked as they made their way towards me. "But after you blew up the Nexus and sacrificed a part of yourself so selflessly... you revived us unknowingly."

Tears filled my eyes as I gave all of them a hug. Solas was shocked, and offered a pat on the back as I let go of him and embraced Nyx and Zyra.

"We wanted to surprise you," Nyx said as I released them. "I think it worked."

"You did," I agreed, wiping my eyes with my fingers. "I'm so grateful you guys are alive."

"We have our abilities back," Solas went on. "You two are the Universal Shamanic Queen Melfina and King Sixus once more."

"That's great." I gave them a sad smile. "But I lost my vampire abilities and can't transform into Hell's Guardian anymore or wield the weapons."

"That's why we're back." Zyra smiled warmly at me. "And they are bringing the twins back."

"They don't control the blue flame?" I asked with surprise in my voice.

"Not the full-blooded Half-Draconian," Nyx whispered to me as Brooke and Trunks handed baby Frudi to Sixus and Xeyva to Zyra. "This baby's life is in danger, Melfina."

"What should I do?" I whispered as I gazed at Tuffara.

"You know," Tuffara gave me a sad smile. "It's what's best for the child."

I looked at Sixus, and he gave me a sad smile. He knew too.

"Nitan and I will adopt Xeyva," Zyra said, making me look at my baby. "We will suppress her Half-Draconian side until she is twenty and can return to Tellus to attend the Abraxas Institute of Union with her sister."

I nodded with tears in my eyes.

"Can you let her know how much I love her?" I asked, as Nitan stood beside Zyra. I watched as she dabbed her index finger against her forehead and she had the scent of a pure blood vampire baby. "Can you do that for me?"

"Of course," Nitan gave me a sad smile. "Exley."

I watched as Exley pulled the Holistic sword out and gently touched the tip of the blade against her arm. The bright blue light flashed, temporarily blinding us. It vanished and Xeyva's eyes were a light gray with blue flakes in the irises. She was now a Stregoni Benefici.

The sound of the astral thread opening resonated beside me, courtesy of Mitrik's skillful grip. Nitan and Zyra ran through it, my hearts pounding in my chest as it shut behind them, sealing their fate.

"We're going back to earth," Nyxie said, drawing my attention back to her. "We'll protect you from the academy, Mel."

"I must protect the Shamanic Queen of Light," Nell said, stepping beside me. "Thank you, Melfina, for your kindness, my queen."

"The honor is all mine, Guardian Nightingale." I kneeled before her. "Thank you all for your service on Tellus."

"That's a first," Varric whispered to Solas as I rose to my feet. "We apologize for the part we played in the destruction of the Nexus Queen Melfina." Varric and A.J. both kneeled before me. "We made a mistake and we apologize for being led astray."

"Rise," I said, and they both stood. "Just protect over Nyxie and Solas and never betray them again, or I will kill you both."

Nell nodded curtly at me for sparing their lives. Varric used his green portal and he, A.J., Nell and Nyx ran through it.

Solas took a step towards me and whispered in my ear. "Thank you Mel," he said. "You are one amazing woman." His lips lightly grazed mine as he planted a quick kiss on my cheek before disappearing through the portal with a leap. In the blink of an eye, it disappeared and darted back to Erda, like a fleeting shadow.

On one hand, I was happy they were alive. But they all left me feeling an emptiness within myself.

I heard snarling behind me. I slowly turned and found Mitrik removing his sharp fangs from Setha's neck. She closed her eyes and when she opened them; they were back to being white with red rings around the edges. She was back to being a Varacolaci.

The Slayers got into defensive stances, and Setha rolled her eyes at them.

"I won't kill her," Setha said with attitude in her voice. "Being her portal, bitch, was something I missed."

While walking over to Sixus and Cy, I wore a sad smile on my face. Fruci was sound asleep in his arms. He pressed a kiss on my forehead and I kissed the baby on her head before taking a step back.

"So Sixus' and my souls are no longer bound by the Holistic and Valistik swords, are they?" I asked Zara and Exley.

"No," Zara shook her head. "Your bound by your mate bond."

"So you'd better not die," Exley said to Sixus and myself. "Or I'll revive you with the Holistic sword."

My intuition kicked in and I sensed danger approaching.

The astral thread appeared and Timbrax leaped out. It closed behind him as he assessed the large group who surrounded me.

He approached me when Brooke, Trunks, Tuffara, and Wren blocked his path by pointing their daggers towards him.

"Who the fuck are they?" Timbrax asked with annoyance in his voice.

"What is your business here Victim Commander?" Brooke demanded. "We know who you are."

"I'm not allowed to talk to my wife?" Timbrax nudged his head towards me and they gave him a confused look before turning towards me. "Your married to *both* of them?"

"I guess," I flashed them my two wedding rings. "It's a complicated situation."

Timbrax sniffed the air and gazed at the vampire hunters who stood behind me. "Zyra was here," he asked. "Where is she?"

"Gone," Zara replied. "Back to the Dark Region with Nitan and my sister."

"You let her take *our* baby?" Timbrax asked me, looking hurt. "I never got to meet her!"

"That's far enough!" Trunks snarled, giving Timbrax the look. "The dragon royals are under the protection of the Slayers."

"Seriously?" Timbrax asked me. "You found fucking Slayers to protect you... from *me*?" Timbrax snarled in rage as he paced before the Slayers.

"Trust me," Tuffara spoke in a scary, calm voice as she glared at Timbrax. "You're the least of our problems, Victim Commander."

"I never should've had you blow up the Nexus Melfina," Timbrax said, shaking his head. "As we speak, the Supernal's are heading here."

"We're well aware of them," Brooke replied bluntly. "Now leave before I kill you... permanently."

"Melfina is in this mess because of me!" Timbrax screamed. "I will not stand by and watch these fucking Supernal's kill *my* wife!"

"As long as you are the Victim commander," Trunks said matter-of-factly. "You are not coming anywhere near the demigoddess or her family."

"What?" Timbrax asked as he stopped pacing and gave them a confused look. "Melfina was a Tribrid, not a damn demigoddess."

"All Half-Draconian's, Half-Breed gargoyles, and Half-Breed vampires will be under the protection of the Slayers and trained as one in the future Victim Commander."

"So, we're... gods?" Sixus asked Trunks.

"Welcome to the family of misfits Sixus," Trunks nodded. "Our parents abandoned us and left us to fend for ourselves in this fucked up world."

Sixus stayed silent. He didn't wanna tell Trunks that his parents actually raised him and his identical twin brother, Feron.

"How long do we have before the Supernal's arrive?" I asked Tuffara since she seemed to be the leader of the Slayers.

"Three days tops," Tuffara shrugged. "As long as the rare blue flame is in your vessel, Melfina," she paused. "You are under twenty-four-hour protection by everyone here, excluding the Victim Commander, of course."

"For fuck's sake!" Timbrax threw his arms up in the air. "I'm not going to kill my wife!"

My music was still blaring, and I had forgotten all about it until I heard the next song.

Scars started playing.

Tuffara gazed up at my dorm room where the music was coming from and looked at me with a smile.

"You like rock?" I inquired.

"I love music," Tuffara nodded. "I am a former pop star before I had to fake my death and become a Slayer, you know?"

"Yeah," I forced a smile. "I heard you had an amazing voice."

"Can I take Frudi to bed, dad?" Cy asked. "My arms are getting tired."

"Go," Sixus said and Brooke escorted her through the crowd with Darby by her side as they walked up the steps and he held the door open for her as they entered the institute. "Our girls are safe, Mel."

"You are more than welcome to stay in the oracle dormitory," I said to Tuffara and the Slayers. "It's the only building we have available for you on such short notice."

"We'll take it," Tuffara smiled as Abel stood beside his wife and daughter. "I need to catch up with my husband."

"You can leave," Brooke said. "Victim Commander."

"I'm not going anywhere. You got that, you demigoddess bitch!" Timbrax snarled.

Brooke was about to say something when Abel, of all people, stepped in to defend him.

"Timbrax has chosen to protect Melfina," Abel said. "Right... Half-Breed vampire?"

"I call bullshit!" Brooke scoffed at Abel. He gave her a look, and she took a step towards Timbrax, who snarled as she entered his personal space. She sniffed his scent and coughed as she stumbled backwards, making a face. "He's a demigod alright."

"Can I see my wife now?" Timbrax asked in a scary calm voice as he shot dagger her way. Brooke stepped to the side and Timbrax tisked his tongue in annoyance as he purposely bumped into her shoulder as he walked up to me.

The Slayers surrounded us and Timbrax rolled his eyes as Velzy brought out his scarlet trench coat. Putting it on, he also wore the scarlet gloves. He popped his collar and Exley handed him the Holistic sword. He clipped it onto his belt buckle and Brooke didn't seem to give a fuck.

"I'm sorry, gorgeous," Timbrax said as he placed a hand on my cheek. "I should've told you that you would lose your vampire abilities."

"The dragon gods didn't intend for me to be a Tribrid Brax." I gave him a sad smile. "I was born to be a Half-Draconian."

"What happened to our daughter?" Timbrax asked quietly.

"Zyra and Nitan adopted her." I blinked back the tears. "They suppressed her abilities."

"Fuck!" Brax shouted, furious at himself. "I've lost everything!"

"That's not true," I whispered as I gently touched his cheek. I felt the tears roll down my face. "You still have me..."

Timbrax crushed his lips against mine and kissed me fiercely. I closed my eyes and returned his kiss before breaking it.

Brooke grabbed me by the arm and pulled me back towards Sixus. He grabbed me and nuzzled his nose into my neck, snarling protectively.

"You're a Half-Draconian Mel," Sixus whispered as he leaned his forehead against mine, locking eyes with me. "You can't be with him after everything he's done to you... to us... to our people."

"Your right," I whispered as I pulled the ring off of my finger. Brooke took it from my hand and threw it at Timbrax. He caught it and I saw the pain in his eyes as I gazed at him. "Sign those divorce papers, Timbrax."

Sixus picked me up in his arms and walked towards the balcony. He leaped up and walked through the open French doors and into my dorm room. Gently setting me down on the edge of the bed, he kneeled down before me.

"I'm sorry Mel," Sixus shook his head. "My heart aches when I see you in so much pain, baby."

Sobbing uncontrollably, I pulled him into a tight hug as he sat beside me on the bed and held me close.

First, I lost two of my daughters.

Now I lost my second mate.

Tuffara, Abel, and Wren all entered the dorm room from the balcony. Wren closed the doors behind her and shut off my music. The room fell silent.

"Timbrax is hiding in the astral thread," Abel sighed heavily. "For what it's worth, Melfina," he paused slightly as I gazed up at him. "Timbrax will fight for you because he loves you unconditionally."

I hoped so.

THIRTY

I was having a hard time sleeping. These Slayers weren't fucking around. There may have only been four of them, but man, they seemed to be everywhere! They were training the dragon knights, assassins, mecha pilots, and vampire hunters to be prepared for the Supernal's when they arrived.

The new, undisclosed location was where they summoned Sixus and me to a royal meeting. We sat in the back of his limousine with the Slayers and Timbrax, who looked even more annoyed that he was stuck across from me with Trunks and Brooke beside him. He kept his eyes closed and his head down with his arms crossed over his chest. The limousine suddenly filled with white gas, and we coughed as we inhaled it. I fell into Sixus before blacking out into total darkness.

***

My eyes shot open, and I sat in my seat at the table in the briefing room, surrounded by the other royals. Sixus groaned as he woke up and took in his surroundings. Cy and the other demigods and demigoddesses woke up as well. Timbrax stood behind me, rocking Frudi as he held a bottle to her mouth. He walked over to Sixus, and he carefully took his daughter.

"Thank you, Brax."

I said in my mind.

He nodded curtly to me as he moved behind me, standing like a guard protecting me and my family.

"More royals?" Feran asked, glancing around the table at the others, who sat up and shook off the sleeping gas. "Who are they and what is their business here, Sixus?"

"They call themselves the Slayers." Sixus cleared his throat as he rocked our daughter in his arms. "A new enemy calling themselves the Supernal's are after Melfina."

"What do they want with the oracle?" Feran asked with a slight frown on his face.

"My powers," I whispered, and all eyes fell upon me. "I absorbed my mother's flame earlier today... as did Sixus and Cy, with their mother and grandmother." I gazed around the table, feeling uncertain. "We're demigods and demigoddesses just as they are."

I nudged my head at the others, and they stared at them in awe.

"We are still in a war against Orion and Victim," Feran went on. "Now we are coming against gods and goddesses?"

"We are here to protect Melfina," Tuffara emphasized. "Removing the blue flame from her body will cause her and her mate certain death."

"I'm not letting that happen," Timbrax said under his breath. "They can't have *her*!"

Sixus glanced at him out of the corner of his eye, but stayed silent. I examined his emotions to gauge if he was pissed. Despite the circumstances, he managed to stay calm.

"And as the only oracle of Tellus," Feran went on. "In times of war, her psychic abilities are invaluable to our kingdoms, which is why we must ensure her survival."

A bad feeling suddenly overwhelmed me and I leaped to my feet without warning, startling everyone in the room.

"Is everything alright, Queen Melfina?" Feran asked as he took a deep breath, trying to calm his racing heart.

"No," I shook my head. "Something is wrong."

A vision appeared in my mind.

I saw Zyra and Nitan hand Xeyva over to Chassin and Mixie Lightborn. He handed them a suitcase filled with money.

The vision faded quickly.

The pit of doom filled my stomach and my eyes widened with terror as I turned and looked at Timbrax.

He already held the astral thread open, and the Slayers leaped to their feet and raced through it. He leaped through it and it stayed open. Sixus and Cy both climbed to their feet, and he pulled her into his arms as I stared at the portal.

The Slayers returned. They were all empty-handed.

"NO!" I screamed as I collapsed to the floor. I looked up as Nitan and Zyra were thrown into the room. The powerful impact of their bodies hitting the wall across the room left them in an unconscious state. Someone threw Chassin into the room next. He also struck the wall and fell unconscious. I turned and saw Timbrax step through the thread, holding Xeyva in his arms. The thread closed behind him. "Xeyva!"

Timbrax rushed over to my side and kneeled down beside me. He pulled me tightly into his arms as I took Xeyva from his arms and she whimpered until she recognized the scent of her parents.

"She's okay," Timbrax whispered to me as he pressed a kiss against my temple. "Our baby is back where she belongs."

"What do we do with them?" Feran asked, pointing his index finger towards the three bodies that lay asleep on each other. "Kill them in the arena, perhaps?"

"Sounds like a plan to me," Sixus nodded curtly at them. "I'm tired of these flip flopping vampires fucking with my family!"

"I have a better idea," I said as Sixus looked at me. "Strip them of their powers so they can't harm anyone ever again." I paused. "And wipe their memories of everything that isn't human."

The Slayers all walked over and grabbed a body. They grabbed an arm and drug them out of the room as soon as the doors slid open.

I saw Timbrax place his index finger on Xeyva's forehead as she slept and he unlocked her Half-Draconian powers. She was back to being a Tribrid once more. He gazed down at her and cleared his throat so he didn't break down.

"She's beautiful," Timbrax whispered as he helped me to my feet after he stood. "Just like her mother." He gently touched my neck and drew his face towards mine. He kissed me fiercely. Returning his kiss, I closed my eyes before he broke it. Gradually, my eyes opened, and I met his gaze. "I love you, gorgeous."

"I love you Brax," I whispered as I turned and gazed at Sixus as I stepped away from Timbrax and stood by his side. "And you too, my sexy dragon mate."

The doors slid open and Nyxie and Solas rushed in, hastening to us. Judging by the looks on their faces, they looked worried.

"What's going on?" I asked as they each took a baby in their arms.

"We miscalculated everything," Nyxie shook her head. "The Tribrid represents a combination of three beings."

"We already know that?" Sixus scoffed. "Can I have my baby back now, please?"

"No," Nyxie shook her head as she and Solas both shifted into their alien forms. The babies transformed back into their tiny selves as their thick dragon shells reformed around their bodies. "These two are joining their sister inside the gateway to be gatekeepers to keep the Nexus from being discoverer'd ever again." she paused. "Each baby will have the important duty of ensuring the safety and well-being of an entire planet."

"No," I shook my head as the shock hadn't worn off of us yet. "You can't do this!"

"We used you three to make this happen." Nyxie looked at me sympathetically. "I'm so sorry, Melfina." They teleported out of the room before any of us could move.

"Tell me," Timbrax snarled as his rage boiled over. "That just didn't happen?"

"Mom," Cy shouted my name, snapping me out of the daze I was in. "Can't you and dad go after them?"

"No," I whispered. "I'm not a Tribrid anymore, Cy."

The building shook violently as we all grabbed onto each other to keep from falling over. It stopped shortly after.

"Fucking shamans!" Timbrax snarled as his rage boiled over.

"I can't believe this happened again," I whispered as Sixus and Cy hugged me tightly. "They didn't even give us a chance to say goodbye to our babies."

"I am terribly sorry for your loss," Feran cleared his throat. "But we have three executions waiting." He paused as we looked at him. "Let this be a lesson for any future traitors of Tellus." He gazed at Timbrax, who snarled at him but kept himself where he stood.

"He's right, Mel," Sixus whispered down to me as I gazed up at him. "Show them no mercy."

***

The arena overflowed with assassins, dragon knights, mecha pilots, repairers, and our guests. The Slayers had placed the traitors in their shackles on the three metal poles. They were waking up.

Zyra, Nitan, and Chassin all took in their surroundings and struggled to free themselves from the chains.

"We made a mistake!" Zyra shouted to me as I stood before her. My expression unreadable. "Show us mercy, Melfina!"

"I've shown you enough mercy," I said in a bitter voice. "You've run out of chances." I walked over and placed my hands on Chassin's head. He struggled to free himself, but it was no use. I was stronger than him and he knew it. He was the contact from Erda and Outer Earth. "As for you," I whispered. "Losing your memories about Outer Earth and Tellus should be enough, don't you think?"

"You won't get away with this shit!" Chassin shouted. "The Supernal's will kill you and take your fucking flame you bitch!"

"I doubt it," I replied. "Goodbye Chassin." I placed my index finger on his Third Eye and closed my eyes. He screamed in pain mixed with fear before he fell silent. I locked his memories away and stripped them from his body. I handed them to Brooke, who placed the bright white orb into a glass box before she closed it and locked it.

Abel unlocked Chassin's shackles and Timbrax held open the astral thread. He tossed Chassin's unconscious body through it, and it shut behind him.

As the rest of us moved past them, we could hear the sound of our footsteps echoing as we stepped out of the circle. The first tunnel beckoned us, and we eagerly sought refuge in its shadowy depths. In awe, we observed as the dragons gracefully landed before us, their scales shimmering in the fluorescent lighting. With a thunderous thud, they touched down, causing the ground beneath our feet to shake.

One word resonated in all our minds.

"Guilty!"

Sixus lifted his hand, and a thick sheet of ice blocked the entrance, stopping inches before our faces. He kept his hand on it to keep us shielded from getting burned. Well, shielded himself from getting burned. Timbrax and I would be fine. Sixus dropped his hand and grabbed me. He wrapped me in his jacket as Timbrax stepped in front of him to take the brunt of the flames once they melted the ice and entered the tunnel. I wrapped my arms around his waist and inhaled his scent deeply as I closed my eyes.

"Focus on me, Mel."

Sixus said in my mind.

I could hear the screams of Nitan and Zyra from the arena. Sixus bent his head and kissed me. I returned his kiss hungrily. His hand dropped to my ass as he pressed my body deeper into his body.

"Hey," Brooke slapped him in the arm. "There's more than just you two in this tunnel, you know?"

Sixus broke the kiss, and I opened my eyes and found him smirking down at me.

"She actually thinks we give a fuck what she thinks."

Sixus spoke in my mind.

"I heard that!" Brooke made a face in disgust as she stepped away from us. "Fucking dragons!"

"I say that to them all the time," Timbrax smirked at me as he held his trench coat open with his back facing the ice that was melting rapidly. "Don't I Melfina?"

"You do," I agreed as I removed myself from Sixus and stood beside Timbrax and held my trench coat open as well. "Move back everyone!"

They raced up the steps and Sixus stood at the bottom with his hands, ready to cool us off when the flames died down. The flames shot past us, and he threw up an ice wall to protect the others and himself. A moment later, it died down and Sixus walked over to us and cooled us down by placing a hand on both of our shoulders.

"Better?" He asked, looking at me.

"Yeah," I gave him a sad smile. "Thank you Sixus."

Timbrax shoved his hand off him and turned and walked back out of the tunnel. I turned and followed him out as we headed towards the arena. Zyra's screams filled the air as fire consumed Nitan.

Sixus touched Nitan's body with his hand, and he turned into an ice sculpture instantly. He punched him in the side of the head before he shattered into a million tiny pieces on the sand beneath our feet.

"Timbrax, please," Zyra begged for her life as tears filled her eyes. She was filthy after being burned. She was a Pyro Lancer. Fire didn't burn her ass. "I love you and our children and our grandchildren!"

Undertow played over the loudspeakers.

The song was fitting for the situation, wasn't it?

"Sorry gorgeous," Timbrax whispered as he gently touched her chin. "You had so many chances and you burned the bridge years ago."

Timbrax stepped backwards a few steps as Sixus formed a thick icicle in his hand. He flicked it, striking Zyra on the side of the neck. She screamed as her body froze, transforming her into an ice sculpture. He punched her in the arm and her entire body shattered into tiny ice fragments on the sand.

Timbrax turned and faced the dragons. "I'm taking my punishment by you dragons," Timbrax shouted, surprising us all. I gazed up at the giant beasts and they burned holes in Timbrax. He didn't give any fucks. "I'm guilty for betraying the Half-Draconian royals!"

"Brax!" I screamed as Sixus grabbed me. Hie ran leaping onto the stone balcony where the other royals sat. "Sixus, he's gonna die!"

Timbrax removed the sheath and tossed it up towards us. Exley caught it in his hand as he held Zara, who was screaming like I was.

"I love you Melfina."

Timbrax spoke in my mind.

In perfect synchrony, the dragons conveyed their verdict directly into our thoughts.

"Guilty!"

The ice dragon powered up his ice ball after he opened his mouth. Timbrax turned his head and met my gaze before turning forward. The dragon released his mighty spray of ice, striking Timbrax head on. He closed his mouth and swung his mighty tail, hitting Timbrax ice sculptured body head on. His body crumbled into many ice crystals, landing on the sand. The dragons shot up and headed back towards the dragon sanctuary.

"NO!" I screamed as Sixus held me tightly.

Let Go was ending over the loudspeaker.

"This concludes-"

"Wait!" Brooke shouted as the white dragon returned.

He hovered over the arena, gazing down at us.

We could hear the dragon's deep, rumbling voice inside our heads as it communicated with us mentally.

"The dragons declared the Vampire innocent of his crimes. His life will be restored!"

"What does that mean?" I asked Sixus, still in shock.

By blowing ice into the ground, the ice dragon reformed Timbrax's body into the perfect ice sculpture. The ice dragon turned and flew back to the dragon sanctuary.

I looked down and saw the ice melting before it exploded. I gasped in shock as I saw Timbrax dripping wet as he fell forward, landing face first on the sand.

"Sedate them," Sixus ordered the Slayers. "Time for a nap, Mel."

A needle pricked the side of my neck before I felt the coldness flow into my vein.

As I was about to lose consciousness, Sixus picked me up and held me.

***

My eyes shot open, and I sat up in bed. The light turned on, and Sixus groaned as he covered his head with a pillow. I didn't know how I had gotten here. The last thing I remembered was Timbrax being revived by the ice dragon before passing out. I shoved the hot comforter off my body and climbed over Sixus. My feet touched the floor, and I crossed the room and pulled open the closet doors. Prior to going into the bathroom, I took a clean double-sided uniform and undergarments.

Pushing open the curtain, I placed my clothes on the banister. I turned the knobs and the water sprayed out of the spout before I stepped in and closed the curtain. Taking a quick shower, I washed my hair and my body before shaving. Turning the knobs, the water shut off, and I opened the curtain. Stepping out, I grabbed a clean towel and dried off before getting dressed.

Walking back into the bedroom, I tossed my dirty clothes in the laundry basket before putting on clean socks and putting on my boots and zipping them up. I brushed my hair. I threw it up in a ponytail I put my two jackets on before clipping on my dagger.

Walking towards the door, they slid open, and I stepped out into the hallway. Tuffara was standing there with Abel.

"How is Timbrax doing?" I asked Abel.

"Pissy," Abel frowned. "He's fine."

"He left this for you." Tuffara handed me a pile of papers. I took them and recognized them as the divorce papers. His signature was beside mine. "I'm sorry Melfina."

Shock mixed with rage filled me as I walked past them and found his hospital room. I entered the room and found him sitting in his bed with an annoyed look on his face.

"What the hell is this?" I demanded as I threw the papers at him. They scattered around the room. "You weren't supposed to sign them, you jackass!"

"I used you, Melfina," Timbrax spoke in a quiet voice. "Stay with Sixus and your daughter."

I walked up to him, balling my hand into a tight fist. I pulled it back before bringing it forward, striking him in the cheek. He sat there and took it. He didn't move.

"Stay the hell away from me!" I spat as I blinked back the tears. "Your such an asshole!" I turned and walked furiously out of the room. My head was spinning, and I just wanted to get away from him.

"Go back to earth and get back the archives the shamans stole from the oracle dormitory, Melfina," Abel said. "Setha is waiting for you."

Setha appeared and held the astral thread open. I leaped through and she closed it behind me as I jumped out. I stood outside the gates of The Sovereign Academy of Shamans gates. It was nighttime, so the academy was buzzing.

"I didn't expect to see you so soon," Solas said as he walked down the steps and opened the gate for me. Upon my entry, he closed it behind me. "I'm sorry we took your babies from you, Mel."

"Whatever." I rolled my eyes in annoyance. "I came to get the archives you stole from my dormitory back."

"Follow me," Solas said as he turned and walked up the cement steps. I followed him as Varric held open the door. We entered the building, and I followed Solas up the hallway. He opened that hidden door with the waterfall. I cautiously entered and he, Nyx, Nell, A.J., and Varric walked in as well. "Tellus is about to be invaded by the Supernal's Mel."

"I know," I sighed heavily. "They want my blue flame."

"You aren't equipped to battle gods and goddesses, Melfina," Solas went on as he handed me the old thick book covered in a new tan bag to keep it from eroding in the light. "They will also take away your powers."

"Are your daggers powerful enough to kill gods and goddesses?" I asked.

"We don't know," Solas shrugged, as they all exchanged glances with each other. "What Nell could find out from reading the archives," he went on. "Was that the dragons have a god or goddess living on Tellus who is capable of destroying the gods and goddesses."

"I'll look for them," I forced a smile as I headed past them. "Thanks."

"You've gotten stronger, Mel," Nyx called after me, making me stop dead in my tracks. "Can you read something for me right quick?"

"Which is?" I asked as she walked over to me. She held out an old parchment paper while Solas held a torch so I could read it.

"Awaken the Dragon Goddess from within."

"What the hell does that mean?" I asked them as Nyxie folded the parchment back up and placed it inside of my jacket pocket. "And why am I able to read this ancient text?"

"You've just awoken the Dragon Goddess on Tellus," Solas smirked at me. "She'll help you defeat the Supernal's."

I felt my flame ignite within my body as I sank to my knees. I felt like my brain was on fire. Solas handed Varric the torch as he picked me up in his arms. I was plunged into darkness as he returned me to Tellus through the blue portal.

THIRTY-ONE

My eyes shot open, and I found myself laying in my bed in my dorm room. I leaped to my feet and rushed towards the door. They slid open, and I stepped out, bumping into Sixus.

"Whoa!" He caught me by the arm to keep me from falling on my ass. "Where's the fire, babe?"

"I awoke the Dragon Goddess when I was with the shamans," I said. "They had me read some old text from our archives book and it awoke her."

"You?" Sixus asked slowly, looking at me. "Could read the text that's over ninety-thousand years old?"

"Yeah." I gave him a strange look. "Aren't you able to read it?"

"No," Sixus forced a laugh. "The language of the ancients died with the elder oracles centuries ago, Mel."

"Really?" I asked as we walked up the hallway and towards the mess hall. I haven't eaten in three days. I was starving. We walked through a line and grabbed trays. We picked out what we wanted to eat. I grabbed a spicy burger with fries and a cola. Sixus grabbed three pizzas, chocolate cake, and water. We walked to our usual table and sat down. "I'm probably able to read it since I'm the oracle or something?"

"Probably," Sixus said as he picked up a slice of pizza and took a huge bite. "We should talk to the Slayers after lunch, Mel."

"What's going on guys?" Tuffara asked as she and the Slayers joined us with Abel, Cy, and Wren.

"Mel can read the old text that died out with the oracles centuries ago," Sixus said as he took a quick drink. "She's amazing!"

"It's not a big deal, Sixus," I whispered as I unwrapped my burger and took a huge bite. The flavors popped in my mouth. I love spicy food. "I'm sure you could read it if you actually tried."

"What did it say?" Brooke asked as she picked at her salad with a fork.

"Awaken the Dragon Goddess from within."

All eyes fell on me, and I gazed around the table, feeling like I was in trouble or something.

"You woke up the Dragon Goddess?" Tuffara asked.

"Yeah," I shrugged. "I'm sure she's in the dragon sanctuary somewhere."

"This is unbelievable," Brooke scoffed. "We actually stand a fighting chance against the Supernal's!"

Everyone talked amongst themselves in excitement. I couldn't join them. Something felt... different. Not in a bad way. Just different. I ate my food in silence and stood. The others stood, and we tossed our trash and stacked our trays on top of the trashcan as we headed for the door. Abel pushed one open and held it for us as we exited the mess hall. I hadn't seen or spoken to Timbrax since earlier this morning.

Sensing the sadness in me, Sixus took me by the hand and interlaced our fingers together as we walked. He glanced at me, and I smiled as he brought me back to him. We've both been through a lot in only a year and a half.

Viz trotted over to us. She was getting along well with Cy and Wren. The three girls were all the same age, so they formed a tight bond quickly. Darby flew down and walked with the girls. I heard footsteps behind us, so I turned and found Velzy accompanied by Rhydian and Timbrax, who looked annoyed that he had to come with us.

I turned back around, and we moved to the front of the group as we walked up the hill. We finally reached the dragon sanctuary and stopped when we saw Orion leaning against the glass.

"What the hell do you want?" Sixus snarled as we walked up to him.

"Our war is temporarily postponed," Orion said as he pushed himself upwards. "We have a new enemy who is nearly upon us, Melfi."

"Are you calling a truce?" I asked.

"For now," Orion sighed. "I see you have aligned yourself with these demigods and demigoddesses."

Abel pulled open the heavy glass door, and we entered the sanctuary. The hot muggy air hit my skin as we walked further inside.

"Where is the oldest dragon, Sixus?" I whispered as I followed him up the long hallway.

"What are you seeking, oracle?"

An unfamiliar male dragon spoke in my mind.

"Can you tell me where to find the Dragon Goddess?"

I asked the dragon in the old language.

"They are dead."

The dragon replied in my mind.

"*Oh. Thank you for your time, guardian.*"

I spoke in my mind.

I turned to leave when he spoke in the ancient language.

"*The Dragon Goddess you seek wields the rare elemental oracle.*"

He spoke in my mind.

"*Only the Dragon Goddess can speak the language of the Celestials.*"

The dragon added.

"*Thank you.*"

I said in my mind.

I turned and pushed past everyone. They stood there shocked that I was speaking to the dragon in an old language that's long since died out on Tellus. As I walked past each room, the sound of dragons roaring reached my ears. Running as I swiftly passed them. I shoved the solid glass door and quickly made my way outdoors.

"Mel!" Sixus caught up to me as I took in the fresh air, trying to calm my racing mind and heart. "What did the dragon tell you?"

The others all rushed outside and gathered around us. They knew something had happened, but none of them spoke the language of the Celestials.

"Why can I understand the ancient language?" I asked Sixus.

"You're the oracle, Mel." Sixus placed his hands on my shoulders, making me look at him. "What information did the dragon share with you?"

"The Dragon Goddess is dead," I whispered. Everyone's faces fell as I gazed at them. "But" I went on. "The new Dragon Goddess wields the rare elemental."

"So, we locate this dragon," Brooke grew hopeful. "We know it's a female, and she wields the rarest elemental."

I gave her a look as I lowered my eyes, and she was the first to realize what I was saying.

"Oh," Brooke said slowly as everyone looked at her. "We've already found her, haven't we?"

Sixus shifted his gaze back to me as the realized hit him like a ton of bricks as well.

"Can someone tell the rest of us what the hell is happening around here?" Velzy asked. "We don't exactly speak dragon, you know?"

"Only the Dragon Goddess can speak the language of the Celestials Velzy," I whispered. "You get it *now*?"

Her eyes widened as she looked at me. Her gaze shifted to Timbrax, who was staring at the ground. He avoided eye contact with me at all costs.

"Shit," Brooke said as she and the Slayers kneeled down before me with their heads bowed. "Everyone bow down before the Dragon Goddess!"

"That's unnecessary," I said as everyone kneeled without hesitation. Even Orion and Timbrax kneeled before me. Sixus did as well. "You can get up, you know?"

Everyone stood in unison, and it made me feel even more uncomfortable in my skin.

We walked down the hill as a group, and I was lost in my thoughts while everyone talked amongst themselves.

"You know," Sixus whispered to me as I glanced over at him as he took my hand again. "It's not a difficult concept to accept that you're the Dragon Goddess, Mel."

"Why can't it be someone else?" I asked. "Why me?"

"Why not you?" Sixus asked me. "Your mother knew that you would be the one to protect Erda, Outer Earth, and Tellus all on your own."

"But" I shook my head. "I can't protect them if I'm dead, Sixus."

"I'm not gonna let that happen." Sixus stopped walking and pulled me to the side as the others walked ahead of us. "The dragon in me will fight for my mate until my dying breath."

"Keep it moving, you two!" Brooke shot back at us. "We need to get her inside where she's safe, Sixus!"

Sixus rolled his eyes, but we started walking again. While being lost in my thoughts, we reached the institute. We stood on the front lawn as the blistering sun beat down on us.

The lights of the shamans dropping from Erda appeared in the sky before they stepped out of them and approached us.

"Who the hell are they again?" Brooke asked, narrowing her eyes at them. "They look familiar, but I can't place from where I know them from?"

"The shamans from Erda," Sixus replied. "You saw them when you arrived yesterday, remember?"

"The Supernal's are coming!" Solas shouted as we looked at him, stunned. "Get the Dragon Goddess inside quickly!"

"Who informed you of her being the Dragon Goddess?" Tuffara gave him a questionable look. "Demigod."

The Slayers pushed me protectively behind them as they stood between me and the shamans.

"They're here!" Varric shouted as all eyes rose to the skies above us. The shamans turned and drew their daggers as they prepared for the gods and goddesses.

Floating down from thick golden clouds were many gods and goddesses descending from the heavens. They slowed down and then stopped fifty feet away from us. There had to be over one hundred of them.

In her strapless, pale blue dress that framed her body, the woman's long, dark flowing hair added an air of elegance to her appearance. Her beauty was breathtaking, radiating from within and illuminating everything around her. With a heart-shaped face, her almond-shaped eyes captivated others - blue pools adorned with swirling purple speckles that shifted with every glance.

"Aphrodite," Brooke spat. "Of course she would show up!"

"There are more demigods and demigoddesses here than I thought there would be," Aphrodite said as she gazed at us. "Where is the rare elemental I sent you to retrieve, Slayers?"

"Someone got to it before we could," Brooke said. "It's been stolen."

"You disappoint me, Brooke," Aphrodite replied. "It's not like you to fail a mission that was so… simple."

"I've heard enough out of you," Nyx said as she flipped her dagger in her fingers before catching it in a tight fist. Setha, Tasia, A.J., and Varric all stepped up to stand beside her. "I'm killing her ass!"

"Nyx, stop!" Solas shouted as she and the others rushed towards Aphrodite. They leaped high in the air, pointing her daggers and guns towards her heart.

Aphrodite caught Nyx and the rest of them by the throat without even touching them. They struggled to free themselves, but it was no use. Her goddess energy was too powerful for them to break free from.

Without effort, the daggers and guns flew out of their hands and stabbed or shot them in their hearts. Aphrodite flung Nyxie and the others and sent them flying towards us. Nyxie and the shaman landed on the lawn in front of Solas' feet. The rest fell before our feet. We stood there, stunned.

"Nyx! Angelina! Varric!" Solas shouted as he pulled the daggers from their bodies, dropping them onto the lawn beside their figures. Before he could touch Nyxie, she evaporated into a thin purple smoke. Her purple shamanic magic seal shot around me before slamming into my body. The other bodies evaporated, and their powers flew back to Erda or their kingdoms. "NO!"

"Where are the dragons?" Aphrodite demanded, without batting an eyelash. "Step forward!"

Sixus and I stepped forward. He interlaced our fingers together as we stood before the goddess.

"Where is the rare elemental?" she asked.

"The dragon who you entrusted the elemental to has passed away," Sixus spoke coldly. "Someone stole the flame earlier yesterday morning,"

"Right before they showed up," I whispered, glancing at the Slayers behind me before I turned my attention back to the goddess. "Your majesty."

"I sense," she went on. "The presence of the new Dragon Goddess."

Aphrodite spoke in my mind.

"Dragon Goddess, step forward and take your rightful place beside us in the cosmos."

Sixus tightened his grip on my hand, telling me not to react.

Nobody moved.

"Hoplites," Aphrodite spoke in a calm voice. "Attack the demigods and demigoddesses and bring the Dragon Goddess to me unharmed!"

Greek soldiers materialized out of thin air, standing before us.

"Shit!" I whispered as Timbrax, and the others stepped in front of us. The alarms sounded around the institute and the assassins, dragon knights, mecha pilots, vampire hunters all emerged from inside. They all drew their weapons and pointed them at the Greek army.

"Attack!" Sixus and Timbrax shouted in unison. Everyone ran towards the enemy at full force. The acid bullets from the vampire hunters' weapons burned the metal shields, striking the soldiers and killing them.

Sixus released my hand and formed thick icicles in his fists. Slamming them into the ground, his ice turned into an enormous wall of ice transforming into ice soldiers. A thick layer of mist surrounded us, and I lost sight of Sixus as he joined the battle.

"Sixus!" I shouted over the screams of death all around me. "Where are you?"

"Don't use your flame!"

Sixus snarled in my mind.

The sight of bright orange flames engulfing the area created a mesmerizing spectacle, leading the way for our army. I strained my eyes, but the thick fog obscured everything beyond a mere five feet in front of me.

"Mel!" Solas shouted as he grabbed me by the hand and began pulling me away from the others. "This way!"

My intuition alerted me that danger was near.

The visibility was practically zero, and I couldn't make out anything, not even an inch in front of me.

"I can't see!" Solas shouted. "Use your flame to light the way!"

"No!" I punched him in the face as he released my hand. I turned and ran, not able to see. "Sixus!"

"Mel!" Solas shouted my name, but I ignored him.

"Brax!" I shouted as panic filled my body. Someone blew pink dust in my face, and I started coughing as I stumbled backwards.

Someone lifted me up into their arms as I started to pass out. I felt them push my head into their chest. I inhaled their scent. Their sweat smelled sweet. Musky. Familiar.

"I have the Dragon Goddess," Solas spoke to someone as he walked past the battle going on around him. "I'm bringing her to you now, mother." He whispered, his voice filled with both anticipation and nervousness.

Just as I slipped into the abyss of total darkness, those words were the last sound that reached my ears.

-SIXUS-

"Mel!" I shouted as I struggled to see through the fog that was growing thicker by the minute. "Someone get rid of this shit!"

The assassins and dragon knights, with the aid of the vampire hunters, formed a wind tunnel that sucked up the fog until it was nearly gone. They placed their hands down and I gazed around at the surrounding carnage. The air was heavy with the weight of lost lives, as bodies lay motionless on both sides.

As I looked up, I noticed Solas walking towards Aphrodite with Melfina in his arms, her unconscious form a stark contrast to his determined stride. Panic shot through my entire body as I met Timbrax's gaze.

"Fucking shaman!" Timbrax snarled as he threw his hand out. The astral thread opened. He leaped through it, and it opened before Solas. Timbrax tried to snatch Melfina's body up as he kicked Solas's feet out from under him, making him fall on his back. A nearby god siting on a cloud punched Timbrax, sending him flying back through the astral thread, and it shut behind him. He climbed to his feet, snarling beside me as he glared at the gods and goddesses.

I snarled at Aphrodite and the two shamans, Nell and Solas as they raced towards her and the other gods and goddesses.

In a soft voice, Solas murmured something into her ear, causing her to momentarily look up at me. However, her focus soon shifted to Mel, who was nestled comfortably in Solas's embrace, wearing a knowing smirk on her face.

"She knew Mel was the Dragon Goddess!" I said to Timbrax.

"Let's go!" Aphrodite shouted to the others. "We got what we came for!"

The demigods and demigoddesses who stood around us stepped forward and Timbrax shoved me behind him as the vampire hunters stood beside him. Cy and Viz stood beside me, with Darby and Mitrik beside them. Viz shed tears for the death of her mother. Orion even stood beside me. He looked annoyed that they had kidnapped his sister and killed his wife.

"You disappoint me," Aphrodite spoke to the demigods and demigoddesses who stood before me. "You've chosen the wrong side."

"We're done taking orders from you!" Brooke shouted. "I hope the Dragon Goddess kills you all!"

"Deliver the Dragon Goddess' two partners to me," Aphrodite cautioned. "Or I will inflict punishment upon all of you!"

"Get the fuck out of my kingdom, you goddess bitch!" I snarled. "I will get my wife back!"

"You've incited a battle with the divine beings." Speaking icily, Aphrodite declared. "The title of victor shall elude you, O dragon king!"

Solas turned his head to look at me, a playful smirk dancing on his lips, as he held Melfina securely against his chest. They joined the gods and goddesses, and together, he and Nell ventured into the unknown.

"We're fucked!" Timbrax snarled. "Is it even possible for us to win a war against powerful gods and goddesses?"

"Melfina will have to tap into her goddess powers," I replied, glaring at Solas's back as he moved further and further away from us. "Or Erda, Outer Earth, and Tellus will fall to the hands of the gods and goddesses."

TO BE CONTINUED.

COMING SOON!
THE ORACLE OF AEON DRA SAGA
BOOK 4

TRIBRID NEXUS PLAYLIST:

From Ashes To New- Live Before I'm Dead
From Ashes To New Ft. Crissy Costanza from Against The Current- Barely Breathing
From Ashes To New Ft. Yelwolf- Monster In Me
From Ashes To New- Breaking Now
Windealkers- Bodybag
Adelitasway- Something More
Adelitasway- All In
Wage War- Magnetic
Self Deception- Dead Water
Lance- From Ashes To New -Post Malone Ft. Ozzy Osbourne- Take What You Want
From Ashes To New- Enemy
From Ashes To New- Broken By Design
Future Palace- Dreamstate
Bad Valentine- Lost Cause
Fame on Fire- Suicide (The Lovers)
The Rock Orchestra- Zombie (The Cranberries)
Bad Wolves Ft. Daughtry- Hungry For Life
Dead By April Ft. The Day We Left Earth & Cyhra- Parasite
Engrave- Fallout
Chrissy Costanza Ft. Voila- 7 Minutes in Hell
Through Fire- Stronger
Escape The Fate- Remember Every Scar
Dead by April- Break My Fall
I See Stars- Calm Snow
The Plot In You- All That I Can Give
Evans Blue- Possession
New Years Day- Done With You
Point North- Nothing Left To Lose
Red- Yours Again
I Prevail- Let Me Be Sad

Point North Ft. Kellin Quinn- Into The Dark
Fame on Fire Ft. Spencer Charmas- Welcome To The Chaos
Set It Off- Why Worry
Bad Omens- The End Of Peace Of Mind
Tommee Profitt Ft. Skylar Grey- Numb (Linkin Par)
Eva Under Fire- Separate Ways (Journey Cover)
Eva Under Fire Ft. Spencer Charnas of Ice Nine Killers- Blow
Ursine Vulpine Ft. Annaca- Without You
Ursine Vulpine Ft. Annaca- Lovers Death
Tommee Profitt Ft. Brooke- Here I Am
Tommee Profitt Ft. Nicole Serrano- Champion
Halestorm- Wicked Waysle
Pop Evil- Breathe Again
From Ashes To New- Dead To Me
From Ashes To New- Legacy
Fame On Fire Ft. Kody Lavigne- Emo Shit
Reddy Redd- Hero
Phix- Came From
Black Veil Brides- Born Again
Written By Wolves- Goddess
Phix- So Alive
Fame On Fire- Halsey Ft. Juice Wrld- Without Me (Rock Cover)
Falling In Reverse- Popular Monster
Bad Valentine- Haunting Me (Alex Pasibe Version)
Fame On Fire- Dead or Alive
Fame On Fire- Katy Perry- Rise (Rock Cover)
Corvyx- Pink- Sober (Male Cover)
Ruelle- Until We Go Down
Motionless In White- Another Life
Tonight Alive- The Edge
Skarlett Riot- Feel
Halflives- Crown
Dead by April- Losing You
Crashing Atlas Ft. Shellby Celine- Too Much
Halflives- Mayday

Halestorm- I Am The Fire
Diamante- Bulletproof
Icon For Hire- Demons (Acoustic Version)
New Years Day- Skeletons'
Tommee Profitt Ft. Brooke- Here I Am
Sleep Theory Ft. Tim Spencer- Numb (Reimagined)
Eva Under Fire Ft. Matt B. From Ashes To New- Coming For Blood
Against The Current- Weapon
Diamante- Ghost Myself
Written By Wolves- Goddess
Like A Storm- Love The Way You Hate Me
No Resolve Ft. Kayla King- Kiss From A Rose (Rock)
New Years Day- Malevolence
Icon For Hire- Gatekeepers
Icon For Hire- Waste My Hate
Escape The Fate- I Am Human
Pop Evil- Breathe Again
Fleurie- Hurricane
Scarlett Riot- The Wounded
Rain City Drive- Cutting It Close
Red- Yours Again
Motionless In White- Another Life
From Ashes To New- Heartache
Fame on Fire- I'm Fine
Red- Breathe Into Me
Evans Blue- Quote
Motionless In White- Sign Of Life
Bad Valentine- Game Over
Icon For Hire- Last One Standing
New Years Day- Half Black Heart
Bad Valentine- Sink Or Swim
Fame on Fire- Stay
From Ashes to New- Let Go
Icon For Hire- Demons
Daughtry- Pieces

Against The Current- Weapon
Simple Plan Ft. Jax- Iconic
Pop Evil- Breathe Again
From Ashes To New- Hope You're Happy
From Ashes To New- Heartache
Vanic Ft. Carmanah King- Run
AID- Who's Afraid Of Little Old Me? X Running Up The Hill (tOTEM Remix) (Mashup by AID
From Ashes To New- Live Before I'm Dead
Bad Valentine- Happy Never After
All That Remains- Let You Go
Nightcore- Battlefield
From Ashes To New -Armageddon
From Ashes To New- Hate Me Too
From Ashes To New- Legacy
From Ashes To New- Echos
Dead by April- Break My Fall (Acoustic)
I See Stars- Running With Scissors (Acoustic Version)
Katy Perry- Rise
Citizen Soldier- Fake Friends
Ekoh Ft. Tech N9ne- Nobody Like Me
Thyrmine- Twinkle Together
Adelitas Way- What It Takes
Sevendust- Unraveling
New Years Day- Defame Me
Black From Ashes To New- Finally See
Black Tide Gallows- Haunted (Taylor Swift Metal Cover)
Rory- Blossom
Villain of the Story- Decade
From Ashes To New- Wait For Me
From Ashes To New- On My Own
Rory- Alternative
Rory- The Apology I'll Never Receive
From Ashes To New- Broken
Tommee Profitt Ft. Skylar Grey- Numb

Like A Storm- Love The Way You Hate Me
Thousand Foot Krutch- Lifeline
From Ashes To New- You Only Die Once
Through Fire- Where You Lie
Breaking Benjamin Ft. Scooter Ward- Far Away
Lewis Fitzgerald- Unlovable
Lewis Fitzgerald- Clarity
Rain City Drive- Heavier
Silent Theory Ft. Josey Scott- Just My Luck
Silent Theory- So Far, So Good
Phix- Alone
Thrymine- Complete Creep
Rose In Doom- Eat Ya (Yummy)
Illenium Ft. Nina Nesbit- Luv Me A Little
Future Palace- Dead Inside
Villain of the Story- Peace of Mind
Vertilizar- With You
Papa Roach- Leader of the Broken Hearts
Pop Evil- Footsteps
Silent Theory- Burn It All Down
Off Script- Thanks for the Misery
These Beautiful Ruins- I Will Rise
Off Script- Enough
Luxi X Synymata- Pretty
Against The Current- Lullaby
Autumn Academy- Reset
Ekoh- The Sound of Falling
The Used- The Taste of Ink
Set It Off- Duality
Slipknot- Vermillion Pt. 2
Through Fire- Breathe
First To Eleven- So Cold- (Breaking Benjamin Cover)
First To Eleven- I Will Not Bow- (Breaking Benjamin Cover)
First To Eleven- The Unforgiven (Metallica Cover)
First To Eleven- The Diary of Jane- (Breaking Benjamin Cover)

TRIBRID NEXUS

First To Eleven- Nothing Else Matters- (Metallica Cover)
First To Eleven—E.T.- (Katy Perry Cover)
First To Eleven- Sweet Child O- Mine- (Guns N Roses Cover)
First To Eleven- Paralyzer (Cover)
First To Eleven- Last Resort- (Papa Roach Cover)
First To Eleven- Crushcrushcrush (Paramore Cover)
First To Eleven- DJ Got Us Fallin' In Love (Usher, Pitbull Cover)
First To Eleven- Decode- (Paramore Cover)
Halocene Ft. First To Eleven- Breaking the Habit- (Linkin Park Cover)
First To Eleven- Animal I Have Become (Three Days Grace Cover)
First To Eleven- Without Me (Halsey Rock Cover)
Starset- Ricochet
Phix- Poison
Halestorm- Love Bites (So Do I)
Sevendust- Karma
Memphis May Fire- Chaotic
Palaye Royal- Dead To Me
Bullet For My Valentine- Your Betrayal
Ovtlier/Motionless in White – Warriors
New Years Day- Hurts Like Hell
Ice Nine Kills - Farewell II Flesh
Catch Your Breath/Ryan Oakes – Perfect World
Kingdom Collapse - Last One Standing
Dorothy – Mud
Jerry Cantrell – Vilified
The Funeral Portrait/Spencer Charnas - Suffocate city
All That Remains- Let You Go
A Day To Remember – Miracle
The Warning – Sick
Beartooth - I Was Alive
Eve 6- Inside Out
Devour The Day- Empty
Papa Roach- Born For This
Bad Omens/Poppy - V.A.N
Sleep Theory – Enough

Sleep Theory- Fallout
Bad Omens- Just Pretend
I'll Nino- What Comes Around
M2M- Mirror Mirror
Beartooth - Might Love Myself
Icon For Hire- Iodine
Papa Roach- She Loves Me Not
Hawthorne Heights – Saying Sorry
Halestorm/I Prevail - Can U See Me in the Dark
Kimberley Locke- 8th World Wonder
Fireflight- Stand Up
Flyleaf- Again
Hoobastank- Running Away
Crashing Atlas- Monster
Against The Current- Weapon
Fire From The Gods - Right Now
Falling In Reverse - Last Resort
Linkin Park- Somewhere I Belong
Pop Evil- Waking Lions
Minute After Midnight – GHOST
Evans Blue- Beg
The Used- The Taste of Ink
Eva Under Fire- Devil in Disguise
Dead By April- My Savior
Icon For Hire- Make A Move
I Prevail- Lifeline
Sleep Theory- Fallout
Breaking Benjamin- Angels Fall
Royale Lynn & Danny Worsnop - death wish
Halestorm- Freak Like Me
Shaman's Harvest- In Chains
Shaman's Harvest- Dangerous
Light The Torch - The Safety Of Disbelief
Halestorm- Rock Show

Bring Me Horizon- Throne
Saving Abel- Addicted
Icon For Hire- Off With Her Head
Falling In Reverse – Zombified
Elijah – HOSTAGE
Catch Your Breath Ft. Ryan Oakes- Perfect World
Catch Your Breath- Shame On Me
I Prevail- Deep End
Trust Company- Downfall
Set It Off- Fake Ass Friends
FLAT BLACK - A Bit of Lightning
Shinedown- 45
Godsmack- I Stand Alone
Wage War- Nail5
Dayseeker – Dreamstate
Framing Hanley- Hear Me Now
The Pretty Reckless- Only Love Can Save Me Now
Highly SuspectNatural Born Killer
If Not For Me - Feel Me Now
Lindsey Stirling- Shatter Me
Diamante- American Dream
Eva Under Fire- Blow
I Prevail- Scars
Chevelle- The Red
Until I Wake- Octane
Archetypes Collide- What If I Fall
Bad Omens- Limits
Archetypes Collide- My Own Worst Enemy (Lit Cover Rock)
Svrcina – Astronomical
MIIA – Dynasty
Ruelle - Game of Survival
Digital Daggers - Still Here
Ruelle - Live Like Legends
Written by Wolves - Let It Burn
Thousand Foot Krutch – Courtesy Call

UNSECRET - Revolution (Ft. Ruelle)
Breaking Benjamin- Until The End
Written By Wolves- Explode
New Years Day- Misunderstood
Shallow Side/Elias Soriano – Filters
Autumn Kings - Sleep When I'm Dead
Bad Omens- The Death of Peace of Mind
Halestorm- Innocence
Motionless In White- Sign Of Life
Archetypes Collide - My Own Device
Archetypes Collide – Undertow
If Not For Me- Demons
FLAT BLACK - A Bit of Lightning
Framing Hanley- Hear Me Now
Red- Breath Into Me
Motionless In White- Masterpiece
Falling In Reverse - Popular Monster
Ovtlier/Motionless in White – Warriors
Wind Walkers- Hangfire
Wind Walkers- Dissipate
Sick Puppies- There Goes The Neighborhood
Silent Theory- Afterthought
Emberlight- Freedom
Pop Evil - Be Legendary
Airhythms Allance- I Need To Forget
Devour The Day – Empty
Fefe Dobson- Shut Up And Kiss Me
Future Palace- Decorabia
Echos- Bruises
Echos- Saints
Jared Land- Holding On For You
Sleep Theory- Stuck In My Head
Rain City Drive- Waiting On You
Beartooth- Riptide
Kingdom Collapse - Last One Standing

TRIBRID NEXUS

Rain City Drive/Dayseeker - Medicate Me
Nothing More - I'll Be OK
Conquer Divide/Attack Attack! – PARALYZED
Crown The Empire - BLURRY (out of place)
Megan McCauley – Fragile
New Years Day - Sorry Not Sorry
Wage War- Manic
Written by Wolves- Let It Burn
Starset- My Demons
DIAMANTE – Sleepwalking
Halestorm- It's Not You
elijah – Virus
Escape The Fate- Do You Love Me
Crashing Atlas- Nothing Left
Thirty Seconds To Mars- The Kill
Crashing Atlas- Thirty Seconds To Mars- The Kill (Cover)
Set It Off- Fake Ass Friends
Pop Evil- Waking Lions
I Prevail- Bad Things
Bullet For My Valentine- Your Betrayal
Eva Under Fire- Until Forever
Halestorm- I Am The Fire
Icon For Hire – Theatre
Sleep Theory- Another Way
Eva Under Fire- Blow
Diamante- Haunted
Disturbed- Down With The Sickness
All That Remains- Two Weeks
Spiritbox - Circle With Me
Bad Omens- Just Pretend
elijah – HOSTAGE
Point North x The Ghost Inside- Safe & Sound
The Warning - Hell You Call A Dream
I Prevail- Lifelines
New Years Day- My Monster

Bring Me The Horizon - Top 10 staTues tHat CriEd blood
From Ashes To New ft Yelawolf - Monster In Me
Until I Wake- Inside My Head
Until I Wake- Octane
Diamante- Unlovable
Against The Current- Weapon
Evans Blue- Cold (But I'm Still Here)
Skillet- Hero
Archetypes Collide – Undertow
New Years Day- Defame Me
Icon For Hire- Curse or Cure
Icon For Hire- Supposed To Be
Rise Against- Re-Education
Thirty Seconds To Mars- Beautiful Lie
Linkin Park- In The End
Breaking Benjamin- So Cold
I Prevail- Scars
Falling In Reverse- Popular Monster
Icon For Hire- Get Well II
Starset- Ricochet
Through Fire- Breathe
Three Days Grace- Right Left Wrong
Through Fire- Breathe
Papa Roach- Stand Up
Pop Evil- What Remains
Sevendust- Driven
The Warning - Hell You Call A Dream
Trapt- Echo
Caleb Hyles Ft. Trevor McNevan- Unparalyzed
Advents – Liminal
Dayseeker- Without Me
Bad Omens- The Death of Peace of Mind
Post Profit - Two Toxic
Galleons – DeLorean
ANBERLIN – Seven

TRIBRID NEXUS

311- You're Gonna Get It
Starset- Echo
Jager Henry/Lil Lotus - Heart of Thorns
Bea Miller - like that
Escape The Fate Ft. Lindsey Stirling- Invincible
Amaranthe- Burn With Me
Dillon Francis & Halsey – Bad At Love
Bad Omens- Like A Villain
Vana - BEG!
Papa Roach- Falling Apart
Avril Levigne- Keep Holding On
Papa Roach- No Appalogies
SYML – Girvan
Ruelle - The Other Side
AIRHYTHMS ALLIANCE - Promises Are Made To Be Broken
Sia- Breathe Me
The Plot In You- Feel Nothing
Bad Omens- The Grey
Breaking Benjamin- Until The End
Alexia Evellyn- Savage Daughters
Nemesea- Stay with Me
Dead by April / Smash Into Pieces / Samuel Ericsson — Outcome
Papa Roach- Leave A Light On
Breaking Benjamin- Never Again
I Prevail- Hurricane
Atreyu - Watch Me Burn
Lakeview/Gideon- Money Where Your Mouth Is
Hillhaven– Sycophants
Linkin Park- Numb
Kelly Clarkson- Stronger (What Doesn't Kill You)
Peach PRC - Time Of My Life
Amy Winehouse- Back To Black
Five Finger Death Punch- Gone Away
Pop Evil- What Remains
Crown The Empire - Someone Else

Dead by April- Calling
From Ashes To New- Lost And Alone
Michelle Branch- All You Wanted
Avril Levigne- I'm With You
Bad Valentine- I (Kinda) Wanna Die
Falling In Reverse- Prequel
Phix- Thunder
Through Fire- Listen To Your Heart (Roxette Cover)
Escape The Fate- Recipe For Disaster
The Ataris- Boys Of Summer
Skarlett Riot- Human
Icon For Hire- Make A Move
Icon For Hire- Get Well
Icon For Hire- Off With Her Head
Adelitas Way- Tell Me
Stone Sour- Song #3
Scott Stapp - Black Butterfly
Beartooth - My New Reality
Starset- Infected
Fleurie- Sirens
Dorothy- Black Sheep
Nothing More- Who We Are
Falling In Reverse - Bad Guy (feat. Saraya)
Bring Me The Horizon- Darkside
Asking Alexandria - Never Gonna Learn
I Prevail- Let Me Be Sad
Bad Omens- Never Know
Black Veil Brides- Fields of Bones
Kingdom Collapse- Half Alive
Dayseeker- Neon Grave
Loveless- I Love It When It Rains
From Ashes To New Ft. Eva Under Fire- Every Second
Fame on Fire- I'm Fine
Silent Theory- What Are the Odds
Memphis May Fire- Somebody

Black Veil Brides- Torch
Wage War- Circle The Drain
Motionless In White- Porcelain
Versus Me- Terrified
Ice Nine Kills- Rainy Day
Asking Alexandrea- Let Go
Crissy Costanza- If Looks Could Kill
Tickle Me Pink- Typical
Linkin Park- Bleed It Out
Skylar Grey- Words
Halestorm- Uncomfortable
Slipknot- Psychosocial
From Ashes To New- My Name
Zero 9:36 – Adrenaline
Ruelle- Madness
Disturbed- Stricken
I Prevail- Blank Space
WARGASM/Corey Taylor - 70% Dead
Call Me Karizma – Madhouse
Jeris Johnson - Kiss From A Rose
Ruelle- Find You
Fleurie - Love and War
Sakoya – Amends
Halsey- Lucky
The Veronicas- 4ever
Asking Alexandria- Into The Fire
Sakoya – Wandering
Saul- King Of Misery
A Day To Remember- Resentment
Thousand Foot Krutch- Lifeline
No Name Faces- Complicated
Through Fire- Breathe (Exstended Version)
Escape The Fate- Lightning Strike
Breaking Benjamin- Ashes of Eden
State of Mine- What Huyrts The Most (Rascal Flatts Rock Cover)

Adelitas Way- Invincible
Crashing Atlas- Graveyard
Archetypes Collide - Your Misery
Future Palace- Heads Up
Ruelle- Game of Survival
Crown The Empire - BLURRY (out of place)
Falling In Reverse - Bad Guy (feat. Saraya)
A Day To Remember- Better Off This Way
Ruelle- Storm
Sevendust- Driven
Ruelle Ft. Tommee Profitt- Hurts Like Hell
Bad Wolves- Lifeline
Saint Asonia – Devastate
Hidden Citizens Ft. Ruelle – Take Over
Ruelle- War Of Hearts
Deadlands- Villain
Adelitas Way- Alive
From Ashes To New- You Only Die Once
Starset- TokSik
I Prevail- There's Fear In Letting Go
Seven Hours After Violet – Radiance
Minute After Midnight – GHOST
Sevvendust- Black
UNSECRET - Heroes Never Die (feat. KRIGARÈ)
Fuel- Hemerage (In My Hands)
Lauren Presle- Americas Sweethearts
UNSECRET - Buried (feat. Katie Herzig)
Thousand Foot Krutch- Curtesy Call
Wage War- Johnny Cash
Wage War- Johnny Cash (Stripped)
In The Moment- The In-Between
Fame on Fire- Back to You
No Resolve- Bad Habits
Breaking Benjamin- Tourniquet
Adelitas Way- Criticize

Gemini Syndrome - Remember We Die
Skillet- Awake And Alive
Dead By April- My Light
Three Days Grace- So Called Life
Bad Omens- Concrete Jungle
Fame on Fire- Spiral: Justice
Reddy Redd- Hero
No Resolve- Come Back Stronger
From Ashes to New- Bulletproof
Dead By April- Dramlike
Linkin Park- Lost
From Ashes to New- Armageddon
Hollywood Undead- City Of The Dead
Fame on Fire- Without Me
Aurora- The Blade
From Ashes To New - Scars That I'm Hiding (feat. Anders Friden of In Flames)
RØRY- Hurt Myself
Escape The Fate Ft. Lindsey Stirling- Invincible
From Ashes To New- Wait For Me
I Prevail- Every Time You Leave
Alive In Barcelona - Bad At Love
Fame on Fire- I'm Fine
Asking Alexandrea- Psycho
Fame on Fire- Without Me
Fame on Fire- Not Dead Yet
I Prevail- Doomed
Pop Evil- Waking Lions
Adelitas Way- The Collapse
UNSECRET - VENDETTA (FEAT KRIGARÈ)
Breaking Benjamin- Follow
Conquer Divide/Attack Attack! – PARALYZED
Until I Wake- Fake
Five Finger Death Punch- Battle Born
Memphis May Fire- Heavy Is The Weight

Fame on Fire- Back to You
Self Deception- Blood & Scars
Ad Infinitum – Surrender
Any Given Sin- Another Life
Poppy- New Way Out
Gemini Syndrome – Remember We Die
Siamese- Utopia
Until I Wake- Fake
The Pretty Wild- Sleepwalkerr
From Ashes To New- Enough
Any Given Sin- Still Sinking
The Veer Union- Empirical
Halsey- Be Kind
Nate Vickers- Bury Me
Fame on Fire—"Chains (The Tower)" feat. SiM
Jeris Johnson- The Story Of Our Lives
Villain of the Story- Losing Control
Fame On Fire- Us Against The World (The Chariot)
Further Within- Fade Away
Nevertel- Losing Faith

Don't miss out!

Visit the website below and you can sign up to receive emails whenever Bria Lexor publishes a new book. There's no charge and no obligation.

https://books2read.com/r/B-A-MGYH-ZSUQD

BOOKS 2 READ

Connecting independent readers to independent writers.

Also by Bria Lexor

Card Masters Saga
Invited by the Elements
Tournament of Wars
Champion of Power

Heir of the Octopus Saga
Hero of the Fallen Empire

Hell's Guardian Chronicles
Crimson Savior
The Force of Vengeance
The Final Glory
Vampire Candidate
Rise of the Cruxim
Reluctant Secrets

Holiday Academy Saga
New Year's Blood

Onizuca Series
Return To Outer Earth

Origins of Onizuca
Fall of the Skraxiz Empire

Shaman Academy Saga
Year One

Shamanic Princess: Ruler of Darkness: Origins of Darkness
Ruler of Darkness

The Enchanted Saga
Twisted Fate

The Gargoyle Redemption Trilogy
Gargoyle Redemption

The Lightworker's Saga
Elysium

The Lyric Lockheart Story

The Flames Omen

The Oracle of Aeon Dra Saga
Rebels Flame
Flight Games
Tribrid Nexus

The Vampire Society Saga
Hunter of Destiny
Kiss of Flames
Sentient of Twilight
Red System Rises
Innocent Hunter
Eternal War

Watch for more at https://brialexor.wixsite.com/brialexor.

About the Author

Bria Lexor is the author of popular Urban Fantasy and Dark Fantasy series. She lives in Colorado and works on her books full time.

Read more at https://brialexor.wixsite.com/brialexor.

Milton Keynes UK
Ingram Content Group UK Ltd.
UKHW021941281024
450365UK00018B/1217